TAKE A CHANCE ON ME

Take a

SUSAN MAY WARREN

Chance on Me

a
Christiansen Family
novel

Tyndale House Publishers, Inc.
Carol Stream, Illinois

Visit Tyndale online at www.tyndale.com.

Visit Susan May Warren's website at www.susanmaywarren.com.

TYNDALE and Tyndale's quill logo are registered trademarks of Tyndale House Publishers, Inc.

Take a Chance on Me

Designed by Erik M. Peterson

Edited by Sarah Mason

Published in association with the literary agency of The Steve Laube Agency, 5025 N. Central Ave., Phoenix, AZ 85012.

Scripture quotations are taken from the *Holy Bible*, New Living Translation, copyright © 1996, 2004, 2007 by Tyndale House Foundation. Used by permission of Tyndale House Publishers, Inc., Carol Stream, Illinois 60188. All rights reserved.

Jonah 2:8 is taken from the Holy Bible, *New International Version,*® *NIV.*® Copyright © 1973, 1978, 1984, 2011 by Biblica, Inc.™ Used by permission of Zondervan. All rights reserved worldwide. www.zondervan.com.

Library of Congress Cataloging-in-Publication Data

Warren, Susan May, date.
  Take a chance on me / Susan May Warren.
    pages cm. — (Christiansen family)
    ISBN 978-1-4143-7841-1 (sc)
  1. Bachelors—Fiction. 2. Women lawyers—Fiction. I. Title.
  PS3623.A865T35 2013
  813'.6—dc23   2012050809

Printed in the United States of America

19   18   17   16   15   14   13
 7   6   5   4   3   2   1

For Your glory, Lord

ACKNOWLEDGMENTS

AUTHORS TAKE A CHANCE every time they write a story. Will they create characters people care about? Will they write story lines that resonate? Will they raise questions and answer them with the right truths? One of my biggest conundrums is getting the facts right. I'm so thankful for the people who take a chance with me and help me solve these dilemmas.

My deepest gratitude goes to:

Molly Hickam, the assistant county attorney in Cook County who walked through all my questions and helped me sort out the law. Any mistakes are all mine.

Rachel Hauck, who worked through every scene with me, faithful on the other end of the phone. I couldn't write a book without her.

David Warren, who brainstormed with me about the custody angle and helped me figure out the tension between Ivy and Darek (and thanks, too, for the name Darek!). You are quickly becoming my secret weapon!

Karen Watson, who always knows just how to round out a story and make it stronger. I appreciate our partnership.

Sarah Mason, for her amazing editing skills. Thanks for catching all the small errors and making me sound good!

Steve Laube, my agent, for his ability to listen and see the big picture. Thanks for always being on my team. You rock!

To my family, who make this life, this adventure, rich and blessed. In my head, we are the Christiansens.

THE AREA OF
DEEP HAVEN
AND
EVERGREEN LAKE

Two Island Lake

The Garden

Evergreen Resort

Gibs's house

Evergreen Lake

Pine Acres

N

GUNFLINT TRAIL

HWY 61

DEEP HAVEN

Minnesota

Lake Superior

My dearest Darek,

Even as I write this letter, I know I'll tuck it away; the words on it are more of a prayer, meant for the Lord more than you. Or maybe, in the scribbling upon this journal page, the words might somehow find your heart, a cry that extends across the bond of mother and child.

The firstborn child is always the one who solves the mystery of parenthood. Before I had you, I watched other mothers and wondered at the bond between a child and a parent, the strength of it, the power to mold a woman, making her put all hopes and wishes into this tiny bundle of life that she had the responsibility to raise.

It's an awe-filled, wonderful, terrifying act to have a child, for you suddenly wear your heart on the outside of your body. You risk a little more each day as he wanders from your arms into the world. You, Darek, were no protector of my heart. You were born with a willfulness, a courage, and a bent toward adventure that would bring me to the edge of my faith and keep me on my knees. The day I first saw you swinging from that too-enticing oak tree into the lake should have told me that I would be tested.

Your brothers shortened your name to Dare, and you took it to heart. I was never so terrified as the day you came home from Montana, fresh from your first year as a hotshot, feeling your own strength. I knew your future would take you far from Evergreen Lake. I feared it would take you far, also, from your legacy of faith.

Watching your son leave your arms has no comparison to watching him leave God's. You never seemed to question the beliefs your father and I taught you. Perhaps that is what unsettled me the most, because without questioning, I wondered how there could be true understanding. I held my breath against the day when it would happen—life would shatter you and leave your faith bereft.

And then it did.

It brought you home, in presence if not soul. If it hadn't been for your son, I might have done the unthinkable—stood in our gravel driveway and barred you from returning, from hiding.

Because, my courageous, bold oldest son, that is what you are doing. Hiding. Bitter and dark, you have let guilt and regret destroy your foundation, imprison you, and steal your joy. You may believe you are building a future for your son, but without faith, you have nothing to build it on. Evergreen Resort is not just a place. It's a legacy. A foundation. A belief.

It's the best of what I have to give you. That, and my unending prayers that somehow God will destroy those walls you've constructed around your heart.

Darek, you have become a mystery to me again. I don't know how to help free you. Or to restore all you've lost. But I believe that if you give God a chance, He will heal your heart. He will give you a future. He will truly lead you home.

Lovingly,
Your mother

CHAPTER 1

Ivy Madison would do just about anything to stay in the secluded, beautiful, innocent town of Deep Haven.

Even if she had to buy a man.

A bachelor, to be exact, although maybe not the one currently standing on the stage of the Deep Haven Emergency Services annual charity auction. He looked like a redneck from the woolly woods of northern Minnesota, with curly dark-blond hair, a skim of whiskers on his face, and a black T-shirt that read, *Hug a logger—you'll never go back to trees.* Sure, he filled out his shirt and looked the part in a pair of ripped jeans and boots, but he wore just a little too much "Come and get me, girls," in his smile.

The auctioneer on stage knew how to work his audience. He regularly called out names from the crowd to entice them to bid.

And apparently the town of Deep Haven loved their firefighters, EMTs, and cops because the tiny VFW was packed, the waitresses running out orders of bacon cheeseburgers and hot wings to the bidding crowd.

After the show was over, a local band would take the stage. The auction was part of the summer solstice festival—the first of many summer celebrations Deep Haven hosted. Frankly it felt like the village dreamed up events to lure tourists, but Ivy counted it as her welcoming party.

Oh, how she loved this town. And she'd only lived here for roughly a day. Imagine how she'd love it by the end of the summer, after she'd spent three months learning the names of locals, investing herself in this lakeside hamlet.

Her days of hitching her measly worldly possessions—four hand-me-down suitcases; a loose cardboard box of pictures; a garbage bag containing *The Elements of Legal Style*, *How to Argue and Win Every Time*, and *To Kill a Mockingbird*; and most of all, her green vintage beach bike—onto the back of her red Nissan Pathfinder were over.

Time to put down roots. Make friends.

Okay, *buying* a friend didn't exactly qualify, but the fact that her money would go to help the local emergency services seemed like a good cause. And if Ivy had learned anything growing up in foster care, it was that a person had to work the system to get what she wanted.

She should be unpacking; she started work in the morning. But how long would it take, really, to settle into the tiny, furnished efficiency apartment over the garage behind the Footstep of Heaven Bookstore? And with her new job as assistant county attorney, she expected to have plenty of free time. So when the twilight hues of evening had lured her into the romance of a walk along the shoreline of the Deep Haven harbor, she couldn't stop herself.

She couldn't remember the last time she'd taken a lazy walk, stopping at storefronts, reading the real estate ads pasted to the window of a local office.

Cute, two-bedroom log cabin on Poplar Lake. She could imagine the evergreen smell nudging her awake every morning, the twitter of cardinals and sparrows as she took her cup of coffee on the front porch.

Except she loved the bustle of the Deep Haven hamlet. Nestled on the north shore of Minnesota, two hours from the nearest hint of civilization, the fishing village–turned–tourist hideaway had enough charm to sweet-talk Ivy out of her Minneapolis duplex and make her dream big.

Dream of home, really. A place. Friends. Maybe even a dog. And here, in a town where everyone belonged, she would too.

She had wandered past the fudge and gift shop, past the walk-up window of World's Best Donuts, where the smell of cake donuts nearly made her follow her sweet tooth inside. At the corner, the music drew her near to the VFW. Ford F-150s, Jeeps, and a handful of SUVs jammed the postage-stamp-size dirt parking lot.

She'd stopped at the entrance, read the poster for today's activities, then peered in through the windows. Beyond a wood-paneled bar and a host of long rectangular tables, a man stood on the stage, holding up a fishing pole.

And that's when Deep Haven reached out and hooked her.

"Are you going in?"

She'd turned toward the voice and seen a tall, solidly built middle-aged man with dark hair, wearing a jean jacket. A blonde woman knit her hand into his.

"I . . ."

"C'mon in," the woman said. "We promise not to bite. Well, except for Eli here. I make no promises with him." She had smiled, winked, and Ivy could feel her heart gulp it whole. Oh, why had she never learned to tamp down her expectations? Life had taught her better.

Eli shook his head, gave the woman a fake growl. Turned to Ivy. "Listen, it's for a good cause. Our fire department could use a new engine, and the EMS squad needs more training for their staff, what few there are. You don't have to buy anything, but you might help drive up the bids." He winked. "Don't tell anyone I told you that, though."

She laughed. "I'm Ivy Madison," she said, too much enthusiasm in her voice. "Assistant county attorney."

"Of course you are. I should have guessed. Eli and Noelle Hueston." Noelle stuck out her hand. "Eli's the former sheriff. Hence the fact that we've come with our checkbook. C'mon, I'll tell you who to bid on."

Who to bid on?

Ivy had followed them inside, taking a look around the crowded room. Pictures of soldiers hung in metal frames, along with listings of member names illuminated by neon bar signs. The smells of deep-fried buffalo wings, beer, and war camaraderie were embedded in the dark-paneled walls.

A line formed around the pool table near the back of the room—what looked like former glory-day athletes lined up with their beers or colas parked on the round tables. Two men threw darts into an electronic board.

Then her gaze hiccuped on a man sitting alone near the jukebox, sending a jolt of familiarity through her.

Jensen Atwood.

For a moment, she considered talking to him—not that he'd know her, but maybe she'd introduce herself, tell him, *I'm the one who put together your amazing plea agreement.* Yes, that had been a hot little bit of legalese. The kind that had eventually landed her right here, in her dream job, dream town.

But Noelle glanced back and nodded for Ivy to follow, so she trailed behind them to an open table.

"Every year, on the last night of the solstice festival, we have a charity auction. It's gotten to be quite an event," Noelle said, gesturing to a waitress. She came over and Eli ordered a basket of wings, a couple chocolate malts. Ivy asked for a Coke.

"What do they auction?"

"Oh, fishing gear. Boats. Snowblowers. Sometimes vacation time-shares in Cancún. Whatever people want to put up for charity. But this year, they have something special on the agenda." Noelle leaned close, her eyes twinkling. Ivy already liked her. And the way Eli had her hand wrapped in his. What might it be like to be in love like that? That kind of love . . . well, Ivy had only so many wishes, and she'd flung them all at living here, in Deep Haven.

"What?" Ivy asked.

"They're auctioning off the local bachelors."

And as if on cue, that's when the lumberjack bachelor had taken the stage.

Ivy sipped her Coke, watching the frenzy.

"So are you going to bid?" Noelle asked.

Ivy raised a shoulder.

The lumberjack went for two hundred dollars—too rich for Ivy's blood—to a woman wearing a moose-antler headband. He flexed for her as he walked off stage, and the crowd erupted.

A clean-cut, handsome young man took the stage next, to the whoops of the younger crowd down front. "That's my son," Noelle said, clearly enjoying the spectacle. He seemed about nineteen or twenty, tall and wearing a University of Minnesota, Duluth, T-shirt. He was built like an athlete and had a swagger to match.

"He plays basketball for the UMD Bulldogs," Noelle said. She placed the first bid and got a glare from the young man on stage.

A war started between factions in the front row. "Should I bid?" Ivy asked. Not that she would know what to do with a bachelor ten years younger than her. Maybe she could get him to mow her lawn.

"No. Save your money for Owen Christiansen."

Probably another lumberjack from the woods, with a flannel shirt and the manners of a grizzly. Ivy affected a sort of smile.

"Maybe you've heard of him? He plays hockey for the Minnesota Wild."

"No, sorry."

"He's something of a local celebrity. Played for our hometown team and then got picked up by the Wild right after high school."

"I'm not much of a hockey fan."

"Honey, you can't live in Deep Haven and not be a hockey fan." Noelle grinned, turning away as the wings arrived.

Ivy ignored the way the words found tender space and stabbed her in the chest. But see, she wanted to live in Deep Haven . . .

Noelle offered her a wing, but Ivy turned it down. "Owen's parents, John and Ingrid Christiansen, run a resort about five miles out of town. It's one of the legacy resorts—his great-grandfather settled here in the early nineteen hundreds and set up a logging camp. It eventually turned into one of the hot recreation spots on the north shore, although in today's economy, they're probably struggling along with the rest of the Deep Haven resorts. I'm sure Owen's appearance on the program is a bid for some free publicity. Owen is the youngest son of the clan, one of six children. I'm sure you'll meet them—all but two still live in Deep Haven."

A redhead won the bachelor on stage and ran up to claim her purchase. Ivy escaped to the ladies' room.

What if she did bid on Owen? Truly, the last thing she needed in her life was a real bachelor. Someone she might fall for, someone who could so easily break her heart.

Maybe she could ask said bachelor to show her around Deep Haven. Teach her about hockey. Certainly it might give her a little social clout to be seen with the town celebrity.

She could faintly hear the announcer stirring up the fervor for the next contestant, then a trickle of applause for the main attraction as he took the stage. She walked out, standing by the bar to survey this hometown hero.

They grew them big up here in the north woods. Indeed, he looked like a hockey champion, with those wide shoulders, muscular arms stretching the sleeves of his deep-green shirt that read *Evergreen Resort—memories that live forever.* He stood at ease like one might do in the military, wearing jeans that hugged his legs all the way down to the work boots on his feet. The man looked like an impenetrable fortress, not a hint of marketing in his face. So much for winning the audience.

In fact, to use the only hockey term she knew, he looked like he'd just been checked hard into the boards and come up with some sort of permanent scowl, none too happy to be standing in the middle of the stage of the local VFW as the main attraction.

"C'mon, everyone, who will start the bidding for our Deep Haven bachelor tonight?"

Ivy looked around the room. It had hushed to a pin-drop silence, something not quite right simmering in the air. She glanced over to where Jensen Atwood had been sitting and found his seat vacant.

On stage, the man swallowed. Shifted. Pursed his lips. Oh, poor Owen. Her heart knocked her hard in the chest. She knew exactly what it felt like not to be wanted.

"One hundred dollars? Who has it tonight for our local hero?"

She scanned the room, saw patrons looking away as if embarrassed. Even Eli and Noelle had taken a sudden interest in their dinner.

Owen sighed and shook his head.

And right then, the pain of the moment squeezed the words from Ivy's chest. "Five hundred dollars!"

Every eye turned toward her, and for a moment, she had the crazy but horribly predictable urge to flee. But the words were out, so she took a step forward, toward the stage. "I bid five hundred dollars," she said again, fighting the wobble in her voice.

Ivy shot a look at Noelle, expecting approval. But Noelle wore an expression of what she could only pinpoint as panic. Wasn't she the one who'd suggested Ivy buy the man?

And then from the stage, she heard, "Well, that's good enough for me! Sold, to the pretty lady in the white jacket. Miss, come up to the stage and claim your prize."

Still, no one said a word—not a cheer, not a gasp, nothing. Ivy swallowed and met the eyes of the man on stage. "I'll meet him by the bar," she said, her voice small.

Owen looked as relieved as she was that they didn't have to create some public spectacle. He moved off the stage and the auctioneer mercifully introduced the band. The men in back resumed their pool playing.

Ivy couldn't help it. She edged over to Noelle. "What's the matter? I know he looks a little rough around the edges, but—"

"That's not Owen," Noelle said, wiping her fingers with a napkin. She shot a glance past Ivy, possibly at the stranger she'd just purchased.

"What?"

"Owen couldn't make it. That's Darek Christiansen. His big brother."

Ivy turned now, found her man weaving his way through the crowd. He didn't stop to glad-hand anyone or even slap friends on the back.

In fact, it seemed she'd purchased the pariah of Deep Haven.

Noelle confirmed it. "Brace yourself, honey. You've just purchased the most ineligible eligible bachelor in town."

Everything inside Darek told him to keep going, right on out of the VFW until he hit his Jeep, and then punch the gas toward the hills.

And hide.

He would murder Owen next time he saw him, which wouldn't be anytime soon, given the kid's celebrity demands. *Sorry, Bro. I can't make it up today—I have a photo shoot.* Owen couldn't have thought ahead to that, maybe rearranged his oh-so-packed schedule? But Owen didn't think beyond practice, improving his shot, and updating his Facebook status. Last time Darek checked, his twenty-year-old kid brother had 32,876 fans.

Darek had maybe thirty-eight friends on his own page. Not

that he was counting, but it seemed like some sort of commentary on his life.

The minute Darek had hung up with Owen, he should have made himself scarce—loaded Tiger into the Jeep, attached the boat, and headed for some pristine lake. Except losing his head and forgetting his responsibilities was how he got here in the first place.

Instead he'd experienced a streak of clearly misplaced hope that the stigma, the gossip, might have finally died and he might once again be an eligible bachelor. Someone who just wanted to start over, for himself and his son.

The near silence in the room when they'd called his name, when he'd stepped up to take Owen's place, confirmed that no, nothing had been forgotten.

Darek stalked past the bar, where, of course, his high school buddies gave him tight smiles.

He hadn't seen any of the former Deep Haven Huskies getting up to sell their . . . well, it wasn't exactly his body, and she certainly didn't expect a real date, right? So he wasn't sure what he was selling up there.

Darek glanced at his father, John, sitting at the end, nursing a Sprite. A linebacker-size man—bigger than any of his boys—he'd played fullback for the Minnesota Gophers back in the day. That he'd ended up with hockey players could only be blamed on the skating rink he'd cleared on the lake every January.

"Great job, Son," his father said, catching his arm.

"This was a bad idea," Darek groused, slowing his exit.

"Five hundred dollars doesn't sound like such a bad idea. You were the most expensive bachelor here. That will make the news."

"Yippee," Darek said. But his father was right—he'd created a bit of buzz, and hopefully it would someday turn into goodwill for their lakeside vacation spot, Evergreen Lodge Outfitter and Cabin Rentals, which most people shortened to Evergreen Resort.

"Do you know the woman who bid on you?"

Darek scanned the room to locate her. He couldn't see her well from the stage with the lights in his face, but he thought he'd glimpsed a redhead wearing a white jean jacket, her hair in a messy ponytail. She wasn't tall, maybe five foot four, and a little on the curvy side.

Now he found her, sitting next to Noelle Hueston and staring at him like she'd purchased . . . well, the devil.

Darek turned away, his lips a grim line. "No, I don't know her."

His father wisely said nothing, took a sip of his Sprite. Then, "She looks pretty."

"Next time you want to sell your flesh and blood, pick a different son."

He caught his father's smirk as he turned to leave, and it only darkened his mood.

No one from Deep Haven, not a soul, had bid on him. What was so different about him from, say, the two previous bachelors?

Okay, maybe that wasn't a fair question. Neither of them walked around with the stigma of being the youngest widower in town, pity and probably the tsk of tongues following in their wake.

He glanced over to the chair where Jensen Atwood had sat, smug, rich, wearing a fancy leather jacket, his hair cut short and slicked back, contempt in his eyes. Yes, he'd seen the man sitting near the back, next to the jukebox, like no one would notice. He had a lot of nerve showing up here, and Darek had just about launched off the stage toward him. That might be a show the locals would bid on—a go-round between Jensen and Darek. Finally.

Instead he'd dark-eyed the guy into fleeing. It fed the heat inside him, gave Darek the strength to stand there like an idiot while the town shifted uncomfortably in their seats.

Until, of course, Moneybags piped up.

Five hundred dollars.

Wow, did she waste her money on him.

And what kind of woman paid five hundred dollars for a man she didn't know? Hopefully she didn't want a real date. He wasn't a real-date kind of guy.

In fact, he was a *never*-date kind of guy.

Darek shook his head and headed out the door.

He paused on the sidewalk for a moment, drawing in the clean air, shaking off the reek of old cigarettes, whiskey, and town gossip that coated him like grime. The moon had risen, hovering above the town, milky light washing over the trading post, the Blue Moose Café, pooling in the harbor, icing the waves of the lake.

He could feel his heartbeat thundering in his chest and hated how easily his guilt took hold of him, turned him surly. At the least, he should swallow his pride—what was left of it—and meet the woman who had forked out good money for him. For charity.

Instead he moved away from the door and dug out his cell phone, about to call home.

"Hey, where are you going?"

He turned, pressing End. His "owner" had followed him out of the VFW. A fireball with green eyes and freckles, wearing the jean jacket he remembered over a T-shirt and a green scarf. She stood about to his shoulder but had no problem slamming her hands to her hips and toeing up to him.

"I thought we had a date."

"Is that what you want? A date?" He didn't mean for it to

emerge so sharp, even angry, and didn't blame her for the way she opened her mouth as if she'd been slapped.

"No, I, uh—"

"Then why did you buy me? And why on earth would you pay five hundred dollars? Sheesh, lady, you must be desperate or something."

Wow. He must have lost control of everything decent inside him. But he didn't like the feeling of being humiliated.

Or owned.

In fact, the entire thing made him feel trapped and small, and he'd had enough of that, thank you.

Her mouth closed. Pinched. "I'm not desperate. If you want to know the truth, I felt sorry for you."

He probably deserved that, despite the way it sideswiped him. He didn't let on, however, preferring to stare at her, something icy he'd learned from his years in the rink. "Okay, then, let's just get this over with. What do you want?"

"I—"

"You should know that I'm not like the other guys in there. If you're looking for some kind of fling, I'm not your man. I can probably hook you up with one of my buddies—"

"Wow. Stay *away* from me." She whirled around, heading down the sidewalk, and he knew he was a first-class jerk.

"Wait!"

She held up a hand. "Forget it! You're right; this was a bad idea."

He ran after her—boy, she had a fast walk for such a short woman. "Listen, I'm sorry. Really. It's just that you don't want a date with me. If you ask, I'll bet you can get your money back."

"I don't want it back."

She didn't stop and he was walking fast to keep up.

"Then what do you want? Why did you buy me?"

She stopped, breathing hard. Pressed her fingers to her eyes. Oh no, she wasn't crying, was she?

He swallowed, his throat on fire, hearing his words and wishing he wasn't the kind of guy who ran full speed into hurting others.

You are so selfish. Felicity, in his head. Always in his head.

"I'm sorry," he said softly, shoving his hands into his pockets. The wind took his words, flung them toward the lake. "It's just that I'm the last person you want to be seen in town with."

She sighed, turning her face away from him. "Well, I don't have anyone else." Her voice emerged small and wheedled in past the anger, the annoyance.

It settled inside, in a place he reserved for Tiger, and he tempered his tone. "Are you here for the weekend?"

"No. I live here." She said it with a layer of determination, as if convincing herself.

Really? "I know nearly everyone in this town—"

"I moved here yesterday. I'm the new assistant county attorney."

Uh-oh. He'd heard that the current assistant CA had resigned to stay home with her newborn child. He'd miss the way she tolerated his monthly phone calls. But someone had to keep tabs on Jensen, right? He looked at this angry sprite and grimaced, imagining her reaction next time Jensen threatened a restraining order.

Darek might be the one doing years of community service.

"Sorry," he said again.

Her shoulder jerked in a halfhearted shrug.

"Maybe . . . maybe I could help you carry furniture or chop wood or mow your grass or something."

She had folded her hands across her chest. "Wow, I must be a real catch for you to offer to mow my lawn instead of being seen in public with me."

"No, I—"

"Like I said, you're off the hook."

"I don't want to be off the hook. You bought me fair and square."

She pursed her lips.

"I have an idea. C'mon."

She frowned at him, and frankly he was done begging, not sure how he'd gotten to this point in the first place. So he turned and headed for the Jeep, parked just down the street.

He didn't look behind him but heard her steps. When he reached the car, he held her door open like a gentleman, although he knew he might be a little late to resurrect any sort of real gallantry.

She looked up at him before getting in, her eyes big and shiny in the moonlight. They caught his and for the first time, he noticed how pretty they were, with golden flecks at the edges.

"I'm safe, even if I'm a jerk."

"I have friends who will hunt you down and kill you if I go missing."

"I have no doubt." He took a long breath and stuck out his hand. "Darek Christiansen, Deep Haven tour guide, at your service, milady."

She regarded his hand for a moment, and he sensed something shifting inside her. "Ivy Madison." Then she slid one of her petite hands into his and smiled.

The full force of it reached out and poured into him, hot and bold and shaking him through. He dropped her grip, swallowed. Stepped back.

She climbed into the Jeep and reached for the seat belt, her eyes on his as he closed the door.

Oh, boy.

Maybe he should have run when he had the chance.

Jensen sat outside the VFW in the Pine Acres work truck—the one he took to town when he wanted to hide—and watched Darek get the girl. Again.

And why not? Darek Christiansen always won.

Tonight, he'd stared Jensen down until he'd had no choice but to slink out. The last thing Jensen wanted was a fight. Especially with only six weeks left on his sentence. He didn't need a judge deciding he wasn't repentant enough and upgrading his community service to a stint behind bars.

Jensen should simply concede that Darek would always win. His streak began in fourth grade, when they'd both started playing hockey, and continued long after Jensen moved away, returning every summer as they vied for Felicity's attention.

Sure, Jensen had a few glimmering moments. Like the summer Darek escaped to Montana to fight the fire in Glacier National Park with the Jude County Hotshots, after Jensen had given up his own firefighting dreams. Jensen and Felicity had nearly become something that stuck then—probably would have if Darek hadn't returned home tan and triumphant.

And of course, there was the simple fact that in the end Darek had *married* Felicity. Jensen hadn't quite seen that one coming. But then again, he doubted Darek had either.

He watched as Darek and the redhead headed out of town in

his Jeep Wrangler. For a moment, he debated going back inside to listen to the Blue Monkeys. After all, that's why he'd braved the auction—Jensen normally slunk in late for the band's events, sitting in the shadows so no one saw him. But today he'd misjudged the time, the auction ran over, and, well, creeping back in now felt too much like tucking his tail between his legs.

He had at least a smidgen of pride left.

Jensen put the truck into gear and pulled out.

One hundred hours and he'd be free; he could leave Deep Haven and never look back. Maybe keep driving all the way to California or Mexico, where he could change his name and leave his past in the dust.

On top of the hill over the town, Jensen resisted the urge to glance out the passenger window at the scattering of lights that made up Deep Haven. Eyes, watching him, blinking, accusing.

He kept his gaze on the road, slowing as he took the truck around a curve carved through the granite, where the shoulder disappeared. His hands slickened and he caught himself holding his breath.

He couldn't wait to leave. But to do that, he'd have to find a few more places where he could go, hat in hand, begging for hours. Deep Haven seemed determined to keep him from fulfilling his community service, especially lately. Volunteer jobs had fizzled to ten hours a week and some places, like the after-school tutoring program, had turned him away.

Apparently the fact that he had graduated from college and managed two years of law school didn't matter to the English teachers struggling to teach their sixth graders to read.

No, if the citizens of Deep Haven had their way, he would have been their first public stoning.

He turned south where the road split around Evergreen Lake and took the paved road to the end, pulling in to the gated community of Pine Acres. The electronic gate and pass card could probably be considered overkill, but his father had promoted safety for the vacation homes when he jumped into the world of property development and created the luxury vacation community, and he kept his word. At least to the residents of the community.

As Jensen drove through the gates, he noticed that deer had snacked on the currant bushes by the entrance. He'd have to reshape them, maybe spray. A bulb was out on the automatic entry lights, and he spotted a tree down along one of the wooded drives. He'd come by tomorrow on the four-wheeler and clean it up.

He had to mow, anyway, and finish painting the Millers' garage—a project his father thought might fill time and create some goodwill. After all, the Millers were one of his father's largest clients in the Cities with their string of cinemas.

Jensen crawled into the driveway of his father's massive vacation home and parked the truck outside. As he got out, the stars created a canopy of brilliance, innocent and bright. They felt so close he wanted to reach up and touch one. The wind hushed in the white pine and birch, the poplar and willow that surrounded the property.

Motion sensor lights flickered on as Jensen moved toward the service door, blinding him for a moment. Then he let himself into the darkness of the garage and didn't bother to turn on the lights, toeing off his shoes and moving from memory up the stairs to the great room. At the top, moonlight streamed through the grand windows that overlooked the lake, waxing the wood floor with light. The ceiling rose two stories, trapping the silences of the grand house, and the place smelled of the walleye he'd cooked for lunch in butter and dill. He dropped his keys onto the granite countertop and opened the double-door stainless fridge, peering inside for something. Anything.

Grabbing a root beer in a tall bottle, he twisted off the cap and padded out to the deck.

The lake rippled in the darkness, fingers of light feathering over the surface. He could barely make out Gibs's light next door, trickling through the woods and across the sandy beach. He should check on the old man. A canoe lay moored on the sand, evidence of a recent visit by his granddaughter, Claire. How she loved to canoe the length of the lake.

Jensen didn't mean to stalk, but he loved watching her. And what else did he have to do, really?

Across the lake, almost directly from Pine Acres, the lights of the Evergreen Resort main lodge blazed.

Once upon a time, he and Darek had been the kings of Evergreen Lake.

He set his root beer on the railing and dug out his harmonica.

The sound echoed across the lake, long and twangy, Johnny Cash's "Cry! Cry! Cry!" Maybe it was a little indulgent, but tonight, he couldn't help it. *"You'll call for me but I'm gonna tell you, bye, bye, bye . . ."*

He listened to the last of the sound lingering as he finished. It was so easy, sometimes, to just close his eyes, lose himself in memories. The heat of the sun on his skin, the taste of trouble in his laughter. Standing on the bow of the canoe, his feet balanced on the edges. Claire and Felicity on the seat in the middle, and at the stern, facing him, similarly balanced, stood Darek.

Jensen had seen that sparking of challenge in Darek's eyes as he said, "You can't knock me off."

"Watch me." Jensen gave the canoe a playful jerk.

Felicity squealed. The summer had turned her hair a rich, luscious blonde, and with her skimpy bikini, he could barely keep his eyes in his head. She faced him, grinning, and he wondered if she could hear his heart pounding in his chest.

Claire grabbed for her side of the seat, and he caught her gaze on him. She always made him feel a little naughty, even when he wasn't thinking anything he shouldn't. Then again, he supposed that's what a missionary kid was supposed to do. Make you behave.

But on days like this, with the sun streaming down his back and both girls smiling up at him, he didn't care about behaving.

Just winning.

Jensen jerked the canoe hard, and Darek's arms windmilled. He nearly went over but found his balance and stamped his foot, making the canoe lurch the other direction.

Jensen caught himself and jerked it back, this time fast, hard, and—

Darek leaned into it, and suddenly Jensen found himself in the air. The chill of lake water swept away his breath, and he kicked hard to right himself.

He found Darek's hand reaching for him when he came up. Jensen took it. And yanked.

Darek flipped over his head and into the lake. He came up sputtering, then launched himself at Jensen. They wrestled until they both hung on the side of the canoe, breathing hard.

"Let's take your dad's boat out, get some dinner down at the Landing," Felicity said as Darek reached for her. She swatted him. Glanced at Jensen. "Please?"

"Sure."

Claire reached out and helped Jensen into the canoe. Darek climbed in after him and they paddled back to shore.

Thankfully, his father wouldn't be back until the weekend to grouse about the boat. Claire and Felicity met him in sundresses and they picked up Darek across the lake, then motored down to the outside grill and restaurant, Jensen's knee propped on the diver's chair as he guided the boat.

"Faster, Jens!" Felicity said, so he pushed up the throttle. Darek frowned, his eyes darkening, but Felicity was laughing and Jensen could feel it in his chest.

Her laughter always felt sweetly dangerous, like if he hung on too long, it might burn him. He could still hear her sometimes, in the darkness across the lake. Taste the memory of that curious summer when he had her all to himself, feel the texture of her kisses. What a fool he'd been, gobbling up the idea that if he did it right, she might belong to him. Believing that he even really wanted that.

Because she'd never belonged to him. Not then, not later.

He opened his eyes, staring into the night, at the lights across the lake, pressing into the darkness.

He should have remembered that Darek Christiansen always won.

CHAPTER 2

IF THIS WAS HIS "Welcome to Deep Haven" face, Ivy would hate to
see what his grumpy side looked like. The man had all the warmth,
all the friendliness, of a pinecone.

Sadly, for a moment there, down at the beach, with the waves
cheering her on, she thought they might become friends. Thought
she saw a crack in his nasty demeanor.

*Darek Christiansen, Deep Haven tour guide, at your service,
milady.*

Right.

She should have asked for her money back after all. Or donated
straight to the EMS department instead of giving in to this farce
of a . . . what? Date?

Maybe she should have taken him up on his offer of yard work.

Most of all, she couldn't believe she'd barely met this guy and he was rejecting her already.

He had taken off the soft top of his Jeep and now sat with his arms folded, mouth grim, waiting to be released from his captivity.

She had the great urge to call it quits and ask him to take her home. But, well . . . the *view*. It glued her to this spot above Deep Haven. "I can't believe we only drove five miles and yet we can see the entire town, practically tuck it into our hands."

"We're on Pincushion Mountain overlook. Teenagers like to make out here."

Well, that wasn't exactly the information she'd expected to hear.

"It looks as if Deep Haven fell into a bowl, spilling out toward the lake." Indeed the lights cascaded down the mountain like a sparkling river toward the blackness of Lake Superior, the light-house the final pinprick against the night. Pine fragranced the air, country music twanged from the radio, and despite the chill creeping under her jean jacket, it seemed a night for romance.

Ha.

Ivy got out of the Jeep, walked to the edge of the cutoff.

"Careful. It's a straight drop down."

I can take care of myself, she nearly said. Had been doing just that for about three decades now. But she didn't want to cause a fight.

"How long have you lived here?" she said, not looking at him. A boat, a single point of light, traveled out on the lake.

"I was born here. Grew up here."

"Made out here?" She couldn't help it and turned to see his reaction. "Oh, c'mon, you were the one who brought it up."

He had his hands on the steering wheel, his eyes on her, narrowed, enigmatic. "Fine. Yes, of course. I was a Deep Haven boy."

That was more like it. She walked back to the car, slid into the seat. "What is your favorite place in town?"

He lifted a shoulder, but she didn't let him off the hook. She knew how to wait out a confession. Finally he glanced at her; then, "I live on a resort on Evergreen Lake. A boy's playground with woods and wild animals and a pristine lake. It's all rocky beach and marsh except for one piece of property at the end that bumps up next to ours. Right there sits an overhanging oak tree with an old rope tied to one of the branches. I spent every summer swinging from that tree or boating on the lake, most nights in front of a campfire, roasting marshmallows."

Look at that. More than a three-word sentence. "That sounds magical."

"Growing up on a resort in a small town has its merits."

"I suppose you know everyone in town."

He shrugged again. "I know enough."

Ivy leaned her head back, tracing the stars, the glorious Milky Way. "I've always wanted to live in a town like Deep Haven. Someplace quiet and safe. Where everyone knows your name, and your neighbors greet you in the grocery store."

"Is that what you want—to be greeted in the grocery store?"

"Maybe. And for the coffee shop barista to know my regular order. For the librarian to call me when my favorite book is in and the mailman to know me by name, maybe come in for coffee."

"My mailman is named Dennis, and he's never come in for coffee once in twenty years."

"I want to have memories. Live someplace where I belong. Where I could stay, forever." She hadn't meant all that to spill out, to sound so desperate. But he clearly didn't appreciate what he had.

"Military?"

"No. Just . . . not the ideal childhood. I was a foster child."

"Sorry."

Ivy closed her eyes. "You can't live in the past. Your life is what you make it." She sat up, then turned. "Take me there."

"Where?"

"Evergreen Lake. I want to see this rope swing."

But he didn't move, his face going a little white. "I can't. I'm not . . . Well, I just can't."

Oh. "So . . . what do you do? Are you a lumberjack like that other contestant?"

She meant it as a joke, but he didn't look amused. "I work at the resort as the maintenance man."

"Carrying on the family business, huh?"

Darek stared at her for a moment. "It's getting late," he finally said, pulling out his phone.

Huh. She wasn't sure what she'd said, but yes, she'd wasted enough time with bachelor number one.

"Oh no," he said, dialing. "I must have muted the ringer. I didn't even hear—Mom, I just got your message. What—?"

He fell silent, something stricken on his face. Then, "I'll be right there."

He hung up and turned the key in the ignition. "I gotta take you home."

Ivy reached for her buckle. "What's the matter?"

He turned, bracing his arm atop her seat. "It's my son. He's in the emergency room."

Son? Darek *was* an eligible bachelor, wasn't he? Her gaze flickered to his left hand. But he didn't wear a ring, so maybe he was divorced. "What happened?"

"He fell off the top bunk. I don't know . . ." The wheels screeched as they headed out of the overlook.

She reached for the roll bar. "Who was with him?"

"His grandmother." They pulled onto the highway. "My mother. She's freaked out."

Where was the boy's mother? "How old is he?"

His hair rippled in the wind, both hands bracing the steering wheel. "Five." His voice sounded choked, panicked. "He's five."

She pressed her hand to his arm. "Go straight to the hospital. I can find my own way home."

He glanced at her, and she saw it again, that chink in his personality that hinted there might be a flesh-and-blood man under there. "Really?"

"Of course." She squeezed his arm. And for a second, he looked down at her grip. Back at her.

Then he swallowed and glanced away, back at the road. "Thanks," he said. Or she thought that's what she heard in the roar of the wind.

She let her hand fall away and held on. When they pulled up to the Deep Haven hospital—a decent size for a community of less than two thousand—he parked illegally in front of the entrance and scrambled out.

Of course he didn't wait for her, but she could take care of herself. Especially around hospitals. How many times had she curled up in a vinyl chair for the night while they worked on her mother?

The ER canopy lights illuminated the entry and the doors slid back as Darek charged inside. Stone columns and the pristine linoleum flooring, muted beige walls, suggested a recent taxpayer-funded update. Ivy followed on his tail, intending to ask at the nurses' desk for directions back to her apartment or even to call a cab. Did they have cabs in Deep Haven? The desk was empty, the nurses probably occupied with their patient.

Across from the desk, an emergency room bay held two beds, one of them cordoned off with a curtain.

Darek plowed right up to a cluster of women standing vigil in the middle of the hallway. The older woman—Ivy would guess she might be Darek's mother—had bobbed blonde hair and smart red glasses, her arms folded over her chest as if trying to hold herself together. One of the girls, maybe his sister, had her blonde hair tied up in a hairnet and sported a short-sleeved black shirt with a Pierre's Pizza logo emblazoned on the breast. The other looked younger, maybe even in high school, petite and brunette. She wore a pink tie-dyed T-shirt, low-hanging sweatpants, flip-flops. Her pink toenails looked freshly painted.

Ivy had correctly pegged them as family judging by the way Darek lit into them. In fact, the entire county might be able to hear him.

"Where is he?"

"Calm down, Darek. It's just a few stitches," the older blonde woman said, but her voice shook.

"*Stitches?* Sheesh, Mom, what happened?"

"I put him to sleep in Owen's old bed, but he climbed up on the top bunk. I didn't even know until I heard him scream."

Darek made a face, something of pain. "You have blood all over you."

At that, Ivy gave the woman a closer look. Blood smeared the collar of her shirt.

"Head wounds bleed a lot—"

"Head wound! Does he have a concussion?"

"I don't know."

Darek pushed the rest of the way through the crowd and pulled aside the curtain.

Ivy saw a man—probably Darek's father for the resemblance to him, with his scowl, blue eyes, wide shoulders under a canvas jacket—holding the hand of a little boy.

A cute little boy. With curly blond hair that hung in spirals around his head and brown eyes. He wore Spider-Man pajamas, his feet bare. And blood saturated his shirt, coated his face. A nurse pressed gauze to a wound over his eye while the child fought back tears.

How well she could remember sitting in a hospital, fighting back tears.

Then Ivy's breath stilled in her chest as the nasty man she'd spent the last hour with transformed before her eyes.

Darek moved around the gurney. "Hey there, Tiger." He forced a smile despite the trauma in his eyes.

"Daddy!" The boy started to whimper and pulled away from the nurse to throw his arms around Darek's neck, burying his face in his shoulder.

Darek held him tight, rocking him.

"Tiger looks just like Darek at this age," Darek's mother murmured. "I can't believe I didn't check on him."

"It's okay, Mom. These things happen. He not only looks like Darek, but he has his father's wild streak." The younger daughter slipped her arm around her mother's shoulder.

"Thanks, Amelia. I just wish he was a bit easier to corral." She turned to the other girl. "Grace, is your shift over?"

"No," the blonde pizza girl said. "But when you called about Tiger, trying to find Darek, I got off. One of the other girls filled in for me. I'll make up the hours later this week."

"Poor Darek. Did you hear that he went for five hundred dollars tonight at the bachelor auction? Some out-of-towner bought him," Amelia said. "Clearly she didn't know what she was buying."

"Oh, be nice, Amelia. Darek is a fine catch for any woman."

"Mom, seriously. Darek is about as dark and wounded as they come. He's never getting married again. He wouldn't have gotten married the first time if—"

"So we're having the party here?"

They turned at the voice, and the sliding doors closed behind a man with dark, tousled hair, sporting a leather jacket, jeans, hiking boots. He strode past Ivy, toward the family.

"Casper!" Amelia went into his arms.

He wrapped her up, kissed her on the forehead. "Hey, Sis."

"How'd you know?" his mother said.

"I texted him," Grace said, kissing his cheek. "And yes, I scored you some leftover pizza, although, by the way, you shouldn't be checking your phone while on your bike."

"I made a pit stop at the Cutaway Creek overlook to call home. Caught your message then." He hugged his mother.

"How long do you have?"

"I leave in a couple weeks. We're diving a wreck off of Key West."

"Bring me a treasure," Amelia said. She had tucked her arm into his.

"How is Tiger?" Casper asked, glancing into the room. "Dare looks like he might keel over. What happened?"

"He climbed up on your old bunk and fell off."

"Where was Darek? Why were you watching him?"

"Darek had a date," Grace said. She had pretty blue eyes and now they shone.

Ivy had already begun to back away, held there only by her crazy, train-wreck curiosity. Why had Darek gotten married—and where was this poor child's mother?

"You're kidding me."

"He filled in for Owen at the bachelor auction. He and Eden couldn't make it, so . . . ," his mother said.

"Darek filled in?" Casper gave a sound of disbelief. "Oh, who is the poor girl?"

Ivy sort of liked Casper—his dark curly hair, the sense of adventure in his aura. With his talk of diving and Key West, he sounded like a modern-day pirate. Why couldn't she have bid on him?

No. Wait. Ivy didn't want a man who was going to leave her for some lost-treasure dream.

What was she thinking? She wasn't in the market for *any* kind of man. Or any kind of relationship that would inevitably end and break her heart.

She edged toward the door, but not fast enough to tune out the little boy's scream. Ivy turned and saw Darek hovering over his son, holding his hand, speaking softly to him as the doctor applied a long needle to the wound, probably to numb it. The child howled.

This was where Ivy checked out.

Besides, Darek had long forgotten her.

It was probably for the best, really. But for the first time since meeting him, she hoped that he wouldn't.

Darek only had to blink and his son seemed to grow another inch. He drew the quilt up around Tiger's shoulders, the child's golden hair like a halo around his head. He looked like a cherub when sleep took him—and it had dropped him hard on the way home from the ER. Darek had removed the child seat from his Jeep in case his mother needed it, so she'd driven Tiger home in her Caravan, Darek following, and Casper behind him riding Darek's old motorcycle.

He'd briefly looked for Ivy as they'd exited the ER, but true to her word, she could take care of herself. He didn't want to think about the crazy hour he'd spent with her, not sure why he couldn't take his eyes off her, nor why it made him feel so miserable.

She wasn't so beautiful that it should knock him over. Nor particularly witty, or even flirty, like Felicity. Just . . . *Direct* might be the word. No games with her. Probably the lawyer in her— although most lawyers he knew hid something.

Still, something about her . . . the way she didn't pity him. Oh, wait, she had—that's why she purchased him in the first place.

Nice.

He probably owed her the five hundred dollars she'd paid, but if he got lucky, she'd chalk the entire experience up to a bad decision and forget him.

At least until he called her office to check on Jensen's hours, with the wild hope that the man might go to jail. Darek would be on his best behavior then.

He had put Ivy out of his mind as he pulled in behind his mother, retrieved his sleeping son, and hiked through the resort to his tiny A-frame cabin tucked on the far edge of the property.

The twelve guest cabins that dotted the lakeshore stood lonely and dark, not a soul occupying them, although a young family was scheduled to arrive on Wednesday for a week. They'd have the run of the place, what with the dismal winter tourist season extending into June.

The lack of snow this year had killed the influx of snowmobilers, snowshoers—even the dogsled mushers had to cancel. Worse, the early spring had dried out the land, turning the forest tinder crisp. Already, the forest service had issued a warning, outlawing campfires in the northern canoe areas. So much for the nostalgia of the north woods that might draw tourists to Evergreen's shores. Thankfully, the forest service still allowed campfires at the resort areas. For now.

Darek had had a powwow with his dad this evening, just before Owen's phone call. He'd unrolled the plans for a sauna, a hot tub, and even a play area for kids. Maybe turn the resort into more of a camp atmosphere for the next generation. And if they could convince Gibs next door to sell his overgrown property, they'd have the only sandy beach on the lake.

But the old man wasn't budging, and they didn't have a single fishing trip on the docket for this month, so even if Gibs had a lightning-bolt-from-heaven change of heart, they couldn't afford to give him anything but a handshake and hope.

After a century of running Evergreen Resort, they just might have to close their doors.

Ivy's words hung briefly in his mind. *Carrying on the family business, huh?* He'd never aspired to taking over the family resort, but God hadn't asked him what he wanted. And now he had no choices left.

He still hadn't made peace with the Almighty over his losses—or his future. Maybe he never would.

Darek never locked the cabin and now pushed the door open to the soaring ceiling of the family room. It collected the shadows of the night, the furry branches of pines imprinted on the walls. He'd built the place for Felicity, thinking she'd like the view of the lake and access to Claire's grandfather's place, but he hadn't counted on how the lights of the Atwood family mansion nearly flooded his front room, turning them blind. Nor how it would make her feel so alone, so remote.

No wonder she hadn't been able to ignore Jensen Atwood. Darek practically pushed her into his arms.

Tiger snuggled closer to him, and for a moment, he debated putting the tyke in his bed with him. But then he'd have to climb into the loft, and he didn't allow Tiger up there anyway. He'd simply sleep on the couch, listening for a whimper.

Darek kissed Tiger on his chubby cheek, tucked his worn stuffed tiger—the one Felicity bought him at the hospital after his birth—into his arms. The hospital had thrown out his precious Spider-Man sleep shirt, too bloodstained to save, so he'd have to head down to the Ben Franklin and order a new one.

Oh, Felicity, he has your nose. Your freckles.

In every other way, Tiger had inherited his father's traits—his recklessness, his sense of danger, his independence. It scared Darek sometimes how much he loved his son. And feared moments like this.

If Felicity were here, none of this would have ever happened. But if Felicity were here, maybe Darek never would have realized how amazing and precious his Tiger was. He'd still be chasing fire, part of the Jude County Hotshot team, possibly working as a fire manager by now. He would be spending even less time at home—and who knows if their marriage would have lasted?

He might have a son who didn't even know his name.

But that couldn't be worse than being motherless, could it? Darek pressed his hand against the burn in his chest and closed the door, after making sure the Spidey night-light was on.

Felicity might have had her faults, but she adored Tiger. She had been a good mother, tried to be a good wife. They might have had a good marriage, been able to figure out their problems, if he'd been a better man, ready for marriage, ready for responsibility. Yes, he could blame this entire mess on himself.

Mostly.

Partly.

He grabbed a blanket and pillow from the hall closet and headed for the couch. The tiny cabin could fit inside his parents' great room. A small hallway connected the open family room and kitchen to the main-floor bedroom. He'd created a loft upstairs for Felicity and himself, but toward the end, she'd slept on the sofa downstairs. She blamed it on wanting to be close to the baby, but he knew better.

She'd furnished the place—it still had her sense of opulence, with the oversize leather sofa and matching ottoman, the red suede recliner, the fifty-five-inch flat-screen TV for the satellite dish he'd long since disconnected. Stainless steel appliances and granite countertops in a kitchen the size of a boat galley.

Cadillac tastes on a firefighter's salary. He was still paying off the credit cards.

He winced as he remembered his accusations. *You should have married Jensen Atwood!*

Yeah, well, you're probably right! But he didn't get me pregnant, did he?

They'd had better times before that. Like when Tiger came into the world. For a brief moment he'd thought it might work.

The lake glistened tonight under the caress of moonlight. The Atwood place loomed across the water, a hulking castle in the woods.

Darek tucked the pillow behind his head. Stared at the ceiling.

Tried to figure out a way to save the resort. It remained the only thing he had to give to his son.

Instead, Ivy drifted into his head. His hand slid to his arm where she'd touched it. He hadn't expected that, a moment of kindness from a woman he'd all but growled at.

He should have given her the attention she deserved. But according to Felicity, he hadn't a clue how to give of himself, how to pay attention to others.

A knock at the door jerked him up. He opened the door to his mother standing on the stoop, holding tight the cardigan wrapped around her. She had her blonde hair pulled back, and her face looked gaunt and tired.

"Mom, what are you doing here?" He turned on the light and moved aside.

She stepped in, and only then could he see that she'd been crying, her eyes void of makeup, a little bloodshot.

"Are you okay?"

She shook her head over and over. "I just keep thinking, what if something had happened? He could have lost an eye. I would never forgive myself if . . ."

Darek drew his mother into his arms. "Shh. I know. And it was an accident, Mom. We can't hover over him every minute." But oh, how he wanted to. To wrap the kid up and protect him from life. From bad decisions. From the mistakes of others. Even from his own father's stupidity.

"He's so much like you," his mother said, disentangling herself from his arms. She wiped her cheeks. "I was always terrified you'd fall into the lake and drown. Or go headfirst over your handlebars and lose your teeth. Or go hiking in the woods—"

"And get eaten by bears?"

She gave him a little push. "You know what I mean. Those woods are dangerous. And none of you boys had a lick of fear in you. I call it boy brain. And Tiger seems to have inherited every bit of yours."

"Um, thanks, Mom?"

She caught his face in her hands. "That's not a criticism. It's a warning."

Even after he'd grown a foot taller than her, she could still make him feel like a small boy, the kind who wanted to say, *Look, Mom!* and get a smile.

She sighed.

"Something else on your mind?"

She walked past him to the kitchen and put the container of milk back in the fridge. It was probably sour by now. "Your father mentioned that you were angry with him."

She had picked up a washcloth and was scrubbing his tiny table, the place where Tiger spilled his cereal this morning.

"Mom, I can do that."

She looked up at him. "Do what?"

Right. "I was just . . . Well, you can't imagine how humiliating it was to stand there in Owen's place, a mule at auction, just for some good press. If Dad wants to boost stays here at the resort, he's going to have to think about updating the place. And maybe you and Gracie could upgrade the lodge canteen offerings to something more than box lunches and s'more kits."

His mother gathered the cereal remains in her hand. "We've always said that Evergreen Resort was an oasis. A place to get away from all the noise of the city." Turning on the water, she began to wash out the rag. "It's supposed to be quiet up here."

"What if people don't want to get away anymore? What if they like—?"

"The busyness? Being constantly entangled in life?"

"Being connected."

"Sometimes a person just has to break away from all that. Listen to their own thoughts, maybe hear a few of God's."

She wiped her hands on a paper towel, then threw it away. "Can I just look in on him?"

Darek nodded and watched as she tiptoed to Tiger's room.

What if someone didn't want to listen to God's thoughts? What if . . . what if someone preferred the chaos, the noise?

It might keep them from looking too deep inside, from being horrified at what they saw.

His mom reemerged and shut Tiger's door behind her. "He's so precious. Especially when he's sleeping."

Darek couldn't disagree. He followed her out to the porch.

The lodge lights flickered in the distance. "You want me to walk you back? Tiger is like a log when he goes out."

"No. I know my way." Of course she did. She'd walked these paths for over half of her life. But as she stepped off the deck, she glanced out over the water, pausing for a moment. "Do you think he sits over there and watches you like you watch him?"

He stilled. "I don't watch him."

His mother glanced at him.

"Much."

"I remember the days sitting on the deck watching you boys waterskiing or hitting a hockey puck around or swinging from that dangerous rope swing. You two had so much fun together."

"Mother—"

"Must be a terrible thing to have to look every day into the faces of the people you hurt."

"Jensen doesn't care who he hurt."

She was silent. Then, "I wasn't necessarily talking about him."

"Whose side are you on here?"

"Why, yours, of course. Which is why I ache for you and all you lost."

"Felicity."

"Mmm-hmm." The wind tugged at her hair, and it whispered around her face.

He glanced at Jensen's castle and a dark boil simmered in his chest. "I still can't believe he got off so easily. He should have gone to jail. Should still be there, rotting. Remembering what he stole from me. Us." He looked at her. "He's never, not once, asked for forgiveness. And he hasn't had to—his lawyer made sure of that."

She considered him, her eyes soft. "Does one have to ask for forgiveness to be forgiven?"

He tightened his jaw. "Is there forgiveness for someone who kills another man's wife?"

She lifted a shoulder. "I hope so, for your sake."

"What does that mean? I shouldn't be required to forgive a man who stole everything from me, should I?"

With a sigh, she patted his arm. "I know forgiveness is a lot to ask." She leaned up and gave him a kiss on the cheek. "I'm glad Tiger is okay. Good night, Son. I love you."

Darek watched until she disappeared into the darkness.

Yes. Yes, it was too much to ask.

He stepped inside and closed the door to the house across the lake, shining in the moonlight.

Claire Gibson wasn't sure what bothered her the most.

The fact that Jensen Atwood no longer lurked in the shadows of the VFW, a ghost in the audience of her performance, or that Darek Christiansen had left with another woman. A woman not Felicity.

A woman not his late wife and Claire's deceased best friend.

She stood at the keyboard trying to concentrate as fellow musicians Kyle Hueston and Emma Nelson churned out a version of "I Heard It through the Grapevine," a cover that always pleased the locals.

Emma finished the last bars of the song as the crowd cheered. Yes, an appropriate song for Deep Haven, where gossip grew like weeds.

Claire expected to know by her shift tomorrow at Pierre's Pizza the name of the red-haired beauty who had purchased Darek Christiansen tonight.

She'd debated bidding herself, the deafening silence nearly squeezing the words from her. She could admit a swell of relief when someone blurted out a bid.

As the applause died, Kyle came around from his drum set and took the mic. "Hello, everyone! Thanks for sticking out the night with us here. Before we play our last song, I'd like to . . . um . . ." Kyle glanced at Emma, gave her a strange look, a grin mixed with a touch of fear.

Claire didn't think Kyle Hueston, local deputy, was afraid of anything.

Suddenly, as Claire's breath stopped, he knelt before Emma and took her hand.

Emma froze.

"Emma Nelson. You put the music in my heart. My life is richer, better, stronger, and more beautiful since you came into it. Please, would you marry me?"

Emma had pressed her hand to her mouth. When he dug out a ring and she nodded, the entire town erupted. She flung herself into Kyle's arms.

Claire smiled, but her throat burned. She swallowed it down, hating the way all that joy pooled in her chest and turned sour.

Kyle had graduated with her. Emma, three years later. Everyone around her had a life, plans, family, friends.

A future.

And she had . . .

"Claire, can you manage the last song?" Emma turned to her, eyes glistening. "I can't sing."

"No problem," she said as Emma took up her guitar. Kyle settled behind the drums again.

Claire spoke into her mic. "Hey, everybody. How about if we end with a little Jefferson Airplane? 'Somebody to Love'?"

No wonder Kyle had picked this set. Claire dug into the chords, leaned into the microphone.

"'Don't you want somebody to love?'"

Yes, actually, she did. But apparently that wouldn't happen as long as she lived in Deep Haven. In fact, everyone around her seemed to be finding the one, knitting their lives together, finding a niche.

Claire had managed to settle into her two-bedroom attic apartment above the Footstep of Heaven Bookstore and Coffee Shop. Beyond that . . . well, she had been voted head horticulturist in charge of the roses in Presley Park.

And she made a mean spinach pizza.

Keeping her smile to the end, she let the last chords fade into the walls as the crowd took Emma and Kyle into their embrace.

She packed up her keyboard without acknowledgment and wished the crazy thought that Jensen might still be here.

Not that she'd talk to him, but at least with him in the room, she knew she existed.

Sometimes she wondered if anyone else knew. For the daughter of missionaries changing the world one life at a time, she'd managed to flop hard into oblivion. What a stellar disappointment.

The night smelled crisp and sweet, a breeze off the lake cooling the June air. Claire drove along the shoreline, then up the hill, and took the north entrance to Evergreen Lake, moving from pavement to a dirt road. The south-siders had pooled their vast resources and had a private paving company smooth out their dirt road. Those on the north side still waited for the city to receive a transportation grant. Someday, maybe.

Gravel and dirt kicked up behind the Yaris, her headlights cutting a trail through the inky darkness. She passed the sign for Evergreen Resort and hoped they had a few guests. But she spied no cars in their parking lot.

She turned in to her grandfather's rutted, two-lane drive, weaving slowly through the trees, past the resort property, and toward the west end of the lake. Beyond the house, the road continued to an old pasture where Grandpop once kept a small herd of dairy cows. The barn had long since been torn down, but the pasture had grown into a beautiful meadow of wildflowers.

She sometimes took her guitar and played in the field, just for the romance of it.

A light burned at the side door, moths flirting with death

around the blaze. Obviously Grandpop held out hope that she might stop by after her gig. He had that uncanny way of knowing when she needed to come home and tuck herself into the familiar smells of the Gibson homestead.

She kicked off her shoes in the linoleum entryway. The kitchen light burned and she smelled the faint scent of grease. *Please, don't let Grandpop have left something burning.*

But the cast-iron pan was cold, a layer of grease hardened, the remnants of a venison burger still in the pan. She picked up a plate left on the round farm table, put it in the sink, then went into the family room.

Grandpop Gibs lay in his recliner, emitting a shallow snore. Claire spread one of her grandmother's knit afghans over him, then considered him a long moment in the pool of light from the standing lamp. He wore his Vietnam years in the lines on his face, his white hair nearly gone now, his skin doughy. His worn, giant hands rested on the arms of the chair, his barrel chest rising and falling.

If she lost him, she'd have no one.

Okay, that wasn't fair. Her parents were still alive, but they had only really shown up in the past ten years in the form of letters, e-mail, and more recently, Skype. They had about as much knowledge of her life as Jensen, next door.

She wondered if he was home.

Turning off the lamp and then the porch light so she wouldn't eat a mouthful of moths, she grabbed another afghan from the sofa and stepped outside. The lake lapped the beach, dark and mysterious, and she walked down the path, letting her bare feet sink into the sand.

She cast a gaze over to Jensen's place, the palatial estate of his father's sprawling log vacation home. The moon slid off the green roof, across the manicured lawn, towering white pine and balsam trees, and a trio of birches. Beyond the massive deck that ran the length of the house, the windows remained dark. Sometimes, however, when she came out here, or even canoed on the lake, she could feel Jensen watching her.

Or maybe she just imagined that he did, with those blue eyes, his lopsided playboy smile suggesting he could have anything he wanted.

No matter what the cost.

Claire sank into an Adirondack chair, wrapping the afghan around herself, shivering as the wind found her hair and untangled it from her ponytail. She leaned her head back to stare at the stars, listening to memories, laughter, tears.

Trying not to hear the accusations.

Most of all, she refused to be upset that Felicity had abandoned them all to figure out how to live without her.

CHAPTER 3

"IF YOU'RE TRYING to impress me, it's working."

The county attorney had cracked open Ivy's office door after a quick knock and stuck his head in. "Second day and you're already burning the midnight oil."

DJ Teague looked and dressed like a man who should be living in a high-rise in Minneapolis and dating some supermodel, with his cocoa skin, soft brown eyes, crisp blue dress shirt, tie and jacket, after a day of meeting with county departments, preparing major cases, and defending the county from lawsuits.

Ivy leaned back in her chair and gestured to the pile of manila folders stacked on her desk. "Oh, I'll be here long past midnight, familiarizing myself with these. I have forty hearings in two days," she said, raising an eyebrow. "How did this happen?"

On the floor, two cardboard boxes held more files, and on a bookshelf along the wall, all manner of legal reference books filled the shelves. First thing she did yesterday morning, after meeting her secretary, Nancy, and her paralegal, Jodi, was start to dig through the piles stacked on her empty desk.

DJ came in and sat in one of the chairs. "We share a judge with the next county, so we have to pack in as many cases as we can during our two days. Ask Jodi to help you catch up and prepare because on Monday, you'll have a new stack of cases to look at."

The afternoon had long since slunk into the horizon, leaving behind pools of light from her lamp. She hated the fluorescent glow and kept the overhead off but had plundered a standing lamp from the reception area to spread light over her shoulder and onto the mess of papers scattered on her L-shaped desk.

Her cursor blinked on an evidentiary brief she was reviewing for tomorrow's hearing.

Ivy forced a smile and debated warming up her coffee, maybe finishing the sandwich she'd ordered from the Blue Moose Café. "I've reverted back to my days as a clerk, I guess. Getting up at 6 a.m. for class, working at the firm at night. I think I lived on coffee and Hot Pockets."

"Daniel said you were his top assistant prosecutor down in Anoka." He smiled, kindness in his eyes. "I have no doubt you can handle this."

A burn filled her throat at the mention of Daniel Wainwright, her mentor/boss/friend. "Daniel might have been overly optimistic about my abilities."

"I always considered him a great judge of character and ability. If he believed in you enough to offer you a junior prosecutor position out of law school, then I believe I hired the right person."

She blinked away a rush of heat in her eyes. "Thank you, Mr. Teague."

"DJ. And I miss him too. The cancer took him too quickly." He leaned forward. "You weren't the only one to sit under his teaching." Ivy could feel the quote before it came. "'You hold justice in your hands. Treat it with respect.'"

She nodded. "I hear him in my head sometimes, even after a year."

He laughed. "I hear him in my head after *ten* years. But I found that everything he said was spot-on. Especially in a small town like Deep Haven. Everyone is watching you here. You have to keep your word and earn their trust one case at a time and never, never abuse your power."

"I wouldn't—"

"Of course not. But justice to one person looks like favoritism to another. This may be the hardest job you ever have."

"I want to get this right. I've dreamed of living here ever since . . ." She grimaced. "Well, since the Jensen Atwood case."

"It was your memo that called for a departure from sentencing guidelines and set up the plea agreement."

"Yes. I still remember the day Thornton Atwood passed it to me—in fact, he gave it to an associate, who gave it to me. Truth was, I didn't know I was doing research on his son's case. He told me to find a way to get the defendant out of jail time. I slaved over that memo, looking for precedent. Daniel was one of my law professors at the time; he read the piece and thought it was a slick bit of legal work."

"And you didn't worry about the ethics?"

"Why? Atwood wasn't representing the case, and I didn't even know Jensen. To be frank, I thought it was a teaching exercise until I saw it on the news after I turned it in."

"You didn't see the headlines?"

"I was clerking and going to law school. I didn't watch television."

DJ nodded. "Daniel told me you were one of his shining stars."

Shining stars. Oh, she missed him.

DJ picked up a file and paged through it. "Jensen still lives here, you know. Still working on his hours. Mitch O'Conner is his probation officer. His office is just down the hall."

"I saw Jensen the other night at the VFW. Nearly said hi, but he doesn't know me."

"Probably better that way," DJ said.

"Why?"

He frowned and slowly shook his head. "He might not thank you for what you did. It hasn't been easy to live here."

"And going to jail would have been better? Listen, Deep Haven should be happy they got anything on him. At least justice prevailed."

"Justice can take many shades, especially in a small town." He put the file back on the stack. "In this job, you get to know your friends, your neighbors, and as their lives weave together with yours, the lines become blurred. You have to always be thinking of conflict-of-interest issues. You get to know the darker side of the community, your neighbors."

"Deep Haven hardly has a dark side," Ivy said with a smile. "Not like Minneapolis."

"You still think that after spending the last day preparing for court?"

Her smile died. "I came here because I wanted to make a difference. Daniel always said small acts of justice can make great ripples in the community."

"Or tear it apart. One of our former assistant CAs left after she had to prosecute her best friend's son. The son went to jail, she lost her friend, and she was dragged through the paper for weeks. She finally left, moved out of town completely."

Ivy stared at him. Oh.

He got up. "Remember, every case is personal. And in a town like this, that means it's about your grocer, your banker, the local barista, your favorite waitress, even sometimes a deacon in the church. People you know and care about. You might have to give them the hard news that their lives are about to change—and you're the one making it happen."

She tried to add a little laughter to her voice. "Well, then it's a good thing I don't know anyone. Not really. I can be impartial."

DJ raised a dark eyebrow. "Hmm. Don't you? Wasn't that you who purchased Darek Christiansen in the bachelor auction?"

Her mouth opened.

He laughed. "It's a small town, Ivy. Besides, I was there."

"It was just for charity. I can promise there is nothing between Darek Christiansen and me."

He held up his hand. "None of my business. You may be playing with fire there a little, but it's your life. I'm just saying that your address book is going to fill up faster than you think." He opened the door. "Don't stay too late. Judge Magnusson is fair, but she doesn't like napping in her courtroom."

"Good night, Mr. Teague."

"DJ." He winked and closed the door behind him.

DJ counted as the second person who'd warned her about Darek Christiansen. He'd been skirting the edge of her brain all day, the way he'd morphed right before her eyes into a man with a heart of flesh. And his family—what might it be like to have a family who rushed to each other's aid? She imagined their Thanksgiving table, loud and noisy, their Christmases messy and cluttered. She could see Darek wrestling with his brother Casper as children, or the two sisters sharing secrets as they polished their toenails.

There is nothing between Darek Christiansen and me.

And there wouldn't be. Because she didn't need darkness and trouble in her life. Especially if there was some kind of crazy ex-wife in the picture.

Except . . . well, it wouldn't hurt to give him another chance, would it? Especially since she doubted very much that his name would ever land on the assistant county attorney's desk.

These were exactly the type of guests Evergreen Resort needed. A young family with four rambunctious children—three boys and a toddler daughter all under the age of eight, not old enough to miss cell phone service or Facebook. Sure, they piled out of their SUV with handheld gaming gadgets, but their smart father ordered the hardware left in the car while Darek checked them in and showed them around the resort.

"There's a playground of sorts by the house. A sandbox and a tire swing, a basketball hoop," Darek said, pointing to the ancient recreation area. "And horseshoes, bocce ball, and a badminton set in the shed."

Overhead the sky had turned into watercolor glory, reds and golds and lavender painted across the horizon. "There's a restaurant down the road, or you can always fire up your barbecue." He had put them in the largest cabin, a three-bedroom with home-made quilts, a tiny kitchen with a retro Formica table and chairs. "There's a canoe down by the shore; feel free to take it out. The life jackets and paddles are in a corral nearby. And of course, a paddle-boat available at the swimming area down by the dock. We also have a floating raft with a slide on it, but there's no lifeguard, so you're on your own."

"No problem," the man said. "We came here to spend time together as a family." He eyed the oldest son, who seemed to be pining for his gaming console. But the boy smiled back at his father.

"There's a booklet of all the nearby hikes and activities in the cabin, and if you want to add a fishing trip, I can arrange that."

"Fishing!" one of the other boys exclaimed. "Cool."

Darek smiled at that. Once upon a time he lived for the hours on the lake with his father and brothers, pulling in walleye.

He walked the family back to the lodge, a towering building that anchored the property, built from hand-hewn logs his great-great-grandfather felled. "You can buy essentials at the canteen." He pointed to a tiny alcove of supplies and snacks, including a small freezer with pizzas and ice cream, next to the resort check-in counter. The front office was actually just an extension of the main lodge, where guests could come and enjoy the view of the lake from the expansive deck or read a novel in the public living room. Darek's family had their own private quarters on the other side of the living room wall, the stone fireplace linking the two sides, their bedrooms upstairs.

"Honey, we should pick up a pizza or two for the kids," the man's wife said, her daughter perched on her hip.

They were leaving outfitted with pizzas and ice cream

sandwiches just in time for Tiger to race in from where he'd been helping his grandfather clean fish. The smells of the lake and fresh air lifted off him and stirred a childhood longing in Darek.

"I caught a fish this big!" Tiger said, eyeing the guests and holding his arms open.

"Already mastering the art of the whopper," Darek said, glancing at the bandage over his son's eye. Seemed soiled but intact.

"Looks like the fish took a bite outta you," the father said, and Tiger laughed.

"We had a little mishap with a bunk bed," Darek said.

Tiger grinned up at him. "Don't forget about the Muffin Man, Daddy!"

The Muffin Man. Right. "Let me get these guests settled, and we'll head out." He picked up the keys to the family's cabin. "Can I help you with your luggage?"

The man shook his head. "That's why I have sons; right, boys?"

The three towheaded boys nodded and scampered outside. Their father took the keys from Darek. "You have a beautiful place here. I came here once with my parents. Best week of my life. I've been looking forward to coming back for years."

"Let me know if you need anything," Darek said as he spotted Tiger helping himself to an ice cream sandwich. "Not yet, sparky. Let's go."

Tiger made a face but hustled out to the Jeep.

"Mom, we're taking off," Darek said, popping his head into the private quarters.

Ingrid looked up from where she stood in the kitchen, making bread. "Are our guests settled?"

"Looks like it."

"I might wander down later and check on them."

Of course she would. With a fresh batch of sticky buns. One of the secret touches of Evergreen Resort—the homey extras.

"Say hi to the Muffin Man for me."

"Right."

Tiger was strapped into his booster seat when Darek climbed into the Jeep. He'd just have to show up smelling like a walleye.

Darek caught a glimpse of the three boys wrestling on the grass near their cabin as he pulled out of the driveway.

Yeah, he remembered when he thought of this place as paradise, when he thought growing up here was the best life a boy could have.

He glanced at Tiger in the rearview mirror, the dirt on his shirt, grimy hands, the hint of a sunburn on his nose, his windblown hair. "How big was that fish?"

"This big!" Tiger held out his arms as wide as they could go.

Darek laughed. Yes, maybe it still could be paradise. Something simple—family. A piece of the northern shore woods to share with the world. The life Felicity had wanted for them. If only he hadn't been too immature to see it.

They pulled up to the library, and Tiger was unlocking his seat belt before Darek applied the brake. "Hold on there—"

But Tiger was out the door and scampering up the sidewalk to the building. Darek followed him and found the ring of kids seated inside the children's reading area, decorated like a zoo, complete with faux bars, cutout giraffes, hippos, elephants. Tiger sat in a molded ostrich chair.

Darek pulled up a child-size chair and settled himself on it, listening to the "Muffin Man"—their creative town librarian—read to the children in her giant cupcake hat, her fuzzy padded costume. She had single-handedly sparked a reading inferno with her Wednesday night story time. And it just might be the only time Tiger sat quietly.

Darek smiled at the other parents as they glanced at him. He tried not to think about the way his son looked like he'd gone a few bruiser rounds with a local bully. *He fell,* Darek wanted to shout, but that would only draw more attention.

At least Nan Holloway didn't sit in the audience, although he wouldn't put lurking in the shadows past her. He glanced around, just to check.

Wait.

His gaze stopped on the petite redhead flipping through a book in the fiction section. He'd been too defensive to really notice how cute she was on their so-called date. Now, dressed in a pair of capris and a pink sleeveless shirt, her hair pulled back, she seemed almost soft, even sweet.

Not at all his vision of a lawyer.

Or of the woman he'd treated so badly. He hadn't allowed himself a moment to get to know her. Just resented her and her intrusion into his life.

It wasn't her fault that he had so much baggage, it could crush any chances of a fresh start.

And it wasn't her fault he'd already blown his opportunity for happily ever after. For a family like the one he'd met today. Maybe if he wasn't so angry and hadn't behaved so badly . . . not just to Ivy, but Felicity, too.

No, he didn't deserve a second chance, but—

Maybe she sensed his gaze on her, watching her flip pages, because she looked up. Right at him.

Her eyes connected, her mouth opening just a little.

He should look away. But he was caught there, his crime becoming more glaring as she blinked, recognized him.

And then, suddenly, she smiled. It was sweet and slow and caught him so off guard he didn't know what to do. Just stared back like an idiot, a deer in the headlights.

"Daddy, read this to me."

Tiger slapped a book onto Darek's lap—a copy of *If You Give a Mouse a Cookie*, one of his favorites. The Muffin Man had finished and now was pointing out her selection of books to the audience.

"Okay, pal," Darek said. No doubt they'd leave the library with a stack of new books, enough for hours of nighttime reading. He hooked an arm around his son, pulled him onto his knee. Opened the book.

Glanced up to where Ivy had stood.

She was gone. And with her, any chance for the smile he should have given her.

Jensen logged five hours and thirty-seven minutes of community service before the sun hit the apex of the blue sky.

He'd started his Thursday morning routine at the harbor beach before 6 a.m., stopping by the Java Cup and bringing Phyllis McCann at the parks and rec department a vanilla latte while he logged in, then arming himself with gloves, a bag, and a stake, managing to fill the bag with the detritus of the week's activities. Banana peels, hot dog boats, candy wrappers, gyro papers, SoBe bottles, apple cores, and even a few Java Cup containers. By the time the sun turned the rocks to gems, the beach shone spotless.

At eight, he headed over to the thrift store, bringing Sharron a freshly fried skizzle from World's Best Donuts, and spent two more hours sorting the five garbage bags of clothing they'd received, checking them for damage, hanging or folding the acceptable pieces on the correct racks and shelves, sending more out to be laundered, pricing them, and listing the best items for advertising purposes on the community intranet. He snagged a pair of rubber boots for himself, something to help him should a sump pump at Pine Acres ever go out again. Sharron signed his card, and he headed over to the Deep Haven animal shelter.

Old Rusty's eyes lit up, his tail cleaning the cement floor as Jensen greeted him. He opened the cage and let the collie lick his chin, rubbing the animal vigorously behind the ears. "I can't believe no one has adopted you yet," he said. "I'd take you home, buddy, but I'm outta here in six weeks, and then what will we do?"

"Take him with you." Annalise Decker stood at the door, a fellow volunteer—although her hours were truly voluntary. She held Arthur, a Persian cat who appeared freshly brushed. "He needs a good home, and you know he loves you."

"I can't. I don't know where I'm headed after I leave Deep Haven."

"Really?" She placed the cat in his cage while Jensen clipped a lead on Rusty. He'd take the dog out for a short run, then clean his cage and return him. He planned to do the same with the pretty half Labrador, half Doberman they'd found running in the woods, collarless. So far, no one had claimed her, and he had half a mind to take her home too. He was a sucker for those sweet brown eyes.

"Yeah. I just need to leave, and once I get free of the county, I'll figure out where to go. Maybe California." He grinned at Annalise as he walked toward the door. "Hawaii. I'll be a beach bum."

"You'll miss this!" Annalise said as the door bumped closed behind him.

Not likely. Apparently she'd forgotten that his time didn't belong to him, that he wasn't walking old Rusty for his health.

But he did like having the collie at his side, especially the way strangers smiled at him, sometimes gave Rusty a pat.

Everyone liked a man with a dog.

He did a mental count of his total hours after today. If he could keep getting days like this over the next six weeks, he'd make his cutoff.

No jail time.

Although, spending three years in a town that hated you felt a little like jail. He didn't blame them—not really. And after three years, they seemed to have built a sort of tolerance for him. Still, he should have seen the future, rejected the plea agreement, and simply endured the four years in prison.

But he was innocent. And innocent men shouldn't go to jail. At least that's what he told himself—told God when Jensen thought He might be willing to listen. But God had clearly already made up His mind about Jensen, just like the rest of Deep Haven.

The smells of fresh battered trout cakes from the fish house tempted him to stop in, and he'd heard that Licks and Stuff was running a special this week—a maple-nut custard cone. But he didn't have time for lunch. Not if he wanted to finish his hours and get home to remove that log, mow, and paint the Millers' place. He should have gotten to it earlier in the week, but by the time he'd finished mowing the high school athletic fields and cleaning the six-mile stretch of highway north of town, he'd arrived home after dark. At least it added to his hours.

He returned Rusty, cleaned his cage, and brushed him down.

Then he doted on the Lab-Doberman mix—he'd call her Nellie—and cleaned her cage. She leaned into his hand so hard as he rubbed behind her ear that it nearly made him weep.

How he hated neglect, hated people not realizing what they had until they lost it.

Jensen hosed down the runs behind the shelter, then wound up the rope and had Annalise sign his volunteer card.

Hat in hand, he stopped by the local Meals On Wheels office. "I'm sorry, Jensen, but we had enough help today. Stop by tomorrow—or maybe next week we'll have an opening." Donna smiled at him when he left, and for a second, he believed her.

He sat in his truck and counted his hours again. Tomorrow he would swing by the social services office and see if they had any shut-ins who needed their lawn mowed or house cleaned. Maybe just needed a friend.

He liked sitting with them, listening to their stories. It made him forget his own.

Back at Pine Acres, he grabbed a ham sandwich, then loaded the mower into the back of the truck and tackled the various lawns that needed attention. He sprayed the decimated currant bush, trimmed it, then found the chain saw in the maintenance shed and went to work on the downed tree.

There had been a time when he detested this kind of work, back when he thought his years in law school might mean some-thing, that he should be respected and admired for his academic prowess. When mowing lawns seemed miles beneath him. But now he found the work refreshing, the sweat honest, and it seemed the one thing he could do to earn his room and board, maybe ease the frown from his father's face.

If that were even possible. He couldn't quite get on his father's good side after the accident. Too many dreams had died that night on the highway.

His father had mentioned, however, that if Jensen could someday talk his neighbor Gibs into selling his shoreline property to Pine Acres, then his little "misstep" might be redeemed.

Misstep. Right. Thornton Atwood often acted as if his son were on some sort of extended, mandatory vacation in northern Minnesota.

That sweet strip of sandy beach *would* be perfect as a private community beach, however. Only problem was, Jensen hadn't talked to Gibs since the terrible accident three years ago. Too afraid, probably. And Claire certainly wouldn't let him get close— she had the temper of a pit bull when it came to her grandfather. He'd never had the courage to cross her.

He cut the tree into foot-long pieces and stacked them beside the house for use when the family wanted campfires. He fed the branches through the shredder, then deposited the sawdust and chips in flower beds near the community entrance.

By the time he considered grabbing the paint bucket, the sun was already cutting long shadows across the paved road of the property. He headed back to the house, unloaded the truck, and hopped in the shower.

Dressed in his sweatpants and a clean cotton T-shirt, Jensen wandered onto the deck overlooking the lake. He listened for the loons calling into the night and dug out his harmonica, answering the call with a mournful tune.

Maybe, okay, he'd miss this. Just this. The quiet of the twilight hour when his muscles ached and fatigue pressed from his mind his mistakes and wishes. When he felt as if he had worked out the stress of the day and earned the right to sink into one of the plush wicker chairs on the deck and watch the sun ignite the lake.

Yes, he'd miss this when he left. This and the tangy memories of summers and life in Deep Haven before it all went sour.

His gaze traveled over to the Gibson place, and he wondered if the canoe still waited on shore.

He put down his harmonica, stood up for a closer look.

A figure lay there. Or perhaps a tarp, but it looked—

No. His breath caught. Gibs lay just beyond the shoreline in the grass, next to his dented four-wheeler, as if he'd hit a tree and taken a tumble.

And hadn't gotten up.

Jensen ran through the house in his bare feet, down the stairs, and into the garage. He slapped his hand on the garage door opener, flicking on the light, then jumped on his own four-wheeler. He'd left the key in the ignition; the engine turned over and he gunned it out of the garage, narrowly missing his father's old boat, now parked on blocks in the fourth stall.

He knew the trail by heart, despite the years. He took it too fast, ducking under branches that had overgrown and narrowly missing the long, shaggy arm of a giant white pine. He came out just west of Gibs's property, near the meadow, and took the road to the driveway. A light blazed on the side entrance, a feeble beacon lit to call Claire home, perhaps. Jensen raced up the driveway and into the front yard, then down to the lake.

Gibs lay in the shadows, shrouded under a hand of darkness. The light from the four-wheeler illuminated his leg at a shattered angle. He wore a work jacket, a pair of gloves, and jeans, but his Huskies hat had tumbled off, leaving a bloody pool where he'd hit his head.

Not far away, his four-wheeler rested on its side, the tree it hit fractured and ready to teeter over. A small trailer filled with cut logs suggested he'd just received a firewood delivery.

Certainly the old man wasn't chopping his own wood anymore?

He crouched beside Gibs, pressed his fingers to his jugular. Please, please—yes, he found a pulse. But the old man wasn't moving.

"Hang in there, Gibs," he said and got up, running toward the house. He found one of Mrs. Gibson's famous knit afghans and scooped up the phone on his way back out. Jensen's thumb dialed 911 and he rested the phone against his shoulder as he reached Gibs and began to tuck the blanket over him.

"Deep Haven Emergency Services. How can I help you?"

He recognized Marnie Blouder's voice. "It's Gibs. He's hurt. I think he hit his head, broke his leg. We need an ambulance up at Evergreen Lake ASAP."

"Jensen, is this you?"

He closed his eyes. "Yes, Marnie. I saw him from my place. Please hurry."

"EMS is on its way. Don't leave him, Jensen."

"I won't, ma'am."

CHAPTER 4

It seemed to Claire that she lived her life always looking in the rearview mirror, wishing she could change what she saw.

Like, for example, the fact that she was spending the two hours she had between her Pierre's shifts trying to coax the town's American Beauty roses back to life.

She could hardly blame herself. Most gardeners faced the late-frost conundrum. Every year, as the days grew longer, the warm sun lured gardeners to uncover their peonies, their hydrangeas, and most importantly, their prizewinning roses. Then, like a thief, a late-season frost would creep in off the lake and kill the buds.

Claire had lost too many beautiful rosebuds before their time by leaning into the season too soon.

So despite the mild winter and lack of snow, she had kept the covers on, not wanting to risk the frost. And her American Beauty roses sweltered under their Styrofoam coverings, broiling instead of freezing to death.

Why, why didn't she just listen to her instincts instead of her fears?

She knelt in the dirt of the city rose garden and lifted one of the containers. Tiny green buds shot out from the cropped limbs, evidence that even in darkness, the roses survived. She pulled the cover off, and the rosebush sprang free as if exhaling.

"Sorry, little rose," she said and sat back on her haunches, brushing dirt from her gloved hands.

"Talking to your plants again, Claire?" Edith Draper strode up the sidewalk on her way to the library, just beyond the garden. She wore an embroidered *Grandmas Are for Hugs* sweatshirt and held an armload of books.

"I'm hoping my decision to keep the covers on and protect them from the frost didn't kill them."

Edith raised a shoulder. "You can't live your life by the what-ifs, sweetie. They look fine to me."

"If I kill these roses, the Deep Haven Horticultural Society will murder me."

Edith had reached the library door. "They put you in charge because you have the best green thumb in town. Not to mention the most energy. Trust yourself." She winked and disappeared inside.

Herself would be the last person Claire trusted. She hadn't made a right decision since . . . well, since she'd convinced her parents to allow her to move stateside and attend Deep Haven High School. But after that . . . yeah, she'd pretty much let down herself and everyone else around her with a string of flimsy life choices.

Claire took off another cover. Again, the rosebush underneath had already started to bloom. Phew. Alive.

She created a stack of Styrofoam containers, then added fertilizer around the roots. Already they looked happier.

She glanced at the sky, the way fingers of twilight stretched out over the heavens. She would have been here earlier, but for the fact that she'd taken an extra shift today. *Please, Lord, help them grow.*

Claire carried the containers into the small storage shed behind the library, left her gloves there, then hopped on her bike and rode it down the street to her apartment. One of the perks of living in a small town—she didn't need a car. Not that she didn't like her Yaris, but sometimes she just loved riding her bike to work and home again, under the starlight.

Her next shift started in ten minutes—not enough time for a shower. She pulled on the black-jeans-and-black-shirt uniform, pinned on her badge, worked her visor over her ponytail, then threw her apron in her over-the-shoulder backpack before scrambling down the stairs and out the back door of the bookstore.

She cast a look up at her new neighbor's place—dark. Apparently the new assistant county attorney worked late hours also.

She hopped on her bike and pedaled to Pierre's, clocking in a minute late. Shoot.

The place looked deserted. No late-night rush tonight, the twenty booths and tables in the main room hosting only a handful of diners. She loved Pierre's, with fishing lures and mounted trout, snowshoes and old Coca-Cola signs, pictures of local hockey teams pinned to the wall. A few framed newspapers heralded Deep Haven events, like the state champion football team and the time their local author, Joe Michaels, won the National Book Award.

Making her way into the kitchen, she breathed in fresh baked calzones, tangy homemade sauce, the scent of fresh vegetables. Tucker Newman stood at the assembly board, working on a Hawaiian pizza. It always cheered her to see him in a hairnet and apron, creating pizza as if it were a work of art. Something had happened to the snowboarder since he started dating Colleen Decker last year. Sometimes she spotted him eating pizza with her family and laughing.

He hadn't exactly laughed in the first few months he'd begun working here. She had thought he wouldn't last.

But that wasn't her call.

Claire read the schedule. They'd put her on the cash register tonight, but with Curt McCormick already manning the counter, restocking cups and napkins and looking as if he might perish from boredom, it seemed that perhaps she could do more damage prepping for tomorrow. She pulled a container of fresh mushrooms from the stainless fridge and headed over to the prep center.

Grace Christiansen stood cutting onions, her blonde hair captured by a hairnet. "I thought you'd gone home for the day," she said, looking miserable.

"Double shift today. I don't mind. I thought you were off tonight." She picked up a mushroom and began to wipe it clean with a paper towel.

"I was, but I got off early the other night and I'm making up hours. Tiger landed in the ER and Mom was pretty frantic trying to find Darek."

Claire stilled, a cold fist in her chest. "What happened?"

"He fell off Casper's old bunk and cut his forehead. Needed seven stitches." Grace shook her head even as she dumped the onions in a stainless steel container. "I think an angel must have caught him because he could have lost an eye. He nicked a pair of Owen's skates he'd been playing with before bed."

"Is he okay?"

"He's fine. He bounces back. I'm more worried about Darek. He practically came unraveled. Blamed himself for not being there—"

"Where was he?"

"Out on a date." She picked up another onion and grimaced.

"Wanna trade?" Claire asked.

Grace shook her head and started to peel the onion. "He was at that bachelor auction—some woman bought him."

Claire had created a nice pile of cleaned mushrooms. "Her name is Ivy. She's real pretty—red hair, shorter, but cute. She told me she's the new assistant county attorney."

"You met her?"

"She lives in the garage apartment behind the bookstore. Our paths crossed yesterday."

Grace nodded, kept chopping.

"What is it?" Claire set the mushrooms on the cutting board and began to slice them.

Grace blinked as if forcing back tears. "I just . . . It's so sad Tiger doesn't have a mom. Wouldn't it be great if Darek could find someone?"

"Tiger had a mom."

Grace glanced at her. Oh, Claire hadn't meant for it to come out so sharp. "I mean, yes, every kid needs a mom. But he has so much family—you and Amelia, your parents, Casper and Owen, Eden."

"He needs a *mom*, Claire." Grace set down the knife, scooping the next batch of onions into the container. "And Darek needs a wife."

Darek didn't deserve another wife. Claire ground her jaw to keep the words from leaking out. "The last thing that Tiger needs is to have another woman take Felicity's place, only for it not to work out."

Grace frowned at her. "What does that mean?"

Claire dumped mushrooms into her own container. "It means that maybe you don't know your brother as well as you think you do."

"He's changed a lot since Felicity died."

Claire put down the knife. "I'm just saying he had his chance, and it's gone. And now he has to make the best with what he has left."

Grace went slack-jawed.

"Please, Gracie. Don't think I'm not compassionate to Tiger. But you have to live with your choices."

"Losing Felicity wasn't his choice, Claire. Accidents just happen. It doesn't mean he shouldn't keep moving on with his life."

Claire stared at her, the words stinging.

"Claire, do you have a moment?"

She turned, wanting to launch herself into Stuart's arms. Probably not an appropriate action for an employee-manager relationship, however, so she wiped her hands, left Grace and her too-forgiving attitude at the prep center, and followed Stuart into his office.

She began an apology before he even sat down at his desk. "I know I lost track of time. I was working in the garden—"

"Really, Claire?" Stuart wore the Pierre's uniform—white apron, black shirt, a contrast to his white hair. The man had been making pizzas for nearly forty years but still managed to keep himself fit. A picture of his family, taken before his wife died, sat on the credenza behind him. "You think I pulled you in here to beat you up for being one minute late?"

Oh.

"What I want to do is give you a raise."

A raise? Her mouth opened to thank him, but he held up a hand.

"But I can't."

She frowned.

"You're already at the very top of the pay scale for a part-time employee, first of all. And second, the truth is, I can't afford you anymore." He actually looked pained.

"Am I being fired because you can't give me a raise? I didn't ask for a raise."

"No, you didn't, but you certainly deserve one. You run the kitchen, the counter, even inventory my supplies better than I do. This place would be a mess without you."

"Then why—?"

"I'm offering you the job of full-time manager. With summer upon us, I have to hire a manager, but I can't have a part-time employee with your salary taking up the budget. Please, will you consider taking the position?"

A full-time Pierre's Pizza manager. She didn't know why she had the insane urge to weep. She pushed a smile through the web in her chest. "I don't . . . I . . ."

Stuart leaned forward, his voice gentling. "I love you like a daughter. Over the past seven years, I've seen you grow and become this amazing woman. But what do you want from your life? If it's to have a career in the food service industry, I can make that happen. Going full-time would give you benefits and a 401(k). A real career. But if that's not what you want . . ." He sighed. "You're twenty-five, Claire. And maybe it's none of my business, but I know your parents, and I know they worry that if you don't make a move out of Deep Haven soon, you never will."

Leave Deep Haven? Her throat tightened as if a hand curled around it.

"I understood it took a few years to get that college nest egg saved, but certainly you have something now. And there are always loans, and—"

"I'll think about it," Claire said. Oh, she didn't want to cry in front of Stuart. Not with his kind eyes looking at her like a father's would.

With expectation. Hope.

She got up. "When do I have to let you know?"

"The sooner the better. But certainly before the Fourth of July holiday. I need to hire someone and get them trained before then."

Perfect. Two weeks to figure out if she wanted to serve pizza the rest of her life.

If you don't make a move out of Deep Haven soon, you never will.

Like she hadn't thought of that every day of her life for the past seven years.

She nodded, put her hand on the door handle just as her cell phone vibrated in her pocket. She grimaced, glancing over her shoulder. "Sorry. I forgot to turn it off."

"No problem, Claire," Stuart said.

She pulled the phone out of her pocket as she opened the door. Read the caller ID.

Deep Haven Hospital. Her breath hitched even as she put the phone to her ear. "Hello?"

"Claire Gibson?"

"Yes." She glanced back at Stuart, who was frowning.

"I'm calling from the Deep Haven ER. Your grandfather has been in an accident. It's not life-threatening, but you should come."

Like a song, the man had embedded in Ivy's brain, and no amount of rereading the last paragraph would dislodge the look Darek Christiansen had given her when she caught him staring at her yesterday in the library.

Staring at her. Like . . . Well, she didn't exactly know how to interpret his expression. It had been as if he were looking at her for the first time. And then the sheer panic on his face when she smiled at him.

She didn't know whether to laugh or cry. At him. Or herself for her own crazy, warm, maybe even painful emotions when she saw him take his son onto his lap and open a book.

It almost made her wish she could rewind her date with Darek and start again.

Such a small, simple gesture. How she would have loved to have a parent read to her. Silly. Stupid. Ivy closed her novel and set it on the coffee table, hating how losses snuck up on her, blindsided her. She wasn't a weak little girl needing a father, a mother, needing a hug.

And she'd simply been reacting to the sweetness of seeing Darek's giant frame propped on a tiny children's chair, listening to the Muffin Man, then bent over reading to his son.

He might be the town grouch, but to his son, Darek was terrific. Kind. Gentle.

So what had happened between him and his wife that she wasn't in the picture?

Ivy got up and walked outside, sitting on her front steps. The sun had set, the stars sprinkled across the inky surface of the water. She could smell the lake in the air, the heat loosening its grip on the day. She glanced at the Victorian bookstore, expecting lights in the upstairs apartment, but apparently her neighbor was working late. She'd met Claire yesterday. A pretty girl, maybe just a couple years younger than Ivy, with dark-brown eyes and hair and a kind smile. She wore a Pierre's Pizza shirt and a black visor, maybe on her way to work.

"How long are you in town for?" she'd asked after Ivy introduced herself.

Forever, Ivy had wanted to say, barely holding the word back. "I just started as the assistant county attorney."

Claire nodded with a smile that seemed to hint at humor on her face. "I'll see you round," she said as she hopped on her red bike and pedaled off.

Ivy hoped so. She could use a friend besides her favorite bestselling authors.

She drew her knees up to her chest, a slight wind soft on her skin. What if she saw Darek again?

What if he smiled back?

Oh, boy. *Now* she felt desperate.

But . . . what if she gave him a second chance? What if he showed up at her house with an apology and an invitation to a second date?

He'd roll up to her driveway and smile—she knew he had it in him—and she'd come off the steps, walk down to the drive to hear him say, *I'm sorry I was such a grouch. How about another try?*

Really? Why, Darek, I'm so glad you asked—

Oh, for pete's sake, she didn't need this. Didn't need Darek in her life, smiling her direction, taking her in his arms.

Because then what? She'd hop in his Jeep and they'd drive off into the sunset? She knew better than that. Happy endings and family didn't belong to a girl like her.

Ivy got up and went back inside, flopping down on the bed in the corner of the room. She turned on her iPod to some Frank Sinatra.

The crooner was singing about moonlight and dancing and falling in love. She turned it off.

Walked to the window and stood there in silence.

Just her and the moonlight.

It would have to be enough.

CHAPTER 5

"TIGER, YOU STAY RIGHT HERE, next to the cart, while Daddy goes to get a watermelon." Darek turned and pointed to his son. Red candy stickiness smudged his cheeks from the lollipop on a string the teller at the bank had given him, and he stood licking his fingers, even as the lollipop sagged in his other hand. His stitches had started to dissolve, leaving a thin red scar. He still looked a disheveled mess, however, his new Spider-Man shirt grimy from a morning of "helping Daddy in the yard."

"Don't move."

"Okay, Daddy."

Darek smiled and rounded the edge of the table, reaching for the biggest watermelon he could find. He slung it under his arm and pulled out his list, just to check.

His mother had this brilliant idea to serve root beer floats on the deck for the one cabin of guests who had checked in last night, as an Independence Day treat.

One cabin for the Fourth of July weekend. He well remembered when they'd had to turn people away.

Darek could barely stand the look on his father's face today when he'd taken two cancellations, both because of the lack of air-conditioning in their "rustic" cabins.

Why couldn't every guest be like the family a couple weeks ago who had fished and swum and hiked and enjoyed the beauty of the north shore without needing the comforts of home?

Not that he blamed the guests, he supposed. With temperatures soaring into the nineties, the tiny cabins could turn to saunas without the right circulation. But they didn't need to be nasty about it. He wanted to strangle the snooty young couple who'd shown up, driven to the cabin, then turned around and left, after calling the resort a dump to his father's face.

While his father smiled and wished them well, Darek wanted to let them know exactly how many hours his mother had scrubbed their cabin. Preferably he'd do it while backing up the skinny, too-slick-looking tourist against his shiny black Escalade.

Ungrateful . . .

Thanks to his mother's hard work, a guest could eat off the floor of any of the cabins, and his father kept them all in tip-top shape. But their homemade breadboard countertops and wooden floors, the rag rugs and old-fashioned quilts could hardly compare to stainless steel and granite kitchens, travertine tiles in the posh condos in town. And never mind the flat-screen televisions.

But oh, they'd serve root beer floats and watermelon. Darek shook his head. He'd never be the host his parents were, despite his efforts, and their hope of handing down the resort to him might be the biggest mistake of their lives. In fact, his dreams, until five years ago, had included seeing the world, finding adventure, and making a name for himself in the world of wildland fire management.

Now, the only flames he saw were the occasional sparks lifting from one of their lakeside fires, snuffed out as they drifted into the night.

He rounded the corner of the table.

Tiger had vanished.

Clearly he would never be the father his son needed, either. "Tiger!" He dumped the watermelon in the cart, turned to scan the produce area. Tables topped with apples, oranges, potatoes, grapefruit, corn, bins of beans, and rows and rows of strawberries gave the five-year-old plenty of hiding places. "Tiger, where are you?" Oh, that kid. Once he'd searched the resort for an hour, finally finding him in the crawl space under the deck.

"Tiger!" He tried to keep his voice down, but the name hissed out through clenched teeth. A woman near the pineapples looked at Darek. He didn't recognize her, so . . . "My son wandered off. He's five and is wearing a Spider-Man shirt."

She shook her head, wearing a look of alarm.

"He does this all the time. He's fine." Really. They lived in a small town. The grocery store had all of seven aisles. But he hated how panic managed to reach up and choke off his breathing.

Darek grabbed the cart and pushed it toward the deli section, casting a look down the canned goods aisle. "Tiger!" Nothing.

He pushed toward the flour, oils, pasta, and did a quick look, then headed for cereals. Tiger loved his cereals.

"Tig—"

There he was, the little scamp, and not alone either. He had his arms around the neck of Nan Holloway.

Of course it had to be Tiger's grandmother who found him. She held on to the boy as if she might never let go.

If she had her way, she wouldn't.

"Hello, Nan."

She glanced at him, her smile vanishing. "Someone could have picked him up and kidnapped him."

"Maybe you could say that louder. I'm not sure Tiger—or the rest of the store—heard you."

"He needs to know the dangers of running off. And frankly, so do you."

"I just stepped away to grab a watermelon." Oh, that sounded brilliant. He wanted to shake away the words the moment he said them.

"That's how accidents happen, isn't it, Darek? When someone takes their eye off the ball—"

"I didn't . . ." He blew out a breath. It didn't matter. Nan and George Holloway had despised him since the day they found out Felicity expected his child. The shotgun wedding that occurred weeks later probably didn't help.

He schooled his tone. "Thanks for finding him."

He reached for Tiger, but Nan ducked her head as if drawing in his little-boy smell. Then she swallowed and affected a smile. "I don't suppose you'd let us take him for the Fourth of July this weekend. Sandra is coming in with her family, and it would be so fun for him to play with his cousins."

The last time he'd brought Tiger over to the Holloways', his son had returned with an entirely new wardrobe, his old clothes probably burned in the refuse pile. Darek tried not to mind, but it made him feel like a guy who lived in his car, panhandling for food for his kid.

And shoot, his pride got the best of him. "Sorry, Nan, but we're having a family get-together too." This time he didn't wait for her to release him but took Tiger into his arms, set him on his hip. "How about the following weekend?"

She tightened her lips as if she was trying not to cry. Oh no. Felicity had the exact same expression. Usually right before she flung something nasty at Darek—objects, words, sometimes even his mistakes.

And true to Holloway form: "Felicity always told me how selfish you were. I just never thought you'd keep Tiger from us."

Now people were staring. Probably agreeing with her.

After all, the Holloways weren't exactly unknown in the town of Deep Haven. Not with George on the school board since the dawn of time and Nan working in the courthouse, issuing building permits and tax liens.

Felicity had been their golden girl—homecoming queen, basketball star, the girl most likely to succeed.

Not get pregnant and marry at the age of twenty.

Nan's eyes sparkled, what looked like tears glistening in them.

"Nan . . . fine. I'll bring him by. How about Sunday, in the afternoon?"

"No. Forget it, Darek. It's time we stepped in and started asking questions. Like how did Tiger get hurt? You never did tell us. At the least I should have gotten a phone call. Just because we were out of town . . ."

He didn't know who to thank for that small gift. No wonder he hadn't seen Nan hovering at the library for the past two weeks—they'd been on their annual trek to some church camp down in the Ozarks.

Sadly, he hadn't seen Ivy, either. Not that he would know what to say to her if he did.

"He fell off the top bunk. But he climbed up there on his own—"

"He was unsupervised?"

"Nan, he's a kid. He's rambunctious."

She tightened her jaw. Then suddenly nodded. "Sunday should work just fine."

She pushed her cart past him, down the aisle.

"Bye-bye, Grandma!"

Nan flashed a smile over her shoulder. Came back and kissed his pudgy cheek. "See you soon, Theo."

Tiger, Darek wanted to say. *We call him Tiger.* But that wouldn't help.

He looked at Tiger. "Don't ever run away from me again."

Tiger's smile fell and his little lip started to tremble. Maybe he should have just let Nan take him home.

Probably he wasn't well supervised, as she said. He softened his voice. "You scared me, pal. Stick with me, okay?" He held up his hand and Tiger slapped it. "Good." He let him down. "Let's get some cereal and finish our list."

"I want Cap'n Crunch!" Tiger reached for the box, conveniently at five-year-old level, and hugged it to his chest.

"No, buddy. Let's try for something healthier, huh? How about Cheerios. Or Honey Nut—"

"I want Cap'n Crunch!" His voice rose.

Darek reached for the box, tried to ease it from his hand. "No. Give it to Daddy."

But the little boy turned away from him, crushing the box in his grip.

"Tiger!"

"I *want* Cap'n Crunch!"

At Tiger's decibel level, Darek expected Nan to come barreling back around the corner at any second, accusing him of some sort of child abuse.

"No," he said sharply, feeling his ire in his veins. He wanted to haul the kid over his shoulder and leave, right now. Just get in his car and floor it—out of Deep Haven, out of this life, this package he hadn't wanted, wasn't prepared for, couldn't seem to get right—

"Can I help?"

He looked up and nearly lost his voice at the sight of Ivy Madison standing there, dressed in a pair of black pants, pumps, and a crisp white shirt. As if she was on lunch break from the office. She looked pretty with her hair tied back.

She crouched down. "Hey there, Tiger. Whatcha got?"

She knew his name. Which meant she'd stuck around the ER long enough that night to hear Darek nearly unravel at Tiger's bedside.

Nice.

"I want Cap'n Crunch," his troublemaker said.

"I see that." She glanced at Darek, then back to Tiger. "Hey, Tiger, I saw you at the library. What were you reading?"

Something lit in those big brown eyes. "The mouse book!"

"Oh, I know that book. 'If you give a mouse a cookie . . .'"

"He'll want a glass of milk!"

"And if you give him a glass of milk . . ." Ivy caught Darek's eye. Nodded to the Cap'n Crunch box.

Tiger bought right into it. "He wants a straw!"

Darek took his chance. He eased the box from Tiger's hand as Ivy asked, "And if you give him a straw . . . "

"He'll want a napkin!"

"That's right! And then he'll check to see if he has a milk mustache." She began to wiggle her nose. "Do I have a milk mustache?"

Tiger shook his head, laughing.

"But he has lollipop lips," Darek said as he scooped Tiger up and plunked him into the shopping cart. "I wouldn't get too close."

"Yum. Can I have a lollipop?" Ivy said, still ignoring Darek.

Tiger stuck out his sticky fist, and for a moment Darek feared Ivy might actually do it—lick the sticky, gooey lollipop.

"Oh no, that's all yours, bud. Besides, if you give me a lollipop, I might ask for . . ."

"A glass of milk!"

She laughed, and Darek did too. And then finally—finally—she looked at him.

Oh, she had beautiful eyes. Green, with golden flecks around the edges. And the prettiest shade of auburn hair, silky and thick. Why hadn't he seen that before?

"You're brilliant," Darek whispered.

She smiled, and for a second, words left him. How he wished he could return to that night two weeks ago and redo it. Be the kind of date she deserved.

"No. I just lived with professional mothers who knew how to distract a kid in the grocery aisle."

He frowned. "Professional mothers?"

"I was a foster kid, remember?"

Oh, that's right. He tried a smile.

"That's okay. It was a trying night. How's Tiger?" She pointed to his forehead. "Seems to be healing okay."

"Seven stitches. I'm sure they're not the last." He winced. "It's been a long shopping experience."

"I get that. One of my foster mothers made us push the cart— that way we couldn't run away. You could try using one of those carts with the little cars built in them."

"This is Deep Haven. They don't have those."

"Right. Then how about letting him do the shopping? Have him help you find things. Kids love that."

"Really? Can I hire you?"

She laughed again. "Thanks, but I already have a job. One I have to get back to."

But—

She turned to Tiger. "Don't give out any cookies."

He grinned.

"Nice to see you, Darek."

And then she was walking away.

"Uh, Ivy?"

He sounded desperate, but he couldn't help his tone. Not when he felt it all the way to his bones.

She turned. Smiled with those pretty lips.

"Hey, I didn't do a very good job the other night."

She frowned.

"I mean, you didn't exactly get your money's worth."

Oh. Whoops. She glanced over her shoulder. Began to shake her head.

"No, I mean . . . I can do better."

No, no . . .

"Really, Darek, let's just forget—"

"How about a real date?"

Their words crossed in the air and hung there. She stared at him, swallowed.

He wheeled the cart toward her, cutting his voice low. "This isn't coming out right. But . . . well, I'd like a chance to redeem myself."

"There's nothing to redeem." She looked genuinely uncomfortable, and now he felt sorry for both of them.

"There is and you know it. So how about this: my family is having a little Fourth of July party, with root beer floats and, who knows, maybe even a few fireworks. Will you join us? I promise, I'm much nicer the second time around."

She wore what he would peg as a litigator face because she seemed to be sizing him up. He was suddenly aware of his ripped, somewhat-dirty jeans—he'd been replacing a few rotted logs from the walking path when his mother asked him to head to town for the grocery run—and his Jude County Hotshots T-shirt with a hole in the arm. Had he even combed his hair or brushed his teeth this morning?

Ivy might have sensed his urge to flee because she gave a quick smile but said, "I don't know. I don't want to get into the middle of anything."

He frowned. "Middle?"

She lowered her voice. "Listen, I understand divorce happens; it's just a little sticky. So . . ."

"Divorce. Oh." He made a face. Shoot, he hadn't exactly explained that. But who would? *My wife was killed*—yeah, that came out great on a first date.

Or whatever it was they'd had.

"I'm a widower, Ivy."

She blinked at that. "Oh. Uh, I'm so sorry." For a second, a shade of pity crossed her face. See, this was why he hadn't—

"I guess I could spend the Fourth of July with you." Then her voice brightened and she faced Tiger. "But only if Tiger is going to be there."

"Yes. For sure," Darek said, a strange warmth coursing through him.

"Good," she said.

"I'll call you and give you directions." He turned his cart away before she changed her mind.

"But you don't know my number."

He gave a quick laugh. "You're in Deep Haven. I'll find you."

As he left her there, he glanced down at his son, who grinned, that sticky red sucker now collecting fuzz on his cheeks. "Good job, Tiger."

Days like today, Jensen thought he might actually survive living in Deep Haven, might even redeem himself, just a little. Erase the legacy of his mistakes and replace it with the man he wanted to be.

"You did a good thing," Pastor Dan Matthews had said that night over two weeks ago when he arrived with the ambulance to bring in Gibs. Meant a lot, especially since Dan had been one of the first on the scene the night Felicity lay dying in Jensen's arms.

He wanted to lean into Dan's words and believe that someday . . . Well, maybe Deep Haven would never forgive him. But maybe they'd start feeling bad about the way they'd treated him.

The memory of Dan's words conspired to give him the courage to stand outside Gibs's hospital room, ready to ask for the impossible.

At the very least, even if his courage failed him, he should check in on the man. Jensen had heard Gibs had returned to Deep Haven today after a two-week stint in Duluth, getting surgery, pins, and a host of other orthopedic care.

Now, with the man back in town . . . Well, he'd been working on his speech all day, along with his offer, and it couldn't hurt to ask, right?

Jensen glanced around for Claire, prepared to retreat if he saw her—she didn't need him here reminding her of her loss. Two weeks ago, he'd made sure to leave the hospital when he saw Claire arrive, still dressed in her Pierre's uniform, her dark hair caught in a net, looking as if her world might be on fire.

But now, the chair next to the bed looked empty, so Jensen tiptoed in.

He'd always liked the sunny rooms at the hospital—the few times he'd had stitches or that one time when his mother's fear of appendicitis kept him overnight. A vase of peonies sat on Gibs's bedside table, probably from one of Claire's many gardens.

Gibs lay in bed, his arms thin and frail on the sheet that covered his barrel body. A large foam pillow shaped like a triangle lay strapped between both legs to immobilize them. He wore an oxygen cannula under his nose, an IV dripping into an insertion on his arm.

Jensen stood there for a moment. He thought he'd seen the old man watching television. But now it seemed—

"I know you're standing there. Just sit down."

Jensen nearly jumped from his skin. "I didn't want to wake you, sir."

"I wasn't sleeping." Gibs opened one eye. "Not with you standing there practically hyperventilating."

Oh.

Jensen sat down.

"So. I guess you're the one who brought me in?"

Jensen nodded. "I'm sorry I didn't see you sooner, sir—"

"Jensen, for pete's sake, I've known you since you were trying to light firecrackers off my dock. You can dispense with the *sir*."

"Sorry, sir . . . Mr. . . ."

Gibs shook his head. Jensen didn't expect the humor, the warmth in his eyes. "Son. Thank you."

His chest loosened. "You're welcome."

"So why the heavy breathing?"

"I . . . Well, see, sir, I wanted to talk to you about your property."

Gibs raised an eyebrow. "Hitting a man when he's down?" But he smiled.

"No, sir—"

"Jensen."

"Gibs. It's just . . . well, I didn't know what your plans were, and you have a pretty big parcel on that side of the lake. My father—"

"I know what your father wants." Gibs's smile dimmed.

"It is the only sandy beach on the entire lake. And really, we only need deeded access so our residents could enjoy the lake."

"Your residential community owns half the lake as it is."

"But you own the best part. And I promise you, we'd pay what it's worth." He handed Gibs an envelope with terms he'd sketched out last night, dusting off his lawyerspeak.

Gibs opened it, read it through. "That's fair."

"You'd still have plenty of private shoreline."

The man nodded. "I would like to give Claire some money for college. I guess I could sell off—"

"You're selling nothing, Grandpop."

Jensen winced even as he turned.

Yep, Claire stood in the door, wearing a green dress, a red knit beret, a pair of high gladiator sandals. She glowered at him, setting a cup of coffee on the bedside table. "I step out for ten minutes to run to the Java Cup and come back to find you swindling my grandfather's land from him."

"I wasn't—"

"No, you can't buy our land, thank you. Grandpop is going to be fine, aren't you?" She looked at Gibs pointedly.

As if he had a choice.

"Honey, listen to me. Jensen here has given me a good offer. And it could help you foot that college bill." He reached out to catch her hand. She moved toward him like a robot, jerkily.

Jensen had to look away from her stricken expression.

"You can't stay in Deep Haven forever," Gibs went on. "We both know that. You have to leave sometime, and maybe this is your chance. The doc says I have three to six months of recovery left, and frankly, I'm not sure I can finagle getting around the house on my own. With this offer, I can recuperate at the care center—"

"No." She ripped her hand out of his. Even Jensen looked up at her tone. "No, you're coming home. You can recuperate there. I'm staying. I'm taking care of you."

"Claire—"

But she ignored her grandfather and rounded on Jensen. "You. Take your offer and get out." She grabbed the envelope from Gibs's hand and thrust it at Jensen. "Now."

Jensen stared at the envelope but refused to take it. "Claire, think this through—"

"Now!"

He tightened his jaw. "You know, you could try seeing past what you think of me to what is good for your grandfather. And for you."

"I know what's good for both of us. To stay far away from you."

Ouch.

He glanced at Gibs. "Thanks for considering it, anyway."

Gibs's mouth tightened to a grim line. "If you ever feel like playing a game of checkers—"

"Grandpop!" Claire's mouth opened for only a second before she charged around the bed, grabbing Jensen by the arm. "Get. Out."

Jensen caught Gibs's wink just as she pushed him out the door.

He stood in the hall listening to the click of the door behind him. The nurse from the station looked up at him, and he felt heat flood his face. He turned and quickly walked down the hallway.

At least the old man was okay. And it hadn't exactly hurt to ask, had it?

Get. Out.

Right. Her words stung. Despite his sins, he would have thought their past still mattered. He could still remember the days when he could make her laugh or when she'd sit with him on the beach roasting marshmallows after Felicity and Darek had left.

He wondered if she remembered those days too.

Probably not.

Jensen got into the work truck and headed to the courthouse, a familiar sourness in his chest. Even after three years, walking into the courthouse and up to his probation officer's office seemed like a walk along the green mile.

He took the stairs two at a time and then turned toward the end of the hall, where he knocked on Mitch O'Conner's door.

Mitch sat at his desk, his blond head bronzed from a recent fishing trip. "Hey, Jensen. I thought I might be seeing you today. Any big plans for the Fourth of July weekend?"

Jensen handed him his weekly time card. "I'll probably see if I can't coax a walleye or two onto my lure in Evergreen Lake." Or not. He hadn't gone fishing since . . . well, before the accident, for sure. But he didn't want Mitch to know that he'd be sitting alone or even tucked into some corner at the VFW or Evergreen Lake Tavern, watching the Blue Monkeys hammer out Cash or Coltrane.

Mitch took out his calculator, began to punch in numbers. "I hear we're supposed to get some rain."

Jensen sank into a chair, watching him tally the hours. "We need it. I drove by the forest service headquarters and they listed today's fire hazard as high. The air even smells dry."

"One lightning strike and the entire forest goes up." Mitch looked up. "Okay, Jensen, we have to talk. According to my calculations, if you don't increase your hours, you won't make it."

He met Jensen's eyes, and every muscle in his body froze. "What does that mean?"

Mitch's mouth tightened. "The terms of your probation say that if you don't fulfill your community service hours, you serve the entire mandatory four years of your sentence. That means prison."

Prison.

Jensen looked out the window, an anvil on his chest. He'd added up the hours, known it was tight, but . . . now he couldn't breathe.

"I know you're working hard these days, Jensen, but you can admit you wasted that first year—"

"I am not guilty!" The words simply burst out of him. "I didn't even see her—believe me, I think about that moment *every single day*. I think through every second, working through my motions. I wasn't speeding; I had just touched the radio—"

"They found your cell phone open."

"I hadn't touched it since I pulled out of my drive, and . . . Forget it. It doesn't matter." He stood. Walked to the window. "It doesn't matter what the truth is. Deep Haven just wanted to crucify me."

"You pleaded guilty."

Jensen rounded on him. "Because if I didn't, I would have gone to prison for four years for a crime I didn't commit! Instead I got three years trapped in this town, facing people every day who hate me."

Mitch didn't refute his words.

Jensen looked out the window. "I would give anything to go back to that night . . ." To not see Felicity suddenly veer out into the road, to not hear her screams as he plowed her over. To not feel his car lurch against her weight. To not hear his own screaming as he found her, broken in the ditch, dying.

Sometimes he felt like he still might be screaming.

"I didn't see her. I didn't . . ." He closed his eyes, and to his horror, he thought he might actually tear up.

"Listen, Jensen, keep at it. Who knows? Maybe a miracle will happen and you'll suddenly get a windfall of hours."

Mitch didn't smile. Jensen couldn't tell if he was joking or not.

"I don't think there are any miracles left for me," he said. "Have a happy Independence Day, Mitch."

The man said nothing as Jensen closed the door behind him.

Ivy closed her office door, the last one to leave. Again. But she'd set that precedent for two weeks now, and . . . well, she had fully expected to come in during tomorrow's national day off. Now . . .

Now she had a date. With an entire family.

She pushed out through the double doors onto the sidewalk, where the moon, already hung in the sky, draped a golden path home. The air smelled of barbecues caught in the fresh wind off the lake. She had chosen to walk to work today, delighted that the courthouse sat only three blocks from her apartment.

The charms of a small town.

Like the sound of live music drifting from a nearby outside eatery. And unknown neighbors who waved to her from their porch. And . . . meeting someone's entire family.

Ivy pressed a hand to her stomach, empty since she'd forced down the deli ham sandwich at lunch. But the waves inside had nothing to do with hunger.

She was suddenly sitting again in a waiting room, about to meet a potential adoptive family. All her dreams curled up into one hot ball inside.

She was ten years old, thinking *maybe*. Maybe they'd like her instantly. Maybe the father would swing her up into his arms, the mother would smile at her, beaming, call her a princess, make her their own.

Yes, and maybe they'd take her home, where she'd never have to leave, where she could have her own bed, maybe carve her name into a backyard tree.

She ran her hand across her cheek, dispelled the moisture there. Foolish maybes. She would harbor no such what-ifs for Darek.

So what that he had those amazing eyes that turned all soft and sweet when he looked at his son. And that more than once she'd let herself wonder what it might feel like to step into those arms, thick with hardworking muscle. She too well remembered the tangy scent of the night when they parked on the overlook, and she simply couldn't erase the way he'd soothed Tiger's fears in the ER with soft, tender tones, or the way he'd taken the little boy onto his lap to read to him.

Or even today, watching his son as he'd recited the book back to Ivy in the grocery store. Pride amid all that affection.

She could be in big trouble if she didn't stop this nonsense before it even started. Tiger was sure to get hurt if Darek decided he wanted to keep redeeming himself.

No, despite his sudden turn away from the dark and crabby side to a man she might actually enjoy, she'd seen his shadows—and not only on their date, but today, when wrestling with his son over cereal. Didn't he know you never fought a battle over food with a child?

Maybe he didn't. Maybe he was just trying to figure it out, trying to be both mother and father. But—oh no. She stopped, wincing. He didn't ask her out for her parenting skills, did he?

This could only be a very bad idea.

She rounded her corner, where the Footstep of Heaven Bookstore and Coffee Shop sat, facing the lake. The hostas had grown up along the walk, the smell of roses fragrancing the air. The light above the porch buzzed with suicidal moths.

Under it, in a pool of wan light, sat her neighbor, the young woman who lived in the apartment above the shop.

"Claire?" Ivy said as she opened the gate. "Are you okay?"

Claire sat on the front steps, arms around her legs, staring out at the lake. Ivy would have continued on the path around to the back, but Claire looked so miserable that she stopped at the bottom of the stairs.

Claire finally glanced at her. "Sorry—yes. I'm okay. I just got back from Duluth."

"I noticed your place looked pretty dark the past week or so. Were you on vacation?"

Claire gave a harsh laugh. "No. I wish. My grandfather drove his four-wheeler headfirst into a tree a couple weeks ago. Our neighbor up at the lake found him." She made a face then and picked up her cell phone. Sighed and put it down. "They transferred him to Duluth for surgery, then moved him back up to the Deep Haven hospital today."

"Are you expecting a call?"

"My parents, checking up on Grandpop. They're worried. They sent me an e-mail and asked me to be available tonight. I get better cell service out here and besides, the night is so beautiful, isn't it?"

Ivy didn't have to look to nod in agreement.

"I used to live in rural Bosnia and there were nights, sitting outside my parents' clinic, when the sky looked close enough to touch. It's the only time I really miss it."

"You grew up in Bosnia?"

"Only until I was fourteen; then I moved to Deep Haven. My parents are missionary doctors."

"Wow. When did they go back?"

Claire glanced at her. "Oh, they stayed there. I lived with my grandparents. They raised me through my high school years. I visited Bosnia when I was fifteen for a couple weeks, but . . ." Her voice trailed off, and Ivy didn't chase the thought. "My parents came home every four years and sometimes for Christmas. We e-mail and Skype, but they're busy, important people. Doctors—did I mention that?"

"Yes," Ivy said. "That's amazing."

"What, that I have such talented parents, or that they have such a waste of a daughter?"

Huh? Ivy had no words for that. She just frowned at Claire.

"I'm sorry. I know you don't really know me." Claire forced a kind of smile. "I work at Pierre's Pizza. And two weeks ago, my boss told me that if I didn't take the manager position, he'd probably have to cut my hours." She looked at the phone again. "I'm twenty-five years old and all I have to show for it are my fabulous pizza-making abilities."

"Some people would love to be able to make a fabulous pizza. Or eat a fabulous pizza." Her stomach growled at the suggestion.

Claire smiled. "You're really nice. I'm sorry. I guess I'm just in a bad mood. I hate when they call. They always ask me if I've applied for colleges or what my plans are. I feel like an idiot." She looked up at Ivy. "It's a terrible thing not to have any plans."

Ivy set her briefcase on the step, climbed up to sit beside Claire. Thought through her life. Yes, maybe. She hadn't ever lived without some idea of her next step. Until she arrived in Deep Haven, her destination.

"It's not like I don't have things I love to do. Like garden. And yes, I love working at the pizza place. But . . . I guess I always thought I should do something big, like my parents. And try as I might, I can't hear God telling me what to do. Where to go. So here I sit, waiting, while people get married, build families and careers around me, and I get offered the job as pizza manager."

"I never considered that God might have an opinion about where I live. What I do. I mean, I believe in God—enough Sunday school and it's embedded in me. And I remember as a child wanting Jesus to 'live in my heart.'" Ivy finger-quoted the words. "But as I got older, I kept looking for Him to show up in my life, even a little bit. I guess it's easier to think that He's not interested."

Ivy didn't look at Claire, instead watching a light on the

water—some distant ship—carving out the horizon. "The spiritual detritus of growing up in the foster system. You never really feel like people are going to stick around. Or that you belong to anyone."

"You can belong to God, if you want," Claire said softly. "God may be silent, but He's never absent."

Ivy turned to Claire. "I've made it this far on my own. I guess I'll keep it that way."

"You're never on your own, Ivy."

"Spoken like a woman who's grown up with family." But she said it kindly, with a smile.

"I suppose," Claire said. "Speaking of, how did it go with Darek the other night? He comes attached with a passel of family."

Ivy stared at her. "How did you know?"

"I was there. With the band. I saw you buy him."

Of course she was. The entire town seemed to be there. "It was so awful. Everyone was so . . . quiet. Why didn't anyone bid on him?"

"Because . . . well, because he is still married in their minds."

"He's not really—"

"No. He's a widower. Three years now. But he was married to this beautiful, strong woman. She was loved by everyone in town. When she died . . . a little bit of everyone else died too. Especially since she left behind Theo."

"Theo?"

"Tiger. Sorry." She checked her phone again. Sighed and put it beside her on the porch. "People probably just can't forgive Darek for moving on."

"Has he?"

She glanced at Ivy. "I don't know; you tell me."

"He invited me over for a campfire tomorrow night."

"Oh, boy."

"Really?"

Claire laughed. "The Christiansens are a force, for sure, but I think they'll like you."

There it was again, the feeling of being auditioned.

"How many are there?"

"Six siblings. There's Darek, of course—he's the oldest. The protector of the family. He used to fight fires with this hotshot team in Montana. Now I think he'll probably end up taking over the resort. And then there's Eden. She's a journalist, or wants to be, although I think she's writing obits for a Minneapolis newspaper. And then Grace, who works with me at Pierre's. She's an amazing chef and is saving up money to attend Le Cordon Bleu. The troublemaker of the bunch is Casper, who is attending college in Duluth. I think he wants to be an archeologist–slash–treasure hunter–slash–adventurer. I suppose they all do, in a way. And after him is Owen, who plays hockey—"

"For the Minnesota Wild. I heard about him that night at the auction."

"Right. He was supposed to be the feature attraction."

"Poor Darek."

"Exactly. Owen is a bit of a legend in our town. Never went to college—he got drafted straight out of high school. He's only twenty and playing in the big leagues. The youngest is Amelia. She just graduated from high school this year and is making a name for herself as a photographer. She did a number of the senior pictures, and occasionally her photos make the front page of the paper."

"I think I saw Amelia and Grace at the hospital a couple weeks ago. They showed up, along with Casper. Lots of drama."

Claire winced. "I should have been there."

Ivy frowned. Why—?

"Darek's wife was my best friend. It tears me up to see Theo without her. I know in my heart that he's in good hands. Ingrid and John are wonderful grandparents, and they own Evergreen Resort, up on the lake. They go to church; John works as a volunteer EMT. Ingrid helps out at the senior center sometimes. They're fourth-generation Deep Haven."

Ivy swallowed, tried a smile. But oh, was she in over her head. These kind of family roots . . .

Claire was checking her phone again. "How is work at the county attorney's office?"

"Busy. I thought Deep Haven would be more peaceful."

Claire laughed. "Oh, the summer is just getting started. We're sleepy in the wintertime, but we grow 200 percent during the summer. That's when the fun really starts."

"Super." She sighed. "How did Darek's wife die?"

"A terrible car acci—"

Claire's cell phone buzzed on the step beside her. She picked it up. Grimaced.

"Good night, Claire," Ivy said as Claire answered it.

She waved to Ivy. "Hi, Mom."

Ivy moved out of earshot and up to her garage apartment. Turned on the light and dropped her briefcase on the table.

Listened to the silence, the waves on the shore, the wind in the poplar outside her window, and wondered what it might be like to have a tribe like the Christiansen family welcoming her home.

"Grandpop's fine, Mom. He survived the trip back to Deep Haven just fine."

Claire watched Ivy walk away in her trim black suit, her auburn hair tied up in a prim ponytail, her heels clicking on the pavement.

Claire didn't own a business suit. She reached up and pulled off her beret, working her fingers through her hair.

"I just keep thinking about what might have happened if he hadn't found him," her mother said. "I always thought he was a nice boy."

Jensen. She was talking about Jensen. The connection was dismal at best, a fifteen-second echo behind every sentence. Claire could hear her own voice repeat her words on the other end. They were probably calling from their hospital line, had probably spent the last thirty minutes dialing over and over to get out. Or maybe they were both huddled over the phone in some still war-torn or primitive village, even at a public phone booth, the smell of dust and heat in the air. She wished they'd just opted to go to the mission headquarters in the capital city of Sarajevo and call over Skype. Then she could read their faces, assure them that she hadn't left her grandfather alone, hadn't been the cause of his accident.

Did they have any idea how hard it was to corral a Vietnam War vet who had a mind of his own?

Or how hard it might be to convince her parents that yes, she had everything under control? An e-mail updating them on his condition should have sufficed.

A mosquito buzzed over her head, landed on her bare leg. She slapped it and flicked it away. Ignoring her mother's comment, she continued. "They expect a three-to-six-month recovery time, but you know Gramps—he's already talking about going home. I am going to take some time off—"

Well, mandatory time off. Because how could she become a

restaurant manager and care for her grandpa? She was still thinking it over, but it felt like the right decision. Right?

"Don't worry about it, honey. He'll be fine in the Deep Haven Care Center. He knows so many—"

"Mom, I have everything under control. Grandpop will come home with me and I'll look after him until he gets back on his feet—"

"Besides, we'll be home soon anyway."

Those last words silenced her. She could hear the overlap of her final words repeated on the far end of the phone. Then, nothing.

"Honey, did you hear me? I said your father and I are coming home. We're working on temporary replacements, and we should be home in a few weeks."

Claire scrounged up her voice. "Why? Grandpop is fine."

Her father's low, solid voice took over. "Darling, we'll be packing up his house, having a garage sale, getting the place ready to sell. We had an offer a year or so ago from the Christiansens, and it's time we moved your grandfather into someplace more secure. And I'll bet you're ready to move on, huh?" Laughter punctuated his words.

She didn't have to smile for their benefit, because, well, they couldn't see her. In fact, she doubted if they'd ever really been able to see her. See how she loved Deep Haven.

She slapped another mosquito. The night had suddenly turned into a war zone.

"I'll bet you've got a tidy nest egg saved up after all those years at Pierre's," her mother said. "It's probably not too late to start applying to colleges. You know, I just read an article about a woman who graduated for the first time with a medical degree at the age of fifty-five. So you're not an oddity, honey. Plenty of people wait to continue their education."

Keep saying it, Mom, and you'll believe it.

"I . . . haven't . . . I'll look into it, Mom."

Oh, what was wrong with her that even at the age of twenty-five, she couldn't just tell them the truth?

Her father's voice came back on the line, softened. "You know, Claire bear, if you wanted to come back to Bosnia with us, you're always welcome."

"No, Dad."

"Your mother could use help in the clinic. Maybe just for a year."

She waited until she heard her voice on the other end; then his own words finished. "I know you love your work, but . . ."

"Honey, are you still bothered by the nightmares?"

Oh, she'd regretted letting Grandma tell them about those. The year she'd woken up screaming, trying to erase that last summer on the mission field. "No. I'm fine." A little lie, but for their own good. "It's just . . . maybe I'm not supposed to be a missionary." There, she said it. After twenty-five years, they should know the truth.

"Claire. Everyone is called to spread the gospel. The Lord said, 'Go and make disciples.'"

She didn't want to have this argument on the phone. Especially since a large part of her agreed with him. When a person became a Christian, the overwhelming grace should prompt her to want to reach out to others.

Not stay at home.

Not hide in Deep Haven.

"We'll talk about it when we get there. Until then, think about where you might want to go to college. Maybe you and your mother could take a trip, make a visit."

Still trying to treat her like she was seventeen, a senior in high school, her whole life ahead of her.

Instead of the superior-size disappointment she turned out to be.

"When are you arriving?"

"We'll e-mail you with our flight information. But we'll rent a car. We don't want to be any trouble."

Trouble was exactly what they were being. "I'll keep you posted about Grandpop."

"That's okay, sweetheart. I talked with Dr. Samson earlier."

Then why—?

"Love you, Claire bear. Go with God."

"You too, Mom." She hung up. Killed another mosquito. Let the night wind rake over her, raising gooseflesh.

Go with God.

To where?

He was probably as disappointed in her as her parents were. She got up and walked around the back of the house to the door, then went inside, climbing the stairs to her apartment. Two rooms, with two tiny bathrooms, the kitchen on the main floor. She had rented it when the landlord, Liza, moved out. The empty bedroom she'd turned into a music room of sorts, her keyboard set up, her guitar on a stand.

She went in, sat down at the keyboard, played the chords of sheet music Emma had recently given her. The Blue Monkeys were supposed to play tomorrow night for the crowds gathered for the fireworks.

Honey, are you still bothered by the nightmares?

Her father's words hung in her mind. She let the sound die out, until only her heartbeat remained.

Sometimes, yes, she still saw them, the three men who broke into her father's office at the clinic. Her hand went to her forehead, to the bump there, still slightly pronounced, where they'd smashed a metal pipe against her skull.

She'd lain there in a puddle of her own blood, watching as they looted the clinic, unable to cry out, only one word on her lips.

Jesus.

She had said it over and over and over until she finally blacked out. Until her father—fresh out of surgery—arrived.

He'd had to wire her jaw shut, but she'd woken the next day without brain damage. She could be thankful for that.

Yes, she still had nightmares. And daymares sometimes, whenever someone walked up too quickly beside her. She fought headaches—probably imagined—and for a long while, maybe a year after the attack, her jaw ached every morning. As if she'd been grinding her teeth at night.

Grandma had purchased her a mouth guard, slept in her room in the other single bed, and held her in her arms when she woke screaming.

Her parents probably never knew that part.

Not when they had so many other concerns, like children without parents, children without eyes or limbs. Children who had seen far worse.

At least Claire had her grandparents.

She got up and sat in the window seat. Looked out at the stars. Wished she could reach for one, hold it to her chest.

But God had apparently stopped hearing her wishes, not to mention her prayers.

She closed her eyes, hearing her words to Ivy. *God may be silent, but He's never absent.*

If only she believed it.

CHAPTER 6

IF HE WERE A SMART MAN, Darek would call Ivy, tell her that he'd made a terrible mistake.

The log split where his ax cracked it, and the pieces fell off the block into the sawdust and pile below.

He'd been charmed by Tiger's lopsided, sticky smile and lost his head a little.

He set another log on the block, stepped back, and swung.

What did he think—that she'd step into his life with her bright, cheery smile and suddenly they'd be a family? Tiger would have a mother and everything would feel right and whole?

The log split, flipped off of the block, landing in the pile.

Darek should stop this before somebody—like Tiger—got hurt.

He picked up another log and balanced it on the block.

"Sheesh, Dare, last time I checked, we were just having a little campfire, not burning Rome." Casper came up behind him wearing an Evergreen Outfitters shirt, the sleeves torn off, and carrying two cans of Coke. He handed one to Darek. "Mom sent this out."

Darek put down the ax and worked off his gloves. Woodchips layered his sweaty skin—he needed a shower before Ivy arrived. He'd called her yesterday at the courthouse, leaving a message with her secretary giving her directions to the resort.

Could he possibly hope that she hadn't received it?

Darek took the Coke, pushed back his baseball hat, and wiped the cold can across his forehead. Closed his eyes.

When he opened them, he found Casper tossing the wood into the wheelbarrow. Oops, he had chopped more than he'd realized. But once he'd gotten going . . .

Casper leaned against the wheelbarrow. "What's eating you?"

Darek shook his head. Setting down his soda, he slid on his gloves and picked up another log.

"Dude, seriously. We have enough wood for the winter. Last time you chopped with such a frenzy . . . well, you and Felicity got married about six weeks later." Casper lifted an eyebrow.

Darek made a face. "I made so many mistakes with her. Starting with getting her pregnant."

Casper took a sip of his Coke.

"It was so unfair to her. I didn't want to marry her—and she knew it. But what could we do?"

"I don't recall Mom and Dad saying you had to get married."

"It felt like the right thing to do."

"Did you love her?"

Darek sank his ax in the wood block. "I don't know. Maybe.

We had fun together. But that summer—well, I'd heard she'd been hanging around Jensen, and . . ."

"You went after her because you didn't want him to get her."

Darek picked up his Coke and finished it, then tossed it in a nearby garbage can. "Move so I can wheel this to the fire pit."

Casper stepped aside, and Darek grasped the handles of the wheelbarrow. He felt his brother's eyes on him as he started to push it.

"Okay, yes. Probably I wanted to win. He had this huge house, the boat, his fancy Mustang."

"So you thought you should have the girl."

"Something like that."

"Except you weren't prepared for what that meant." Casper finished his own Coke, tossed the can in a recycle bin beside the path. "Move over. I got this."

Darek relinquished the wheelbarrow to his brother.

Crickets chirped in the forest as they walked along the path, through the heat trapped between the trees. His feet crunched on thick, dry needles, tinder to a fire if a blaze ever started.

It was days like this that raised the hair on the back of his neck. All of Deep Haven County could go up in flames with one careless camper or a well-placed lightning strike.

"You miss firefighting."

He glanced at Casper.

"It's the way you pick up the needles and break them, testing their moisture levels. And the way you watch the sky. You miss it. The adventure, the hunt for fire, the battle."

He and Casper had that in common, at least. The love of adventure. Being four years older than his middle brother had always seemed to distance them. Casper and Owen were a better fit—especially with their love for hockey. Darek hadn't loved the game, just played it because he didn't like basketball. He did love the ice, the cold frost on his face on a crisp winter day.

Shoot, he just loved being outside, the world in his grasp.

"Yeah, I guess. I'll never forget that day I walked into our apartment, about two weeks after we got married. There was a message from my pal Jed from the Jude County Hotshots, and they needed me for a fire. Felicity looked at me like I had said I was going to war. Then she cried; I packed and left. Didn't see her again for three months."

"The Colorado fire, right?"

"Montana. The Colorado fire was the next June. Tiger was about three months old. That time I was gone until September."

They'd reached the beach area, where their father, long ago, had created a fire pit with benches that circled it. It looked out over the lake, where the afternoon sun turned the water to a rich sapphire, a few boaters spraying diamonds into the sky. He could smell barbecues and hear laughter trickling across the lake.

Almost on reflex, his gaze went to Jensen's place. No barbecue there; it looked uninhabited.

Casper parked the wheelbarrow and Darek began to load wood into the pit, creating a tepee.

"I didn't want to come home. I didn't miss her—didn't even miss Tiger. He was just this nuisance to me. I had my plans. I wanted to be a fire manager. And I didn't care that Felicity hated it. I was a real prize back then."

"I remember," Casper said, starting to unload the rest of the wood in a neat stack to one side.

"Yeah, well, I'm not proud of it. The worst part is, the last thing she said to me was 'You're so selfish.' And . . . I was." He looked at Casper. "I was. I can't believe I seriously considered letting the Holloways have full custody of Tiger. I nearly walked away from him. Now he's my entire life."

"So you're not a selfish jerk anymore. That's a good thing."

Darek's encounter with Nan Holloway rushed back at him. Maybe he still was. He stuffed birch bark and woodchips around the base of the fire tent. He'd leave it there until tonight, when they were ready to have their campfire. Then they'd head to town, where they'd watch fireworks over the harbor.

Casper had finished emptying the wheelbarrow. "So why the mountain of wood?"

"Because I hardly deserve a second chance with a woman."

"What woman?"

Darek got up, brushing off his hands. "The woman who bought me the other night." He made a face. "That came out wrong. I mean, at the VFW fund-raiser. Her name is Ivy—she's the new assistant county attorney."

"Does she know about Felicity . . . and Jensen?"

He frowned, shook his head. "No. I don't think so. Why would she? I told her my wife had died, but frankly, I don't want to go back there. I'm trying to move on. To build a new life." Or at least considering it. "I saw her at the grocery store, and she was . . . she was nice. And good with Tiger. I guess something took possession of my brain and I asked her over tonight."

Casper raised an eyebrow. "To hang with the family?"

"I know. What was I thinking?"

"I think you're either partaking in some self-sabotage or you really like her."

"I don't know her well enough to really like her."

"After tonight, you will." He clapped Darek on the shoulder.

"You might be surprised. This could be a good thing. A fresh start. You aren't the guy you were five years ago. Take a chance, Dare." Casper gave him a smile. "So she's a looker?"

Darek let his memory roam over the woman he'd seen at the VFW, then at the grocery store, trying to decide which version he liked better.

"Yeah. She's got this pretty red hair, green eyes, a smile that could knock the wind out of a guy—"

Casper was shaking his head.

"What?"

"You're right. You don't deserve her. I think you need to introduce her to me."

Darek grinned and reached for him, but Casper danced away.

"You know, I bet she'll take one look at me and forget all about you anyway, Dare."

"You think so."

Casper took off running.

"Yeah, you'd better run, punk!" Darek yelled after him, grinning.

Take a chance.

Okay. Maybe it was time to leave the past behind, start over.

He stopped in at the lodge and found his mother tossing together fruit in a giant watermelon-boat salad. Tiger sat at the counter, working on a flag coloring sheet she'd downloaded from the Internet.

"I'm going to take a shower. Can you keep an eye on him a little longer?"

"Tiger and I are doing great. And Gracie should be home soon to help with the potato salad, so take your time."

He landed a kiss on her cheek, then headed out to his cabin.

Overhead, he heard a peal of thunder. Maybe they wouldn't have a campfire tonight. But that was okay—they'd congregate on the veranda at the picnic tables near the grill. Maybe their guests would swing by for the root beer floats his mother promised them. Casper would probably regale them with some recent diving adventure story, and Grace would add in a tale about a tourist down at Pierre's. Darek would wrap Tiger in a blanket and the tyke would fall asleep on his lap, or maybe Amelia's, and . . . and then he and Ivy would watch the fireworks.

Maybe the chaos of his family was too much for a first date.

But he was a package deal, so she should know that from the start.

He showered, shaved, and pulled on a clean T-shirt, a pair of cargo shorts, and sandals. He debated, then added some of the aftershave his mother had gifted him at Christmas.

He was returning to the lodge when he spotted a car in the gravel parking lot, something unfamiliar. A red Nissan Pathfinder.

Darek slowed, pushed away the strangest twinge in his chest, and entered the lodge through the deck.

There she stood, leaning over the granite counter, a crayon in hand, helping Tiger fill in the red stripes of his flag. She wore a lemon-yellow sundress, a pair of beaded sandals, and her hair was gathered into a messy ponytail. Flag earrings dangled from her ears.

Ivy looked up at him and smiled, a sweetness in her beautiful eyes.

Right then, everything stopped. His breathing, his heartbeat. His words.

This was it. Everything he wanted, right here. A fresh start with a woman who didn't know him, didn't know his past.

His last, and best, chance.

Darek had no idea what kind of paradise he had here.

The Christiansen family owned the most gorgeous swath of two hundred acres in northern Minnesota. The resort sat on the shore of a glorious lake, and a woodchip path edged by rocks wound through the property, connecting twelve log-sided cabins, all with freshly painted red or green doors, a spray of impatiens in the window and deck boxes. They all faced the view, Adirondack chairs on the decks perfect for reading a book or listening to the loons at night.

A lodge house featured a giant stone patio with a built-in grill and picnic tables under a pavilion, and beyond that, a trail led down to a point where a campfire ring suggested long conversations while sparks flickered into the night.

"It's beautiful, Darek," Ivy said as she walked with him. He'd given her a tour, pointing out places where he'd played as a child, trees he'd climbed, the rope swing. She pictured him as a teenager, swinging out over the water.

What might it be like to grow up in one place, to see your history every time you stepped outside?

Tiger would have that. He ran ahead of them on the path, chasing a yellow Lab.

"What's the dog's name?"

"Butter. Actually it's Butterscotch. My father got the dog for my mother after she lost a baby."

"Oh, I'm so sorry."

"Yeah, it was after Amelia, a surprise pregnancy. Of course, a dog's no substitute for a child, but Butter seemed to try. She followed my mom everywhere. She's about fourteen, and we live in fear that she's not long for this world."

The dog ran up to them, holding a slimy ball in her teeth. Darek pried it out but only tossed it down the trail. Butterscotch waddled after it.

"This is an amazing place to grow up."

"That's the bulk of our business—return guests who spent their childhoods here and want to share it with their children. Too bad the kids aren't interested in their parents' legacy."

She looked up, troubled by his words. "Why not?"

"They want the conveniences, the excitement of life plugged in. They don't yet realize what they're missing."

"Which is?"

He smiled at her. "Evergreen Resort, of course."

She laughed, and when Butterscotch returned, Ivy bent down and rubbed the dog behind the ear.

"Oh, she likes you."

"No. All dogs like this. You just have to know where to rub."

"Dogs, kids. You have hidden talents."

"You learn to adapt when you live out of a suitcase," she said, letting the dog go.

He frowned as they came up to the patio.

His father, John, manned the grill, flipping burgers and brats. Definitely the patriarch of the family, he was a tall man with broad shoulders under a brown plaid shirt, rolled up to the elbows, a baseball cap over his shaved head. John had the kind of smile that would have made a little girl want to call him Daddy.

Ingrid, Darek's mother, directed traffic. She wore a green sleeveless blouse, a pair of black jean capris, her blonde hair held back by a headband, like some sort of fifties housewife.

Ivy's mother had looked ancient and worn from the day she gave birth to her, it seemed. Her last memory of the woman had been at the foster care offices, relief drawn into her mother's face as she said good-bye.

Grace, the blonde daughter from Pierre's Pizza, stirred the potato salad, wearing a white chef's apron. Amelia, Darek's youngest sister, snapped photos of the activity, capturing the image of Tiger jumping off the deck railing into Darek's arms.

"Careful, pal. I might not have seen you. What if I didn't catch you?" he said, swinging the boy up on his shoulders.

"Daddy, you'll always catch me!" Tiger raised his arms high, towering over them.

Casper, who'd ridden in on his motorcycle, looked no more tame tonight than when she'd seen him at the hospital. He came over and gave the kid a high, high five. Tiger laughed.

The air smelled of burgers, rich and thick, and with the exception of an occasional rumble in the sky, nothing could mar this perfect Independence Day celebration.

That was, if Ivy didn't screw it up. *Don't be overeager.* She kept rolling that mantra through her head as she smiled, laughed, listened. She wanted to drink it in, try to understand their expectations before she cracked open the door to her life.

Fourteen different foster homes did that to a person. Yes, she wanted them to like her so much she could taste it.

She'd thought she was past this.

"I've got to run down to the fire pit. I'll be right back," Darek said, putting Tiger down.

He left her as Ingrid came through the sliding-glass door holding a giant Tupperware bowl of Grace's potato salad. "Ivy, could you grab the pitcher of punch that's on the counter?"

"No problem," Ivy said and ducked inside to grab the punch. She added it to the table of goodies, then returned for the cups.

"Smile!" Amelia snapped her picture just after she turned.

"Oh. I wasn't ready."

"I like the impromptu ones best." She turned the camera around. "See how cute you are?"

In the shot, Ivy wore a strange, unfamiliar smile, and it raised a lump in her throat.

She set the cups on the table and watched Darek come up the trail from the fire pit. "I put jugs of water out, just in case something happens and the wind takes the blaze out of our control," he said to his father, who nodded.

But she couldn't help asking, "Why? It seems like it's going to rain."

He looked at the sky. "I don't know. It's been thundering for an hour, but the air doesn't feel like rain. It just feels sharp. Like flint."

"Darek has Spidey senses when it comes to reading the weather for fire hazard," Casper said, waging a thumb war with Tiger. He let Tiger pin his thumb. "Oh, you got me!"

Tiger erupted into giggles.

"Dare used to be on the Jude County Hotshot team," Amelia said, capturing the tussle with her camera.

"What's that?"

"The United States has a number of specialized hotshot teams around the country whose job it is to fly in and assist the local population fighting wildland fires," Darek said, opening a bag of potato chips, stealing one, and then dumping them into a bowl.

"Darek was training for a fire management position," John said. "Someone hand me a serving plate."

"Scared me to death to see him on the news—or pictures of him. All covered in soot, wearing a bright-orange Nomex helmet, looking as if he'd walked through hell." Ingrid held the plate as John slid juicy burgers onto it. "I felt better when Jens—" She cut herself off, smiled. "Never mind. Should we pray for dinner?"

Darek shot a look his mother's direction. Then he bowed his head.

Ivy closed her eyes as she listened to John bless their dinner. She'd lived with many families who shared this tradition, but listening to John's voice as he asked for God's blessing on their day and food seemed . . . well, not at all like a tradition. But as if he might truly mean it.

They *amen*ed like a football team, announcing it together, and then Darek handed her a plate.

He put his strong hand on her back and nudged her toward the serving table as he leaned close and spoke into her ear. "We eat big and fast here. I'll run interference for you."

She glanced over her shoulder at him, and he winked.

She could see him then—raccoon eyes, dirty, strong, heroic. Yes, fighting fires would have been his element.

"How long were you on the team?" she asked Darek as Ingrid set her burger in a fresh homemade bun. The sight could make her cry. She'd had a piece of toast and a yogurt for breakfast while sitting at her desk at the courthouse, cramming in a few hours before she let herself escape.

DJ was right—the traffic citations and other disturbance complaints had doubled, just this week.

"Three years, but I started fighting fires here, in Deep Haven. We had a terrible fire about eight years ago, on a lake near Canada, on the east end of town. Smoke covered the entire county."

Grace swiped a chip. "A bunch of the nice houses and resorts in Moose Valley burned before they could stop it."

"That's terrible." And then it happened, the stupid question she'd feared might slip out. "Why did you stop firefighting?"

A hush descended around the patio. Amelia concentrated on applying mustard to her burger. Grace scooped up potato salad.

"He got married," Casper said, sliding off the table and grabbing a plate. "And then Tiger came along."

She layered lettuce and tomato on her burger, hating that she'd reminded them of so much pain. "I see."

"But once a pyromaniac, always a pyromaniac," Casper said, clapping his brother on his back. "He only learned to fight fires because he spent years setting them."

"That is not true," Darek said. He picked up two plates—one for Tiger, probably.

Ivy added fruit and potato salad to her plate and headed over to the condiments.

"Really. Then who was it that burned down the garage, huh?" This from Grace, and Ivy suddenly wanted to thank her—and Casper—for rescuing her.

"I didn't burn down the garage—"

"It wasn't his fault. Not exactly," Ingrid said, setting Tiger on a bench. "I'm the one who told him to make a nice bed for the dog."

Huh? She must have frowned because Casper laughed and said, "We're just confusing her." He came up beside Ivy, slid his arm around her. "We had this outbuilding, see. Something my grandfather built years ago. More of a workroom. My grandfather called it his doghouse—he even installed a little heater and electricity in there so he could listen to the Husky football games in peace."

"My mother was a baseball fan," John said. He turned off the grill.

"Anyway, this was before we got Butter—we had this old dog

named Chester, and he used to love to sleep in there. We even put in a dog door. One day, Mom was cleaning out the basement and found this old foam pillow from one of the sofas we'd long since destroyed. She thought it might make a good bed for Chester."

"I just wanted him to go put it in the outbuilding—"

"She told Darek here to make a good bed for the dog. So he did. Shoved that foam pillow right up against the heater."

Ivy glanced at Darek. He shrugged, but a smile played on his face. She sat down at the picnic table next to Casper, across from Ingrid.

"I looked out the kitchen window about three hours later and saw this strange glow from the woods," Ingrid said. "Right about then, Darek, who'd long forgotten about the dog bed, came through the house asking about dinner. He saw the glow, opened the door, stood there for a moment, and then said . . ."

As if they'd planned it, in unison, every person recited, in a long, awe-filled tone: *"Wow."*

"'Wow'? That's *it*?"

"That's it," Ingrid said. "Then he shut the door."

Ivy stared at Darek. "What were you thinking?"

Darek set Tiger's plate in front of him. "I was thinking, *Wow.*"

She laughed and picked up her burger. The juices dripped onto her plate as she took a bite. She just barely stopped her eyes from rolling back in her head. "Delicious," she said to John.

"Thank you."

"What did you do?" Ivy asked Ingrid, taking another bite.

"Well, I asked, 'What's wow?' then opened the door. The garage was an inferno, two stories tall, engulfing the building."

"Oh, my." Ivy nearly choked and wiped her face with a napkin. She could have eighty more of those burgers.

"Yes. I yelled to John and grabbed the phone. By the time the fire trucks got here, we'd decided to douse the surrounding forest with hoses, knowing the place was long gone."

"It didn't catch anything else on fire?" She dug into the potato salad.

"Nope. We were lucky. But I was more specific in my instructions the next time."

"I was a very obedient child," Darek said.

Ingrid rolled her eyes as John coughed, pounded his chest. "What? It's Casper who caused the most trouble. Didn't he steal a car at the age of seven? How about sink his snowmobile in Lake Superior in July? And what about the time we came home to find him and the entire Deep Haven hockey team skinny-dipping in Evergreen Lake in February?"

"That was Owen's fault, not mine, and it was a dare."

Everyone laughed. Ivy had never felt so full, so satisfied.

"Did someone mention my name?"

She looked up, past Ingrid, and saw a young man, a younger version of the broad-shouldered Darek, come around the house to the porch. He wore a Minnesota Wild T-shirt, a pair of loose athletic shorts. Behind him came a pretty woman with her mother's signature blonde hair, wearing loose faded jeans and a sleeveless orange shirt.

"Owen!" Ingrid jumped up, stepped over the picnic bench, and hurtled toward her youngest son.

He wrapped her in his arms, twirling her around.

Casper had also risen and now hugged the other woman tight. "You should have called us!"

"I wanted to surprise you," she said.

"That's Eden, my sister," Darek said quietly. "And Owen. I stood in for him that night at the bachelor auction."

"So he was the one I was supposed to buy," Ivy said.

Darek glanced at her, but she winked.

He smiled then, his blue eyes twinkling, something sweet and dangerous in them. And although she was full enough to burst, she drank it right up.

So much so that she hurt.

Yes, Darek probably had no idea what he had here. But Ivy did. And she had no intention of letting that go.

CHAPTER 7

Jensen watched as Claire stood at the back of the stage like a ghost, a shadow of herself, playing the songs, adding backup, but without life. Pale, almost as if she hadn't really shown up for tonight's gig.

For the first time in three years, he wanted to talk to her. He sat at a back table on the open-air deck, nursing a glass of raspberry lemonade and listening to the Blue Monkeys twine out a rendition of Fleetwood Mac's "Go Your Own Way," the sound seasoning the flavor of the night. Behind him, tourists and locals fought for space along the rocky beach, unfolding blankets and chairs in anticipation of fireworks.

He should probably leave after this set, before people noticed him enjoying his freedom.

Emma leaned into the mic, her Fender over her shoulder, the sun draping a long shadow behind her. "'You can go your own way! Go your own way . . .'"

Jensen shook his head at the irony of the words.

No, if the people of Deep Haven had their choice, he wouldn't go anywhere. In fact, he'd better start bracing himself for a stint in the clink. He imagined that the county prosecutor was already writing the violation complaint. Hopefully he wouldn't go to Oak Park, a level-five prison. Maybe he'd end up at Stillwater or Faribault. Or maybe they'd simply send him to the local lockup, here in Deep Haven.

They'd probably prefer to put him in stocks in the public square.

He took a sip of lemonade, the bitterness watered down by the melting ice, then motioned to the waitress for a refill.

The song ended and Jensen added his applause. One more song and he'd bug out, head home. Try not to think about Claire's reaction to him at the hospital.

He couldn't explain why he still dragged himself down here tonight to listen to her, why he still hung on to the faint hope that she might forgive him, be his friend.

Yes, he was a lonely, pitiful man.

The applause died as Emma stepped up to the mic again. "Thanks for coming out, everyone! We're going to take a ten-minute break before the fireworks start, and then we'll come back at you with another set—this time with a little Skynyrd."

They received more applause as Jensen dug out his wallet. The night air smelled of campfire and celebration and he wanted to stay.

He put a ten on the table, sure that covered his drink and more. He was rising when—

"What are you doing here?"

He looked and saw Claire barreling off the stage toward him. Her voice carried in the air, although probably only he heard it, with the clatter of conversation on the deck and the music piped out over the radio. She wore a blue tank top, shorts, a long crocheted vest, and a pair of black flats and looked like she wanted to finish what she had started at the hospital.

He held up his hand. "I was just leaving."

But that didn't seem good enough. She came right up to him, put her hands on her hips. "Jensen, I swear. What's going on? I see you at every single gig. Sitting in the back like some sort of stalker. Why?"

He hadn't expected that. She *saw* him? Every time? Oh, he was a crazy, sorry lot because the tiniest spark lit inside him. He tried to swallow it away, but there it was, all warm despite the way she glowered at him.

"I . . . I like your music." That sounded right, and he chased his words with a smile.

She narrowed her eyes.

He braced himself.

And then, to his horror, her eyes began to fill, her jaw clenching. "Claire?"

"Leave me alone." She stalked toward the steps to a grassy path that led down to the lake.

He knew her better than that, thank you. "Claire!"

She didn't stop, but he didn't expect her to. He ran after her, caught up. "What did I do?" Wait, that wasn't the right question. He added, "This time."

She brushed her hand across her face, quick, sharp, as if to wipe a tear. "It's not you, Jensen. I'm sorry. I shouldn't have yelled at you."

She shouldn't have yelled—? "I . . . Well, you can yell at me anytime, Claire, if it helps."

Oh, that sounded stupid. And martyrish. Maybe he should have left her alone.

But she stopped, considering him for a long moment. So long that *he* had the urge to turn and run.

"People do that to you, don't they?"

She had such pretty eyes. Amber, really, in the right light. He'd forgotten that—or maybe not, but he'd tried to. "I—"

"You're a scapegoat in this town."

Now she had his attention. "I don't know about that. I think Deep Haven has their reasons." Even if he was innocent of the crime they accused him of, he could certainly agree with their anger. Their grief.

"I know. But the truth is, you probably don't deserve what they handed down to you."

Who was this woman, and where had they put the Claire he knew, the one who hadn't talked to him in three years?

"I don't understand. I thought you agreed with—"

"With how you were treated? No. I believed that it was an accident. I'm mad at you for other reasons."

Well, now that they had that cleared up . . . "What reasons?"

She pursed her lips, turned away from him. "I'm not a fool."

Wow. Not a clue. Still . . . "Listen . . . the reason I keep coming to your gigs is because I miss you."

Now he might as well open up his chest, let her take a good look at the ache inside. But he didn't know when, out of some cosmic misalignment, he might find himself talking to her again, especially in a moment when she wasn't hating him completely, so he went on. "I used to love to listen to you play, and . . . I know I come to all your gigs, but it's just because I miss you and Darek. I'm sorry if it makes you uncomfortable."

She was staring at him, her mouth open a second before she closed it. Then her face began to crumple.

"What did I say?" He winced. "I'm sorry, Claire. I don't mean to hurt you. I'll go."

She drew in a shaky breath. "No. Don't go."

Don't go?

He couldn't breathe. Okay.

She looked at the harbor and let out a trembling sigh. "Do you remember that Independence Day we made a campfire on Paradise Beach after the fireworks and stayed out all night, sleeping under the stars?"

"Your grandfather drove by three times that night."

"He knew you and Darek were red-blooded males and never understood how we could be just friends."

Yeah, him either. In fact, if he were honest, despite his efforts he'd never really thought of Claire as just a friend. And Felicity . . . she'd been more of a conundrum.

"You told us the story of Bosnia that night." He'd wanted to climb out of his sleeping bag, take Claire in his arms, tell her that he'd never let anything like that happen to her again. Never let her feel trapped, overwhelmed, abandoned. But Felicity kept looking at him, tossing rocks onto his sleeping bag, and, well, he'd been tossing them back, just for fun.

It seemed Felicity always had to have his—and Darek's—attention. Even in Claire's most desperate, vulnerable moments.

"That's right; I did," Claire said. He got a hint of a smile.

"Then we stayed up all night and played truth or dare."

"Mostly truth," she said.

"Except you dared Darek and me to go for a midnight swim."

"I saw the way Felicity was flirting with you. I thought you needed cooling off."

He laughed, but a little heat pressed his face. And then, for some stupid reason, he reached up and thumbed away the tear glistening on Claire's cheek. "What's the matter?"

Her smile faded, something haunted in her eyes. Then she turned away.

"Claire?"

"My parents are coming home."

He stalled at this, and she glanced back at him.

"Yeah. From Bosnia. To sell my grandfather's place."

He didn't know how to react, hating the traitorous leap his heart took.

"Not to you, Jensen. To Darek and Evergreen Resort."

See, she could see clear through him. "What? No."

"That's what they said. They're going to use the money to put him in a home, and . . . and they expect me to move on with my life."

Move on. He hadn't really noticed it before but . . . yes. She should move on. Beyond Felicity, beyond her grandfather. Beyond Deep Haven.

"What are you going to do?"

"That's the point!" She held up a hand as if in apology. "Sorry."

"I don't understand."

"I don't *want* to move on. I like it here—and I have nowhere else to go."

Jensen frowned at this. "What are you talking about? Don't you want to leave? Go to college or move away, start a new life?"

"Why? This is my home. I like it here."

He just stared at her.

"Don't you?"

He raised an eyebrow.

"Of course not. I get that. But . . . see, I don't know what I'd do. Play music? Make pizza? I do that here. And my grandfather's here. I don't want to go. I want to stay and take care of him."

"Then stay." Jensen didn't know where the words came from, but they came out of him with power. "Stay."

"How? Grandpop can't live in that house, at least not until he's better—"

"What if we installed ramps, made it handicap accessible?"

"I don't have money for that."

"But I do. I have my entire trust fund, just sitting there gathering interest. And believe it or not, I'm pretty good with a saw and hammer."

Jensen still couldn't believe the words emerging from him, but he let them hang there, not caring that they were edged with a sort of sad desperation. And hope. He could nearly taste it. *Please, let me help, Claire.*

He could admit a small bit of satisfaction that Darek wouldn't win again, wouldn't take the land Jensen wanted. But even more, he wanted to help Claire. Anything to make her come back to life. Maybe the last good thing he did before they took him away in handcuffs. He wasn't going to fulfill his hours before the deadline anyway. This felt like a better project than a useless fight for his freedom.

"You'd do that for me? Help me take care of my grandfather?"

His smile emerged slowly, from deep inside. "If you'll let me stay and listen to you sing."

A beat passed before, "I don't sing much."

"You should. You have a beautiful voice."

She blinked at him. "I do?"

He lowered his voice, met her eyes. "You do, Claire. Why do you think I keep hanging around the back of the room?"

She stared at him. Then her mouth clamped shut and she turned away.

And he'd blown it. He knew it in her posture, the way she watched the dark water, the moonlight catching the waves like the glint of a blade.

He'd moved in too fast, reminded her too much of . . . of what they should have had, maybe.

Then, suddenly, she nodded. "Okay."

"Okay?" Good grief, too much surprise in that. He made a face but erased it fast when she smiled.

There was a softness, a touch of friendship in it. Even a hint of what might have been.

"Okay, Jensen. You can stay."

Ivy fit into his family so easily that it felt to Darek as though she might have always belonged. She laughed at his mother's lame jokes and asked his father a million questions about the resort, acting genuinely interested in his endless stories of days gone by. She praised Grace's new potato salad recipe and posed for Amelia's photos. She and Eden exchanged favorite hot spots on the University of Minnesota campus, Ivy's alma mater, although clearly she'd spent more time in the library than his sister. She asked the right questions about hockey to Owen and didn't even act annoyed when he went on about his new digs and shiny new sports car.

She pried stories out of Casper while she helped Tiger roast a marshmallow and create a gooey s'more. She even laughed and cleaned him up when he showed her his sticky fingers.

Now, Tiger sat beside her on the beach of the Deep Haven harbor, on a stadium blanket Darek remembered to bring. She'd donned a University of Minnesota sweatshirt over her lemon dress, and the wind had tugged her hair down from her ponytail, whispering it around her face and sending him the slightest hint of some clean vanilla scent.

She'd purchased a neon-lit glow stick and fashioned it into a circular crown, which she placed on Tiger's head. A sea of fellow spectators surrounded them, sitting on blankets or folding chairs, waiting for the Elks Club to start the annual fireworks across the bay. The Christiansens had arrived in time to stake out their traditional perch—next to giant boulders that cordoned off the beach from the rest of the shoreline. As children, Darek and his siblings had loved to climb on the rocks, daring each other not to fall into the lake.

Sometimes, looking back at his childhood, he wondered how they'd ever lived through it. Or how their mother hadn't lost her mind with worry.

Darek picked his way through the crowd, holding a tray of cones from the local Licks and Stuff. He hunkered down next to Ivy and Tiger, handing them their orders.

Ivy took her cone—butter brickle and vanilla, double scoop. "Thank you."

"You're welcome. Tiger, let me . . ." He tucked a napkin into his son's jacket. It stuck out like a beard, but maybe it would keep the five-year-old from walking away a sticky mess. At the rate Tiger had been eating tonight, he'd probably be sick, but Darek had never seen his son so happy—and easy to control. He hadn't wandered away once, and there wasn't even a hint of a meltdown on his face.

Yes, Ivy wielded some kind of magical powers with children.

The night had turned into jeweled perfection, the sky washed with diamonds, glistening on the dark velvet surface of the lake. The thunder had rolled off into the distance, dying without a hint of moisture.

Grace and Casper had climbed onto the boulders to watch the show, Amelia standing on the pathway behind them, snapping shots destined to appear on the Deep Haven Facebook page. Their mother and father had brought their folding chairs and now sat like royalty among their subjects. Owen, of course, vanished the moment they hit town—probably stirring up trouble with his buddies. Eden sat next to her mother, fiddling with her smartphone.

"This is amazing," Ivy said, catching dripping custard with her tongue. "The harbor beach is packed."

"People come in from all over the county to watch the fireworks," Darek said. "It's the hottest ticket in town—to watch the display over the harbor, reflected in the water."

"You're so lucky to live here. I read about Deep Haven—there are articles in the Minneapolis paper sometimes about events up here. But I never dreamed it would be so quaint."

Events. Like crimes? Felicity's death—and Jensen's guilt—had made the news even in Minneapolis. But that had been three years ago. Certainly she wouldn't remember that.

No. This was a fresh start with a woman who'd slipped into his life without baggage, without the headlines standing between them. A woman who didn't see his mistakes but his future.

He licked a chocolate drip running down the side of his cone. "Deep Haven is a great place to grow up." For him, at least. He wanted to believe those words for Tiger, too.

"I never lived in one place for more than a year," Ivy said. Tiger scooted off the blanket and went to sit on the rocks.

She finished the top of her ice cream and started in on the cone. "After the state severed my mother's rights, I spent about a year bouncing around the system. I'll never forget my first long-term placement. I arrived just before Thanksgiving. There were three other foster kids who lived there, but the family had six grown children who all brought their spouses and children with them. The house was packed, about fifty people over for dinner, and I remember listening to the noise, the laughter, the way they all knew each other, and . . ." She raised a shoulder, then looked away, her voice thickening just a little. "It was nice."

Nice. But he could hear so much more in those words. He grabbed a napkin and wiped his wrist, working on the edges of the cone. "How long did you stay?"

"Until the next June."

That was a long-term placement? Eight months? He swallowed down a tightness in his throat, his appetite gone. "How many foster homes did you live in?"

She looked at him, found a smile. "Fourteen, total."

Fourteen. He couldn't help himself. "I'm sorry, Ivy."

She shook her head. "It taught me to be resilient." She finished her cone and reached for a napkin.

"Is that why you became an attorney? To help kids in the system?"

"And women like my mother, too. And to make deadbeat dads like mine help raise their own children. There's nothing worse than a man who has a child, then walks away."

"Yes," he said, feeling a twist of shame. He finished his cone without tasting it, glad for it to be gone. "Is that what happened to your mother?"

"She got pregnant at fourteen, ran away from home, and I landed in foster care for the first time before she turned twenty-two. By then, she'd lived with two other men, had an abortion from the first man, and was nearly killed by the second one. In between boyfriends, we lived in boxes and abandoned cars, and she did anything she could for money. . . .

"We ended up in Minneapolis, with a guy she met in Des Moines. He was a trucker and, I think, took pity on us. He had three kids of his own. I liked it there; I shared a room with his daughter, who braided my hair and let me play with her Barbies. He tried to help my mother, and it worked for a while. She got a job at a mail-stuffing place and stopped using. It was a real home, you know? I started going to school, making friends, believing that finally I might have a dad. Then my mom got hurt on the job—lifting something, I think—and it put her on her back. She started taking pain meds and it all started again. One day I came home to find her passed out, hardly breathing. I called 911 and that was the beginning of the end. I was permanently removed when I was nine."

At nine, he'd been in third grade, spending his summers learning to swim and fish with his dad while Ivy tried to figure out why she didn't have one.

Tiger came toward him, his hands extended and dripping with vanilla custard. Darek intercepted him, grabbing napkins to work off the paste. His mother handed him a wet wipe and he went to town on the boy's face.

Ivy waited until he turned Tiger loose and the boy ran away

before she continued. "My mother finally ended up in jail. I looked her up when I turned eighteen and visited her in the women's prison. She . . . she was sad for the way our lives turned out, but sometimes it's just the way it is. She didn't expect her life to turn out this way either—she just let defeat take over and rule her. Severing her rights was probably the best thing that could have happened for me."

"You're not angry with her?"

"Bitterness only eats you alive." She looked at him. "Right?"

He frowned, then gave a quick nod. "Right."

He checked on Tiger, who was climbing a rock. Casper hauled him up.

"Keep him out of the water, Casper," Darek called.

"Anyway, I get to choose my own life, my own path. And I chose Deep Haven. I'm here now, and I'm not leaving." She leaned back on her hands. "Ever."

Not leaving.

"You know, you can see the fireworks better from the lighthouse out there." He pointed to the break jutting out from shore. "Would you like to go for a walk?"

"What about Tiger?"

Darek glanced at Casper. His brother was already looking at him, wagging his eyebrows. See, this was what happened when you lived in a small town. Everyone watched as you fell in love with the new girl.

No, not fell in love. Just . . . started over. He wasn't sure he even knew what it felt like to fall in love. What he and Felicity had shared felt more like . . . well, it certainly wasn't love at the end.

"Tiger's okay with Casper."

"Then sure," Ivy said.

He held out his hand as he got up, intending to help her, but when she slid hers into his grip, he didn't let go.

She had soft, tiny hands, and he felt like a clod with his work-worn calluses. But he held on and led her through the crowd to the sidewalk, then down the beach and around the block to the lighthouse pathway.

The streetlights didn't reach far enough, and he slowed so she could pick her way along. He climbed onto the breakwater and helped her up.

"You know this area so well."

"Deep Haven boy," he said simply.

"Right." The breakwater was wide enough to walk side by side. "Thank you for letting me meet your family. They're great."

"*You're* great." Oh, wow . . . um . . . "I mean, thanks for being so great to them. Casper thinks he's going to discover some hidden treasure, and Owen just wants to flex for everybody to fawn over his physical prowess. Grace is always looking for people to try out her recipes, and Eden thinks she's going to be a superstar reporter. You listened to them all. Even posed for Amelia." He slowed, turned. "Thanks for that. And especially for being so nice to Tiger."

"Tiger is a wonderful little boy. You've given up so much for him." He frowned.

"Your firefighting dreams. It's so romantic that you gave it all up for love. I'm so sorry about your wife, Darek. You don't talk about her, but I can imagine that you miss her."

The wind trailed a long strand of hair into her eyes, and he brushed it away. Wished he could tell her the truth without sounding like a jerk.

"I do, yes." For Tiger's sake. And for himself. Felicity's death had stolen from him the chance to make it all right. To fix his mistakes.

No, Jensen had stolen that.

"But I'm trying to move on. To build a life for Tiger. I hope that we can build up the resort so he can take it over someday."

"It's a beautiful place. But . . . was it full?"

"No. We had a terrible winter—no snow. And spring came early. It's been so hot and miserable, and without air-conditioning or Internet in our units . . ."

"People don't appreciate the idea of an oasis in the woods."

"It's hard to update your Facebook status from Evergreen Lake. No cell towers."

"I rather enjoyed the luxury of being off the grid today."

"You're among the rare, then." He glanced at her, his words finding soft soil. Rare, indeed. "You know, the only thing I miss about my hotshot days is my motorcycle." Okay, that wasn't true. He missed the camaraderie, the challenge, the urgency of fighting fires. But admitting it only revived the ache.

And how could he compare that life to the life he had with Tiger? His family?

"You had a motorcycle?"

"The one Casper's driving. The Kawasaki 300. It was mine. I traveled to Montana and back quite a few times on that thing."

"Hard to strap a car seat to a motorcycle."

"Exactly."

They'd reached the end of the breakwater, where the lighthouse perched. He tugged her underneath the giant girders and beyond, to the edge.

From here, looking back along the shoreline, the town sparkled, lights sprinkled around the bowl of the harbor and against the hill.

"You know every great view in town," Ivy said.

"Just about," he said, turning to her. Oh, she was pretty, with those freckles that belied her job as a prosecutor, those big green eyes, staring at him.

There was something about her that made his breath leave him, warmed everything inside him. Maybe it was just the longing for something to be different and good. For someone to look at his broken life and put it back together.

For God to finally let him start over.

Darek licked his lips, tried to find the words. "I'd like to . . . ," he said softly. He touched her face, running his thumb down her cheek, meeting her eyes. "Can I . . . ?" He drew in a breath as the fireworks started behind him. He could hear the murmur of approval from the audience echo across the harbor.

"I'd really like to kiss you."

Ivy looked at him, blinked. Swallowed. Then a smile slid across her face. "I . . . I'd like that."

I'd like that.

So he started with something gentle, tentative, brushing his lips against hers. A sweet chill ran through him at the taste of butter brickle ice cream, the vanilla fragrance of her skin lighting a blaze inside. She reached up and hooked her hands lightly around his jacket collar as if to pull herself closer, and he ran his hand behind her head, into that thick, soft hair, just barely holding himself back from deepening his kiss, from allowing this heady rush of emotions to scare them both.

Because holding her like this, kissing her, awakened an awareness in him of just how long it had been since he'd let himself wonder, let himself want. Let himself believe in grace.

Yes, standing here in the glow of the brilliant plumes of celebration, his arms wrapped around this beautiful woman who molded herself to him and kissed him with such tenderness, could only be something he didn't deserve.

The fireworks went by too quickly. And not just the display in the night sky over the harbor, but the ones that happened inside Ivy as Darek held her in his arms.

She couldn't remember the last time she'd been kissed the way Darek just kissed her.

Okay, never. Because the truth was, she never had real time for dating. Not with keeping up her grades for her scholarships and clerking at Atwood and Associates and then her junior partner position in Daniel's firm and the hours and hours she'd studied for the bar.

Nope, with the exception of a very sloppy sixteen-year-old prom date, this was it. Her first real kiss. The kind to wait for.

She couldn't believe how sweetly he'd kissed her. Nothing like the prickly man she'd first met, wearing his anger on the outside. No, this man had asked her permission before he kissed her, savored the kiss, made her feel like he meant it.

Please, let him have meant it. Because she surely did.

They sat on the edge of the breakwater, watching the fireworks arching across the sky, holding hands. And then, when she shivered, pulling her knees up into her dress, he'd moved behind her and pulled her against his chest, wrapping his arms around her.

That kept her warm. On fire, really.

She felt his heart thump against her back, reveled in the woodsy campfire scent of him, and felt only a little guilty that his wife had missed out on so much, her life cut short.

But Ivy didn't want to think about her. Not tonight.

When the fireworks ended, Darek helped her down the breakwater and through the mass of crowds toward the beach. "I can walk home from here," she said, but he had her hand and didn't let go.

"I'll walk you home. I just want to check in with Tiger, make sure he's okay."

What a great father. She could melt at the sight of Darek with his son, the way he'd gently wiped Tiger's face and hands tonight.

The smell of firework debris seasoned the air, the crackle of faraway contraband celebrators in the distance. Darek stopped on the beach, turned to look.

"What?"

"I'm going to call the sheriff's department, see if they can track them down. It's a great way to start a forest fire."

"Seriously?"

She and Darek continued along the shore, rocks falling away under their feet. "The forest is one big tinderbox right now. And people can be so careless."

Oh, she loved the responsibility—

Wait, not loved. Liked. A lot. She couldn't fall in love with a guy on the first—okay, second—date. But the fact that he worried touched her anyway.

"You loved firefighting, didn't you?"

He glanced at her; then a curious smile appeared on his face. "Yeah. I love the forest, and reading how a fire moves through it is fascinating to me. It's like a battle, and you just have to outsmart the fire. But there are so many factors you can't control—weather and wind. You have to always be thinking what it wants, where it wants to go."

"You talk as if it's alive."

"It is. It breathes air, needs fuel to stay alive, is hungry for more."

"But it takes a spark to get it going."

"Right. And that's what I'm hoping we can avoid. Because as much as I love fire, I don't love it enough to wish it upon the beautiful forests. Forest fires are terrifying and dangerous, and I don't miss the part where people could lose their homes or die."

"Do you think you'll ever go back to it?"

He shook his head. "That part of my life is over." He said it in a way that sounded a little like he'd been punched in the chest, fighting to catch his breath.

"I'm sorry."

He looked at her again, gave her hand a squeeze. "Thank you."

As they came closer to where the family had parked, they saw a crowd—nothing big, but a few people turned, watching something.

"Oh no," Darek said.

"What?"

He dropped her hand and jogged up the beach. She couldn't run in flip-flops, so she clambered after him. She worked her way in from the edge and then wanted to weep at what she saw.

Tiger stood in the middle, soaking wet and shivering, his lip fat and bleeding. Casper was wrapping the picnic blanket around him.

Darek knelt before his son, finished wrapping the blanket, then clutched Tiger tight to his chest. "Buddy, what happened?" Darek looked up at Casper as he asked, a darkness descending across his expression.

"I fell!" Tiger began to cry and Darek picked him up, held him in those big arms.

"He was climbing on the rocks, and even though I had ahold of him, he slipped, hit his mouth on the rock, and went in."

"Dude," Darek said, visibly trying not to raise his voice, "you shouldn't have let him climb on the rocks."

"What are you talking about? We did it our entire lives. Besides, he's fine, aren't you, champ?" He rubbed Tiger's back; the little boy gave him a mournful look.

Ivy made her way to Darek. "I can walk myself home. I just live across the street behind the Footstep of Heaven."

Darek glowered at Casper like he wanted to take his brother apart piece by piece.

"Meet us at the car, Son." John Christiansen reached out for Tiger.

Darek seemed to hesitate, and Ivy was about to insist again that she could make it across the street on her own when Darek kissed the top of Tiger's head and handed him over. "I'll be right there."

Tiger curled against his grandfather's shoulder.

Darek caught Ivy's hand without ceremony and headed toward the sidewalk.

"Darek, really. I'm a big girl."

"My dad is trying to keep me from pummeling my brother."

Oh.

Around them, families packed cars with coolers, blankets, folding chairs. Others hiked home, catching the hands of their children. Cars began to move down the street. Darek kept hold of her hand as they crossed between traffic. They walked in silence down the sidewalk for a moment, his face tight.

"Is he going to be okay?"

"Yes, but Casper might not live through this," he growled.

"It was an accident. Kids fall."

He shook his head. "My son looks like he's been beaten up. Between the stitches and fat lip . . . they're going to call child protective services on me."

She frowned at him. "No one is going to call CPS."

But he wasn't kidding, not by the grim look on his face. "You don't know the Holloways."

"Who?"

"Felicity's parents. His grandparents. After she died, they sued me for custody but lost. Since then, they've accused me of negligence twice. I have to bring Tiger over on Sunday and . . . Oh, this is bad."

His expression was so defeated that she took his face in her hands. Looked in his eyes and said what she'd said to herself every time a social worker appeared at the door. "Everything is going to be fine. No one is going to take Tiger away from you. You're his father, and he's a normal, rambunctious five-year-old boy. I don't know the Holloways, but certainly they can see that."

He looked at her as if drinking in her words, longing to believe her. Then, softly, "You are so beautiful."

Oh, she hadn't expected that. Or the way he slid his hand around her neck, leaned down, and kissed her.

Right there, in front of his family.

When he let her go, he surrendered a smile. "When can I see you next?"

Tomorrow? She held that word in. "Call me."

"Don't just show up on the Footstep of Heaven doorstep?"

She smiled as he took her hand again, headed down the street. In the distance, thunder began to roll once more.

"Maybe it'll rain after all." She glanced up to see two figures at the gate. She recognized Claire and then . . . Jensen Atwood?

Yes. Jensen was unloading Claire's portable keyboard from his truck parked in front of the house, now carrying it toward her apartment.

And then, to Ivy's surprise, she heard, "What's he doing there?"

Darek was looking at Jensen, his expression dark. He let go of her hand. "What is Jensen Atwood doing at your house?"

She stared at him, his tone so abrupt, so angry. "What? I—"

"Do you know him?"

"Why are you yelling at me?" She took a step away from him, suddenly seeing the man from the auction, angry and rude.

He must have seen her face, for he cringed and looked away, his voice falling. "Sorry, I . . . You're right. I just . . ." He looked back down the street, where Jensen was returning to his truck. "Who is your roommate?"

"I don't have one. I live behind the house in the garage apartment. But Claire Gibson lives above the bookstore."

"Claire." He shook his head, his voice going softer. "I should have known."

"Should have known what?"

He drew in a long breath, turned back to her. "Nothing." He reached out and touched her hand. "I'm sorry. I just . . . Jensen Atwood brings out the worst in me."

"Why? Who is he to you?"

"It's a long story, for another time. I don't want it to wreck our night. Let's just say that if there is anyone you should stay away from in this town, it's Jensen Atwood."

"You used to say that about you." She tried a smile.

Darek gave a harsh chuckle. "I did, didn't I?" But his laugh died. "I actually mean it about Jensen."

His words slid inside, settled under her skin like a burr. "Why do you hate him so much?"

"Because he stole my life from me."

She frowned, but he leaned close to kiss her on the cheek. "I'll call you."

Then he dashed across the street to where his family waited in their Caravan. Casper roared off on his motorcycle.

And Ivy stood there on the sidewalk, an icy hand around her heart.

How did Darek know Jensen Atwood?

CHAPTER 8

She could at least make him a sandwich. Claire peeked out the window to where Jensen was building the long ramp that would replace the steps to the backyard. True to his word, he'd arrived about an hour ago, unloaded wood and power tools from his truck, and begun work as if she wasn't even in the house.

As if he didn't need her.

And maybe he didn't because while she worked a double shift at Pierre's yesterday, he'd already modified the front stoop. A tiny ramp sloped from the ground to the house, peaked at a new landing, then led into the entryway.

Or maybe he was simply used to working alone, used to being—or trying to be—invisible.

Not that people wouldn't notice him, in his baseball cap,

a button-down shirt cut off at the arms—threads loose where the sleeves should be—and a pair of ripped and faded blue jeans perfectly seasoned for his physique. He clomped around in work boots like a real carpenter and even wore one of those leather tool belts, a square pencil behind his ear, which looked like it might be getting sunburned.

In fact, the man looked like he'd walked off an L.L. Bean cover.

Yeah, real inconspicuous.

She'd popped her head out once and offered him a glass of water—just to be polite—but he'd waved her away.

He'd smiled, though, as he did it, and it conjured up the memory of him driving her home after the gig. Normally she would have let Kyle drive her home—he usually picked her up to help with her equipment—but with Jensen offering . . .

You have a beautiful voice.

Oh, she shouldn't have let that go to her head quite so easily.

She needed to remember exactly why she hadn't talked to him for three years. And it wasn't because he'd caused an accident that took Felicity's life.

No, that she blamed on Felicity.

Not that Jensen shouldn't be blamed for his part in that terrible evening. The fight that caused Felicity to don her running shoes and take off.

Maybe he thought Claire didn't know. That no one except Darek knew.

But Claire had been sitting on the beach that night, heard every word of the fight as Darek's and Felicity's angry voices echoed over the lake.

She knew exactly what part Jensen really played in Felicity's death.

That thought had fueled her as she spent the morning cleaning out the entry hall, moving boxes of old boots and hats, fishing gear, snowmobile helmets. She'd even moved the rough-hewn bench, sitting there since the dawn of time, out to the garage. Then she went to work on the kitchen table, lifting it onto cinder blocks so Grandpop could move a wheelchair under it.

Taking a break, she searched the fridge for something edible for lunch. In the freezer she found leftovers from a ham, a hunk of cheese, and a loaf of bread she'd baked a while back. Hopefully it wasn't freezer burned. She thawed it all, constructed a couple sandwiches, added some condiments and pickles, arranged them on two plates, and with her back to the door, eased it open.

"Jens?"

Oh, the old nickname just slid out. She didn't mean it.

He looked up, a hint of surprise on his face, and for a second, she felt it—the past, easy and fun, perfect. The sunshine baking into her skin, the scent of evergreen in the breeze, gooey sweet marshmallows on her tongue, the crackle of a bonfire as it ate away the darkness.

She wanted to devour those days, let them nourish her, but she swallowed them away.

Jensen stood, turning his hat backward so that a clump of his blond hair stuck out in front, curly and thick. "Whatcha got there?"

"How about a little lunch?" Claire balanced the plates, but with the steps destroyed, she was stranded on the stoop.

He reached for the plates, then turned his back to her. "Hop on."

She didn't know what to make of his offer, nearly lured by the nostalgia of their past.

"I got this," she said and jumped down. She tried not to notice the disappointment on his face.

He was just here to help. And the sooner he finished, the better for everyone.

He set the plates down at a nearby picnic table and examined his sandwich.

"It's all we had. I'll do better tomorrow."

Jensen slid onto the bench. "You don't have to feed me, Claire. I could go home for lunch." He picked up the sandwich. "Not that I'm complaining."

"It's the least I could do," she said, sliding opposite him. She bit into her sandwich. It did taste freezer burned. "I'll get us some milk."

"I have water." He gestured toward a jug in the bed of the truck.

"You're turning into quite the handyman for a big-city boy." He was tan, his arms a nice bronze, and he looked anything but a city boy. "I remember that first summer you came back after moving, and I barely recognized you. You had your hair long—"

"As I recall, you called me Jenny until I got it cut."

"Tough love, baby."

"You were tough, all right. Yelled at me for a week for quitting football."

"You didn't even try out for the team down in Wayzata."

"They're a state-ranked team. I barely got any playing time, even here."

"And hockey? You played decent hockey."

He gave her a look. Well, she'd thought so.

"Moving my senior year pretty much destroyed any sports aspirations for me."

"I'm sorry. I thought you were good."

"Thanks for that. But I think it was just you being nice to me."

Oh. There he went again, stirring up the past. She blew out a breath, tried to remember his many sins. "Well, I didn't know anyone except you, Felicity, and Darek. I had no choice."

Not true, but it kept him at a distance.

"I couldn't believe that you came back after your trip to Bosnia that first summer. I thought you were gone for good, and then one day you appear on the dock. Fresh from Europe, all exotic and curious and . . ."

"And you came over in your boat and immediately tried to get me into trouble."

He grinned at her, wiping his mouth on his arm. "What trouble?"

"You nearly got me killed! I'd never been tubing before."

"You kept yelling at me to go faster. You don't say that to a teenage boy with a fresh boat license!"

Claire laughed. "Yeah, maybe." She looked out at the lake lapping at the sandy beach as if reaching out to pull them into the past. "Those were good days."

Jensen was silent as he finished his sandwich. Then he went over to the truck, picked up his bottle of water, and drank it down. "Want some?"

"I'll get some from the house."

"Suit yourself. It's well water. Yum." He grinned and replaced the cap.

This not liking him, not letting him inside to nudge her memories, might be harder than she thought.

He picked up a board.

She got up. "So what will this look like when you're finished?"

"Well, any single run of a handicap access ramp can't rise more than thirty inches. The back door is too high, so we'll have to make two. The maximum slope ratio is one-to-twelve, so I'll make them both twenty feet long with a landing in the middle." He held the board at the angle from the house. "Like this."

"That's a big ramp."

"Your grandfather loves his yard."

Yes, he did. Claire found herself smiling.

"Once we finish this, we'll have to move inside and adopt some universal design elements. Nonbarrier showers, and I might have to widen the entry doors, lower the handles."

"But I'll be living here with him."

"What if he needs to get out on his own? You don't want him to depend on you for his freedom, do you?"

"Where did you learn all this?"

He had put the board down and picked up a shovel. "Learn what?"

"Building. Handicapped access rules."

Jensen walked over to the corner of where he'd sprayed an orange square. Planted his shovel in the ground. "I worked at the senior center a year ago for my community service doing some repairs."

Right. "What are you doing?"

"We have to pour footers for the landing."

"So you have to dig holes?"

He was already making a dent in the earth. "It won't take long. I'll pour the footers tonight, then tomorrow start working on a deck base."

"How long do you think it'll take?"

He glanced at her. "We'll get it done before your parents come home, if I have to work day and night."

Her throat tightened. Wow.

She picked up the paper plates, then went to the cold campfire pit and dropped them in. Stood looking at the charred black wood.

"What about your community service hours?" She winced when she said it, but . . . well, all this time working with her couldn't be good for his sentence.

He was moving dirt behind her; she could hear him grunt. But he said nothing. So she turned, stuck her hands in her back pockets. "Jensen? What about your community service hours? Or are you all done?"

He had created a substantial pile and now sank the shovel in deep, letting his foot rest on it. "I'm not going to make it."

Huh? "I don't understand."

"I have too many hours to complete by the end of the month. I'm not going to make it." He began to shovel again. "I was kinda stupid when I was first sentenced. Angry, even. So I didn't have my heart in it and I pretty much wasted my first year. Thankfully Mitch got ahold of me and made me see the light, made me turn my hours in every week, even though the court didn't mandate it, but . . ." He dumped out another spadeful of dirt. "I have too many left."

"What does that mean?"

He didn't stop shoveling. "It means that in a few weeks, I'll be in violation of my probation and they'll send me to jail."

Jail.

She didn't know why the word took her like a fist in the chest, squeezing out her breath. It wasn't like she hadn't thought about that after the accident, but she'd nearly cried with a sort of tangled relief when he'd only been sentenced to community service. Because despite his sins, he suffered too. People just didn't see it.

She hadn't really seen it. Not until the other night when he'd been willing to leave the concert because he was bothering her. Bothering Deep Haven.

Maybe . . . maybe he *had* changed. She watched him work, his strong muscles rippling across his back, down his arms, and remembered the boy who had made her laugh with his stupid jokes or occasionally ventured out to his deck and serenaded the night with his harmonica. Who had asked her to prom her senior year when he discovered she didn't have a date and returned from his sophomore year in college to take her.

Maybe he wasn't the man who'd had an affair with Felicity Christiansen, who had broken her heart and gotten her killed.

No. Felicity wouldn't have lied about that, would she?

Claire blinked back the strangest rush of tears and headed toward the side of the house.

Jensen didn't look up, just kept digging as the hole grew deeper.

One person at a time, Ivy would quietly enact justice in Deep Haven.

Like working out a plea agreement for Devon Ford on his juvenile petty offense—aka underage drinking—charge. He was a good kid, just needed a wake-up call, so she'd offered probation with a deferred sentence. As long as he kept his nose clean for a year, the charges wouldn't appear on his record.

And then there was the matter of Krista Brown and her first-offense possession of marijuana. Ivy offered Krista's defense attorney a deal for his client: a fine and an agreement to seek treatment.

All that in between her five criminal traffic complaint arraignments, three initial appearances, one pretrial, and one sentencing. After lunch, she had three probation violation hearings, two omnibus hearings—all in traffic court—one contested omnibus hearing, and a review hearing.

Then came the CHIPS—children in need of protection or services—cases: two review hearings, an admit/deny hearing, and a number of permanency review hearings.

The docket repeated itself tomorrow.

By the end of the month, she'd probably know half the people in Deep Haven, at least the ones who drove without a license, sped through town, or were fighting to keep their children.

"That's your third Diet Coke." Diane Wolfe, the county social worker, slid onto a wire chair overlooking the harbor, holding her basket of fish-and-chips. A taller woman, she kept her dark curly hair short, wore little makeup, and had a no-nonsense way about her that suggested she looked at the facts—a good thing when dealing with the intricacies of families. Diane's office was just down the hall, and she and Ivy spent the better part of these court days together. Daniel had always encouraged a positive relationship with local social workers and law enforcement. Hence why Ivy had also invited Mitch O'Conner, the probation officer, to join them for lunch.

Mitch sat facing the harbor, eating his batter-dipped french fries, letting the sun bathe his face. Or maybe dreaming of fishing. His office sported a number of mounted trophies.

Seagulls called over the water, the sun high and glorious. The lake seemed so blue, it could reach out and woo her into its cool waters. Ivy wore a pair of black dress pants and a pink sleeveless blouse, her hair up, but sweat still began to trickle down her back. The one nice thing about being trapped inside a courthouse all day—air-conditioning.

"I'm trying to keep my energy up," Ivy said, attempting to balance the ingredients of her crab sandwich. "When I first arrived,

I thought this might be a fluke, but no, it's like this every week. A marathon of cases."

"And the summer is just getting going," Diane said.

"People keep saying that. It's July."

"Wait until August. It's our high season."

Ivy kept trying not to glance over to the lighthouse, not to let Darek tiptoe into her mind. He hadn't called all weekend, and she'd spent the early part of the week working on cases, preparing for today, and hardly noticed.

Okay, she'd noticed.

But maybe, as it had with her, when they kissed, the smallest spark of fear had lit inside him, compelled him to step back, take a breath.

"Judge Magnusson certainly keeps the docket clipping along."

"No wasting time with her," Diane said. "She expects you to be prepared. Whenever she's presiding, I spend the days before cramming like I am still in college, remembering specific incidents so I don't look like a fool on the stand."

"Don't let her lie to you," Mitch said, looking at Ivy through his aviator glasses. "She'd do that if Santa Claus was presiding."

Diane wiped her mouth with a napkin. "It only took once for a defense attorney to tear me apart on the stand, and I never let that happen again."

"The children of Deep Haven are fortunate to have you," Ivy said.

"Agreed." Mitch smiled, and Ivy instantly liked him.

"By the way, just a heads-up." He looked at Ivy. "Jensen Atwood isn't going to finish his community service. I think we'll have to file a probation violation complaint." He mopped ketchup with his fries while everything stilled inside Ivy.

Diane sat back in her chair, sipping her strawberry lemonade. "I can't decide how I feel about that. I see him around town, working hard. And yet, I see Nan Holloway with Tiger, and my heart goes out to the entire family. I know Darek is probably doing his best, but he's a single dad. I know it can't be easy for him."

Darek? Ivy set down her sandwich, trying to sort out their conversation. What did Darek have to do with Jensen's probation violation?

"I can still remember that horrible night," Diane said.

"What happened?" Ivy said, reaching for her glass. She knew some of it—that kind of story stuck in a person's memory. But maybe they'd fill in the details.

"Oh, it's a terrible story," Diane said. "It was late at night, and Felicity Christiansen was out running on the highway north of town. Jensen came around the corner too fast, didn't see her, and hit her."

Felicity Christiansen.

Ivy's head swam, the world curving in, back out, watery. Felicity was Darek's wife.

"He was driving one mile over the speed limit," Mitch argued back to Diane.

"And he was texting."

"They never proved that."

"Only because it never went to court! He pleaded out. There are folks in Deep Haven who are still angry over that."

Ivy couldn't breathe. Clearly neither Diane nor Mitch knew that she'd been the one who helped orchestrate the plea agreement. Or at least suggest the parameters.

"He never would have gotten a fair trial here, Diane, and you know it."

Diane's lips gathered in a tight bunch. "Maybe."

"Diane—"

"I just feel sorry for the family. Darek raising that sweet little boy all by himself. He and Felicity had their whole lives ahead of them."

Bile pooled in Ivy's chest. She just might throw up.

"I still can't believe the judge granted a departure from the sentencing guidelines."

"Blame it on timing," Mitch said. "Judge Carver was leaving, and he'd driven that patch of road too many times to agree with a vehicular homicide ruling."

"If Jensen's dad hadn't been a lawyer—"

"He wasn't represented by his father," Ivy said softly.

Diane glanced at her. Frowned. "You're familiar with the case?"

"It made all the headlines in the Cities, Diane. Of course she is."

No, that wasn't it. But she couldn't . . . "It was handled by another firm."

"Well, someone knew their law because they dug up some precedence and produced quite a memorandum. Otherwise Carver would have never allowed the plea bargain to go through."

Ivy looked at the water, where otters skimmed along the surface, ducking under to hide, reappearing in the shadows under the dock.

"He might not have gotten jail time, but the guy has certainly paid for his crime," Mitch said.

Diane poked at the ice cubes in her glass with her straw. "How?"

"Can you imagine living in a town that hates you? That wishes you were in jail? He's toed the line, and now he'll violate his probation by less than a hundred hours."

"That's a lot."

"Not when you consider he had three thousand hours to fill."

DJ's words trickled back to Ivy. *Justice can take many shades, especially in a small town.*

Indeed, from Darek's—and Tiger's—viewpoint, perhaps justice hadn't prevailed, not at all.

She hadn't gotten the case wrong, had she?

"He could file a motion for clemency," Mitch said.

"What?" Diane shook her head. "Listen, a crime was committed, and he had ample time to complete his community service. Let him go to jail."

Ivy must have gone a little white because Mitch glanced at her. "Are you okay?"

She nodded.

But how could she possibly be okay with Darek's voice in her head? *He stole my life from me.*

And she'd made it worse. She kept Jensen out of jail.

How could she not have figured it out? Darek had talked about his wife, how he lost her so young. But . . . Ivy hadn't asked because she hadn't wanted to know. She'd been so desperate for him to like her . . .

She was smarter than this. She should have pieced it together. Why hadn't she?

The question dogged her all afternoon after she escaped to her office, closing the door to pull herself together. Now, she stood at the window and fought the urge to pack her things, take off back to Minneapolis.

Before Darek found out.

Before she had to tell him.

Maybe . . . maybe she just wouldn't tell him. Did he really have to know?

A knock came at her door. "Come in."

She turned to find DJ entering. "Just stopping in to check on you."

"Did you have a nice weekend?"

He slipped into a chair, grinning, teeth white against his dark face. "I should ask you the same thing."

"What?"

"First you buy Darek Christiansen and then you kiss him?" He leaned back, crossed one leg over the other.

She winced. "You saw that?"

"All of Deep Haven saw that. Right there on the sidewalk in front of the harbor."

Ivy sank into her desk chair. "Tell me the truth—now do you think it's a conflict of interest? Me seeing him? Especially after I wrote the memo on Jensen's case?"

Clearly she'd knotted her brain too tight on this because DJ frowned. "So you *didn't* know about the connection between Darek and Jensen. I wasn't sure." He sighed. "No, it's not a conflict of interest. Your firm wasn't the attorney on record, and you didn't even know Darek at the time. So . . . no."

"And if I have to bring a complaint of probation violation against Jensen?"

"Really? He's violated his probation?"

"No. But he is short of his hours. So maybe."

"I still don't see a conflict. You're just responding to the court's mandate. However—" he leaned forward—"does Darek know you were involved in his wife's case?"

She made a face, shook her head. "Does he have to?"

"That's up to you, Counselor." He picked up a rock that Ivy

used to hold down a stack of police complaints. "I'm not the one trying to build a new life here, finding a niche, falling in love—"

"I'm not falling in love."

He raised an eyebrow.

"I've known him for two weeks. Two."

"Mmm-hmm." He put the rock on the desk. "All I know is that secrets don't last for long here." He got up. "By the way, I don't know if you remember, but I'll be leaving for vacation on Friday—I'll be gone two weeks. But it's July; everything grinds to a halt in July—"

"I know. The summer is just starting."

He laughed. "You'll be fine."

Ivy picked up the rock after he left, feeling the weight of it in her hand. Eyed the phone.

And for the first time, hoped Darek Christiansen wouldn't call.

"Four days. You're a real prize, big brother."

Eden sat down next to Darek at a picnic table in the harbor park, her gyro sandwich in a foil wrapper, a malt from Licks and Stuff in her other hand. She wore her long blonde hair down, a sleeveless shirt, a pair of dress pants. She'd inherited the elegance from their mother. Darek always thought she should've aspired to be in front of the camera, not behind it. But she loved words and thirsted for a great story.

"What did I do?" he asked.

"You haven't called her yet, have you?" Someday Eden would be a crackerjack journalist. Especially since she went right for the jugular with her questions.

"No, all right?"

"Sheesh, I'm just saying, I liked her. We all did. It's been *four days*. Call her."

But his hearing had stopped on *We all did.* "You had a conversation about my date?"

"You kissed her in the middle of the sidewalk. What were we supposed to do? Look away? It's like a train wreck—we couldn't help it."

"Thanks. Nice analogy." He had already unwrapped his double cheeseburger and spread his fries on the tray; now he opened the chicken nuggets meal for Tiger, who was busy stalking seagulls across the lawn.

"Okay. Let's try: it's about time, and it was all we could do to not cheer from the sidelines."

"It's not a sporting event either."

"Apparently it is. And you're losing. To yourself. Call the girl." Eden unwrapped her gyro, watching Tiger. "You almost got that last one, Tiger!"

"Don't encourage him. He's already a mess. If he falls, he'll split open that lip again, and the swelling is just starting to go down." He took a bite of his burger.

"You can't wrap him in bubble wrap, Dare."

"I'd like to." He put down the burger, wiped his mouth. "You should have seen the way Nan looked at me when I brought him over on Sunday. Like I'd let my son wander out into traffic."

Darek winced as the little guy tripped, lurching forward onto his hands and knees. But he got up laughing.

Tough kid. So much like himself. Except it seemed like Darek hadn't gotten up the last time he went down.

Until Friday night. With Ivy.

For the first time in three years, he'd glimpsed the man he wanted to be.

Still, Eden was right. He was losing. Every day that slipped by felt a little like the magic died. He couldn't seem to stir up the courage to call her, and he couldn't figure out why. Especially since she'd wandered into his brain and set up camp there. He kept seeing those green eyes, widening just before he kissed her. Kept tasting her lips, feeling her hair between his fingers—

"Nan's just being overprotective. Like she was with Felicity." Eden bit into her gyro, yanking him away from Ivy, back to reality, where he should stay.

"No wonder she hates me, then," he said.

Eden reached for a napkin. "Felicity made her own choices, Darek. You're not entirely to blame."

Yeah, well, his sister hadn't been there that night on the beach when Tiger was conceived. Fresh from a month fighting fires with his hotshots, Darek had blazed into Deep Haven like a hero—or at least he thought so.

And it didn't help that Felicity confirmed it in the way she smiled at him, flirted with him, kissed him. Still . . . "Trust me, I'm the one to blame. Not that she wasn't willing, but . . . at the end of the day, I'm the one who should have said no. I knew what I should—and shouldn't—have been doing." That night, he'd stolen Felicity's future from her. Her dreams and plans . . . and the chance to marry someone who truly loved her.

"Well, you made it right."

He pushed his double burger away, his appetite gone. "Did I? I married her, but maybe that was just making the situation worse." He stared at his little boy, so much of Felicity in him—those big brown eyes, the way he held up his arms to embrace the world. "I should have done better by her."

"You were young too, Darek. And you had man brain."

He glanced at her. "You and Mom. Do I want to know what that is?"

"Oh, you can figure it out," she said, taking another bite.

He rolled his eyes.

"Just don't let that same brain keep you from calling Ivy. I like her. A lot. And I have a feeling you do too." Eden set down the gyro. "This thing is so messy!"

Exactly what his life might become if he called Ivy. Let her in any further. Tangled. Dangerous. Terrifying.

Messy.

And that thought planted him right there, stuck. His phone in his pocket, burning a hole, reminding him that he was a jerk.

But last time he'd let his heart take charge . . . "Tiger, come over here and eat your nuggets! They're getting cold."

Tiger looked at him, then ran to the table, climbing onto the bench. He reached for the toy, but Darek pulled it away. "After the nuggets."

Tiger frowned but dug into his lunch.

The sun had climbed to the apex of its path, a slight dusting of clouds in the sky. A skim of smoke tinged the air—probably local campfires or even the fish house, smoking their daily catch. The lake never looked so blue—a rich, deep indigo. On the harbor beach, a couple children threw stones into the water or skipped them across the surface. A husband held his wife's hand, swinging it between them as they strolled along the rocky beach.

"When do you head back?" Darek picked up a fry, bathed it in ketchup.

"This afternoon. Owen has an appearance tomorrow, even though I have the week off."

"How's he doing?" He hadn't spent much time with his kid brother, Casper and his father commandeering all the conversation, spinning it around the Wild and new plays and stats and play-off hopes and . . . Well, that had never been Darek's life.

"He's young. And it's a little too much glamour for someone his age. He's got a cameo in an upcoming *Sports Illustrated*, something about the hockey stars of the season. And the Wild press team has him playing in charity events and appearing at festivals all summer long."

Darek took a sip of his Coke, finished the can, then crushed it in his hands. "I never thought I'd see one of our siblings on the cover of *Sports Illustrated*."

"He's not there. But he will be."

"And you? When will I see your byline in some magazine?"

Eden finished with her gyro, closing the leftovers in the foil. "I wish. If I could just get into the news department, start reporting real stories. Obits is such a dead end . . ." She winked, but he saw the frustration in her eyes.

"You'll get there, Sis."

"One story. I just need one story. In the meantime, I guess I'm in Minneapolis to keep an eye on Owen."

"Good luck with that," Darek said. "It's like keeping Tiger out of trouble. Right, pal?"

Eden laughed as Tiger grinned at them. Poor kid looked like he'd been hit by a truck, his fat lip now smeared with ketchup, the stitches almost completely dissolved over his eye. He ate his fries with grimy hands and had a skid mark on his knee from where he'd gone down in the grass.

Nan's words from Sunday burned into Darek's brain. *Can't you take better care of him?*

Maybe not. Maybe it would have been better for him to concede that Nan and George Holloway could take much, much better care of Tiger. Could give him the attention he needed, fill his world with the touch of Felicity he lacked.

And then . . . then Darek would leave. Do something with his life, like fight fires again. Or finish his fire management training.

When he came home, he'd be his son's hero. The man who trumpeted back into his life and took him fishing and taught him to swim and hunt and love the forest.

Instead of the guy always tired, always a little less of a father than he'd like to be.

"The place looks nice. You and Dad did a good job rebuilding the deck on cabin four. And did I see sauna plans—finally—in the office?"

"Finally, yes. And a new playground. But what we really need is Internet."

She made a face.

"Eden, you're not there. It's isolated. Remote. Families want to be connected; teenagers want to update their Facebook status."

She stirred her malt. "I noticed we only had two cabins full this week."

"The Schmitts and the Iversons arrived yesterday. The same week every year for the last decade."

"God bless them."

"But their kids don't come. We gotta do something. Nobody wants to go to Evergreen Lake and rent a paddleboat or sit on the dock and read."

She considered him. "So what do we do? Convince Mom and Dad to sell the place? What would they do? Where would they go?"

"Sell? No. Of course not."

She held up her hand. "Sorry. I just thought . . . Well, it felt like you wanted to move on—"

"I want to make it better, Sis. I'll do whatever it takes to put Evergreen Resort back on the map, to pack out the house like in the old days. For Mom and Dad. And for Tiger."

She raised an eyebrow. "That's a change. Are you convincing yourself, or do you mean it?"

"I mean it. Don't you think Tiger deserves the childhood we had?"

Eden finished her malt, then picked up her trash. "You want to make Tiger's childhood better? Give him a future? Call Ivy." Getting up, she walked around to Tiger and wiped his mouth. "C'mon, pal. Did you know if you put salt on a seagull's tail, you can catch him?"

"Really?" Tiger talked with his mouth full, climbing off the bench.

"Nice, Eden."

She gave Darek a toothy smile and led Tiger off toward the beach.

Her words netted in Darek's chest. *You want to make Tiger's childhood better?*

Yes, he did.

Darek took a breath, pulled out his phone, and walked away from the table, toward the parking lot. He just had to call her. Ask her what she was doing this weekend. Maybe take her fishing.

Fishing? Oh, c'mon. He could do better than that. He stared at the phone, wishing for words. Anything.

Hey, Ivy, it's Darek. He'd gotten that far in his head when he heard a vehicle pulling into the lot. He stepped back onto the grass and looked up just as it rolled to a stop beside him.

He stilled. It couldn't be.

The vehicle resembled an ambulance, with two bay doors in the back that opened to supplies and beds. Along the outside of the truck, door handles indicated four compartments—he knew from memory that the other side contained identical spaces for personal gear, foodstuffs, medicine, firefighting supplies.

A fresh coat of lime-green paint covered the surface, with the words *Jude County Hotshots* painted along the top.

Darek lowered the phone.

The Jude County Hotbox had just rolled into town.

And then—he should have expected it—the door opened and from the passenger side jumped the man who'd been his squad leader. Now Jed Ransom wore the word *Foreman* on his shirt pocket.

"I told you we'd find him, guys." Jed approached Darek, hand out. "Dare, how you doing? Feeling like fighting some fire?"

CHAPTER 9

"WE HAD A FLYOVER SIGHTING on Sunday morning, around six."
Jed unrolled a map on a large conference table in an interior room
of the National Forest Service building. He always stood a foot
taller than other men Darek knew, not just in size but in stature.
Dark-haired and from Montana, with the slightest Western drawl,
Jed could read a fire like no one else. He'd started as a ground
pounder when he was eighteen, risen up the ranks, graduated from
Butte College with a degree in fire science, and now trained and
worked as the ramrod of one of the tightest crews in the West.

He was the man Darek had once hoped to be.

The Jude County Hotshots trained in Ember, Montana, but
deployed out of Boise, from the National Interagency Fire Center,
their type-one crew often called first when a fire started to blaze.

Especially one in the tinder-crisp forest of the Boundary Waters Canoe Area, where a blowdown ten years ago had left dead trees like matchsticks across a million acres of forest.

Darek could barely contain the adrenaline shooting through his veins as he heard the conversations of arriving hotshots, the buzz of radios in the NFS office. "Where did it start?"

"They think here, on the southeast corner of Swan Lake." Jed pointed to a place on the map twenty-three miles northwest of Deep Haven, thick in the BWCA. "Weather service pinpointed a thunderstorm there Friday night with somewhere in the neighborhood of a thousand lightning strikes. Could have been one or more, but no one noticed any activity until the morning."

Darek remembered the air that night—crisp, almost a sizzle to it.

That was the night he'd kissed Ivy.

"Right now, it's inaccessible by land; we'd have to paddle in. So far it looks to have incinerated over thirteen thousand acres of boreal forest."

All that black spruce, jack pine, balsam fir, and paper birch, gone. Darek could imagine the fire almost as if he were there— sweat pasting his yellow shirt to his back, Pulaskis swinging, dirt flying, chain saws roaring, the searing breath of the dragon on their backs. He could smell the acrid odor, feel the embers falling like snow, dusting his helmet. The furnace would dry his throat, make him tuck his handkerchief over his nose and keep digging right beside twenty other of his fellow ground pounders, battling together.

Yeah, he missed it.

"We estimate, with the debris left by the blowdown, that there might be fifty to a hundred tons of dry fuel per acre. The fire is jumping lakes by connecting with islands, and a flyover this morning estimated flame lengths up to a hundred feet."

Around them, Darek recognized a few of the hotshots who had filtered in—Graham, a seasoned Native American sawyer built like a fortress, and Pete Holt, former military who did a couple tours in Afghanistan and had a kid on the way right about the time Darek left. He looked like he might be a crew boss now for the way he was hollering at the youngsters, college kids looking to pay for their tuition.

One woman on the team, a blonde who wore her hair in a long braid down her back, immediately made friends with Tiger, who was admiring their Pulaskis, helmets, and gear. She offered Tiger her whistle and he blew on it while everyone laughed.

Tiger was having the time of his life.

So much like his father.

The NFS command center buzzed with activity, flyover reports from spotters coming in, the weather report rattling away on a nearby radio.

Jed alternated between listening to the weather and to an explanation of the terrain from a local NFS fire supervisor. "If we can contain the fire before it gets here, to Bower Trout Lake, then we won't have to evacuate. There're about seventy homes located on Trout."

"There haven't been any prescribed burns in this area—ever," Darek said, skimming his hand over the region between the fire zone and Trout, then farther to Two Island Lake. "We need to stop it before it gets to Two Island. South of Two Island, we start to encroach on residential areas. There's a group home here, the Garden . . ." He pointed to a large area just north of Evergreen Lake. "And then, of course, Evergreen has about 120 homes, not to mention our resort."

"From there it's a straight shot to Deep Haven," Graham said.

"We'll stop it long before it endangers Deep Haven," Jed said. "We've asked to deploy a Bombardier CL-215 tanker plane— should be here later today. We'll get that in there and see if we can make a dent in it."

Darek looked at the map, traced the fire road, then the portage line into Ball Club Lake. "You could start a prescribed burn on the north side of Ball Club, see if you can use up the fuel, shut it down."

Jed leaned over the map. "Good call. After the plane gets in, we'll assess whether we need to send in the crew." He turned to Darek. "By the way, it's great to see you. How've you been?"

"Good."

"We miss you on the team. No one can sing Johnny Cash like you and Jensen."

"I miss 'A Boy Named Sue'!" Pete Holt yelled.

Darek refused to let his smile dim. Maybe they didn't know, or remember, how everything between Jensen and him had gone south. Yet those had been good days.

The energy in the room, the way the men congregated around the fire stats, seemed contagious. They'd sent in a crew because of the last fire, years ago, near Sea Gull Lake that took out so many resorts and homes. Apparently the NFS wasn't taking any chances in this dry season.

Indeed, the entire county could go up in smoke if they didn't snuff out the fire, and soon.

Someone had put an orange Nomex helmet on Tiger, was letting him dig through a backpack of equipment. Darek had no doubt there might be a dream igniting inside his five-year-old.

A man came into the room carrying a large box. A little under six feet, he had dark-blond hair, a military build. He set the box on the floor, then came over to the table and opened a laptop. "I've already pulled up the map and plugged in the weather conditions, the fuel loads. That should tell us a little about how the fire will run." His screen came to life, the fire box surrounded in red, a map underlying the burning area.

"Dare, I'd like you to meet Conner Young. He hitched on board with us last year doing some advanced communications work. He developed a program to help us read and predict fire behavior."

"Hard to do that from twenty-plus miles away. Better to get close to it, see it, hear it." Still, the program might save precious time and resources if they could predict the run of the fire. "Does it work?"

"We're still testing it, but he's able to upload his data right to the handhelds." Jed pointed to the box. "Sort of like smartphones but with better service."

"Like the kind that can survive being dropped in the dirt, kicked, and burned?"

"Oh no. We leave that to the hotshots," Conner said, smiling.

Darek put him in his late thirties, maybe early forties, experience around his eyes. He liked him. "How often does the data refresh?"

"Right now, it's dependent on satellite—the same Doppler the weather service uses. But we can also receive data from airplanes, and in Montana, we are developing a remote video surveillance system that is affixed to the fire lookout towers." He glanced at Jed. "But we admit, there is no substitute for experience and hands-on surveillance."

Darek leaned in, got his bearings, then touched the screen. "If we had to, we could go in through here—" He traced his way up the portage route, moving his finger east, then south. "There's a large clearing along Forest Route 153. A great place to set up a fire camp."

Jed checked his route on the map. "Dare, I'd love for you to jump aboard and help me work the fire—even at the command center. If you want, you could hike in with us. You know this area, know how the fire might react with this fuel."

Yes. The word was nearly on his lips. Nearly . . . "I . . . I'd love to, but—" He glanced at Tiger. "I can't."

"You don't have anyone to watch him?"

"I don't know. Maybe." Surely his mother wouldn't mind. Or Nan. She'd jump at the opportunity to keep him. Even overnight.

Except wouldn't that give her perfect evidence for her belief that he didn't really want to be a father, that he would rather race out to fight fire than take care of his son?

"Daddy! I gotta go!" Tiger had run up to him and was holding himself, doing the potty dance.

Darek steered his son by the shoulder toward the bathroom. He could hear the guys laughing behind him. He stood in front of the door, his neck hot, while Tiger took care of his business.

"No problem, Dare. You have your hands full," Jed said. He gave him a kind, almost-pitying smile.

Or maybe Darek just imagined the pity.

He drew in a long breath. "Where are you guys staying?"

"Dunno. Know of any good places in town? Forest service is picking up the tab."

Darek smiled. There was more than one way to get in on the action. "As a matter of fact, I have just the place."

"Why on earth would you want to spend your lunch hour losing at checkers? I think this was a bad idea." Gibs jumped two of Jensen's red chips. "Crown me."

"You're better company than the seagulls," Jensen said, adding a black chip to Gibs's. "Besides, I've won a couple times."

The sun streamed in through the man's hospital window, across his bed to the red recliner, where Jensen sat opposite the bedside table. His half-eaten sub sandwich lay on the nightstand.

Actually, what he might call this, if anyone really put him on the rack, was cowardice. He hadn't known that Claire would be there when he arrived two days ago to build the ramp. Being around her made him lose his focus—if he didn't watch it, he'd slice off a finger or slam his thumb with a hammer.

Or say something stupid, like his comment about going to jail. After that, she'd looked at him just like he deserved.

That's why she stayed inside, never came out again. Why today he couldn't bear to head back up there until he knew she started her shift at two o'clock.

He could work late into the evening, no problem. He was good at working in the shadows.

"Jensen, pay attention. I just double-jumped you. If you're not going to play to win, then don't bother."

He glanced at Gibs, but the man wore a smile. "You want me to beat you, old man?"

"You can at least try."

Jensen moved his piece, waited for Gibs to move, then double-jumped him. "Crown me."

"That's more like it. You're playing like a whipped puppy. That's not the Jensen I used to know."

"The Jensen you used to know was reckless and dangerous and got everyone in trouble."

"No, the Jensen I used to know was a young whippersnapper who was just trying to get the girls to like him."

Jensen's mouth opened a bit.

"The first time I met you, you were doing a backflip off the dock. As I remember, it was May, the lake too cold to swim in, but you—and Darek—were showing off for the girls."

"I never—"

"Please." He moved his piece, blocking Jensen's next jump. "All you and Darek did all summer was flex and show off your tans to Claire and Felicity. Even when you weren't driving your father's speedboat around the lake, you seemed to be hanging around. But while Darek was always trying to find the next great adventure, you were the one who made sure the girls got home safely. You always had a smile for Nelda and me. And don't tell me you weren't the one who came over early and stacked my shipments of wood. I'm not stupid."

Jensen moved a piece across the board, affecting some semblance of strategy.

"It's nice to have you back, is all. I'm just wondering if my granddaughter has anything to do with that."

Jensen looked up, tried a smile. "Nah. You saw her last time I was here." He wasn't sure Claire had mentioned her household improvements to her grandfather. "Besides, I never left, Gibs."

Gibs moved his piece forward, a strategy that made no sense to Jensen. "Sure you did."

"I've been living in the same place, my father's house, for three years. You know that." He moved his piece closer, attacking.

"Just because you've been living there doesn't mean you didn't disappear." Gibs moved his piece back, away from Jensen's. "The day you walked out of that courthouse, bound to Deep Haven, you vanished. The Jensen I knew simply died. And this strange boy who walked with his face to the ground took his place."

Jensen studied the board. "What was I supposed to do? I had to live here. But I didn't have to like it. You can't imagine how terrible it is to walk around with a target on your back, people talking about you, accusing you of something you didn't do." He moved his piece.

Gibs moved his king across the board, flanking Jensen's position, should he jump Gibs's piece. "I know exactly how you felt, son. I'm a Vietnam vet. I came home to a country that hated me, accused me of killing children, of burning villages. They threw blood and paint on me, and they refused to serve me at the VFW. I was a pariah in this country, even this town. I knew I hadn't done what they accused me of, but it didn't matter. They believed what they wanted. Your move."

But Jensen couldn't move. He stared at Gibs. "I'm sorry."

"Once people form an opinion, it's very hard to change it, and the frustration of that went inside, became a battle I faced every day. For a while there, I let it eat at me. I turned to drink, made a nuisance out of myself. I still can't believe Nelda hung on to me. Booted me out of her bed but not the house. I thank God for that. And then one night, I came home, buttered. Took a smoke on the sofa and fell asleep. My son, Ricky, woke me up, yelling—he was about eight at the time. Scared the tar out of me, but the rug was on fire. Nelda and I carried it outside, beat out the flames on the sofa, and then she lit into me."

He met Jensen's eyes. "I nearly lost them both that night because I was angry at how I was treated. My Nelda cleared through the fog in my head when she told me that I might not have killed any babies in Vietnam, but I was still a sinner back here in Deep Haven."

Jensen frowned.

"She pulled her Bible off the shelf and shoved it at me. I'll never forget her words. 'No one is righteous, not even one. So stop acting all wounded and realize that you're a mess, Jack Marshall Gibson'—scared me half to death when she used my full name. 'The good news is that God still loves you. And so do I.'"

He made a face. "That's when she finally threw me out of the house and barred the door."

"Ouch."

"I went straight to my little church there on Third and Third, got down at the altar, and wept. See, she was right. I was angry at how I'd been treated, calling it unjust. But it didn't matter what they accused me of; I was still a sinner. I wasn't guilty of war crimes, but I'd done plenty to be ashamed of. The truth is, if we had to walk around with our sins taped to our backs . . . well, we'd all be finding ways to hide in the woods, huh, Jensen?"

Jensen stared at him, not sure who he might be talking about. Just once he'd like the town of Deep Haven to take a good look at *Darek* and *his* part in the nightmare that destroyed so many lives.

But they'd never looked hard at the golden boy to see the truth. Just found it easier to point to the rich kid.

Gibs's face softened. "As unjust as their accusations were, God used them to remind me that Nelda was right—no man is right before Him. I'm not saying that I—or you—didn't get a bum rap. But the Bible says that if we claim we have no sin, we are only fooling ourselves and not living in the truth. God sees your heart, Jensen, and He knows the truth. And yes, that thought should cripple you. I know it did me."

Jensen glanced at his unfinished sandwich, then at the time. Tried not to think of how many nights he woke, shaking, sweating, a scream on his lips. How he sat on the deck, waiting for the sunrise.

"Now, some people get angry that they even need to ask for forgiveness. Especially for being human, for making mistakes. They go around doing community service, trying to make it right."

"I was *sentenced* to community service," Jensen said, but Gibs rolled over him.

"But here's an even better truth: God knows you can't make it right. None of it. But He can. The day I took a good look at my sins—my real sins—was the day I discovered 1 John 1:9. 'But if we confess our sins to him, he is faithful and just to forgive us our sins and to cleanse us from all wickedness.'"

"I'm not wicked."

"Jensen, you've spent three years lying low, trying to make everything right. But you can't redeem yourself. You can't make yourself and your life whole again. God can."

Maybe the old man was right—it was a bad idea to get beat at checkers over lunch. Better to face Claire. At least she didn't make him want to hit something, hard.

No, wait . . . yes, she did.

Jensen looked away.

"Has it occurred to you that God might be trying to get your attention? He longs for your heart more than your good acts."

"He can't have my heart. Not after what He did to my life."

"It seems to me that you are doing to God exactly what the town is doing to you. Unfair blaming."

Jensen picked up his sandwich, considered it, then wrapped it up in the paper.

"The longer you keep walking in anger toward God and your lot in life, the longer you will stay broken."

"I'm not broken, old man. It's just that . . . I'm tired of feeling like I'll never escape that one mistake."

Gibson leaned back against his pillows. Met Jensen's eyes.

"Okay, fine. I know I'm not perfect either. But I'm trying—"

"No one is doubting that."

"Then why the sermon?"

"Why the checkers?" Gibs said softly.

"I don't know. Maybe because I want . . ." Oh, none of it made sense. "Forget it."

"For a guy who doesn't think he needs forgiveness, you're certainly trying hard to earn it. Maybe you start with an apology."

Jensen got up. Grabbed his sandwich. Ground his jaw so tight he thought his molars might dissolve.

"You can't walk around with a smile plastered on your face when there's so much debris inside. It's going to come out, and someone is going to get hurt." Gibs's eyes darkened, something of the old Marine in them. "Someone like my granddaughter."

The threat felt like a punch to the throat, quick and sharp. "I would never hurt Claire. You don't know anything, old man."

Jensen turned, about to stalk out, but stopped and rounded on Gibs. "The minute Felicity died in my arms, her blood on my hands—the minute this town stopped listening and started pointing fingers—they silenced any apology they might get. Of course

I was sorry! In so many ways, you can't begin to count. But when they blamed me, I had to start defending myself. I couldn't turn around and be sorry or they would have crucified me." His voice trembled, but he didn't care. Nor did he care that his entire body felt like he might indeed crumble, his eyes burning with what felt disgustingly like tears. "This town stole my right to grieve."

He swallowed. Drew in a long breath. "You try killing the woman you loved and see how you sleep at night. See how you look at yourself in the mirror. All you want to do is run, pretend you aren't the person you see. But I can't, can I? Trust me, it's much easier to be angry." Jensen stormed from the room, down the hall, and into his truck.

Sat there in the heat of the day, sweat rolling down his back.

If they wanted to blame him for a crime, wanted a reason to put him in jail, maybe he'd give them one.

CHAPTER 10

IF JENSEN DIDN'T WANT HER to eavesdrop, then he should stop visiting her grandfather. Or shouting. Claire could have heard him in the next county, maybe even in Wisconsin.

You try killing the woman you loved and see how you sleep at night.

Jensen's words had riveted her to a spot in the hallway by the nurses' desk, where she'd been trying to nail down a conversation with her grandfather's doctor.

Loved. Of course he'd loved Felicity. She knew that. But to hear him admit it . . .

Hours later, Claire still couldn't shake away the anger clawing at her—mostly at herself for doubting Felicity. No, her friend hadn't actually said the words, but she knew the truth in the way Felicity suggested it—she and Jensen had an affair. He'd loved her.

Loved.

When she nearly sliced off a finger, she set the knife down on the cutting board, shaking.

Next to her, Grace stretched out crust, a ticket lined up in front of her. She glanced at Claire. "I'd offer to trade places with you, but this order calls for a thick crust, not something beaten to a pulp."

Claire managed a smile. "Sorry."

Tucker ran the register out front, although at the moment, he was cleaning the microwave. The dining area was empty, their lone order a takeout.

Claire probably didn't need to be chopping onions, but she'd store them for tomorrow. Besides, it gave her someplace to put the ache.

What a fool she'd been letting Jensen back into her life to roam around and kick more holes in her heart.

Maybe she should leave town. When her parents arrived and sold her grandfather's home out from under her, she'd have nowhere to belong anyway.

She blinked back the burn in her eyes.

"What's eating you?" Grace ladled out white sauce, running it around the dough. She must be making one of her signature spinach pizzas.

"It's nothing."

Really. Because how could Claire admit to anyone how betrayed she felt? How in her head over the past few days Jensen had . . . well, maybe simply become less of a villain, more of the friend she remembered.

And then, with one sentence, he'd reminded her exactly why she hadn't talked to him for three years.

"You nearly added a finger to the toppings." Grace glanced over as Claire clasped her fist tight. "Yes, I saw that." She dusted the top of the pizza with shredded provolone. "We missed you in Bible study last night."

"I was with my grandfather."

"We prayed for him. How's he doing?"

"I don't understand. He's bedridden, in pain, and he's acting like he's having the time of his life."

"Your grandfather always made me smile. Always had a kind word for me at church. But you missed a great study. It was on Psalm 145, verses 17 through 19. 'The Lord is righteous in every-thing he does; he is filled with kindness. The Lord is close to all who call on him, yes, to all who call on him in truth. He grants the desires of those who fear him; he hears their cries for help and rescues them.'"

Trust Grace to have memorized it.

She dotted spinach on the pizza. "We talked about what it means for God to be righteous in everything He does and to be filled with kindness."

Right. Kindness. Claire didn't want to argue, but frankly, God felt anything but kind these days.

She scooped the onions into a stainless steel container, wrapped it with plastic, and put it in the oversize fridge. Stood there, the cool air washing over her.

She hated how the rest of Jensen's words sat in her head, threat-ening to dissolve her anger.

See how you look at yourself in the mirror. All you want to do is run, pretend you aren't the person you see.

Claire understood not wanting to be the person she saw. Looking in the mirror every day, wearing that stupid black visor, the black polyester shirt emblazoned with *Pierre's Pizza*. Yes, she knew what it felt like to go to bed with disappointment weighting down your chest. She even understood the desire to run.

But she'd done the opposite. Stayed in Deep Haven, paralyzed. Always paralyzed.

Still, how did a person forgive himself for destroying so many lives? Even if it had been an accident? She'd watched him stalk out to the parking lot, sit in his truck, and for a moment . . .

Yes, for a long moment, she wanted to forgive him. And that, perhaps, made her most angry. Jensen didn't deserve it. Hadn't even asked for it.

She needed to remember that while he might not have been guilty of reckless driving, he'd broken up Felicity's marriage, driven her out of her home that dark night.

Jensen was right. It was much, much easier to be angry. Especially at herself for nearly falling for that signature Jensen charm.

Grace put the finished pizza in the oven, the rollers sending it through the heat. "No more orders?" she asked Tucker.

He shook his head. "The place is dead."

Claire sprayed her stainless steel workstation with cleanser, ran a cloth over it. "Grace, do you want to go home?"

Silence.

Grace was giving her a long, strange look. "I, uh . . . Stuart promoted me to summer manager. I need to stay until close. But you can leave if you want."

Claire opened her mouth, the words absent. Oh. Silly tears edged her eyes. "Right. Congratulations." She hadn't exactly gotten back to Stuart—apparently he tired of waiting for her answer. She should have told him, but the fact that he filled the position without hearing from her . . . "Okay then." She unknotted her apron. "Sure. I have things to do."

Things. Like . . . ? She hung up the apron, punched out, and headed out the back door into the night. Her bicycle was propped against the side of the building.

She stood there in the dirt beside her bike, blinking back more tears. It wasn't like this job meant anything.

Claire pedaled off toward her apartment, but the windows looked dark, forlorn, no lights even from Ivy's place in back.

The night arched above her, a few clouds blotting out the moon. She could smell the tinge of campfire in the air, hear the complaining of seagulls.

She turned and began to pedal toward the cemetery.

Claire parked her bike at the entrance by the wrought-iron gate. Moonlight dappled the Deep Haven cemetery in variegated shadow, but she knew the route by heart—four rows up the path, cut to the right, seventeen spaces over.

Felicity rested near a towering tree of heaven, the yellow blossoms dropping like tears on the pathway. The summer after Felicity's death, Claire had planted a garden. It seemed such a small gesture, but it kept Felicity alive somehow, especially after Mrs. Holloway thanked her.

She'd started with hostas around the base of the simple marble stone, then dug out around it and every Memorial Day added annuals—blue ageratum and white sweet alyssum, purple lobelia and hardy pink geraniums. This year, she'd added red salvia around the edges.

Next year, she'd plant a rose of Sharon. She'd taken a clipping from the garden in town and had it rooting in a container at home.

Claire stopped in front of the grave to wipe grime from the

stone. Maybe she shouldn't have come out here at night—she could hardly tell the weeds from the flowers—but the wind reaped the fragrances, and just sitting here, working the soil by the feel of her hands, seemed to untangle her anger and let her experience her grief.

She felt around the soil, found a thistle, worked her fingers to the roots.

You try killing the woman you loved and see how you sleep at night.

She heard Jensen's words again, this time with pain at the edges.

No. Jensen didn't belong here, at the foot of Felicity's grave, and Claire refused to feel sorry for him. He'd known that Felicity was married, known exactly what he was doing.

And Claire had watched it happen, right there at Pierre's Pizza.

Felicity hitching Tiger to her other hip, then offering Jensen a one-armed hug, her eyes in his when she let go. She'd given him that cheerleader smile. "I didn't know you were back, Jens."

Claire wasn't sure how Felicity did it. She possessed a sort of bewitching power over men, but Jensen, who knew better, walked right into it. Tall and tanned, his blond hair cut short, fresh out of his second year of law school . . . the sight of him in the Pierre's lobby had turned Claire dumb. She longed to hide, mortified when he turned to her and spied her wearing her uniform.

Yeah, she was still here. Still hawking pizzas. Still wearing the silly visor, still—

"Sure, I'll help you," he'd said to Felicity. He'd tickled Tiger in the stomach then, the two-year-old dissolving in laughter.

Claire hadn't wanted to know what happened after that.

You are so selfish!

She remembered that thought curling inside her as she watched Jensen help Felicity tuck Tiger into his car seat, watched her throw her arms around Jensen's neck, press her body to his. Hating her best friend for—

No. *No.* It wasn't Felicity's fault. She'd been lonely, and who could blame her, with Darek off for weeks at a time—the entire summer, really—fighting fires?

When Felicity explained it, it made perfect sense.

"He's been helping me with a few things. And, well, Jensen just knows me. Understands. He's always been that way, hasn't he?" She'd dipped her feet into the cool, sun-tipped lake, Tiger asleep in the portable crib under the shadow of a trio of paper birches in her yard. "He's always been so . . ."

"Nice?" Claire had filled in the word, searching for innocence.

"Charming." Felicity winked. "And handsome. Don't you think?" She made that humming sound, the one she used to make when she talked about Darek.

And that's when Claire knew.

Claire yanked a thistle from the graveyard garden, threw it. "Yeah, handsome," she said into the night. Too handsome. Just as handsome as Darek, only different. More refined. Less hard-edged and dangerous.

Sweeter.

Charming. Another word, probably, for *slick.* Or *slimy.*

Playboy. Yes, that was the word.

She felt along the soil, rooting for another thistle. No wonder Felicity had fallen for him, cheated on Darek. Jensen had always wanted her and finally grabbed his chance.

A thistle pricked her fingers, and Claire jerked her hand back. Brought it to her mouth, tasting blood.

She should come back with gloves. But the weed would only weave its roots around her bedding plants and choke them out.

So she went after the thistle again. Finding it, she dug in, ignoring the pain.

It just wasn't fair.

"I don't get it, Felicity. Why? You had everything. Everyone loved you and yet you just had to have Jensen, too, didn't you?" Claire tried to work out the weed, but it snapped in her hand, leaving the root embedded.

Perfect.

Stupid town. Stupid garden. Claire felt around, grabbed the stalk.

Came up gripping a lobelia. She threw it away, angry, and reached in again. "You couldn't just admit that you'd made a mistake marrying Darek."

She pulled out another stalk, found an ageratum flower in her fist.

Fine. Claire got up on her knees, leaning in with both hands. That thistle was still there; she just had to find—

A bunch of alyssum came out in her grip. She sat back, looked at it, and heat rose up inside her. Feeling wetness trickle off her nose, her chin, she dumped the flowers and leaned in again, rooting for the thistle. "I hate you for leaving me here." She grabbed more of the flowers, not caring, yanking hard, tossing them aside. "For taking so many lives with you." She pricked her finger again, and the pain sent her into a frenzy. "I hate you!" More flowers, her hands filthy with dirt. "I hate you!"

"Claire, stop!"

Arms went around her, grasped her wrists, held them tight. "Stop!" Jensen said into her ear. Soft and strong and smooth and—

"Don't touch me!" She twisted to push against his chest. "Stay away!"

Jensen held up his hands. "I'm not going to hurt you."

That shook her. Brought her back to herself.

He was on his knees, worry in his eyes. He'd showered or something since she saw him last, his hair tousled and clean, the smell of soap and cologne radiating off him. For a second, she just wanted to sink into him.

But she backed away. Tried to slow her breathing.

"Why are you destroying Felicity's garden?" He reached down and eased her fists open. She made out two handfuls of alyssum.

"Oh." Claire sat back, letting the flowers fall. "I don't know. I . . ." Her voice trembled then, and a whimper escaped. She was so pitiful, it only made it worse. "Go away, Jensen. Please—just leave me."

"No," he said softly. "No." Then he put his arms around her, pulling her into his embrace. She didn't have the ability—or perhaps the desire—to resist.

He put his chin on her head, tucked her in close. "Shh."

Jensen. She closed her eyes and breathed in the strength, the essence of him. He might not have Darek's rugged appeal, but Jensen always possessed a gentleness, a way of listening—

Claire pressed her hand to her mouth. She should lean away before she lost herself completely.

"You don't hate Felicity," he said softly, his heart hammering under her ear. "If you should hate anyone, it's me."

Well, that was true. But she didn't feel it. Not anymore. "I don't hate you, Jensen." She took a long breath, listened to it shudder out. "And you're right. I don't hate Felicity either. It's just . . . nothing feels right since she died."

She pushed away from him. His gaze held her, his lips tight.

"I can't seem to . . . I can't seem to forgive."

He nodded.

"No, you don't understand. It's not Felicity I can't forgive. Or even . . . even you."

He swallowed at that, something desperate in his face. But it seemed she couldn't stop herself. That right now, with the flowers she'd planted lying in ruin around her, she couldn't keep it in.

"I can't forgive God, Jens. I don't trust Him anymore. I . . . keep blaming the fact that I'm stuck in Deep Haven on Felicity or my grandfather. But the truth is, it just . . . it just confirms that I was right."

He frowned.

"God isn't kind." She clamped her hand over her mouth, horrified at her own words. But she kept going, speaking through her hand. "He's not kind. He took away Felicity—"

"*I* took away Felicity."

"No. God could have protected her on that road. He could have . . . Why didn't He protect her? Why didn't He stop—?" Her voice grew soft. "She. Was. So scared."

Jensen licked his lips, swallowed. "She never woke up, Claire. She died almost instantly."

She closed her eyes. "I know."

His touch on her cheek startled her. She opened her eyes and he cupped her face. "We're not talking about Felicity, are we?"

She stared at him, began to tremble. "No."

"We're talking about you, in Bosnia. About the men who attacked you, beat you, scared you. Nearly killed you."

She drew in a shaky breath.

"We're talking about the fact that a terrible thing happened and you haven't felt safe since. Even here in Deep Haven."

He knew her that well? She swallowed, nodding.

"Because . . . it's not about Deep Haven," he said softly. "It's about God. How can you trust Him, put your future in His hands, when He lets bad things happen to . . . people like you?"

She clenched her teeth together, but a moan emerged and her control broke. "Yeah. Me." She gulped a deep breath. "It shouldn't have happened to me."

Jensen touched her forehead with his, his arms still around her. "You're safe here, Claire. I won't let anything happen to you. I promise. I'll figure out a way for you to stay. You don't have to leave Deep Haven."

Oh, she wanted to believe him. Especially when he pulled her to himself. They sat there in the pocket of the night as she listened to his heartbeat, strong against her ear.

It wasn't until she finally looked into his eyes, ever so briefly, that she realized the truth.

She was jealous. All these years, despite her best efforts, she had hated Felicity, at least a little. Because Felicity had what Claire had always wanted.

The heart of Jensen Atwood.

Claire had turned Felicity's gravesite into a debris field. Flowers littered the lawn, and tomorrow, the cemetery gardener would think wild dogs had trampled on Felicity Christiansen's grave.

Unless—worse—someone had seen his Mustang parked outside the entrance, done the math, and again assigned blame.

Jensen had no doubt that there might be formal charges, at the very least some sort of probation violation cooked up.

See, he didn't have to leave town to find trouble. But he didn't care. Not really. Not with Claire in his arms.

Not that it didn't seem a little awkward, sitting here at Felicity's grave. He couldn't escape the irony. Felicity, between them again.

He probably should have kept driving tonight. Should have put the past behind him, at least until the authorities caught him. But he'd seen Claire's shiny red bike leaning against the entrance, and . . . well, he worried.

He always worried, just a little. Ever since her story, so many years ago. It kept him up at nights sometimes, how close she'd come to being killed.

Of course she felt betrayed by God. He did too, although he knew better. The only person who'd let him down was himself.

"I never asked . . . what are you doing here?" Claire said.

"Uh . . ."

He didn't want to let her go. But she pushed away from him. "Jensen? Why are you here?"

He leaned forward, began gathering the flowers. "Can these be replanted?"

"No," she said. "I'll have to buy more."

He scraped them all into a pile.

"Were you following me?"

"Nope." He pricked his hand on a couple thistles at the bottom of the pile.

"Jens!"

"Okay, fine." He got up, holding out his hand, the other still gripping the flowers. "I . . . I was out for a drive."

She took his hand, let him pull her to her feet. "A drive." Her gaze went past him, to the entrance. "Is that your Mustang out there?"

His attempt at a smile fell flat, so he walked toward a receptacle and dropped in the mutilated flowers.

She followed him. Then, quietly, to his back, said, "You were leaving, weren't you?"

He closed one eye, a half wince. "No," he lied.

"Please. Seriously? I know you, Jensen. You haven't driven that car for three years."

And how could he? First, the police had impounded it, and then he didn't want to see it, even once his father had it repaired. It sat in the garage until today, when Gibs turned on him.

Jensen had driven home, changed out of his work clothes, packed a bag, and bidden this town good-bye. He'd had plans to at least get to Duluth. Maybe hop an airplane.

Try to live with himself in Jamaica. Or the Bahamas. Or . . .

"Where were you going?"

He sighed and told the truth. "I don't know. I just . . ."

"You just decided after all this time, with only a couple weeks left on your probation, to ditch town? To throw your future away? To give up and finally land in jail?"

"I don't want to go to jail, Claire!" He took a breath, hitched his tone lower. "I want this to be over. I'm tired of being a disappointment. Of walking around like I've got a wanted poster hanging from my neck. I'm never going to redeem myself, as your grandfather so nicely pointed out."

"What?"

"He reminded me that no matter what I do, I'm a mess—"

"My grandfather loves you. He's probably the only one in this town who fought for you." She made a face when she said it. "Sorry. But we had a huge fight over the editorial letter he sent in to the *Deep Haven Herald*."

"What letter?"

"You never read it? It took up nearly an entire page. He talked about the boy you'd been, the man you'd become, reminded people that they couldn't convict on circumstantial evidence—"

"It's true!"

"Yeah, well, he got two death threats, and someone dragged one of our canoes out in the middle of the lake and shot it full of holes."

He sobered. "I didn't know that."

"Maybe you also didn't know that he went to your initial arraignment. And that he spoke to the county attorney on your behalf."

Now he felt a little ill, his conversation with Gibs replaying in his head. "No, I didn't."

"He missed you, you know." She swallowed and bit her lip as if trying not to say something more.

"It doesn't matter. I don't know why I keep trying. This town will never forgive me."

"For pete's sake, Jensen, you never asked!"

He stared at her, his mouth open. "I couldn't—I . . . Listen, the second I stood up there and asked forgiveness, it would have been over for me. I . . . I wanted to," he said softly. More than anyone could know.

Her eyes were shiny. "Don't quit, Jensen."

"I'm not quitting, okay? I'm staying. But it doesn't matter, Claire, because the truth is, I'm going to jail anyway." He held out his hands as if in surrender. "So whether I violate my probation by going on the lam or simply wait out the inevitable, it's happening."

She was staring at him now, her eyes bright, her face still a little soggy. "No. You're not."

"Claire, unless you have some sort of secret pull with the court system, yes, in fact, I am."

"My neighbor is the new assistant county attorney. We'll just talk to her. She's really nice. You'd like her."

"In case you've forgotten, my *father* is an attorney. Believe me, if he wanted me off, he'd get me off."

Who knew but his father had orchestrated the entire community service bondage. Jensen couldn't prove it—not with another firm handling his case—but he believed his father had somehow come up with the plan to indenture him to Deep Haven.

Maybe he'd been trying to help. At the very least, avoid the embarrassment of having a son in prison.

And although Jensen had been ready to defend himself, when his lawyer blindsided him with the plea agreement, his father pulled his financial support. Right then, Jensen had looked at his future, and what choice did he have?

"I don't think your neighbor can help me."

"Maybe you could let her try?"

Oh, he wanted to believe the hope in Claire's eyes. The way she looked at him as if she saw something more than the man he was.

"I'm sorry I let you down," he said softly, not sure where that came from.

"You didn't . . . I mean . . ." She shook her head. "Listen, the past is the past; let's try to move on."

It cost her something to say that—he saw it on her face. "How?"

But she stepped up to him, pressed her hand to his mouth. Smiled, something honest and without judgment.

The sense of it swelled inside him, washing over the wishes and the regrets.

He smiled back. "Okay. Yes."

"Yes?"

"Let's go talk to the assistant county attorney. What's her name?"

"Ivy. Ivy Madison."

Ivy sat in her yoga pants, eating a bowl of ice cream, staring at her cell phone. The night pressed against her windows, only her overhead fixture splashing light onto the table. Dishes were piled in the sink, and in the next room, a bath filled.

Maybe Darek would never call. After all, after four days . . .

Could she live with that? Only one date, no explanation, even after he'd kissed her so sweetly?

Yes. Maybe.

Or not.

Especially when she thought of Tiger, the way he nestled into her lap, throwing rocks, then playing with the glow stick she'd purchased for him.

He had a sweetness about him, a little-boy charm that he must have inherited, at least in part, from Felicity.

Felicity Holloway Christiansen.

Her file lay on the round pine table. Ivy had pulled it after lunch today, in between writing up complaints, summonses, and evidentiary briefs, not to mention following up on cases and answering about a hundred e-mails. Her brain had turned to mush, and the accident report and evidentiary briefs and memorandums in Felicity's case couldn't be considered light reading.

But she had to know.

So she'd read every detail, remembering it from when she'd read it the first time. Although, instead of Felicity being labeled as "the victim," as Thornton Atwood had done in the file she'd been given, and Jensen as "the accused," in this file, she'd discovered names. And witnesses. Including Darek.

If she'd been less eager three years ago, she might have dug around a little, instead of wanting so much to please her boss, to impress him. Though she hadn't known the accused was his son until after she handed in her recommendation—Thornton had masked the entire file and made her believe it was just a teaching exercise.

She easily pieced the scene together—a fight with Darek put Felicity in a running mood, and she'd ventured out, probably still angry, just after 9 p.m., in her Jeep, parking at the Cutaway Creek overlook. Maybe to just sit and think. They'd discovered her Jeep there, later that night.

Sometime after 9:35, she took off running, downhill, toward town. With traffic.

Jensen, on his way into town for pizza, came around the curve and an oncoming car's headlights hit him in the eyes. He'd blinked and taken the curve too tight.

That's when he felt the car hit Felicity. Investigation indicated that he hadn't run into the ditch—on the contrary, they supposed she might have been crossing the road and hadn't seen his lights.

She died almost immediately, her skull shattering.

Ivy had read the obit, too, and every single article she could dig up on the court case. Jensen had been accused of texting, a thin case built around negligent driving, and Ivy used that to tear holes in the prosecution in her memorandum. Still, with his cell phone open, a text recently sent . . .

She could still remember turning in her memo on the community service option to her junior associate, the pride she'd felt as she handed it to him. Then she'd marched into Daniel's adjunct professor office at the University of Minnesota and shown it to him.

He was impressed, especially when the plea made the evening news.

She took another bite of ice cream, and it shivered through her. Yes, maybe it would be best if Darek never called again.

Ivy put the bowl down, her appetite souring. Oh, why did the world have to be so terribly small?

She'd always known that fate—or God—was against her. And this was just more proof. No matter what she did to reach for her dreams, something always destroyed it.

I've made it this far on my own. I guess I'll keep it that way.

You're never on your own, Ivy. Claire's words, in her head.

Yes, she was. Because God certainly wasn't on her side, and with Daniel gone . . . No, she had no one.

She got up to stop the bathwater.

"Ivy?" A knock came at her door. "It's me, Claire."

Claire? Ivy went to the door, flicking on the outside light. "Hey—"

Her gaze stopped on the man standing behind Claire. Jensen, offering her a sheepish smile. Shoot. How she hoped her face didn't fall, that he didn't see the minute hiccup of breath. "Hello."

"Hello," he said, reaching past Claire to shake her hand. "I'm Jensen Atwood. I'm sorry to bother you—"

"We need some help," Claire said. "Can we talk to you?"

The moths bounced around the light, a big one dive-bombing the open door. "Come in," Ivy said, shooing it away.

Except now Jensen Atwood stood in her tiny kitchen. With his sun-bleached and tousled hair, she saw the arrogant playboy the media had portrayed him as three years ago. No wonder Deep Haven wanted to crucify him.

Claire looked at him and smiled. So maybe not *everyone* in Deep Haven.

"How can I help you?"

"I was wondering if we could ask for some legal advice."

Advice? Oh, please let it be about a traffic ticket. Or a recovered wallet. Or maybe they'd saved someone's life, needed to know about Good Samaritan laws.

Ivy had a sick feeling here.

"It's late, Claire. We shouldn't bother her," Jensen said. He put his hand on her shoulder.

If there is anyone you should stay away from in this town, it's Jensen Atwood. Ivy couldn't tear her gaze from that hand on Claire's shoulder.

Wow, how quickly small-town prejudices tangled her thoughts, her opinions. She stepped back. "No, that's okay. How can I help?"

"It'll only take a minute," Claire said. "I know it's late, but . . . well, us being neighbors, I figured it was okay."

Huh. "Sit down."

Ivy turned toward the table and froze. The file on Felicity Christiansen. She rushed over, closed it. Dumped it all onto a chair. "How about on the sofa?"

She'd inherited the sofa from the previous tenant, something green and a bit smelly, but she was rarely here . . . Still, she cringed when Jensen and Claire sat down, their faces so expectant. As if somehow she might save the day. As if she hadn't had a conversation with Jensen's probation officer about the very real threat of his probation violation.

And then there was the little matter that she'd set up his probation in the first place. At least that he'd be behind bars if it weren't for her.

Which, if she stood in Darek's shoes, might be a good thing.

But she wasn't dating Darek, and right now, Claire had a clear grip on Jensen's hand.

This town had suddenly become microscopic.

Ivy tried not to look at the file, some of the papers scattered on the floor like grenades.

Brilliant, Ivy.

"What's going on?" She crossed her leg, her foot tapping. Forced a casual, neighborly, how-can-I-help? smile.

"Well, Jensen is on probation."

"Mmm-hmm."

"And he has a bunch of community service he has to fulfill."

"Hmm."

"The problem is, he doesn't have time to complete it, so we were wondering if there is any way to get more time."

"Mmm."

Claire smiled at Ivy.

Oh, her turn. "Jensen . . . uh, do you have a defense attorney? He could file a motion on your behalf to extend your probation."

"I'm self-represented, ma'am."

Oh, boy.

"Okay. Have you talked to your probation officer?" She hated this part.

"I have. He . . . Well, see . . ."

"The thing is, Jensen was unfairly charged. He—he didn't do what they accused him of," Claire said, a little too brightly.

Ivy swallowed. "Hmm."

"Vehicular homicide," Claire said.

Jensen cringed, looked away.

"But he was innocent—it was an accident."

Ivy nodded.

"No, really!" Claire said.

Jensen had his eyes closed now.

And that's when Ivy's heart went out to him. Wasn't that why she came to Deep Haven? To help people? And frankly, when he met her eyes and offered a sad smile, she wanted to like him. Once upon a time, she'd read his statements as a mere clerk, unbiased, and in her dark cubicle, she'd believed in his innocence so much, despite the circumstantial evidence, that she'd spent hours and hours finding him a way out.

Maybe she was naive, but back then she'd believed in second chances, in the law helping people change their lives, and most of all, in doing her very best to see that justice won, even in no-win situations.

Which was why the words came to her. "You could try for clemency. It's rarely given, but sometimes—"

"Clemency!" Claire sat up. "Yes!"

"But I can't file that because I'm a *prosecutor*. I'd be the one filing the complaint *against* him." She spoke her words slowly, clearly.

But she did want to help. She just didn't want anyone to know.

Like Darek. Although he hadn't exactly chased her down, wooed her heart from her, had he?

Maybe him not calling was all for the best, before she got too entangled in a conflict of interest.

"Listen. Go online. There's a form and instructions. If you follow that, you can submit a motion for clemency. I can't make any guarantees, but . . ."

"Thank you, Ivy. You're the best!" Claire jumped up from the sofa and wrapped her arms around Ivy.

Jensen held out his hand. "Thank you, Ivy. I have to admit, I wasn't expecting any help."

Of course not. "Glad to meet you, Jensen."

She turned off the floodlight after they let themselves out.

Watched as Jensen walked over to a shiny black Mustang and Claire gave him an awkward wave as she wheeled her bike away.

Hmm.

Okay, so living in a small town might be a smidgen more complicated than Ivy had thought, but she handled that without any land mines, right? She'd simply offered them advice. Hadn't gotten her hands dirty, hadn't run into any quagmires of ethical violations.

Just doing her job, one life at a time. Staying impartial.

She heard water running as she shut the door.

No! Ivy ran into the bathroom, nearly went down on the slick tile. The water ran over the top, had already flooded the room, and was now cascading into the hall.

"No, no, no!" She waded in, reached over, and shut off the faucet. Plunged her hand into the depths and pulled the plug.

The water began to gurgle out.

Grabbing clean towels, she threw them on the floor to mop up the water.

From the kitchen table, her cell phone rang.

She ran toward it, nearly slipped again, stepped on one of the papers, and with it stuck to her foot, picked up the phone to look at the caller ID.

Darek.

It rang again and she stood there, her thumb hovering over the button to answer.

So much for staying impartial.

CHAPTER 11

Ivy DESERVED BETTER and Darek knew it. He forced a smile as she stopped by an artist's booth displaying suncatchers and other jewels on a fishing line.

Ivy caught one in her hand. "Pretty." She held it up to capture the rose gold of the setting sun.

Darek tried to act interested in a piece of jewelry but mostly just intercepted Tiger's grab at the pieces. "Hands off, pal."

Tiger made a face. "I'm hungry."

"I know, bud. We're going to get some supper in a bit here."

"I want ice cream!"

"Not before dinner. You'll ruin your appetite."

Ivy let go of the suncatcher. Glanced at the vendor with a smile and then turned away. "We can get it now, if you want."

"No. We can finish walking through this row of merchants. This is fun."

She raised an eyebrow but moved on to the next booth. At least this artist he knew and could make some small talk. Liza Beaumont, the potter, wore her black hair up in a ponytail, a long wrinkled skirt, a tank top that revealed her strong arms.

"Hello there, Darek." She leaned down. "Tiger."

"Hello, Miz B."

Liza met Darek's eye as she straightened. "Tiger's preschool class came to my studio last year and they all made bowls."

"I painted it too!"

Ivy was holding a bowl, looking at the bottom. "I have a few of these in my apartment."

"Let me know if you need any replacements." She winked. "So, Tiger, they are painting rocks down at the beach. You and your daddy should head down to the booth."

Just what Tiger needed. Paint. Rocks. A lethal combination. But Darek managed a smile.

"Don't look so ill, Darek. It's just watercolors," Liza said. "Maybe you should paint something. Could be good for you. Loosen you up."

"I don't—"

"C'mon, it'll be fun," Ivy said as if she'd been waiting all her life to paint rocks. Or maybe she was simply as miserable as he was.

Maybe she, too, longed to be somewhere else.

Ivy took Tiger's hand. "C'mon, let's go show your daddy the amazing artists we are."

The sight of Tiger looking up at her, adoration in his eyes—yes, that could pull Darek out of his self-pity and into a happier place.

And he could admit to losing himself in a happy place for a

long moment tonight as Ivy met him outside her apartment, wearing a pretty orange sundress with a pair of flip-flops.

She'd smiled at him, her green eyes in his, as if searching for something. If he didn't know better, he might have called her expression fear or even sadness. As if he'd nearly blown it by not calling her for four days and now stood at the precipice of losing this chance completely.

But then Tiger asked her if she wanted a cookie, she laughed, and the fist in his chest eased.

Especially when Ivy accepted his outstretched hand.

Her soft grip in his should have been enough to distract him from the orange haze along the far horizon, the scent of smoke in the air. From the knowledge that Jed and the rest of the Jude County Hotshots were holed up at the forest service office reading maps and weather reports, constructing fire behavior scenarios and a plan of attack.

But the last day had sucked him right back to the past. It felt somehow like he hadn't lost a day of his life as Jed and the crew unpacked their gear at Evergreen, sat around the lodge swapping stories. Darek fell into the hive and had them all laughing at the rookie escapades of their superintendent.

Most of all, it made him feel normal. Or at least like the man he'd wanted to be. It bolstered his courage to finish that phone call, to talk to Ivy and ask her out to the opening night of the art show.

Art. What had he been thinking? The chamber of commerce had blocked off the street, allowed locals to put up booths, and now he'd sentenced himself to an evening of examining pottery, trying to be impressed by woven baskets. Deep Haven and its penchant for festivals.

He'd rather be studying flame lengths and fire behavior. Even out on the fire line, trenching for twelve hours, hot, acrid air burning his throat.

Okay, maybe not entirely, but . . . if he had to look at another piece of painted birch bark . . .

"Cheer up. No one is going to make you paint, Picasso," Ivy said.

Her smile could stop the constant, frustrated boil in his head, and for a second, it all washed away. He should simply enjoy his evening out with this beautiful woman who represented everything he needed. A fresh start. A mother for Tiger. A woman without guile.

"Just you wait. I took three years of art in high school," he said.

"Really."

He leaned close, catching her vanilla fragrance. "It fulfilled my art credits. My mother has a closet full of scary vases and ceramic plates."

She laughed and it felt like a fresh breeze to his soul.

They cut across the sidewalk and into the harbor park, where a flautist played from a stage, the music soft against the breeze and the wash of waves on shore. Nearby, the children's tent hosted various activities, one of them the rock-painting contest. He settled Tiger at a table while Ivy retrieved a painting kit for him: a bucket of rocks, brushes, and a tin of watercolors.

"Hey there, buddy, are you here to paint?" Caleb Knight came over, wearing a baseball hat and his Huskies football shirt.

"Hey, Caleb," Darek said, catching his hand. Although he'd graduated long before Coach Knight came to town, he'd watched him transform the Huskies football program into a championship team. Some year soon, they'd win state. "I didn't know you were an artist."

"We're fund-raising for the school," Caleb said, pointing to a donation bucket.

Darek dug into his pocket, came out with a ten, and dropped it in.

Caleb tied an apron on Tiger and showed him how to dip his brush in the water, then the paint. Tiger reached for a rock and began to turn it green.

Darek stepped out of the tent, watching the waves. The water turned platinum in the light of the setting sun. A slight breeze bullied the collar of his polo shirt.

Conditions like these could be most dangerous on a fire line. Winds could be deceptive, lull firefighters into believing they had the upper hand. He'd known fire crews to take naps too near a line, nearly find themselves caught in a firestorm.

He'd have to stop by the forest service office and—

"You're not really here, are you?"

Ivy's voice cut through his thoughts and he turned, tried to focus on her. It was a moment before he found words. "There's a fire north of Deep Haven, back in the BWCA. A bunch of hotshots from my old crew are in town, and . . ." He lifted a shoulder. "They're staying at the resort."

"And you'd like to be with them."

He slipped his hand into hers. "No. I'd rather be here with you."

She took a long breath. Didn't smile. "I'm a lawyer. I know when people are lying."

Oh yeah. His smile fell. "Okay. Yes. But that's not my life anymore."

"And you're kicking yourself for still wanting it." Her voice grew soft. "We can't blame ourselves for wanting something. Just for what we'll do to get it."

She had such amazing green eyes, the way they shone in the sun, and for a long moment, he forgot exactly what he'd been pining for.

Yes. Right now he would rather be here, with her.

"Thanks for coming out with me tonight," he said. "I'm sorry it took so long for me to call."

She smiled, but that sadness touched her eyes again. Oh, he'd hurt her.

"It's not that I didn't want to; it's just—"

"With Tiger it gets tricky."

"Yeah," he said. "I . . . don't want him getting hurt."

She had her fingers woven with his. "Me either." Then she pulled away from him. Wrapped her arms around herself. "It was probably a good thing because I need to talk to you."

He made a face. "Please don't tell me I totally blew it. Really, Ivy, I wanted to call you, but I—"

She held up a hand. "It's not that. It's just, this town is so small. . . ."

Small. His chest tightened. Of *course* she had heard about him and Felicity. The kind of man he'd been, why he'd lost his wife, why he didn't deserve a woman like Ivy. His hopes betrayed him when he said, "What did you hear?"

She frowned. "I didn't—"

Behind him, Tiger laughed. And then he heard a voice lift above his son's, deep and resonant, raking up memories.

He whirled around.

Couldn't believe what he saw.

Claire Gibson was crouched beside Tiger, painting rocks with him, and beside her . . . Jensen Atwood. Feeding Darek's son cotton candy.

"What the—?" Darek sucked in the words, but they fueled the burn in his chest as he strode toward the tent. "Get away from my son!"

Ivy somehow beat him to the tent and now stood between Jensen and Tiger. She gave Darek a look that stopped him, made him blink. "You're scaring Tiger," she hissed.

For a second, he felt slapped.

Then she crouched beside Tiger. "Hey, bud, how about we wash those hands, maybe get some ice cream, huh?"

Tiger was staring at him, his hand sticky with red cotton candy. He got up with Ivy, who glanced again at Darek.

He forced a smile, feeling as if he'd been read his rights. "Go with Ivy, Son."

He watched her lead Tiger out of the tent, then rounded on Claire and Jensen, the rush of fury back, flooding his mind, his chest.

"Stay away from my son," he said, keeping his voice low, taut.

Jensen wore a hard glint in his eyes. "I was just talking to him—"

"You have no right to talk to him."

"Dare," Claire began. "It's my fault. I saw him painting, and he looked so cute with his apron. He has Felicity's nose, and—"

"Don't talk about Felicity." His gaze hadn't moved from Jensen's. "Ever."

"She was my best friend. Of course I'll talk about her," Claire said. "You're not the only one who lost her."

He tightened his jaw. "I don't want to see you in my town, Jensen."

"Believe me, I don't want to be here. But I am, and I'm just trying to enjoy this festival with Claire. Sorry we upset you—"

We? Darek felt as if someone took a scythe to his body when he saw Claire put her hand on Jensen's arm.

Were these two . . . *together?*

Jensen made to walk away, and Darek should have let him. But he couldn't. Not with so much steam inside, not with Jensen walking around, a free man, unpunished.

Unapologetic.

And even worse, with Claire.

He grabbed Jensen's arm.

It was a fight just waiting to happen. He saw it in Jensen's eyes, the way he whirled around, yanking his arm out of Darek's grip. He wasn't sure who started it then. If it was Jensen's fist in his face that made him launch himself at him in a full body check, or if Jensen had simply been trying to protect himself.

Whatever the spark, Darek had enough fuel inside him to light up the entire place. He took Jensen down on the painting table with a crash, rolled, and landed beside him on the pavement. Jensen slammed an elbow into his jaw as he struggled to get up, and pain strobed against Darek's eyes. He reached out, clawed at Jensen's collar.

He heard ripping but didn't stop, flinging his arm around Jensen's neck.

And then Darek simply held on. He'd stopped thinking, just acted on pure adrenaline. Closed his grip on Jensen, squeezing out his air.

But Jensen had always fought dirty—Darek forgot that. The man landed another elbow in Darek's gut, this time enough to wheeze the breath out of him. Darek gasped, let go, and Jensen scrambled away.

His former best friend stood above Darek, his shirt ripped, breathing hard.

Darek pushed himself up, still wheezing, his heart slamming against his rib cage.

Around them, even the seagulls had gone quiet. Save for one lonely, wretched cry.

"Daddy!"

The entire date had been a bad idea, and Ivy knew it. Especially as she pulled Tiger away from Darek, who lay sprawled on the ground, covered in paint, so much anger in his eyes, it even scared her a little. She turned Tiger around, crouched down to pull him against her, to hide him from Darek's violence.

His little body shook, and she didn't blame him.

No child should see a parent disintegrate. No matter the reason why. Parents were required to be strong, capable, in control.

Her throat tightened. Tiger had wrapped his arms around her, breathing into her neck.

Okay, maybe there had been a few good parts to this date. After all, she couldn't remember the last time someone had held on to her like this, so tight, as if they needed her. She breathed in his cotton-candy, sun-soaked body trembling in her arms. "It's okay, Tiger. Shh. Your daddy's fine."

She looked at Darek then, fire in her eyes, hoping he could read her mind.

Get up. You're scaring your son.

And worse, *Your mother-in-law is watching.*

She glanced over to where Nan Holloway stared at Darek, her mouth open, not even bothering to conceal her horror.

Not such a great way to meet Felicity's mother, perhaps. Ivy had been washing Tiger's hands in the fountain when the woman came up behind them and introduced herself. Tiger had flown into his grandmother's arms as if in confirmation.

Felicity's mother. Nan Holloway.

Hadn't Darek said something about how she'd wanted to take Tiger from him?

And then this incident capped off what felt like one badly timed event after another.

Ivy should have just told him the truth right off, ripped the scab from the wound, dealt with the blood and gore. They'd get it over with, and he'd walk out of her life, stop wasting their time.

Unless Darek could forgive her . . . and it was that thought, and the way Tiger greeted her, that had silenced Ivy. Maybe three years was long enough to grow forgiveness in his heart. Maybe he'd listen to her story and realize . . . what, that she hadn't meant to set Jensen free?

Although, really, how free could the man be?

Especially now, standing in the middle of the crowd, looking like he wanted to run.

Jensen looked at her. Then to Tiger. Back to her.

Like she had betrayed him.

He turned, pushing through the crowd, Claire on his heels.

Darek was just climbing to his feet. The man with the football emblem on his shirt helped him up. Patted him on the back as if Darek had simply fallen.

For once, she didn't want to know the gory details.

Tiger still clung to her.

"Let me take him," Nan said, so close to her that Ivy jumped. She crouched beside them and Ivy released Tiger into her arms—after all, she had no right to him. But she ran her hand down his back as he clung to his grandmother, still crying.

"Shh," Nan said, glaring at Darek.

He strode over to them, his mouth a grim line. He was breathing hard and almost looked as if he might cry, his eyes reddened. *She* nearly wanted to cry at the sick expression on his face.

"Give him to me, Nan," Darek said.

But Nan picked Tiger up, holding him as he wrapped his legs around her waist. "I think you need to cool off, Darek," she said with something just short of a snarl.

He took a breath, glancing at Ivy, then back to Nan. "I'm fine."

But Nan wasn't having it. "You're not fine. Brawling in public? What's next, Darek? First you show up on Sunday with Theo looking like he's been dragged down the street by a pack of wild animals, and today, I see you wrestling like one! I'm not sure this is the kind of parent my grandson needs."

Ivy saw a spark of heat in Darek's eyes and just about put her hand on his arm.

"I know Felicity wouldn't approve, God rest her soul. She'd be horrified to see how you're behaving."

"Maybe she should have been thinking about that before she decided to run out—" He clipped off his words.

But Nan looked like he'd struck her. "I know you never really loved my daughter, Darek. But she adored you, and don't you dare go desecrating her memory! She was a good wife to you, a wonderful mother—"

"Nan, I'm sorry. I didn't mean—"

Nan seemed just short of snapping herself. She tightened her hold on Tiger, took a step back. "I'm taking Theo home with me. I'll get him cleaned up, feed him, and bring him back to you tomorrow."

This time, Ivy did slip her hand onto Darek's arm.

"No."

"Darek, he's upset—"

"I'm upset! Did you not see the man who killed your daughter playing with your grandson?"

His voice came out booming, and Tiger wrenched around in Nan's arms, so much horror on his face that it made Ivy want to weep.

"Darek!" Nan snapped.

Tiger turned back to Nan, wrapped his arms tighter around her neck.

Darek winced. Gritted his teeth. Turned away.

His breaths rose and fell in his shoulders, and Ivy wanted to press her hand to his back. But suddenly, with Nan looking at her—the entire town looking at her—she had the sense that she might be a villain in this story.

Taking Felicity's place.

The truth rushed up at her. Ivy didn't belong here. She should leave. Now.

She couldn't breathe.

Run. Away.

Her feet crunched on the rocks as she backed up, and the sound made Darek glance at her.

Please. He said it with his eyes, the pain in them rooting her to the spot. *Don't go.*

Or maybe she just hoped he was saying that. Nevertheless, she stopped.

Darek slowly turned back to Nan, his shoulders rising and falling. He rested his hand on Tiger's back and said quietly, "Tomorrow. By noon."

Nan seemed speechless for a moment. Then her voice dropped. "You're doing the right thing, Darek."

He nodded, nothing of agreement in his face, and bent to kiss Tiger on the cheek. "Be good for your grandma."

Darek stood there as Nan walked away with Tiger, so much heartbreak in his eyes that Ivy couldn't help but take his hand.

He didn't look at her. Just wove his fingers together with hers.

"C'mon," she said quietly. "I've had enough art for today."

He said nothing as she led him up the street, past vendors, past the crowds. She wasn't exactly sure where she might be going, and when they ended up at his truck parked outside her place, she thought he might simply leave her there.

Then, inexplicably, he turned to her. "I know I haven't been very good company today. But—" he looked at his fingers still laced in hers—"would you be willing to have dinner with me?"

Dinner?

It's getting late. I have to work tomorrow. She should have said either of those things. Instead, she nodded.

Climbed into his truck. Rode beside him to Evergreen Resort. She knew exactly where Felicity had died now and found herself measuring the road as they drove silently around the curve.

Darek's fists tightened on the steering wheel and he took a long breath.

Finally, when they reached the dirt road that led to the resort, he said, "I'm sorry." He had his face glued to the road, but his words flickered in his expression.

"What happened?" Ivy said softly. "One minute you were standing there; the next, I return to find you on the ground with Jensen."

"I don't know."

He pulled into the parking lot, now filled by the hotshots' trucks and cars.

Darek sat there a moment, then looked at her. "Jensen killed my wife."

She knew that, but hearing him say it felt so blunt, so raw, that the hurt registered on her face anyway.

"He was driving, and she was out for a run, and . . ." He closed his eyes, shaking his head. "I don't want to talk about this."

She swallowed, nodded, pretty sure this wasn't the end of it.

Darek got out of the truck. "I have a couple steaks in the fridge, and my sister made some fresh bread yesterday. I'll just be a moment." He left her standing on the path while he disappeared inside his parents' lodge home.

The woods trapped the heat, the scent from a lush blanket of pine needles, the wind filtering through the paper birch. She walked out past the lodge and saw a canoe pulled up to the beach, a pontoon boat at the dock. A crow called from a nearby perch.

"A man can forget up here," Darek said behind her. He held a stainless steel bowl with a head of lettuce, tomato, red onion, and cucumber. From his fingers dangled a bag with a loaf of bread.

She took the bowl from him. Considered him a moment. "Or he can try."

Darek tried a smile and then nodded, walking past her.

Ivy fell in step with him, their feet soft on the path. Roots crisscrossed the trail as it wound through the woods to his little house.

Darek set the fixings down at an outside table. "I'll be right back."

Ivy waited on the porch, looking out at the lake. What might it have been like to grow up here, at a place embedded with so much peace? With legacy? With his family right down the trail, his name carved into the trees? This was Darek's land—Evergreen.

He had no idea what it felt like to be uprooted.

Darek emerged from the house with a cutting board, plates, a couple knives, two napkin rolls with silverware, and two fresh steaks on a serving platter. On a second trip he brought a couple Cokes, salt and pepper, garlic, blue cheese salad dressing, setting it all on a table on his deck.

"That's quite the place," she said, gesturing across the lake.

He didn't look up.

Oh, this might be a bad idea after all.

"Jensen Atwood lives over there, in that big house." He unwrapped the steaks and turned to light the grill, a six-burner gas affair. It roared to life, and he turned down the heat, closed the hood. He stared at it for a moment; then, "We grew up together."

"You and Jensen?"

"And Felicity and Claire. They were two years younger than us, so they were always a little off-limits. We spent every summer right there, out on that lake." He pointed with his tongs. "We were best friends, even after he moved away."

She picked up a knife, began to cut the cucumber into slices. "Why did he move?"

"His parents got divorced and his mother remarried. His father was bitter, moved him down to Minneapolis." He salted the steaks. "Jensen hated it. He loved living here, and moving to the Cities tore his life apart. He came back every summer."

She glanced at him, surprised at the lack of rancor in his voice.

"He was here the summers I was working on the hotshot team in Montana. Well, most of them. He came to Montana the first year, but . . . it didn't work out."

She reached for a tomato.

"I remember the year I came home for a visit during the summer, hearing rumors that he and Felicity were an item." He took the onion, began to slice it. It came off in thin rounds. "I wasn't surprised. He was always competing with me for something. Hockey. Grades. Felicity."

"You and Felicity dated in high school?"

Darek blinked as if trying to fight off the sting of the onion. "No. Not really." He looked away, widened his eyes. "Wow, these are strong."

Ivy reached over to steal the onion from him and finished slicing. She'd never been susceptible to the power of onions.

He set down his knife. "We went to senior prom together—double-dated with Jensen and Claire. I think Felicity got it in her head then that we should be together, and . . . well, she came on pretty strong after that, and especially when I got back that summer, despite the fact that she was dating Jensen." He lifted the hood on the grill, dropped the steaks on with the tongs. Seasoned them with garlic. "Not that I wasn't willing." He sighed. "You should probably know that Felicity and I weren't married when Tiger was conceived."

Ivy hadn't expected that. But, well—

He looked at her then, something of pain in his eyes. "The truth was, I didn't want to get married. I was angry at her—I felt like she trapped me." He closed the hood, turned the heat down more. "I wasn't exactly a great husband. I was angry and resentful and gone most of the time on the hotshot crew. I worked year-round back then, training when I wasn't working for the forest service. No wonder she turned to Jensen."

His words made her look up. "Did she and Jensen—?"

"I don't know. After three years of thinking about it, I don't think so, but at the time . . ."

That seemed so . . . forgiving for a man who had just tackled said nemesis in public. Ivy added the onion to the bowl. Picked up the lettuce and began to tear it with her hands.

He took a long breath, gazing toward the house across the lake. "Deep down, I was so angry at her, at life." A muscle pulled in his jaw. "I accused Felicity of having an affair the night she . . ." He sighed. "I can't believe I did that. I can still hear it sometimes, my own voice in my head telling me to stop. Telling me to just shut my mouth. But I can't take the words back. I can't stop the rush of accusations—so many of them. I blamed her for everything. For getting pregnant, for stealing my life. And she threw it right back at me. Told me that I should be more like Jensen. That he wouldn't run out on her. That's when I suggested that maybe she was looking for a do-over with the boy next door."

Ivy had stopped tearing the lettuce and now just watched him deflate, wearing his defeat on his face.

"Sadly, she was right. Jensen was the kind of guy she could depend on. He'd always been that guy, and I knew it. Despite his parents' broken marriage, Jensen was a guy who would have settled in Deep Haven, made a life with her. He's small town at heart, and in a way, I stole Felicity from *him*."

His words left her a little hollow, unsure how to respond. "Did he love her?"

"I don't know. Maybe. He had a soft spot for Claire, but Felicity was always shiny and bright. She attracted all our attention." He let out a wry chuckle. "Jensen was the best man at my shotgun wedding."

"Shotgun?"

"No, not really, I guess. Although I'm sure Nan and George wished they had one, maybe to run me off." He gave her the smallest smile.

She hesitated, then smiled back.

Behind him, smoke trickled from the grill. "The steaks!" He heaved open the lid. Smoke billowed out as he grabbed the meat, turned it.

"I hope you like your meat charred," he said. "Sorry."

I didn't come for the food. Not that she let herself say that, but as she watched him begin to toss the salad, she wanted to slide into his arms. Mold herself to him, taste his lips on hers.

Make him forget all his mistakes, his regret, and . . .

Stay here as if she belonged.

Maybe someday, if he could forgive Jensen, then Darek could also forgive her. In fact, maybe she should just tell him the truth— tell him that, from a distance, Jensen looked innocent. Probably was, but she'd leave that out. She'd come clean, let Darek see that she never meant him—or Deep Haven—any harm.

She was just trying to be impartial. To help justice along.

"I forgive you," she said, reaching for the salad. "Just don't set anything else on fire."

He laughed, rich and delicious.

Oops. Too late for that.

Darek wasn't sure how he'd gone from the turmoil inside to a place where he just wanted to forget the steaks roasting on the grill and wrap his arms around Ivy.

What had he been thinking, opening up his regrets, his mistakes for her full-on scrutiny?

Ivy was just so easy to talk to. She listened without judgment. With compassion. And talking to her somehow unknotted the anger in his chest.

Darek took a breath and turned back to the grill, waving his mitt through the smoke. "They're going to think we've started the forest on fire." He could feel his heart thundering through his ribs, sense her standing behind him.

It was just the adrenaline of the day, the way she'd taken his hand, helped extricate him from the embarrassment in town. Agreed to join him for dinner, giving him yet another chance.

He glanced across the lake, where a light flickered on at Jensen's place.

A strange, unbidden longing went through him. *Hey, Jens, wanna go fishing?*

Darek blew out a breath, checked the steaks. Despite their crispy exteriors, they still seemed juicy. He slid them onto the serving plate. "Want to eat down by the lake?"

When he turned, he found Ivy already holding the bowl of tossed salad, plates topped with the napkin rolls in her other hand. He picked up the Cokes, tucked the dressing under his arm, and nodded toward a picnic table at the water's edge.

She led the way, looking so pretty in that sundress, the wind playing with her hair. She'd probably be cold now that the sun was nearly gone. Maybe he'd help solve that.

Oh, see, here he was, moving too fast again.

Ivy set the bowl on the table and added the plates, side by side so they could watch the lake together. She set down the napkins and climbed onto the bench.

"When I was twelve, the foster family I lived with went camping. I lay in my tent all night, shivering, terrified of the sounds.

But I loved the idea of eating outside. And by the end of the week, I couldn't wait for the next year's adventure."

"And were you scared the next time?"

She dished salad onto her plate, then forked one of the steaks. "Yum. This looks delicious."

He frowned. "Ivy?"

"I was moved three months later, right before Christmas. I never saw that family again."

Oh. "I'm sorry."

She lifted a shoulder. "It was okay most of the time. I got used to moving. The hardest was the time I almost got adopted." He watched her tackle her steak, cutting it into tiny pieces before she picked up a bite.

"What happened?"

She sighed. "It was an older couple. Professionals. They didn't have kids and wanted a son and a daughter, so they took in me and a boy about a year older. He was cute, athletic. Stayed out of trouble. Me, I was bookish." She looked at him, a smile on her face.

Darek didn't feel like smiling.

"One day the man left his money clip on the kitchen table, and twenty dollars went missing. I wasn't sure if Brooks had taken it, but I certainly hadn't. They interrogated me, and although I told them the truth, they didn't believe me. I have a feeling Brooks pinned it on me, but . . . they sent me back about a week later." She took another bite of her steak.

He'd lost his appetite. In fact, he felt sick. "I'm so sorry."

"It's okay. I survived."

"You're an amazing woman, Ivy."

She gave him a little frown. "Why?"

"Why aren't you broken and angry and . . . ? You're so put together."

The laugh she gave sounded nothing like humor. More like chagrin, maybe. "I . . . just kept dreaming of something more, you know? I made sure I didn't get attached. I had to believe that someday . . . well . . ." She seemed to be searching his eyes. Across the lake, a loon mourned, low and long.

"Had to believe that someday . . . what?" he said softly.

Ivy looked away, shook her head. "It's so beautiful. I would never leave if I lived here." She closed her eyes, drawing in a breath.

"I don't want you to." He didn't know where that came from, how it even emerged from him, but it surprised her as much as it did him because her eyes flew open.

He cupped his hand on her soft cheek. "*You* are so beautiful," he said. Then he leaned in and kissed her.

It was just as he remembered from their date under the fireworks, just as he'd been trying to forget—not wanting to, but feeling like he'd probably had no right to kiss her in the first place.

Maybe it was a fluke, all of this. This woman, who now surrendered to him, letting him kiss her, moving her hands to palm his chest. The way, with her, he felt redeemed. As if the last five years might be healed in her embrace.

His arms went around her, and he pulled her to himself. *Ivy.* He tried out her name on his lips, whispered it against her neck. Then he leaned back, held her face in his hands.

She swallowed.

"You make me feel new, Ivy. Like I don't come with all this baggage. Like I didn't tackle the guy who used to be my best friend today. Like I didn't scare my son. You make me feel like I can start over and maybe someday be the guy I should have been all along.

With you, all the roaring anger in my head goes away, and I can forget. Even move on."

She swallowed again, her eyes glistening. Then she closed them, turning her head away.

What? "Are you . . . upset?"

She made a face, shook her head, but untangled herself from his arms.

"Ivy, what's the matter?" See, he *was* moving too fast, setting things on fire he had no business igniting.

"I didn't . . . You should know that I didn't plan this. I didn't . . ." She looked at him, took a breath. "I came here because I wanted to help people. I wanted to change lives. I wanted to do some good. I never wanted to hurt anyone—" She clamped her hand over her mouth and leaped up from the bench.

Darek followed her. "You're not going to hurt anyone."

"I just . . . Listen, maybe this isn't a good idea."

He caught her arm. "What do you mean?"

But she pushed against him. "Nothing. I'm sorry." She walked away from him. "I think I need to go."

"Go? No, Ivy. What's going on?"

Her face had crumpled, a strange twist to it as if she might be trying not to cry. "You don't get it. I do that. I have a good thing going, and suddenly I wreck everything. And then it's just over." She was backing away. "Just . . . over."

Oh. He got it then. "Social services shows up and yanks you away."

She went a little pale. But nodded. "I don't have baggage because I know that nothing really lasts. Ever. People just . . . They give up on me. So I learn to not expect much. And now you . . . and Tiger and . . ."

She gave a harsh, almost-bitter laugh. "Or maybe it's God who gives up on me. Who hates me."

"What? Ivy, why would God hate you?"

Another sharp laugh. "No, wait; He doesn't hate me. That would involve caring. He just doesn't . . . Well, He's not on my side."

"Ivy—"

"It's not that I care. It's just . . . I want a break, you know? For just one thing to go my way."

"I don't understand."

"It doesn't matter. I shouldn't let it matter."

She was walking away, toward the parking lot as if—shoot, she wasn't leaving!

"I'm going home, Darek." Her voice shook. Was she crying?

He caught up to her, turned her. Tears cut down her face. What in the world—? "Listen, I admit that God and I aren't necessarily on speaking terms, but I know that He doesn't hate you. And I'm not going to let you walk away from me. I'm not going to give up on you. Or . . ." He swallowed. "Us. I'm not going to give up on us."

She frowned as if flummoxed by his words. "Us?"

Us. The word lodged in his brain too. But he'd really said that, and there was no going back now, so he nodded.

"I . . . I've never been a part of . . . us."

He ran his thumb down her cheek, found the words easier than he thought. "Maybe it's time you were. Maybe it's time someone believed in you, held on to you, made you believe you matter."

She blinked and a tear dropped off her chin.

He felt the words even as he said them. "You do matter, Ivy." He nudged her chin up and bent down to brush her lips. "To me. I want an us."

He kissed her sweetly because it felt right, and then more because his heart took hold of him.

She didn't respond, not at first. Then she slipped her arms around his neck. A sigh shuddered out of her as she kissed him back.

She was small and perfect in his arms, and as the shadows carpeted the forest around them, he let himself believe that yes, he could be a good man. The man he should have been with Felicity.

The kind of man Ivy deserved.

CHAPTER 12

WHAT DAREK HADN'T DONE physically, he'd accomplished mentally. Or perhaps spiritually. Because looking at Jensen, Claire knew something had shattered inside him.

He stood on his deck, unmoving, watching shadows fill the nooks and crannies of the lake. As if caught in that moment when Darek grabbed his arm.

Claire had the overwhelming urge to go up to him, put her arms around him. Tell him that he wasn't the man Darek accused him of being.

She believed that. Whoever Jensen had been, ever so briefly three years ago, he'd changed. He wasn't the man who would steal another man's wife. Wasn't the man who would betray a friendship.

That kind of man didn't work from dawn till midnight building his neighbor a wheelchair ramp or widening doorways or raising the table and lowering the bed. Didn't set down his hammer for an hour to accompany her to an art festival.

How Claire wanted to return to the nightmare in town and erase it.

"I'm so sorry I got you into this, Jens."

"It's hardly your fault that Darek hates me." Jensen didn't turn from the railing. "I don't know what I was thinking. I know better than that."

"What, going into town?"

"Running the risk of being seen in public. Especially by Darek."

She handed him a glass of lemonade. "That was my fault. I saw Tiger and missed him so much . . ."

"He looks so much like Felicity—those cute freckles, that nose. He has her eyes, too."

She didn't know what to make of that.

"The last time Darek and I got into a fistfight was the day I walked off the hotshot crew."

"You never told me that."

"It wasn't a fight really. He got in my face about leaving, called me a coward—and it turned into something ugly." He stared at his glass. "I didn't even ask my father before I went—just took off right after graduation with Darek, dreaming of being a hero with him. My father tracked me down—literally got on a plane and found me. We'd just come off a month of training and fighting a fire in Idaho, and he appeared at the camp in Montana." He shook his head. "I didn't want to leave, but . . . but I didn't have anything else. My mom had moved to California with her new husband, and maybe Darek was right—I was a coward."

"You weren't a coward—"

"I was. I should have stood up to my old man. But I bought right into the idea that I should be something more than Deep Haven. That I should be above it."

"Then why did you come back every summer?"

He looked at her, then swallowed, looked away. "I had my reasons."

Oh, right. Like Felicity. She could never dodge that subject.

"I think I was jealous of Darek living his dream, becoming a hotshot. And then, of course, he married Felicity."

She sighed, desperate to change the topic. "Thank you for all your hard work on the house. I can't wait until Grandpop sees it. He's going to love it."

Jensen took a sip of his lemonade. "Are you sure you're up for this? Taking care of your grandfather will be a big job and—"

"Yes." She didn't mean for it to emerge so fast, but . . . "Yes. I am. It's why I'm here."

He nodded, studied his glass. "Of course. Your grandfather is lucky to have you."

"I'm lucky to have him. I keep thinking about what would have happened to me if they hadn't taken me in—if my parents had made me stay in Bosnia."

"They should have stayed home for you," he said, his voice shifting.

"I couldn't ask them to do that. They were missionaries. Doctors." She shook her head, trying not to hear the past. The moments she'd cried herself to sleep in her bed. Or her mother's words: *We have a job, a duty, to the Lord, Claire. You can't ask us to betray God.*

Which, of course, was why God hadn't been talking to her. She'd betrayed Him with her accusations. Her doubt.

God isn't kind.

She still couldn't believe she'd said that out loud. She'd sat in her bed last night repenting of her words. Hating that deep down, yes, she felt that sometimes.

But she had to believe in a kind God, a God who cared. Otherwise life was out of control. Random. And no safety could be found in a random, chaotic world.

"You were more important. They should have come home."

Oh. Silly tears pricked her eyes. She turned away.

True to form, Jensen rescued her. "You didn't have to make dinner."

Claire drew in a quick breath, found a smile. "It's one of the things I do well. The pizza will be ready soon."

He glanced at her, his gaze roaming over her face, those kind blue eyes that always made her aware of the woman she wished she could be. Beautiful, flirty like Felicity. Strong. Taking what she wanted from life, instead of letting it take her.

"From what I remember, you do everything well."

She made a noise, something that resembled a laugh.

"What? You do. You made great grades in school. Weren't you like number six in your class?"

"Five." Funny how he remembered that.

"And you can play nearly any instrument. I used to sit out here on the deck at night, hoping you'd make an appearance on the dock with your guitar. Sometimes I'd take out my harmonica and play along."

"You should play with me sometime."

Now he gave a humorless laugh. Shook his head.

"Why not? You could join the band—"

"The minute I'm done, I'm leaving."

The harshness of his tone stilled her. He must have noticed because he looked at her.

"I just . . . I thought you loved it here," she said softly. Tears burned her eyes again. She turned away from him, faced the water. "You told me once that you couldn't wait to live here. Said you planned to come back after law school, open a practice, save the world."

"That's before I needed saving."

Right. She swallowed the knot in her chest.

"Yeah, I wanted to live here, once. But now . . ." He shrugged. "I like the idea of Hawaii."

She didn't match his smile. "It's hot there."

From the kitchen, the oven buzzed. Claire tore herself away and retrieved the pizza, slid it onto a wooden cutting board, returned to the patio table.

Jensen pulled up a wrought-iron chair, lighting the electric lantern. She set down plates and pulled up her own chair.

"Yum." He reached for a piece and grinned as if trying hard to brush off the horror of the day. He caught the dangling cheese, piled it on the pizza.

Oh, he was a handsome man. He'd changed out of his ripped shirt into a blue button-up, a pair of low jeans, flip-flops. Dressed like this, he looked every inch the rich city kid he'd become.

The lawyer he'd wanted to be.

Hard to think of him like that, especially when he rolled up his sleeves, wore his faded Huskies cap backward, clomped around in those boots.

"I downloaded the clemency application." She pulled a piece of pizza onto her plate. "It looks simple."

"I read it over." He took a sip from his glass. "I don't think it'll work, Claire. It asks for letters of reference. And after today in town . . ."

"Not everyone agrees with Darek. Not everyone sees you as a villain."

He considered his lemonade. "When are your parents going to be here?"

She watched him, not sure why he'd changed the subject. "They said a couple weeks. I don't know. With luck, they won't come."

"You don't mean that."

She drew her legs up in the chair. "They'll just start making me feel like a failure. Remind me of how I didn't do anything with my life."

"If you could do anything, what would it be?"

"I don't know. Be a professional gardener, maybe."

"Not play music?"

"No. I don't have a passion for it like Kyle and Emma."

"But flowers you love."

"I love working the soil, seeing the seeds come to life, watching them bloom. I love the weeding and pruning."

"You keep the Deep Haven roses, right?"

She nodded.

"They're beautiful."

"Resilient. Every year, we have a debate about when to take off the covers. This year, I . . . well, I nearly killed them. I was afraid of a late-season frost—we get them almost every year. But it never came, and they nearly suffocated."

"But you coaxed them back to life." He studied her, a strange look in his eyes. "You do that, Claire. Coax things back to life."

She couldn't move, not sure about his words, the texture of emotion in his eyes.

From across the lake, a loon called, and the sound of it echoed off the water.

"I owe you an apology," she said quietly.

He frowned.

"I thought you had an affair with Felicity." Claire felt him tense in the small intake of breath. "Felicity . . . She told me about how you came over and helped her construct that play set for Tiger. And she was talking about you like . . . like she had feelings for you. Then that night . . ." She winced, not sure if she should tell him. "Well, I think Darek might have thought so too."

He had closed his eyes as if he'd just received a blow.

"I'm so sorry—"

"I didn't, Claire." He opened his eyes, met hers. "I swear to you, I didn't."

"I believe you," she said, perhaps too quickly. But then she offered a smile. "I believe you."

"So if you could do anything, it would be grow gardens?" His words rushed out fast.

"Yes. I think so. I would love to open a nursery in town, maybe do private landscaping. I know it's not as glorious as my parents' work, but . . ." She let her words fall off, realizing that no, actually, it wasn't glorious at all.

She picked at a pepperoni on her plate. "So there's no chance of you staying in Deep Haven?"

"I won't have a choice in a couple weeks."

"Don't talk like that."

"We need to get real about this, Claire. I need community service hours in the worst way. And they just aren't available here. And after today . . . there's no clemency for me. I kept thinking

that if I just worked hard enough, someday the town—Darek—
might forgive me. Or at least stop hating me."

"No one hates you, Jens. They're just grieving."

He looked at her, something so raw in his eyes that she pushed
her plate aside, leaned closer to him.

"I don't hate you."

He swallowed. "Thank you, Claire. You have no idea . . ." He
looked away. "I've missed your friendship, you know. The way we
used to hang out. You always took me seriously. Seemed to see the
real me."

She touched his hand, unable to stop herself.

He looked down at it. Back to her.

"I still see you, Jens," she said softly.

I still see you.

Jensen couldn't escape the way Claire looked at him, the tone
of her words; he wanted to drink it all in, let it nourish him.
But . . . no, she didn't really see him. How could she?

Maybe Gibs had been right. He wasn't guilty of the crime Deep
Haven accused him of, but he had darkness in him. He had certainly wanted to turn on Darek today and hurt him.

Really hurt him.

And that scared him. It should scare her, too, if she only knew.

There was more—things inside him that he feared acknowl-
edging. Like the fact that, deep down, he'd been glad that Felicity
and Darek weren't happy. That she'd turned to Jensen for an ear,
a friend.

But no, he hadn't gone as far as to betray Darek physically. To tempt Felicity to destroy her vows. Claire's apology, her admission, had nearly leveled him, but he could see how she might think . . .

He withdrew his hand from her touch. Got up and walked to the deck railing again. Spied a light glowing from Evergreen Resort, cutting through the twilight.

"What's the matter, Jens?" Claire followed him to the railing, and he hated how much he needed her there, beside him.

"I . . . I'm not the man you see."

She said nothing.

"I keep thinking that if I just keep doing the right thing, keep smiling, keep working out my sentence, I'll break free of all this anger—this hurt—inside."

"My grandfather says when we try to work out our own redemption, that's when we find ourselves far from God. Christianity is the only religion that says our works actually do nothing to save us. It's only our acceptance of grace that makes us whole. We have to draw near to God and let Him do the redeeming."

Grace. He wasn't exactly sure what that looked like. As for wholeness . . . he would settle for peace. The kind that allowed him to sleep through the night and look at himself in the mirror in the morning.

"I don't think there's any grace for me." He took a breath. Might as well tell her the truth. "I'm so angry all the time, Claire. And not just at Darek or Deep Haven, but myself. I can't figure out how to live with what happened. And I feel worse with every hour of service I put in. Like that will bring Felicity back. It's such a farce. Then I start arguing with myself that it wasn't my fault, and then . . . then the anger sets in. It's a cycle I can't break."

She stared into the darkness. "You start to see the things you should have done. The ways you should have been more careful. Locked the door. Screamed."

"Not checked the radio, or maybe gone slower around that turn."

"Keep reliving the moment when you turned around, and they were right there."

"When you heard her scream, the sickening thud."

"When the world started to move in slow motion."

"And stopped."

She closed her eyes. "And stopped."

God isn't kind. He heard her words, a soft echo inside. Felt them, like a dagger in his soul. No wonder he was angry all the time.

At the touch of Claire's hand on his, he opened his palm. Folded her fingers into his.

I love you, Claire.

The thought stilled him, froze his breath in his chest.

But with her standing there, the wind stirring up the dark hair around her face, the past seemed so close, so . . . redeemable.

"Thank you for being my friend today." Oh, how lame. But what else was he supposed to say? *I've been in love with you since you moved to Deep Haven but I was too scared to tell you? Instead, I dated—even fell in love with—your best friend?*

What a fool he'd been, and he'd known it even then. But being in love with Claire was a little like being in love with a saint. Just a little unseemly. Because then she'd see him, know him . . . and of course there was Felicity. It was easier, somehow, to flirt with her, tease her back. Mostly because Felicity's rejection wouldn't have torn him apart.

Because he hadn't really loved her. Not the way he loved Claire. And in fact, he had a terrible suspicion that he'd always been a tool for Felicity to get who she really wanted—Darek.

All the same, his words to Claire felt a little like he'd taken a piece of his heart and pinned it to the outside of his body. *Thank you. For being my friend.*

She shivered as a sudden gust of wind shook the trees.

And because she hadn't rejected him, because she hadn't looked at him like he didn't deserve a moment of her presence, he couldn't stop himself from pulling her to his chest. Wrapping his arms around her. Like a miracle, she tucked herself against him, her arms around his waist.

So maybe they could forget the past, just like she said.

Maybe he wouldn't have to leave Deep Haven to start over. "Claire . . ."

She looked up at him. And in the light of the rising moon, the smell of summer lingering in the air—in the way her mouth tilted slightly—he felt young again, taking pretty Claire Gibson to her senior prom and wishing she was his girl.

His gaze roamed her face just for a moment. Without waiting to think, to hear the warnings in his head, he bent down and kissed her.

He expected something of hesitation. Even feared that he'd gone too far, that she'd push him away, the old sense of guilt rising up to paralyze him.

But she kissed him back. Lifted her face to his, curled her arms around his shoulders, and molded herself to him. He had his arms around her back and pulled her close, deepening his kiss, tasting the lemonade on her tongue, feeling the whisper touch of her hair against his cheek.

She was delicate and perfect, and why hadn't he done this years ago?

In truth, *she* was the reason he'd returned every summer. *Claire.*

She made the softest sound of enjoyment, as if no, he hadn't just blown it with her. Not at all. So he lifted his head, found her eyes. "I might have a lot to apologize for, but I'm not going to apologize for that. I've been wanting to kiss you for years."

Her eyes widened. "Really?"

He nodded and then, fueled by the smile that lit her face, lowered his mouth again to hers.

Yes, he was kissing Claire Gibson. On his deck, with the beauty of the forest around him, the call of the loons as serenade, the wind rushing through the trees as if in cosmic approval.

Maybe, indeed, this was the definition of grace.

Us. Darek let that word hover in his mind, over the growl of the chain saw in his hand.

He and Felicity had never been an *us.* A *them,* perhaps, but . . .

Yeah, that had been his fault too. How many times had she said she wanted a real marriage, the kind in which they actually meant their vows?

Us.

He stepped back from the tree, nearly six inches in diameter, and gave it a push. It went crashing down into the forest, taking out poplar branches and the furry arms of evergreens. He revved the chain saw, then began to dice the trunk into stackable pieces. Wood shavings splattered into the air, the smell rich with freshly hewn sawdust, mingling with a tinge of the far-off wildfire.

Too far to be a worry, but it never hurt to clean up the property.

He turned off the chain saw, removed his goggles, and reached for the logs, tossing them toward the wheelbarrow.

"Casper! Bring me the stump grinder!"

Casper, dressed similarly in a pair of leather logging chaps and gloves, an orange hard hat and goggles, hiked over with the tree stump grinder. "Next time you decide to fireproof the grounds, please send me an e-mail, and I'll remember not to come home."

"Go take out those saplings I marked."

Casper lifted the chain saw. "Yes, chief. Anything else, Your Fire Highness?"

The finest prickles of sawdust layered Casper's chin, feathered into his dark hair. He smelled like a swamp and wore a fireman's tan.

"Hard work is good for you. All that archaeology is going to make you soft. Digging in the soil with a toothbrush. Whatever."

Casper pulled down his goggles as he fired up the saw. "The Swan Lake fire is still twenty miles away. You heard Jed—they'll put it out long before it gets to Deep Haven."

Darek ignored him, began to grind down the stump, listening to the replay of his conversation this morning with Jed.

He'd come into the lodge just after dawn and found Jed and Conner Young, the new Jude County communications guru, huddled over a map. His father stood at the head of the table, cradling a cup of coffee, his face knotted in concern as Jed pointed out the fire's growth over the last week.

Indeed, this morning, smoke seemed to saturate the air, as if overnight the wind had whipped it into a new frenzy.

Jed had drawn a red wax line on the fire map, only a small portion of it in blue, where the hotshots had hiked in yesterday and contained the edge. Most of them still camped out on the line. "Last night's winds caused the fire to surge. Flyovers this morning show the fire hopping across Ball Club Lake, from island to island." He pointed out the places. "And it's made land here, twenty miles north of Deep Haven."

Casper had walked in then, wearing a pair of shorts, his shirt open, his hair on end. He stood beside his father, arms folded over his chest. Darek's mother was listening in the kitchen, wearing oven mitts, as if waiting for something to finish baking. The house smelled of cinnamon and nutmeg.

"We have a few natural fire breaks between the head of the fire and any residential areas." Jed pointed to a couple logging roads, a smaller lake, and the larger Two Island Lake to the south that spanned miles. A roadblock to the residential areas of the county. "We'll get an air tanker in today and see if we can slow the head down, but the forecast calls for wind gusts, and with all the deadfall, the fuel load is thick in this area. We need to be ready for some torching and spotting." He circled a section of uninhabited forest where he predicted the fire would run.

Beyond the blue line, just down the road, the wilderness became dotted with cabins.

Darek leaned over the map. "I think this part of the line can be controlled by a hand crew. Our best line of attack is to get the crews in here—" he drew his finger along a logging road about two miles south of the flames—"early this morning, while the wind is still at five miles per hour. You may even be able to get a dozer in there. But I'd start a backfire, see if you can't drive the fire toward Hand Lake."

Jed seemed to consider it.

"The crew hiked in and posted video at the two fire stations, here—" Conner Young pointed to a mark on the map—"and north, up here. We should have fresh footage this morning that'll give us a glimpse of how it's moving."

"Do you think it will get this far southeast? It's coming at a pretty good clip," Darek's father said. He'd worked crews back in the days of national park fires, had stories of brave men fighting with just Pulaskis and shovels. Today's equipment included saws, dozers, planes, and torches. But the hard work remained the same.

"It's a remote possibility. It could hit Evergreen Lake, but we hope to stop it by then," Jed said. "I'd make sure the place was fireproofed, just in case." He turned to Darek. "Sure wish you were joining us."

Him too. Although, after last night . . . "Sorry, Jed. I have to stick around, make sure our resort is ready."

"Fair enough. By the way, we have a crew from Sacramento coming in today, along with a couple pilots and smoke jumpers out of the Jude County base in Ember. I told them they could stay here. We're setting up a fire camp on Forest Road 153 for the ground pounders and command central. But I want my pilots and dozer operators fresh. I hope that's okay." Jed rolled up the map.

"We'll make room," Darek's father said.

Jed swiped a piece of cinnamon bread that Darek's mother offered him on a paper napkin. "Thanks, Mrs. C."

"You boys be safe out there."

"Videos?" Darek asked Conner. "Really?"

"Technology," Conner said. "You might want to consider installing it up here."

"We have indoor plumbing. What more do you want?" his father said, and Conner laughed.

Yeah, well, not a bad idea.

Although, for once, Darek had enjoyed watching the sunset with no Internet, no television, no cell phone to pull Ivy from his arms.

Now he shut off the stump grinder, brushed sawdust from his arms, and worked off his goggles. His stomach roared—he hoped his mother had a sandwich waiting. And Tiger should be returning soon.

Probably he owed Nan a thank-you. He hadn't been at his best yesterday, and she'd sort of saved him. Although he'd never, in a thousand years, intentionally do anything to scare Tiger.

He looked up as his father emerged from the edge of the forest, gloved, wearing a long-sleeved flannel work shirt, hauling a dead log. He dumped it near the wheelbarrow, then turned to the lake, wiping his forehead with his shirtsleeve. "Sure makes me wish we'd taken the government up on that grant to install a sprinkler system."

"We couldn't afford the system, even with the grant," Darek said. "It's for . . ." He gestured across the lake toward Pine Acres. Then he walked up to his father. "They'll stop it before it gets to Evergreen, Dad. Jed knows what he's doing."

"So do you."

He did? Darek fought a strange swell of warmth.

"I wouldn't trust this property to anyone but you, Darek. You know the forest; you know fires." He turned to his son. "This property is over one hundred years old. It was the hottest place on the shore fifty years ago. We used to have dances right there, in that old pavilion." He pointed to the broken shelter, the one Darek longed to tear down. He'd forbidden Tiger from playing under it, had roped it off, away from guests. A yellow flag fluttered in the breeze, connected to the rope.

"Your great-great-grandfather built the lodge with his own hands, and your mother and I got married right there, on the point." His father looked up to the sky then, to where a dark, smoky cloud rolled over the lake. A haze had settled over the forest, probably blown all the way to town, turning the air to ash. "Do whatever it takes to save Evergreen Resort, Darek. I'm trusting it into your hands."

Casper was watching them, had his ear protection removed and hanging around his neck.

"Don't worry, Dad; I got this."

His father clapped him on the shoulder, squeezed. "Evergreen is in the good hands of my sons. By the way, I was thinking, with your men staying here, we might be able to scrape up enough for a down payment on Gibs's place. He's back from the hospital but staying at the care center for a while. I thought I'd stop by, see what he says—"

"Darek!"

Darek looked up and frowned at the sight of Diane Wolfe striding down the path.

"She's got her game face on," his father said.

Indeed, this seemed a business visit—he'd seen that expression before. Like the time the Holloways had sued for custody. And twice after that, when they'd accused him of neglect.

He ignored the knot in his chest, tried to keep his voice cool. "Hey, Diane. What's going on?"

"Hello, Darek. John. Casper." The social worker, never a woman to flinch, came out hard and fast with her words. "There's been a complaint, Darek."

Nice. "What now?"

"I have to say, there are grounds. Tiger looks pretty beat up."

Beat up? He felt his father's hand on his shoulder. "He fell. Off the top bunk a couple weeks ago. And then at the Fourth of July fireworks. But he's fine now."

"We have pictures. And then there's the complaint from yesterday."

Darek stepped out of his father's touch. "What kind of complaint?"

"Brawling. Violence. The allegation is 'egregious incident involving a child.' It alleges emotional trauma—"

"Tiger was fine!" Darek throttled his voice to low. "Listen, he was a little scared, is all."

Her lips tightened into a thin, unforgiving line.

He took a breath. "Diane. Nan hates me. You know this. She hates the fact that Felicity died and I didn't. And she's been trying to take Tiger from me since the day of Felicity's funeral."

"I have to investigate every complaint, Darek."

"You tore our lives inside out last time. Tiger had to stay with a foster family—do you know how crazy that made him? He started wetting the bed again and—"

"These are serious neglect and egregious emotional injury allegations, Darek. You know you have to cooperate. I advise you to simply submit to another home study—"

"So you can what? Observe me as I feed my son, put him to bed? Read him a story? Explain to him why his grandmother thinks I would hurt him? Diane, it's me. You know me. For pete's sake, you go to my church."

"We're not saying you'd hurt him—just that there may be neglect." She shot a look at John, her face pinched. "Especially this time of year."

"What, you think running the resort will result in my *forgetting* I have a child? If anything, Tiger is better cared for with all of us home. No. This is stupid. I'm done cooperating. Back off, Diane. And tell Nan that if she ever wants to see Tiger again, she'll have to stop accusing me of hurting my own son!" He didn't care that his voice rose, reverberated through the forest. "Get off my property!"

She stood there.

He looked toward the empty parking lot. No wonder Nan was late bringing back *his son*. He tore off his gloves, dropped them in the wheelbarrow. Stalked past her.

"Where are you going?"

Darek turned around, walking backward. "I'm going to get my son before his grandmother skips town with him."

Diane narrowed her eyes. "I'm warning you, Darek—"

"You'd better not be here when I get back."

Ivy had wasted half the afternoon staring at her computer screen, listening to Darek's words roll through her head.

I'm not going to give up on us.

Such strange, unfamiliar words, they almost didn't make sense to her. *Not give up. On us.*

She simply couldn't embrace them like this, couldn't let them settle inside. Not when she had so much to push against them.

Like the truth. Her past. Jensen. Felicity.

With you, all the roaring anger in my head goes away, and I can forget. Even move on.

She wanted to cringe when she thought about her tirade. God wasn't on her side? It was true, of course, but she'd never let that truth leak out. It sounded so . . . weak. Pitiful. Woe-is-me.

She'd learned early on in the foster system to hold in those kinds of moments. No one got anywhere with self-pity.

And she was getting nowhere with this warrant.

She saved it, reviewed it again, finished typing up the incidents of the complaint, and then printed it off.

A stack of DUI complaints from last weekend and one custody hearing still waited for review. She wanted to sink her head onto her desk.

"You picked a fine time to leave me, DJ."

He'd stopped in this morning, on his way out of town, to ask, "You got this?"

"Of course," she'd said as if she wasn't sinking under piles of complaints to review. "Have fun in Yellowstone."

"We'll be out of cell range until Tuesday. But you have this under control. And Jodi will help you."

"No problem." Ivy had actually said that and waved him off as if, indeed, sixteen cases still to review by five o'clock tonight would be no problem at all.

Except she couldn't get her mind off Darek.

She should have told him about Jensen. Should have just let the truth spill out, end things between them. But, well . . . *You matter,* he'd said, and her heart bought it. Turned her common sense off.

And when Darek held her like that, she never wanted to let go.

No, she'd done the right thing in not telling him. It seemed Darek wanted to leave it all in the past anyway, and what good was there in bringing up some remote, what's-done-is-done memory that could only rake up the grief?

She'd let it go, and Darek would never find out. After all, clearly not even Jensen knew she'd been involved in his case.

See, she didn't have to wreck anything.

Because despite her panic attack, the one that nearly had her running away, leaving before she got left . . . *I'm not going to give up on us.*

Yeah. She just might build a life here, with Darek Christiansen and his adorable son.

Ivy smiled and pulled out the next report, reading through it. A third-offense DUI. She opened a blank complaint form and began to type.

Darek had driven her home late, walked her to her door, kissed her again, holding her in those firefighter arms.

Oh, shoot. She deleted that last sentence.

For a long, crazy moment, she'd almost invited him in. By the look in his eyes, he might not have said no.

But—call her old-fashioned—she'd always wanted to wait until . . . what, marriage?

She shook the thought away. Marriage? She'd known the man for three weeks, tops.

Three amazing, breathtaking weeks—

A knock startled her right out of Darek's embrace. "Come in." Oh, she hoped she wasn't blushing.

Diane opened the door. "Do you have a minute?"

"Sure, of course. Sit down."

Diane took a chair, a folder on her lap. She wore her hair in a tight bun, and added to the business suit, she looked like one of those social workers who could decree your future and make you live with it. Ivy had never liked that type—they scared her.

But she had the power now. She folded her hands on her desk. "What can I do for you, Diane?"

"I think we have a situation we need to review." She rested her hands on the file.

"Oh?"

"Yes. It's a local. He's . . . Well, this is his third complaint. And normally I wouldn't think anything of it, but this time there's some reason to believe the child might be in danger."

A fist grabbed Ivy's insides, tightened. How she hated children at risk. "Who reported it?"

"A relative. I went to talk to the father today, and he ordered me off his property. Refused to even listen, let alone allow a home study." She opened the file. "I think we need to review it, see if there is enough for an emergency removal of the child from the home."

Emergency removal. Ivy had been on the receiving end of that, once. She could still hear her tiny voice on the phone to the 911 operator, still hear her mother cursing as the social services agent tore Ivy from her arms.

Sometimes, could still feel the fear curling through her body as they deposited her in a new home, with foreign smells and too many people, too much noise.

"I'll look at it right away."

"With the weekend upon us, we have no time to waste," Diane said. She handed over the file. "The child is currently with his grandparents, but I'm not sure how long that will be the situation. I'm suggesting we issue an emergency removal, place the child temporarily with his grandparents, issue a no-contact with the father, and then proceed with a home study and review of his case."

"Sounds about right. I'll review the case, and if it warrants it, I'll write up a report and issue an emergency removal request immediately."

"Good."

She expected Diane to get up, but the woman just sat there. As if waiting.

Hmm. Ivy took the folder, opened it.

No . . . Her breath stopped. She reached for her reading glasses, pulled them on. Tried not to let her hand shake.

"There are three complaints in total, all filed over the past two months. She also took pictures for each complaint. They're in the file."

Indeed, pictures of Tiger betrayed a rather brutal story. With the injuries on his face, he looked positively abused.

"And there are two accounts of an altercation Darek had last night." Diane pressed her hands together, reaching out to Ivy with her eyes. "Listen, we all know that it's a little tough on Darek with all that's been going on. But Nan has raised real concerns, and we at CPS take every report seriously."

Ivy wanted to throw the entire file against the wall. These were not the situations that needed intervention. No, kids sleeping in cars and in flophouses and begging on the street for food—now *there* might be a case deserving an emergency status.

Still, her head told her that, had she not known Darek and the circumstances, she might be equally concerned.

And that was the problem. She did know Darek.

Worse, as she looked up, she had the sense that Diane knew that.

Ivy took a breath and came out with the truth. "I can't fairly evaluate this report. I . . . I have personal knowledge about this situation, and I can tell you that—"

"You have personal knowledge, which means you'll have to recuse yourself from this evaluation."

"Agreed, but again, I know Darek—"

"It doesn't matter. The facts are the facts."

"But that's what I'm saying: the facts are wrong."

"You're not impartial." Diane sighed, something of compassion crossing her face. "Listen, I know Darek too. And I don't necessarily believe these allegations. But they are strong enough that we have to take a closer look. Here's the problem: if you dismiss them and Nan pushes, she can say you had prejudice against the report, refused to protect the child, and suddenly Darek's being looked at by the state, not just the county. Then Theo gets taken from his home and Nan's home, gets put in foster care in Duluth, and it becomes a nightmare for everyone."

"But I can't issue an emergency removal order if I know there isn't a reason."

"Then pass the case to someone else. How about Jodi? She'll review it and write a recommendation for you."

Which Ivy would have to obey or, again, look as if she had prejudice against the report.

"Why are you telling me this?"

"I'm not uncaring here. I've known Darek for years, and despite a few wild escapades in high school, he seems like a good father. But people change when they're under the stress Darek's been under, and we have to act in the child's best interest."

"It is not in Tiger's best interest to be taken from his father."

"You want to believe that. But it's not your decision. If we don't follow the letter of the law on this, Nan will press it. Who knows but Darek could lose custody of his child."

"Why is Nan doing this?"

Diane got up. "I probably shouldn't say this because Nan and I are friends, but the fact is, Nan is angry. She still blames Darek for stealing her daughter's heart away from the man Nan wanted her to marry."

Ivy stared at her. "Who?"

"Jensen Atwood, of course. They were dating when Darek came home and got Felicity pregnant. Nan's never forgiven him for that."

"It seems to me that Felicity made her choice." Oh, shoot, did she really say that? So much for impartial.

"Depends on who you talk to. But the minute Felicity died on that terrible night, this town took sides. And Nan is on the side against Darek. If you want to help him, you have to stand back and trust the system."

Trust the system. Sure. She became a lawyer because she *didn't* trust the system. Because she knew that it failed people. Her.

And now Darek and Tiger.

"Give the report to Jodi," Diane said. "And whatever you do, you can't tell him."

Diane closed the door behind her as Ivy sank her face into her hands.

For a long moment, she wished she'd never set foot in Deep Haven.

CHAPTER 13

Gibs wouldn't leave him alone. Jensen felt as if the old man sat in his head, digging at him, his words like a lawn mower, churning away.

For a guy who doesn't think he needs forgiveness, you're certainly trying hard to earn it.

He'd finished widening the doors of Gibs's house before the sun peeked over the far horizon and now was drinking a cup of coffee while standing on the Gibson beach. Overhead, a smoky orange haze evidenced the fires to the north, the smell of burning wood pungent in the air.

He drove the four-wheeler back to his house, then went through the gated community and tested the sprinklers, just in case. His father had installed a state-of-the-art fire-protection system throughout the acreage years ago, after the Moose Lake fire.

The system pumped water from the lake and could be rerouted to douse both the houses and the forest.

Jensen heard the phone ringing as he showered and came out to find a missed call from his father. The old man had likely gotten word of his upcoming failure and incarceration. Jensen knew his dad still had connections in this town. Probably Mitch himself, calling up to inform on him.

Before heading to Gibs's place yesterday, Jensen had cleaned cages at the animal shelter, sorted clothing at the thrift store, and tried to figure out what he could do to add hours to his time. Anything to stay out of prison, stay in Deep Haven.

And to think, a few days ago, he'd been ready to run. But that was before he'd kissed Claire. Before he remembered just why he'd wanted to stay in Deep Haven. What brought him back every year after he'd left.

Claire. Not Felicity. He knew that now.

Last night he'd dropped his measly time card off for Mitch, who added the hours to his chart and told him, "You have seventy-four left."

Seventy-four in two weeks. He could accomplish it, if he had enough places, maybe.

Now he got into his work truck—having parked the Mustang back in the garage—and headed to town.

He stopped in at the donut shop, found Lucy Brewster behind the counter and her husband, Seb, the current mayor, in the back, powdering donuts.

"I'll take a glazed raised and a skizzle," he said. "And how about a couple sugar cake donuts?"

He didn't exactly know what Gibs liked these days, but he'd once been a pushover for skizzles.

"How are you, Jensen?" Lucy asked. She was always so kind to him, even after the accident. "Can you see the fire from your place?"

"A little over the horizon, but I'm sure it's nothing."

Seb was looking at him, nodding. "I hear they're bringing in more type-two fire teams. I wish they'd call for volunteers—"

"No, it's technical work; trust me," Jensen said. "People think being a wildland firefighter is just digging, but being on a crew is much more. You have to understand fire, how to take care of yourself—"

"Were you on a crew?"

"Not long enough," Jensen said. "Thanks for the donuts."

The seagulls called after him as he climbed into his truck. The haze had filtered into town, turned the air murky as he drove to the Deep Haven Care Center. Claire had mentioned that Gibs moved to a private room earlier this week.

He owed the guy a rematch in checkers.

And okay, he wanted to ask a few questions. Like how did someone shake free of the past? Really shake free?

Jensen pulled up to the care center, parked the truck, grabbed the donuts, and went in through the double sliding doors. He glanced in a couple rooms as he walked down the hall, his heart bleeding a little at the sight of so many elderly waiting out the last years of their lives.

He was tired of waiting for tomorrow. Waiting for his sentence to be over.

He wanted to learn how to live.

He found the right room, could see Gibs in bed, talking to a man out of view. Jensen paused. Listened. Froze.

"I'd like to sell the land to you, John. I really would. But I already promised it to Jensen. He's offering a nice price, something that would help Claire go to college. Finally."

John . . . Christiansen? Oh no.

And that's when Gibs looked up. Glanced at the bag and smiled. "Donut delivery, just in time."

Funny how Gibs always made Jensen feel like he'd done something right. Except . . . well, except last time, when he'd driven him from the room.

But now Gibs perked up, gesturing him inside. Jensen didn't want to look at John Christiansen, sitting there in a chair, his legs crossed. But John didn't seem to have a problem getting up, reaching to shake his hand. "Jensen. How are you?"

Huh. "Fine."

"Keeping busy?"

"Yeah. Here and there."

"Your dad's place sure looks nice. You're doing a great job there."

"Thanks."

No malice. No hatred. John even smiled at him, nothing of accusation on his face.

"See you round, Gibs. I'll be by to check on you when you get back home." John shook his hand.

Jensen watched him go.

"Those donuts for me, son?"

He held out the bag, and Gibs smiled as he pulled out the skizzle. "You remembered."

"John Christiansen wants to buy your land?"

"Apparently my son told him he could. But I'm still entertaining your offer." He winked. "Much better."

"But, Gibs, I . . . Claire is really looking forward to you moving home, and . . ." He didn't want to give away her project, but clearly she hadn't told him. "She's made a few preparations."

"Yeah, I know. Like planning to quit her job at Pierre's."

She was?

"And putting her apartment up for lease."

How did he not know this? Was he still so mired in his own world that he hadn't listened to hers?

"But I have news for her. I wasn't able to give my son much, but if you're serious about your offer, then I am serious about taking it. It would give Claire a future, and I put in a request to move to the senior center in town. All my friends live there, and I wouldn't mind being a little closer to the VFW."

Jensen went blank. Claire would murder him if—

"I don't think I can buy your land, sir."

Gibs frowned, drew in a long breath, set down the skizzle, which had dripped sugar on his pajamas. "Then I guess I'll have to take the offer—"

"No. Don't do that." Oh, shoot. "Listen, Claire doesn't want to leave Deep Haven."

"You know, God says there is a time for mourning and a time for rejoicing. Claire's been in mourning too long over this thing in Bosnia. She needs to move on."

Move on. But—

"God expects us to keep moving forward, even when terrible things happen. I was just sitting here, reading Joshua 1. God tells Joshua, who is still mourning Moses, to go into the land, to possess it. He says that He already had the victory planned out. Every place Joshua's foot touched, He'd already given him. God has a plan for Claire, and she has to keep moving toward it."

"But what if that plan is here?"

Did he sound desperate?

"With you?"

Apparently he did. "I . . . No . . ."

"She came in yesterday, looking spunky and pretty, and I had to wonder if you had something to do with that, young man."

Funny, when Gibs said it like that, Jensen felt about sixteen. "No . . . Maybe. Yes, I've been seeing Claire. But I'm not going to stand in her way, if that's what you're thinking."

"Oh no, of course not. You're already doing that for yourself."

Huh? "Every time I visit, you start harping on me—"

"It's because I love you, Jensen. You're like a son to me. And I've sat there, watching you waste away, your mistakes eating at you for three years. It's time you stopped mourning too."

Like a son. The words nearly burned, deep inside him. He looked away. "I can't. I don't know how."

"Yeah you do. You've got to ask for forgiveness and repent."

"For something I didn't do?"

"No, for all the things you *have* done. You might not have killed Felicity intentionally, son, but you are still guilty of taking a life. And if it's not that, how about the hate in your heart for—?"

"I don't hate Deep Haven."

"I was going to say yourself."

Oh.

"You're so angry at what happened, at not being able to blame anyone, that you have nowhere to put it. So you've bottled it up and tried to tell yourself that you're innocent, but the truth is, none of us are. We're all wretched sinners, no matter what we're accused of. And whatever we've done, Satan wants to keep us there, trap us in the past. God wants to set you free to the future.

But you gotta confess that you need Him, regardless of the crimes you're guilty—or innocent—of."

Jensen closed his eyes. Drew in a breath. He did want a future, but . . . "I don't know. I've managed to mess up my life pretty badly."

"So plan A is a bust. God can make plan B better than plan A ever would have been."

Plan B. Or even plan C. As in Claire.

The old man reached out, took Jensen's hand. "That starts with letting God heal you. Learning to forgive yourself, to believe in God's love for you."

Oh, he didn't know if he could go that far. "I know I'm not a good man, Gibs. I'm pretty sure God doesn't love a guy like me."

"God doesn't love you because you may or may not be a good man, Jensen. He loves you because He chooses to. Because He wants to. But you're right: you'll never be a great man without God forgiving you and setting you free. And you're not a failure, you're not trapped in your sins, until you stop reaching out for Him."

Reaching. Yeah, he could do that.

At least, he wanted to.

"Gibs!"

No wonder Gibs wanted to stay in town. He had more visitors here than Jensen had ever seen at the cabin. Joe Michaels walked into the room dressed in jeans and a blue T-shirt with *Deep Haven Fire and Rescue* printed on the front.

"Jonah, my friend, how are you? Want a donut? Jensen brought me breakfast." Gibs held up the bag.

Joe peeked inside. Took out one of the cake donuts. "Dan's down the hall—we're doing visitation. Hey, Jensen."

"Hey." Jensen only knew Joe by his fame—an author whose

wife owned the bookstore where Claire lived. But then again, Jensen might be called famous too. Or infamous.

To his surprise, Joe turned to him. "I was going to call you. My friend Mitch told me that you might be willing to do some volunteer work. I need help fireproofing the Garden. It's a group home where my brother lives, just out of town. In case the fire turns east."

"Glad to help. What do you want me to do?"

"Can you dig a hole?"

"It seems to be one of my specialties."

If the court spent one day with Darek and his son, Ivy was sure they'd know what a terrible mistake it would be to tear them apart.

Tiger squealed, caught between Darek's legs as his father tickled him, the glow of the campfire in his delighted expression. Darek grinned, blew a raspberry into his son's neck as Tiger turned, pressed his hands to his dad's shoulders.

"Daddy!"

Daddy. Perhaps this was what Ivy loved—no, *enjoyed*—the most about Darek. The way he loved his son.

Ivy would erase that terrible file from her brain. And the fact that she'd waited until after five o'clock, after Jodi left for the day, to put it on her desk.

Tiger wasn't in danger and Jodi would figure that out, right?

"Have a s'more, Ivy." Ingrid sat down beside her, handing her a long fork and the bag of marshmallows. Across the fire pit, in the glow of the light, Amelia and Grace were laughing over pictures Amelia had taken of Tiger, viewing them on her digital camera.

"I'm so full, Mrs. Christiansen. I can't eat another bite."

"Please call me Ingrid, and I promise these just sort of sneak into the nooks and crannies, fill you right up with warmth and sweetness."

No. This family filled her with warmth and sweetness. They'd greeted her today like a sister, roping her into making punch, stirring another of Grace's potato salad concoctions, and setting the table on the deck for dinner. Tiger had come running up to her, holding a pansy picked from his grandmother's garden, and Ivy couldn't help but draw the child into her arms. And when he kissed her on the cheek, she had no words.

When Darek called and invited her over to the resort, she'd had no idea it meant she might be adopted.

Adopted.

Her throat tightened and she swallowed hard. "Do you do this every week? Have a campfire?"

"Or something." Ingrid poked a marshmallow onto the end of her fork. She wore leather mules, jeans rolled up at the ankles, a flannel vest over a Deep Haven Huskies hockey T-shirt. "I like to have the kids come home at least once a week to check in, see how they're doing. Of course, with Casper staying at the lodge for another week—"

"Maybe two, Ma," Casper said from across the fire, where he sat on a bench, appearing mesmerized by the flames. "I have to fix the bike—I'm waiting on a part."

"You didn't break my motorcycle, did you?" Darek said, now wiping Tiger's face with a napkin. He only succeeded in smearing marshmallow goo into the dirt on his face.

"*My* motorcycle," Casper said. "It cried in relief when you gave it to me."

"That Kawasaki and I have fond memories together. Like many trips out to Montana and back."

"Exactly my point. You wore it out." He picked up a stick. "It needs a new muffler, maybe a timing chain. I want to work on it a bit before I head down to the Keys."

Tiger turned in Darek's arms. "I wanna ride on the 'cycle, Daddy!"

"Daddy doesn't ride the motorcycle anymore, champ." Darek was still trying to corral Tiger's hands.

"Then I want to ride the dozer! Please!"

"The dozer?" Ivy asked.

Darek finally had his son's hands captured in front of him. He looked up. "I took out the old bulldozer to widen the logging trail around the property. Just to get rid of any extra wood fuel."

"It's because he likes to drive heavy machinery," Grace said. "Don't let him lie to you."

"Me! I'll drive the dozer!"

Darek caught Tiger's eyes. "No. It's too dangerous."

"Do you really think the fire could come this far south?" Ivy asked.

"It could," Casper said. "I was talking with Jed today. He says they are bringing in four type-two crews, two more hotshot crews, and three Beavers for transport."

"Beavers?"

"Floatplanes," Darek said. "Jed said they've got a virtual tent city set up on 153, just east of the fire. There's a couple hundred fire personnel hunkering down there. Jed's letting the pilots and some of the supervisors bunk in the cabins, but pretty much everyone's on the line now, twenty-four hours a day."

"Really? They fight through the night?"

He smiled, twirled his marshmallow in the flame. "There's something about watching a fire at night, the glow against the blackness. It's alive, and it sees you—"

"You're scaring me, Dare," Grace said.

"I guess you have to see it. But there's an eerie magnificence to fire, especially in the woods at night. The line of fire simmering in the darkness, the trees like torches. And it hums and crackles. Like I said, alive. It's almost magical."

"Except that it can kill you," Amelia said.

"And burn down your home," Ingrid added.

"But . . . it couldn't really come all the way here, to Evergreen, could it?" Ivy asked again.

Silence.

"It could come all the way to Deep Haven if it isn't stopped," John said. "Fire does what it wants if it's not contained. It can consume anything and takes no prisoners."

Ivy watched the campfire flicker, sparks dissolving into the darkness.

"But don't you worry, Ivy. Evergreen Resort knows how to survive," John said quietly. "Like the flood back in '87. And about ten years ago, three cabins were destroyed by the blowdown. Don't worry. No forest fire is going to wipe us off the map."

"Owen called, by the way," Ingrid said. "He was worried about the fire. I told him that Darek had cleaned up around the resort."

"Darek and *Casper*, sheesh," Casper said, rolling his eyes for effect.

"Darek cleaned up?" Ivy asked.

"I thought I'd widen the logging road around the property. It's just a precaution, but we have about three miles of property back into the woods and, well, it doesn't hurt to be prepared."

"Such a Boy Scout," Casper said.

Darek threw a marshmallow at him.

"Eden's working on an article about the fire, hoping to pitch it to her editor," Ingrid said.

"Poor Eden," Grace said. "It's tough to work so hard for a degree and then be relegated to the obits."

Ingrid's marshmallow was browning to a beautiful amber. "See? Our weekly campfire keeps us connected. Checking in with each other's lives. A family."

A family.

Ivy wedged her hands between her knees, wishing she'd brought a jacket.

Tiger moved over to Ingrid. "Can I have your mellow, Gran?"

Ingrid laughed. "I think you forgot to eat the last one, kiddo. It's all over your face. Let's get you cleaned up." She glanced at her husband as if hoping he'd be willing to take her fork.

"I'll take him to the house," Ivy said. She held out her hand. "C'mon, Tiger."

Indeed, he was covered in marshmallow—her hand glued to his as they made their way to the house.

"I like you," Tiger said, looking up at her. "Are you going to be my new mom?"

Oh. Uh . . .

She scrambled for words, not sure how to answer. Thankfully, the dog emerged from the deck where she'd been hiding/digging/chasing squirrels, and Tiger let go of Ivy's hand to race after her.

"C'mon, Tiger!" Ivy said as she reached the deck. "Let's get cleaned up."

"Oh, he's a boy; he'll never be clean." Ingrid came up behind her carrying the potato salad bowl and leftover hot dogs. "I think my boys spent their formative years covered in leaves, dirt, and woodchips." She winked and headed toward the house.

Tiger came running up, and Ivy held open the door for him. Ingrid was piling dishes into the dishwasher. Ivy grabbed a rag and wiped Tiger's face, his hands.

As she rinsed the rag, she saw Tiger head out the door, back to the fire pit. "I'm going to have an 'venture," he said as he went outside.

"I'm glad you came tonight, Ivy." Ingrid was still loading dishes. "You're good for Darek."

She was?

"I haven't heard him laugh like that for . . . well, for years."

Ingrid closed the dishwasher and began to fill the sink with hot water for the dishes that couldn't fit. She picked up a sponge and a cup. Ivy grabbed a dish towel.

"He changed after he married Felicity. I think he realized that just because you make one mistake doesn't mean you should make a second. But he had to make his own decisions. I think he thought we expected him to marry her, but we just wanted him to take responsibility for his action. Marriage only made things worse. He puts such pressure on himself."

She handed Ivy the cup. "That's why it's so good to see him loosen up." She met Ivy's eyes. "I'm glad you're here."

Ivy gave a little laugh. "Yeah, well, I used to be the best little scullery maid in the foster system."

A tiny frown crossed Ingrid's face. She turned back to the sink. "How long were you in the system?"

"I had fourteen homes altogether, from the time I was nine to eighteen. Thankfully, the system also helped pay for college, along with my grants, so it turned out okay." She set the cup on the counter.

"Fourteen. Wow. I thought the system tried to adopt kids into homes."

"I wasn't adoptable."

Ingrid glanced at her, frowned again.

"Oh, it's not like they didn't try. But . . . it never worked out." She took the next cup from Ingrid's hand and began to wipe it. "I realized pretty early that the foster care system is like a business. The families gave me a bed and food, and I gave them a paycheck. I was a commodity, worth a little more every year."

Ingrid stilled. Drew her hands from the water, dripping with soap. "That's not how it's supposed to be at all. You're not a commodity, Ivy. You were a little girl who needed a mom and a dad and a family. To be loved and hugged and cherished."

Ivy's eyes began to burn, and she let out a laugh, anything to loosen her breath. "No. It was fine. I was fine. It worked out just . . . fine. I didn't need any affection. It wouldn't have been real, anyway."

She looked away, blinking, put the cup on the counter.

But Ingrid didn't move. Water from her hands dripped onto the wood floor. "No, it *wasn't* fine. You should have been cared for. Loved. You should have been adopted into a family."

Ivy looked down, glanced at the open door. She should check on Tiger, see if he made it back to the fire pit okay.

Her voice sounded small as it emerged. "I did fine on my own. I learned to fit in, to not make trouble—at least until they figured out I didn't belong, and then, well, I adapted. Learned to fit in somewhere else." See, the terrible rush of heat had passed. She reached for another cup, but Ingrid caught her hand in her wet one.

"You don't have to learn to fit in here, Ivy. Just be who you are. That's enough for us. And it's enough for God. You're not a commodity to Him. You're His precious child whom He loves."

It was back, the tightness in her chest, the burn in her eyes, and now . . . Oh no, she had to look away because her face had begun to crumple. She wanted to say it—*No, God doesn't love me*—but it felt too . . . raw. Pitiful, maybe. She blinked, trying to shake it all away.

"Oh, my sweet girl. I'm so glad God brought you to us." Then Ingrid reached out and pulled Ivy close, into her flannel embrace.

And Ivy didn't know what to do. Because it just felt so . . . so . . . Aw, shoot, Ingrid had such a tight grip on her, was holding her like she really meant it, and Ivy couldn't stop it. Couldn't stop herself from tucking her head into Ingrid's shoulder, from covering her face with her hand, from letting the tiniest hiccup of sound escape.

And then she was crying. Really crying and not sure why. She just couldn't stop this terrible, ugly rush of emotions that bubbled up and out of her. She came out of herself and could hardly believe that, indeed, she was holding on to Ingrid, weeping, and becoming an awful mess right there in the kitchen.

Ingrid kept holding her. Not shushing, not becoming uncomfortable with the tragedy of Ivy's emotions, just holding her. As if Ivy belonged there after all.

So she closed her eyes and let herself feel Ingrid's embrace, breathing it in. Just breathing.

She finally hiccuped back a breath and pulled away, pressing the dish towel to her eyes. She might even have a bit of a runny nose.

"Sorry," she said, removing the towel.

Ingrid nodded, her eyes so much like Darek's—blue, compassionate. She caught Ivy's face in her hands, now dry, although a little cold and wrinkly. "No sorrys. You feel free to come and get a hug anytime. Or maybe I'll just come after you with one." She winked.

Ivy smiled, not sure what to do with that.

Ingrid turned back to the sink, running more hot water. Dumping in the hamburger serving platter.

Ivy stood there, wrung out.

"There you are." Darek came in through the sliding-glass door. He held a jar of pickles, the bag of marshmallows. "Where's Tiger? I wanted to show him the northern lights."

"The northern lights are out?" Ingrid said, grabbing a towel.

"Isn't he with you?" Ivy said at the same time.

Darek froze. Then he set down the pickles, the bag.

"I cleaned him up, and he went back out to the lake. I saw him—"

"He didn't come back," Darek said.

Ingrid set down the towel, said, "He was playing with Butterscotch. Maybe he's with her."

Darek disappeared out the door. "Tiger!"

Ivy ran after him into the yard, while Ingrid went out the front door. The air smelled thicker with smoke, but maybe that was just the campfire. In the darkness, the hover of orange flames on the far horizon seemed more ominous, as if Mordor might be just beyond the trees.

"Maybe he's at the cabin," Darek said and took off down the trail.

Casper and his sisters had come up from the fire—John also, carrying a flashlight. He handed it to Casper. "Check the other cabins."

"I'll see if he's in Butter's doghouse," Grace said.

Amelia headed toward the lodge. John went around the back. Ivy could hear Tiger's name called in the air.

How could she have lost Darek's son? So much for fitting into the family.

If she ever needed fate to be on her side . . .

Or . . . *You're not a commodity to Him. You're His precious child whom He loves.*

Okay, if God loved her—really loved her—then . . . then He'd help her think.

Think.

Once, when she was about ten, she'd wandered away from her foster home, following a labyrinth of alleyways, dreaming up the families living inside the homes.

I'm going to have an 'venture, Tiger had said.

What was an adventure for a five-year-old? A motorcycle?

Or maybe . . . the dozer.

Where had Darek said he'd left it? On the old logging road around the property? She'd seen a rutted trail across the road from the parking lot when she drove in.

In the wan light, she headed toward the lot, hoping to find John, but it was empty. Still, she spied the trail and ran toward it, feeling the ruts of freshly churned-up dirt.

"Tiger!"

She didn't want to think of what might happen if they didn't find him, if they called in search and rescue. Especially with the CPS file sitting on Jodi's desk.

Her career would be over. At least in Deep Haven. Worse, Darek might lose custody of his son.

But that all paled against the reality that in these woods . . . "Tiger!" She picked up her pace, saw the dozer in the distance, a dark hulk against the darkness.

She reached it, found her footing, and climbed up to the cab, yanking open the door. "Tiger?"

Empty. She stared into the darkness, her heart sinking, her breath catching up to her.

And then she heard the sniffles. She closed the door, climbed down. Listened.

They came from the front of the dozer, near the scoop. She moved around the side. "Tiger?"

There he sat, his hands scraped, a raw place on his skin where he'd scuffed it hard on something. She couldn't see the full extent of his injuries, but he seemed more scared than hurt.

Ivy crouched next to him. "Are you okay, bud? We were so worried."

"I fell."

"I see that." She took his hands. "We'll get you cleaned up, make it all better."

And then he launched himself into her arms. She held him there, rocking him. "It's okay, buddy; we found you."

His body was warm, his grip iron around her neck. She gripped him back just as tightly and stood, his legs going around her. Then she hiked down the trail carefully, feeling her way along the rutted surface.

She could hear the voices calling before she emerged from the trees, but she didn't want to scare Tiger. So she waited until she reached the parking lot, spied John, and called, "I found him!"

John ran over to her, Casper and his flashlight waving erratically behind him. "Where was he?"

"At the dozer. On an adventure, right, bud?" She tried to meet Tiger's eyes, but he had a pretty good hold on her.

Darek came running down the path. "You found him?"

"Ivy did," Casper said. Grace had joined them, coming from the fire pit.

In the distance, Ivy thought she heard a siren. But it could just be in her head, in her heart.

Breathe, just breathe.

Darek reached her, bent to check Tiger.

The little boy lifted his hands. "I fell!"

Darek was breathing hard, but he kept his voice calm. "Where did you go? Daddy was so worried."

Tiger leaned back in Ivy's grip. "I went on an 'venture."

"Buddy, you can't do that. You could get hurt."

Ivy had to admire how Darek kept his emotions, the ones playing across his face, out of his voice.

The siren grew louder. Ivy glanced at John. That wasn't . . .

"Ivy followed my footsteps." Tiger gave her a sloppy, wet grin.

"She did, huh?" Darek said. He looked at her with so much gratitude that she had no words. "Well, Ivy knows how to find lost little boys."

"I wasn't lost, Daddy. Next time, give me a map."

"Okay, pal," he said and pulled Tiger into his arms. He buried his face in the boy's shoulder.

Ivy pressed a hand to Darek's back. He was trembling.

And then the siren cut through the night, trumpeting into the parking lot with lights flashing.

Darek whirled around. "What . . . ?"

Amelia came bounding out of the house. "Oh, you found him!"

Butterscotch ran up, barking. Casper made a face.

John blew out a breath, shook his head. They all stood in tight silence as an officer got out of the cruiser.

Beside her, Darek sighed, a sound of defeat. "Hey, Kyle."

"Darek. We got a 911 call about a missing child."

"We got him," Amelia said. "He just wandered off—"

Ivy didn't know how it happened or why, just that suddenly

Darek's future—her future—rose up in front of her and the words rushed out. Fast.

False.

"Actually, I'm so sorry, Officer. Tiger and I were just off on an adventure, and we forgot to tell the family."

The officer, about her age, approached the group. Took a look at Tiger, who turned in his father's arms. "That true, Tiger? You have an adventure?"

Bless his heart, the little boy nodded. "Ivy and me were at the dozer!"

Kyle laughed. "Okay. Well, Amelia made it sound like it was an emergency."

"Sorry," she said. "I panicked."

"Next time I promise to tell you if Tiger and I go for a walk," Ivy said.

"And you are?" Kyle asked.

Darek touched her shoulder. "This is Ivy Madison, my girl-friend."

Girlfriend.

"Okay then. I'll call it in as a false alarm. You folks have a nice night," Kyle said.

No one moved as they watched him leave, his lights disappearing into the night.

"Girlfriend?" Casper said when he turned and glanced at Darek. "Finally." He leaned over and gave Ivy a kiss on the cheek. "Welcome to the family, Ivy League."

Family. She stood there as they headed back to the house, reveling in a feeling like marshmallows, hot and gooey, filling all her empty spaces.

CHAPTER 14

IVY WOULD SIMPLY SNEAK into her paralegal's office as soon as the janitor unlocked the courthouse, under the cover of early morning shadows, and remove the file from Jodi's desk. Certainly she hadn't looked at it yet. Not this early on a Monday morning.

And certainly she wouldn't have received any follow-up report from the Deep Haven sheriff's department about a 911 call regarding a lost child at Evergreen Resort.

The thought, however, had Ivy by the throat.

Along with the fact that she'd lied. *Lied.* To the *police.* At the time, the words rose up and slipped out, as easy as a summer breeze, natural and fresh.

Tiger and I were just off on an adventure, and we forgot to tell the family.

Now every word of that sentence felt like a land mine, and they'd begun exploding shortly after the glow of Darek's words wore off.

This is Ivy Madison, my girlfriend.

He hadn't mentioned it again after the cop pulled out of the parking lot. Darek had held Tiger long enough for him to wiggle out in protest. He reluctantly handed his son to Amelia, who took Tiger off to clean him up and tuck him into bed.

Darek drove Ivy home. In silence.

But the word *girlfriend* thundered between them.

That word had turned her hot, glued any response to her chest, made her long to look in his eyes, maybe dismiss the rumble inside that had begun to churn.

And then he'd reached across the seats and taken her hand.

He'd kissed her again on the porch, much of the evening's emotion—fear, panic, relief—in his touch, and she hung on, feeling the same thing. It helped her forget herself and her colossally stupid words long enough to stand at the door and wave good-bye.

Sort of like a girlfriend.

Only as he drove out of the driveway did the magnitude of her lie roar to life inside her head. The scenarios replaying in her brain consumed her for the remainder of the weekend. Loud enough for her to turn off her cell phone, avoid Facebook, and dive into an old John Grisham novel.

She might have gotten through two chapters.

Mostly, she just plotted what she might say should Diane appear at her office on Monday with a copy of the 911 dispatch in her hand.

Was Ivy at Darek's house this weekend? Um . . .

Yes, Deep Haven had become a microdot.

And so much for staying impartial. Ivy had taken sides,

practically set up camp on Christiansen turf the moment the lie exited her mouth.

She'd never thought she would leap so high and fast over that line of ethics.

But Darek didn't deserve to lose his son, and perhaps only she knew it. Only she knew that the right and just action would be to get the complaint dropped.

Ivy caught her reflection in the glass and grimaced as she pushed through the doors of the courthouse. She looked like she'd pulled an all-nighter at the U of M law library cramming for an exam, half-moons of worry under her eyes, her hair pulled back in a messy ponytail, wearing a pair of yoga pants and a T-shirt. But she'd just get in, take the file, and lock it in her desk drawer. Then—okay, she was a coward—she'd call in sick.

She felt sick.

Deathly ill, actually.

By the time she came in tomorrow and gave the file to Jodi, Ivy would be able to get ahold of DJ—didn't he say he'd be reachable by Tuesday? DJ knew Darek and his family. He'd remind Diane of that and deny the emergency removal.

And Darek would never know how close he'd come to losing Tiger.

Or rather, Ivy wouldn't be forced to choose between Darek and her job. Darek and Deep Haven. Darek . . . and . . .

Girlfriend.

Yes, her entire world turned complicated on that word.

The hush of the morning was broken by her flip-flops as she dashed across the floor to her inner offices.

Nancy's desk by the door was cleaned off, dark. Of course, Ivy's office door remained closed. Thankfully, so did Jodi's.

Just as she'd left it on Friday at 5:37 p.m.

She beelined for Jodi's office and knocked, just in case.

Nothing.

She eased the door open. Light streamed in through a side window across Jodi's clean desk—the calendar, the closed laptop, the black in- and out-boxes, the files . . .

Ivy stilled. The Christiansen file wasn't on top. She picked up the small stack, looked through each one.

Nothing.

Maybe she'd put it in the out-box by mistake.

No.

She stood there, her heart in her throat. Jodi must have come in over the weekend and—

"We'll get the paperwork moving as soon as Ivy signs the order for emergency removal."

Ivy froze, a bandit caught in bright lights. Diane's voice. And then Jodi's.

"I'm glad you called me."

Ivy didn't even have the sense to move behind the door or affect a casual, yes-I'm-supposed-to-be-here pose.

After all, where exactly could she run? Hide under the desk? Oh no, that wouldn't look suspicious.

So she just stood there as Jodi entered.

"I thought I closed—oh, hi."

Ivy forced a smile. Managed to look like she might belong there. In her yoga pants.

Casual day.

"Hi, Jodi. I'm glad to see you in so early. I came by to check on a file."

Diane had come in behind her. "Ivy. Great, you're here. Jodi did the research on the Christiansen case over the weekend."

"Oh . . . good."

Jodi handed her the file. "Are you looking for this one? It's the complaint you left on my desk Friday. I'm sorry I didn't get to it—I had to leave early."

Diane raised an eyebrow.

"No problem," Ivy said. She took the file. Could barely read it, her throat so thick she thought she might drop right there, asphyxiating.

Breathe.

But just as she feared, Jodi had written a sound recommendation for temporary removal of Tiger from Darek's custody. She'd even drawn up the petition for the emergency protective services order.

"And you're recommending the child be placed with his grand-parents?" Ivy said, her voice soft. Hopefully it came off solemn and not as if a cleaver sliced through her chest.

"Yes. There will be an emergency hearing in seventy-two hours to determine further action."

Ivy just stared at the complaint, listening to the roar in her ears, seeing Darek's eyes when he'd emerged from the woods and seen her with Tiger.

He might not live through this.

"All you have to do is sign it, Ivy. Jodi can notarize it, I'll fax it to Judge Magnusson's office, and they'll add it to her docket this morning."

Ivy didn't move.

"Ivy—"

"He's not in danger," Ivy said softly.

"And you know that because . . . ?" Diane asked, her voice soft despite the words. "You know you have to recuse yourself because of Darek. And because you were there this weekend when Kyle responded to the 911 call."

She closed her eyes.

"Kyle mentioned it in church yesterday. I'm sorry, honey, but this is a small town."

So small it just might strangle her.

"If you don't sign it, I'll have to bring this to someone who can—and will—in Duluth. And then Tiger might not end up with his grandparents, but in an emergency group home. Who knows what will happen after that."

"This is wrong."

"This is the system. And if Darek deserves Tiger, he'll get him back. Don't let your emotions cost you your job. Or cost Darek his son."

Girlfriend. The word lodged in Ivy's throat and cut off her breathing as she signed the petition.

Jodi notarized it and handed it to Diane. The social worker stood at the door for a moment. "Go get cleaned up. You have to represent your petition in court in an hour."

Not if Ivy left town first.

The air thickened the farther north Darek drove on Forest Route 153, like a fog descending upon the land, blotting out vision even as his headlights cut through the smoky layers. Only late afternoon and it looked like nightfall.

Just ten miles north of Evergreen Lake, the northern boreal forest resembled a war zone—and smelled it, too, the acrid, sooty air pricking his nose, stinging his eyes.

How easily the misery—and triumph—of working on the hand crews returned to him. The gritty, bone-tiring work that seemed endless as crews assaulted the forest, cutting down shaggy conifers, maple and myrtle, scouring the earth down to the mineral soil and then drip-lighting the once-towering forest, backburning to quench the assault of the fire. He effortlessly conjured the buzz of chain saws, the rattle of bulldozers chewing away the forest, the crackle of the fire, burning just beyond the edge of trees as an occasional drift of spray from the hose line drenched hot spots that jumped over the line.

It always felt like righteous work, backbreaking but honest, and seeing Jed methodically map out the fire line every morning on the lodge kitchen table stirred a military camaraderie inside Darek.

But Casper's words about additional crews had finally made him climb into his Jeep for an updated incident report. Especially since Jed had moved to the camp, leaving the cabins for the pilots and supervisors who either headed out to the airport or down to the forest service office in Deep Haven every morning.

His mother held Tiger's hand as Darek drove away, and for a moment, he'd seen Felicity, Tiger at her shoulder, watching him exactly the same way.

He'd left three messages on Ivy's phone yesterday, and frankly if she didn't call him back soon, he intended to head to town, track her down.

See if he'd scared her off with his use of the word *girlfriend*.

He let it settle into the hollow places and discovered it didn't sting. *Girlfriend*.

And maybe, someday, *mother*. *Wife*.

Okay, wait—he breathed away the tightness in his chest but let the word linger just a bit.

Wife.

Yeah, maybe.

He turned left onto a now-well-carved fire service road. Traces of recent use scarred the trail—broken tree limbs, the tread of hotbox trucks hauling equipment into base.

The road opened into a meadow the size of a couple football fields, an old pasture now turned into a small city of two- and four-man pup tents lined up in rows against the edge of the forest. A row of porta-potties on the opposite edge evidenced the nod toward sanitation, as did the makeshift showers set up with tarps and five-gallon hanging bags of water warmed only by the sun. The showers weren't meant to soothe but to scrape off a layer or two of the ash and soot embedded in a fire bum's skin after a week on the line. Real clean came only on R & R away from camp.

A lineup of grimy yellow-shirted men and women stood outside a window cut into the tractor-trailer-size mobile kitchen unit, looking miserable, exhausted, and battle worn. They carried plates of food to mobile picnic tables under a giant military-style tent that suggested a modicum of protection and relief from the blazing sun.

Darek had always preferred to eat his meals in the open air, the heat and odors of too many ripe bodies conspiring to steal his appetite.

Along the rear of the trailer were maps duct-taped to the side, next to whiteboards with weather and incident updates, all protected by a long yellow tarp, propped at lengths with poles.

Darek parked in the grass, finding a space beside a beater pickup amid the forty or so other vehicles, and climbed out, adjusting his cap. He felt a bit naked without his orange hard hat, his yellow NFS shirt. And nothing of soot on his face.

He found Jed standing with a woman wearing a bandanna tied over her long, dark hair, a pair of aviator sunglasses protecting her eyes. They were staring at a map of the area as she ran her finger along a red line drawn in wax pencil.

Darek stepped up to the map, his breath catching at how the fire had grown, how close the red line came to the edge of his family's property. He must have made a noise because Jed turned.

"Hey, Dare. Good to see you. I was hoping to stop by and thank your mom for all the cookies."

"She made more. They're in the Jeep."

"God bless her. This is Katie Whipple—we call her Whip. She's got a fire management degree, is working on one of the crews." He turned back to the map.

"So as you can see, right now the fire's only about 30 percent contained, with around ninety thousand acres gone. We hoped to steer it west, to Two Island Lake, figuring that was big enough to shut it down." He pointed to a lake eight miles northwest of Evergreen. "We've spent quite a bit of energy to cut in line on this fire service road here, connecting Pine and Two Island." Now he traced a green line about two miles from camp. "We started a back burn, managed to destroy most of the fuel to the east of this line. Unfortunately . . ." Jed took off his hat, wiped his arm across his brow. "Last night, the fire jumped the line right here."

He pointed to a narrow lip of earth between the fire line and a tiny outlet of Two Island Lake. "The crews had some torching, and with the wind whipping up, we're seeing significant growth just south of Two Island."

South of Two Island. On the way to Evergreen.

Darek studied the map, tracing the path of the fire. "There's a lot of blowdown debris still not cleaned up in there. And that's getting awfully close to a few outlying cabins, not to mention the county group home, the Garden. They might need to evacuate."

"We've alerted the Deep Haven sheriff's office of that possibility. Meanwhile, we're going to head south and see if we can't reinforce the line, maybe start another back burn, turn the fire west toward Dick Lake."

"That might work." Darek debated, then added, "But with the winds out of the northeast, if we don't turn the fire, it will continue to push south. It'll burn all the way to Evergreen Lake."

He left the rest unsaid but saw in the rise and fall of Jed's chest that he'd connected the dots.

If it skirted the lake, nothing stood between the flames and the village of Deep Haven.

Except . . . "What about reinforcing the line here, between Evergreen and Thompson Lake?" Darek pointed to the lake just beyond Evergreen to the west, little more than a droplet, but not densely populated. "There's a fire road, and if the fire turns south, we could pinch it west, toward Thompson. Eventually it would run into the Cascade River."

Jed glanced at him, frowned. "That fire road is south of your place, Darek. A back burn might take out your property."

"Not if I finish the dozer work around the property. We'll start the back burn here, just north of Evergreen, and drive the fire west, to Junco. That way, if the fire jumps the river, it will have nothing to consume. It'll starve."

"You've dozed around your property?"

"I still have a couple miles left, but I can finish that, start cutting a line here. And if I got a crew down there, we could get a line cut in maybe forty-eight hours." He picked up a green wax pencil and drew on the map. It seemed like such a tiny line of defense, but if they cut through Gibson's old cattle pasture, then widened the fire road, started a back burn, and met the fire head-on . . .

"It could work," Whip said. "But frankly, that's a lot of what-ifs to apply to our limited manpower. We already have a natural fire line here, at Junco. I say we put our manpower here, starve the fire, and push it back toward Dick Lake." She drew her own green line like a net around the fire.

"Not a bad plan if the wind is from the south, but—"

"Who are you again?" Whip asked, rounding on him. "I'm sorry, I'm not trying to be rude, but we've been working this fire for about ten days now. Unless you want to grab a hard hat and a Pulaski, you're just a civilian looking over our shoulders. Let the NFS handle this. Trust me; we've got it."

He saw Jed raise an eyebrow, maybe in warning, but the flashover came quick and hot.

"Really. So tell me, have you ever seen a peat fire? It's underground like the fires of hell and can burn for months, even years—under pavement, under houses, under vast acres of land. Even under the snow, surviving until spring, when it comes back to life. When it's that deep, it destroys tree roots and soil; the only things that will grow after a peat fire are thistles and briars. Peat is hard to ignite but nearly impossible to put out. We have about six million acres of peatland up here, in dried swamp and old, overgrown marshes. And guess what Dick Lake is?" He pointed to the map, on the south end of the lake. "A marsh. At least on this end. So if you want to turn the northern shore of Minnesota into one giant ember, ignore everything I have to say and drive the fire back that way."

She just blinked at him, her jaw taut.

Beside Darek, Jed took a deep breath. "Dare used to be one of the Jude County Hotshots, Whip."

Her mouth tightened to a thin line. "Sorry."

The apology nudged Darek a little from the crazy darkness that had risen and gripped him. Maybe she hadn't deserved all that—no, for sure she hadn't deserved all that.

In fact, just when he thought he'd licked it, maybe he had a peat fire of his own smoldering inside. He took a breath. Forced a smile. "Listen, it's not a bad idea to try to cut off the fire here. I'm just saying, for backup—"

"I've got a Beaver taking off in about thirty minutes to scout the fire and the lay of the land. Why don't you join me and Whip?" Jed said.

Behind Darek, a truck had pulled up, and a few newly outfitted warriors climbed in the back, headed out to the line.

Join them.

Or . . . or he could go home to Tiger, finish dozing. Then he and his son could motor down to Deep Haven, find Ivy, maybe head over to Licks and Stuff. Not that he didn't care about the fire, but . . .

Girlfriend. He stared at the map, the markings, Jed's grubby raccoon face, the distant glow of fire even at the apex of the day, and suddenly it vanished. The coating of regret, the simmer of frustration inside. As if someone had reached in and stirred up that peat fire, only to douse it with something fresh and clean.

Ivy. He saw her holding Tiger on Saturday night, saw her standing up to Kyle and the way she looked at Darek when he kissed her. Wide eyes, that sweet smile.

He could give her the home she'd never had, build a future with her. And they could be a family.

"No. I gotta get home." He clapped Jed on his shoulder. "You got this." He glanced at Whip. "Be safe."

She nodded. "Thanks for the input." Her face seemed to relax then, a smile at the edges. "I'll keep your idea in mind."

He returned to the Jeep and retrieved his mother's cookies, left them on the table in front of the maps. Jed waved to him, his radio out.

And then Darek was heading home, away from the fire, the clatter of the camp, the lure of the past. As he drove south, the lake fanned out before him, a glorious blue, fingers of sunlight cutting through the smoke to caress the earth.

Maybe he'd take Ivy out in a canoe to the middle of Evergreen Lake, tell her about the time he'd caught a walleye as big as his arm. Or the time he and Casper had gone bear hunting for the first time. Or when he and Jensen—

Jensen.

Yeah, maybe he'd tell her about Jensen and how, once upon a time, they'd had a friendship closer than brothers. How he did stare across the lake sometimes, at Jensen's house, just as his mother accused him of.

How, sometimes, the urge to let it all go, to forgive, seemed so big it could consume him. Yes, he'd tell her that, too. Not that Darek would forgive him, but . . . what if he did?

What if being with Ivy turned over a fresh grace inside?

He turned down his road, smiling. She could do that—help him forgive, help him start over.

He slowed as he came into the parking area, a sweetness stirring in him when he saw her Pathfinder. So she'd gotten his messages. He imagined her sitting in the kitchen with his mother, maybe trying out one of Grace's newest recipes.

But then, beside her car, he noticed . . . a cruiser?

He parked, shut off his Jeep. Climbed out. And that's when he heard them.

"You can't take him without letting him say good-bye—"

"Don't make this harder than it is—"

"Just cooperate, John, please—"

"Mr. Christiansen, I promise we'll get this figured out—"

"Wait for Darek—"

"I want my daddy!"

Darek took off in a full-out run toward the house. The voices came from around the rear, so he took the path to the deck.

They all turned as he vaulted the steps, found Tiger clinging to his grandmother's neck. Ingrid looked furious—Darek had always feared that face—and his father seemed moments away from being thrown into the back of Kyle's cruiser.

Kyle met Darek's eyes, something of regret in his own even as he held up his hand. "Calm down, Darek."

"It's going to be okay." This from Ivy, who stood slightly away, dressed in her lawyer clothes, her arms folded across herself, her face almost white.

"Daddy!" Tiger reached for him, and of course Darek pulled him into his arms.

And then he rounded on Diane, who wore her lips tightly bunched, held a file in her hands. "What's going on here?"

"The court has issued an emergency removal for Theo, Darek. I'm sorry, but he's going to have to come with us."

For a moment—an eternal, bloodletting second—his heart simply stopped. Refused to beat as he stared at Diane.

Then at Ivy.

She swallowed, her expression wretched, tears glazing her eyes. "I'm sorry," she whispered.

"I . . ." He closed his mouth, tried to get his wind back. "Over my dead body."

"Darek—" Kyle started.

"You don't have a choice," Diane said. "That's why Kyle is here. You'll be taken into custody if you don't release your son."

"What are you talking about? Why—? I don't understand." He turned to his mother, but she had a hand pressed to her mouth. His father looked at him, his jaw tight, and gave a small shake of his head.

"We know about Saturday night, about Theo getting lost in the woods."

Ivy looked away.

Darek blinked at that, not sure . . . "He wandered off."

"It doesn't matter. The court has decided that CPS needs to take a closer look at Theo's situation. There will be a hearing in seventy-two hours to discuss further action."

"Three days? And where is Tiger going to be during those three days, Diane? Please don't tell me a foster—"

"He'll stay with Nan and George."

Of course. "No."

"Please, Darek," Ivy said, coming to life now. "Trust me."

He stared at her, and everything inside him settled into one dark, glowing coal. "What's going on, Ivy? Did you know about this?"

"Don't blame her, Darek. She's just doing her job."

Doing her—? "What do you mean? Did you—did you *agree* to this?"

He reached out and yanked the file Diane held, opened it, reading over Tiger's shoulder.

He wanted to howl when he found Ivy's signature, petitioning for the emergency removal order.

"Darek—" Ivy started, but his expression must have scared her because she closed her mouth. Winced.

"I promise we'll take good care of him," Kyle said. "Tiger, would you like to see my police car?" He leaned toward Tiger, glancing at Darek. Mouthing, *I'm sorry.*

It was the only thing that kept Darek from landing his fist in the deputy's face, right there, and facing who knew what kind of charge.

Instead, he took a breath and glanced at his mother, who nodded. Oh, he couldn't do this.

But despite the clawing in his chest to just run, to take Tiger and strap him into his car seat and vanish, he forced a smile.

"Hey, buddy. Would you like to go see your grandma and grandpa for a few days?" Darek leaned back, met his son's eyes.

"No. I wanna stay with you!"

"I know, pal. But your grandma really wants to see you. And Ivy will bring you there; won't you, Ivy?"

"Yeah. Sure, bud. Maybe we can stop and get ice cream." She ran her hand down Tiger's back.

Tiger looked up, so much trust in his eyes that Darek wanted to strangle Ivy. But perhaps this was the show she put on for people. Making them believe in her, trust her, before she decimated their lives.

A true prosecutor. A manipulator.

He should have figured that out. Hadn't she told him, even warned him away? *I have a good thing going, and suddenly I wreck everything. And then it's just over.*

Yes, it certainly was.

"Go with Ivy." He kissed his son and, despite the boy's grip, managed to pry him off, put him on the ground. He gave Tiger's hand to Ivy.

She took it, smiled at Tiger. "I promise, everything is going to be just fine."

When she glanced at Darek, he took a second to narrow his eyes at her before he stepped away.

"We'll be in touch," Diane said. "C'mon, Theo." She led them off the deck.

Darek followed the troupe to the edge of the parking lot and watched as Kyle buckled his son into the cruiser, as Diane slid in beside him. He barely had the courage to lift his hand and smile as Tiger pressed his little palm to the window.

Oh, he might crumble, right here.

His father's hand rested on his shoulder.

Ivy walked to her car, opened the door. Paused. "Darek—"

"Get off my property," he said quietly, a fire under his skin. "You don't belong here."

CHAPTER 15

Ivy saw nothing as she drove back to Deep Haven.

She shouldn't have gotten involved. Why did she get involved?

She just had to keep from dissolving. Just had to pull herself together. Stay unattached.

She followed Kyle's squad car all the way to Nan's house, saw Nan standing on the porch, and felt like a traitor. Diane got out of the car, holding Tiger's hand, but the tyke broke free and ran to his grandmother.

Ivy didn't wait to listen, didn't want to hear what Diane said. Never mind her broken promise about buying Tiger ice cream. In the vast array of betrayals, that seemed minuscule.

She put the Pathfinder in drive and headed home. She'd call in sick.

Or maybe she'd just quit.

When she swiped her hand against her cheek, it came away wet. That stupid Darek, drawing her in, making her care about Tiger. About him. Making her believe that she could belong in his life.

Oh, she knew better. She'd eviscerated her one rule—*don't care. Don't get attached; stay impartial.*

But she'd make it through this. She didn't have to fall apart.

Ivy pulled into her driveway, still shaking. Still hearing Tiger crying, seeing the way he'd held on to Darek.

Yeah, she knew that feeling. She wanted to wrap her arms around Darek herself and hold on. Get him to listen to her, trust her. Tell him that he didn't have all the facts.

Make him take back his words. *You don't belong here.*

But she didn't blame him, not really.

Ivy's hand still shook as she opened her door, going inside to stand in her quiet apartment. The faucet dripped water into the sink; the refrigerator hummed as if in disapproval. Outside, the sun had unlatched from the sky and begun a slow descent, scrubbing the floor with shadow.

She had enough money in her bank account to move to Minneapolis. Or Chicago—or how about Rhode Island?—as far as she could from Deep Haven. But what good would that do?

Yes, God clearly hated her.

She closed her eyes, feeling the old rush of panic inside. The one that came every time a social worker appeared on her doorstep.

Again. It was happening again, and she was an idiot this time for letting it happen.

Ivy managed to make it to the tiny bedroom, where she lay down on the comforter, pulled her knees to herself, and held on.

Just hold on. The panic, the emptiness, would pass. She'd figure out how to get up, wash her face, keep going.

I'm glad you came tonight, Ivy. Ingrid's voice, now burning inside her. *You're good for Darek.*

Right.

I'm not going to give up on us.

She wanted to cover her ears.

She toed off her shoes. Pulled out her hair band, letting her hair fall to her shoulders. Closed her eyes. Yes, it would pass. She drew in a breath.

Leaving felt right. It wasn't like her absence would leave a hole in anyone's life. It never had before.

Boxes. She needed her boxes. Tonight, after everyone left the courthouse, she could collect her belongings, meager as they were. And by morning she'd be gone.

Vanish. Just as she had fourteen other times.

Ivy sat up, rested her hands against her stomach. Better, much better.

She caught her reflection in the mirror as she stood. Oh, boy, she appeared even more bedraggled than she had this morning. Her hair stringy around her face, her cheeks splotched, her eyes red. She turned away, unable to bear herself.

Yes, she needed boxes. And she'd write a note to Liza and tell her she could keep the rent. Leave the key on Claire's doorstep.

"Ivy?" The voice jolted her from where she stood in the middle of her bedroom, unmoving.

"Ivy, are you here? I knocked, but—"

Ivy had no words for Ingrid as she turned and met her eyes.

Ingrid looked like she'd been crying. "Oh, sweetheart," she said. "Are you okay?"

Ivy just stared at her, blinking hard, a terrible rush of heat through her body, filling her throat.

"I'm . . . I . . ." And then she felt herself crumpling. Pressing her hands over her mouth, she sank onto the bed. "I'm so sorry."

"Ivy," Ingrid said, the softness in her voice enough to unravel every last hardscrabble bit of control.

Ivy shook her head. "I'm sorry. I'm so sorry."

Ingrid's hand touched her back.

"I didn't have a choice. If I didn't sign it, it would only be worse for Darek. This way . . ." She looked up. "If there was any other way, I would have found it."

"I know." Ingrid sat on the bed and pulled Ivy to herself. "I know."

"You do?" Ivy leaned back. Met Ingrid's eyes. "But—"

"Ivy, I believe in you. I know you care for Darek—and Tiger."

"But my signature is on the petition."

"And the truth is in your eyes."

"Really?"

"Yes. Of course. I know you wouldn't intentionally hurt Darek or Tiger."

"But Darek—"

"Darek is angry. He's been angry for a long—very long—time. Mostly at himself, but he has a hard time seeing that. Sometimes it's just easier to blame others than to look inside."

"He's a good father."

"Of course he is. But he's going to be a better father once he lets go of all that anger, when he starts to rely on God. Could be that God is using this to bring Darek to his knees."

"I don't understand. Why would God let this happen to him?"

"God sees more than we do. And I don't understand the mind

of the Almighty. But I do know His heart and the fact that He longs to rescue His children, to show them how much He loves them."

Ivy looked away. "I'm not a child. I don't need God's love."

Ingrid said nothing for a moment. Then, "It's a terrible thing to believe that. We all need to believe God loves us. Otherwise, yes, we are alone."

Ivy blew out a breath, wiped her hands on her dress pants. "It doesn't matter what I believe. And it doesn't matter what the truth is. Darek is going to blame me for taking Tiger away from him, no matter what I say. People believe what they want, despite the facts. Emotions get in the way."

"Indeed."

Ivy frowned.

"Oh, Ivy, you and Darek are so much alike. You're basing your belief that God doesn't love you on emotions. On your experiences. On what you think God's love for you should look like. I felt that way once too. I lost a baby after Amelia. I'd done everything right, and I'd dedicated my life to being a mother. I was so angry at God—He didn't have the right to take my child. I thought surely He didn't love me. If He had, He would have saved my baby."

She touched Ivy's hand. "I'd forgotten, in that moment, about the other children He'd given me. But even that wasn't the bigger truth. Because of God's love for me, I would see my child someday. It was that fact—and that emotion—that finally healed me."

Ivy frowned. "I don't understand."

"Here are the simple facts. God gave us a law, and we break some aspect of it every day. We are greedy or selfish; we love ourselves more than God. The Bible says if we think we are without sin, we are lying to ourselves. The law, which we've broken, condemns us. To death, actually. But see, God, in His mercy, doesn't want that—so He offered Jesus in your place. You get to live because Christ paid your penalty. God's not impartial. If He was, He wouldn't have sent Jesus. In fact, you could say God operates almost entirely on emotion—love."

Ivy stared at her.

"God loves you, Ivy, and He has every day of your life. You might consider that He even saved your life by putting you in foster care. He hasn't given up on you, hasn't let you go, and He has brought you here, to this moment, for you to hear this truth. You have *always* belonged to Him." She leaned in, pressed a kiss to Ivy's cheek. "That truth should set you free to love, no matter what the cost."

"I don't know. Emotions get me into trouble."

"God is a God of emotion. And it's good. You don't have to be afraid of caring. Of loving my son or my grandson."

Ivy glanced at her.

"You look at him like I looked at John. Like I still look at John. As if he is my tomorrow. Where I belong."

No, she didn't . . . did she?

"I don't know what to do. I don't know how to fix this."

Ingrid squeezed her hand. "Take a chance on God. After all, He took a chance on you. I'll bet He can fix this."

Maybe God had meant for Claire to stay in Deep Haven all along. Maybe His silence had nothing to do with what she had or hadn't done with her life, and everything to do with—how had Jensen said it? *You do that, Claire. Coax things back to life.*

Those words settled inside, nourished her, and for the first time, she could believe that she hadn't just failed herself, her parents, God.

She took off her gardening gloves, setting them beside the pruning shears, and felt deep in the soil for moisture to know how long to set the sprinklers. With the heat of July upon them, the roses needed extra TLC. Replacing her gloves, she picked up her shears.

Perhaps, all this time, she'd just been waiting for a purpose. Like caring for her grandfather. And standing by Jensen.

Loving Jensen.

She smiled at that, letting the words seep through her. She'd always loved him, really, but how could she tell him that with Felicity in the way? He had a gentleness, a way of caring for others that no one else saw. And he didn't condemn her for wanting to stay, to be safe. Yes, that he understood.

She was still trying to convince herself that she hadn't dreamed the moment when he'd said her name, drawn her close. Kissed her like he'd been holding his breath for three years—maybe more—and finally was drinking in air.

But after days with no word, not even a hint that something magical had happened between them on the deck, she was trying to fight off the taste of panic. Yesterday she'd driven to her grandfather's cabin, but even by nightfall, Jensen's place remained dark. Maybe she should call him—or head up to his house and find the courage to knock on his door.

It bothered her a little, not knowing where he was.

Claire clipped off eager suckers shooting from the base of a rose, then a couple flimsy shoots that only stole life from the plant.

It wasn't like she hadn't been busy, too, with her double shifts on Saturday and Sunday, feeding the extra firefighters holed up at various resorts around town.

Certainly Jensen had an explanation. She'd simply trust him. Believe in him.

He deserved that after all this time.

She worked fertilizer into the soil before adding a fresh layer of loose mulch. Then she moved to the next plant.

"Why are you hurting the flowers?"

The voice turned her, and she found Angelica Michaels behind her. The ten-year-old wore shorts and a yellow T-shirt, her blonde hair in two braids, concern in her almond-shaped eyes.

"Hello, Angie. I'm not hurting them. I'm pruning them so they'll grow better. See, I'm cutting these tiny, thin stalks because they only make the plant weaker. And to give it big, strong flowers, I'm pinching off these little flowers. That way all the nutrients go to make this one bud strong."

Angelica's mother, Mona, came out of the wellness center. "Hello, Claire."

"Mrs. Michaels."

"I thought I'd see you at the Garden. The staff is worried they'll have to evacuate, and they're digging up a number of strawberries in order to save their different varieties. I would have thought they'd ask for your gardening expertise. Joe's been there for three days, cutting back the forest, and I think he's set up a sprinkler system to save the house."

"I had no idea the fire was that close."

Mona nodded. "I'm driving up to get Joe's brother and bring him to town. If they have to evacuate, it will stress Gabriel even more to be in a new location."

"We're going to get Uncle Gabe," Angie said.

Mona kissed her on the forehead. "That's right, honey." She turned to Claire. "Think you'll start up the reading group again in the fall? Angie loves listening to you read at the Footstep."

Claire smiled. "As a matter of fact, I think I will."

Because, yes, she'd be here. For the first time in three years, the answer, the decision, felt right. Even perfect.

She snipped one of the flowers just starting to bud and handed it to Angie. "Put this in water, and it'll open in a day or two."

Angie's eyes glowed.

"Thank you, Claire. You always make everything so beautiful." Mona took her daughter's hand and they headed down the street.

The Garden. Hadn't Grandpop said something about Jensen working there with Joe on Friday? Maybe he'd stayed over to help them fireproof the place.

See, she too easily read into things. Like Jensen's so-called affair with Felicity. She should have known he wasn't the kind of person to do that. Betray his best friend.

No. Jensen was a good man, a kind man. She'd always known that.

Claire finished fertilizing, pruning, and mulching, then set the timer on the sprinklers to come on in the cool of the day. By the time she cleaned up, the sun hung low over the horizon. To the north, smoke from the fire plumed in the sky. It did seem to be closer, but perhaps the wind only pushed the smoke toward the lake.

She changed into jeans and a T-shirt and headed to the care center. She hoped to catch Dr. Samson on his late-afternoon rounds, corner him about releasing her grandfather into her care. With the ramps done and the house cleaned, it was time for him to come home.

The geranium pots by the care center's front door needed watering, the soil caked and hard. Good thing geraniums were hardy.

Inside, Mrs. Westerlind was sitting by the window, staring out to better times. Claire crouched by her wheelchair, touched her paper-thin skin. "Good afternoon, Minnie. The flowers down at Presley Park are beautiful. I saw Timothy in the newspaper on Friday—he won the Fourth of July fishing contest. Such a handsome great-grandson you have."

Minnie blinked, slowly turned her head. Claire smiled at her. "God loves you, Minnie," she said.

Then she got up and waved to Ellery, sitting in a chair by the table. He was working on a Scrabble board, one gnarled hand arranging the pieces.

She headed down the hall to her grandfather's room. Maybe she'd find a way to volunteer here after Grandpop moved home.

Stopping by the nurses' station, she asked, "Is Dr. Samson in yet?"

The nurse made a face. "Sorry, Claire. He's gone for the day. But he already spoke to your parents, I think."

"They called?"

"Honey, they're *here*, with your grandfather."

Claire stilled. Here? Now?

Deep breath.

That didn't have to change anything. Once they saw the house, saw that she could care for her grandfather . . . Claire found a smile. "Thanks."

She took a quick, full breath and headed down the hall. *Mom, Dad. I'm so glad you made it. It's so great to see you!* She cycled the words through her head until she meant them and then opened her grandfather's door.

"It's my property. I will do what I want with it."

She stopped just over the threshold, letting the door whoosh shut behind her. What—?

"Claire bear!" Her mother, dressed in jeans, a white blouse, and a pair of dock shoes, got up from her chair and headed for Claire, arms open. Wanda Gibson didn't believe in hair dye, so there were strands of gray tucked in with her dark hair, cut into a manageable shag. The years had gained on her, but not by much, and she still had the strong grip of a trauma surgeon used to making hard decisions. She pulled her daughter into a hug. "I've missed you, sweetheart."

Claire took the chance to sink into her mother, to cherish her embrace, however fleeting this moment might be. Because she had no doubt her grandfather had just laid down the law—and he was right. It was his property, and they couldn't fly in here and yank it from him.

Her father had also risen and come over to greet her. He'd put on a couple pounds overseas, but it didn't show much on his tall frame. His hair was thickly salted, his eyes still warm—he resembled a wizened old professor rather than a missionary general practice doctor. He kissed the top of her head.

"We just got into town or we would have called," her mother said. "You look good. Have you been gardening again?" She picked up her daughter's hand, examining her fingers.

"Working the roses at Presley Park."

"Claire does many of the gardens around town, Wanda," her grandfather said. He looked at her with a smile, her partner in revolution.

"Well, that's a fine hobby," Wanda said. "I can't keep a cactus alive."

"That's okay, darling. Just stick to people." Rick Gibson pressed a kiss to his wife's cheek.

Claire knew he didn't mean it as a slight. Really.

"How are you today, Grandpop? I'm sorry I missed the doctor. Did you talk to him about going home? Did he give you the all clear?"

She'd raised something from the dead there because the room went silent. Grandpop reached for her hand.

She stared at it, his grip in hers, the way he tightened it. And . . . Oh no. She started shaking her head.

"Claire, we all know that house is getting to be too much for me. The wood heater, the plowing just to get out in the winter. Truth is, my bones are tired."

Her throat tightened. "But I could take care of all that—"

"No, darlin'. You need to stop worrying about me and start figuring out what you want to do with your life."

But . . . Grandpop was her life. And Deep Haven and Jensen—

"Besides, Jensen has offered me a tidy price. Enough to purchase a place at the senior center condos—and enough to pay for you to start college."

Jensen offered . . . "When?"

"I talked to him on Friday."

She couldn't move, couldn't breathe for the coils around her chest. Friday. After he'd kissed her. After he'd acted like maybe he'd stay. Here in Deep Haven. With her.

Her mother's hand curled over her shoulder. "It's for the best, honey. And it's so generous of your grandfather to give you this start, isn't it?"

Claire tried to smile—she did. But her eyes were clouding.

"We need to get settled at the missionary house the pastor

rented us for the rest of the summer, and then tomorrow we'll start sorting through your grandfather's things." Her mother reached over and touched his leg. "Don't you worry, Dad; we'll get you moved in before we leave."

She turned back to Claire. "And you—I think we need to start getting some applications filled out. What about St. Scholastica? Or even the University of Minnesota, Duluth?"

Her grandfather met her eyes, a hint of compassion in his. "Claire—"

"I can't believe Jensen did this. I never should have trusted him." She turned, pushed past her father.

"Claire?"

She had no words for him, for any of them. Not with her heart lodged soundly in her throat, threatening to choke her.

Claire stalked out the door, down the hall, ignored the residents in the lobby, and hit the doors, straight out into the heat of the late afternoon.

Jensen did this.

If he'd never intended for her grandfather to move home, why did he keep working?

She stood in the parking lot, in the glaring sun, realization pouring through her. Of course. To get to Grandpop. The more he wooed Claire, the easier she'd get out of his way. Long enough to convince her grandfather to sell.

Long enough to betray her.

Another deception. Another hit-and-run by Jensen Atwood. Why had she believed his words? He'd probably even lied about his affair with Felicity.

Oh, she was such a fool.

Claire climbed into her Yaris. Sat in the sweltering heat for a long moment, then started the car. The air-conditioning blasted tepid air, and sweat ran down her back as she headed toward her grandfather's cabin.

She barely braked at a stop sign, then headed up the hill, her eyes watery. Oh, God must be laughing now. She'd been blind-sided again. Knocked in the head, taken to the floor, kicked.

God *wasn't* kind, and that realization sank deep into her bones until she wanted to wail. But this time, she didn't have her grand-parents to soften the blow, to embrace her, to keep her safe.

She took Evergreen Road, turning on the north branch. Her grandfather's place was dark, of course. She climbed out, still shak-ing. Walked to the dock.

Jensen's house remained dark, not a hint of life. Just like his heart.

"I really hate you." She wasn't sure to whom she might be talking—maybe Jensen, maybe life, but the words echoed back to her.

Ignoring Jensen's new ramp, she took the side entrance, feel-ing her way into the house in the darkness. She knew where every chair, every lamp, every knickknack sat and now sank into Grandpop's chair, feeling the grooves in it.

How many times had she emerged from her room late at night to see him here, rocking. Praying. She'd climb into his lap, even at fifteen, and he'd tuck her close and pray for her, quote Bible verses over her.

"'For I know the plans I have for you,' says the Lord. 'They are plans for good and not for disaster, to give you a future and a hope.'"

Claire shook the memory away. Then she reached for one of her grandmother's knit afghans, bunching it under her head, inhaling the sweet aroma of her childhood.

She didn't care what plans God had for her. She wasn't leaving.

After days of digging into the earth, sawing down trees, and creating a fire perimeter around the Garden, Jensen wanted nothing more than to crawl home, take a shower, and sleep.

He'd call Claire first. The memory of her holding on to him, her pretty eyes in his, her smile—yeah, that had kept him going as Joe the Overseer directed him and a small crew of church volunteers during the past few days. They'd cleared twenty feet of forest around the edge of the property, and Joe had laid down hoses across the grounds, setting up sprinklers to face the lodge.

The smoke hovered like a specter, weaving through the trees, descending lower upon the property with each hour. Jensen wore a bandanna over his nose, a pair of goggles that one of the volunteers had gone to town to purchase, and now held a chain saw, wearing earplugs to soften the noise as he mowed down a tall white pine that could turn into a deadly torch should the fire light it. It could topple onto the house, the green perimeter they'd created, and burn the lodge to a crisp.

He'd slept little, the fear in the residents' eyes pressing him to keep working, and now exhaustion turned his body to ribbons of agony. But at night, he could make out the glow of fire against the sky. Growing.

He knew about the Garden, of course, the group home in the woods for adults with mental challenges. The residents earned some of their own income with an acre of strawberries they picked and sold all summer.

What he hadn't known, however, was that Gabe, Joe Michaels's brother, lived here. In his late thirties, Gabe had lived in the area for over a decade. Joe had introduced Jensen to his brother as "a friend from Deep Haven."

A friend.

He'd liked the sound of that, probably too much. But the combination of Joe's words and the memory of Claire in his arms conspired to make Jensen believe it.

The saw bit through the tree trunk, nearly to the other side. He backed it out, then shut it off, leaning hard against the cut tree.

At first, it didn't want to budge. But he picked up a sledge and gave it a good whack. The tree shivered. Another blow and he heard a sharp crack. Then the tree began to list. He pushed against the trunk, just to give it encouragement, and the pine began to fall, faster as it headed toward the ground. Branches caught in the arms of the forest, ripping other trees as the momentum lashed them until the pine landed with a terrible shudder.

Jensen pulled off his hard hat and dragged an arm across his forehead. Sweat slicked off onto his shirt—long-sleeved and covered in dirt and woodchips. He picked up the saw and tromped back to the perimeter of the property where he'd left his shovel. He'd dug a five-foot swath, as Joe instructed, but it seemed an inadequate defense to stop the onslaught of fire that cracked and shot off flares in the distance.

Jensen was downing the tepid, nearly hot water in his canteen when Joe came up. He looked as exhausted and grimy as Jensen, dirt caught in his three days of beard growth, his jeans dirty and ripped. Jensen recognized Pastor Dan, aka the fire chief, trudging up behind Joe, carrying a map.

"'Sup?"

"We got a call from the NFS. They're worried the fire is headed this way. They're recommending we evacuate."

"We've got the sprinkler system ready to go," Joe said. "And Ruby, the house manager, has the residents packing some belongings."

"Where are they going?"

"Don't know yet," Dan said. "We have calls going around the church prayer line. We'll find homes for them."

Joe coughed. "I don't know, Dan. We had a fire here about ten years ago. We had to ship the residents to group homes around the state until we rebuilt. It was hard on all of them. My brother nearly came unglued." He shook his head. "Mona is coming to get him, but the fact is, all of them need stability. Something familiar. It would be best if they stayed together."

"There are twenty residents, Joe. The hotels are full, and they can't live in the church—"

"How about my house?" Jensen said. The idea formed as quickly as it tumbled out. "I've got a big place—five bedrooms— and we could haul in more mattresses. I know the thrift shop has a few in the back room—and blankets and pillows too. There's plenty of room and they could all be together."

A slow smile creased Joe's face. "That's a great idea. Thanks."

"I'll set the sprinklers to go while you load up the residents."

Joe nodded, and he and Dan headed toward the house.

Jensen picked up his tools, jogged to his truck, piled them in. He hollered at a couple of the other volunteers to add to the pile, just in case they needed to do any more work around his place.

But his house came equipped with state-of-the-art sprinklers, a trimmed boundary that he meticulously maintained in accordance with the NFS, and besides, it was south of Evergreen Lake.

Yes, the residents would be safe there.

Seemed like a better use for the house—a sanctuary rather than a hiding place.

Jensen ran to the Garden house, found a spigot, and turned it on full. Water began to spray the house and the grass to the perimeter of the property. He ran through the spray, relishing the cool water, and turned on the next line of sprinklers at the spigot behind the house.

In the strawberry gardens, the automatic sprinkler system rose from the ground. Joe had repositioned the heads so that they now sprayed to the farthest edges, creating a rim of water.

By the time Jensen reached the final spigot, the residents had packed themselves into the volunteers' trucks, vans, and SUVs.

Jensen climbed into his truck, Joe sliding in beside him. He backed out, headed south. Smoke drifted across the road like fingers against the beam of his headlights.

"Thanks for doing this, Jensen," Joe said.

"I'm glad to help." More than glad, really.

"Well, I know this town hasn't exactly been kind to you over the past three years."

Jensen glanced at him, an eerie tightness in his chest. During the days at the Garden, he'd been able to forget, at least briefly, his pariah status in Deep Haven, working in camaraderie with volunteers from the community church. But now . . .

"The truth is, I didn't know what to think. I was on the EMS team that responded that night, and I saw you weeping over Felicity. Felt like an accident to me."

Jensen stared straight ahead, his hands tight on the steering wheel.

"I have to give you props for staying here."

"I didn't have much choice." He didn't mean for that to emerge with such a sharp edge.

"No, but I've watched you. People like you. You're kind, and you do the work."

"People don't like me, Joe. They tolerate me, at best."

Joe made a funny noise, one that sounded like disagreement. Jensen glanced at him.

"Gibs doesn't tolerate you. He thinks the world of you."

"That's because I saved his life."

"I think you should stop right there and take a look at your words. You saved his *life*."

"Okay, not his life, but—"

"I'm not arguing with you. I'm trying to help you see the truth. You're not the pariah you see yourself as."

"You don't understand, Joe. The town wants me to apologize. And I can't."

"Why not?"

Jensen looked at him. "Because . . . I'm not guilty?"

"Can't you apologize and admit sorrow? That if you could, you'd change everything?"

Jensen turned onto Evergreen Road, not glancing at the resort. Darek's resort.

Last time he'd been there, he'd been helping Felicity put together a plastic play set for Tiger. He'd swung the boy in the air, met him at the bottom of the slide. He'd sat at a picnic table facing the lake and listened to Felicity cry about her failing marriage.

He'd held her in his arms, brushing back her hair. And deep inside, he'd relished the fact that Darek had failed. The great and mighty Darek Christiansen had blown it.

But . . . he'd also stood beside his friend at his wedding. Pledged to help him be a good husband.

He shook his head.

"You wouldn't change it?" Joe said.

"I would. Of course I would. But how can I fix it now? Frankly, if I were Darek, I'd hate me too." The words settled over him, and he breathed them in. Yes, Darek probably had a reason to hate him, to blame him, and not just because he'd killed Felicity, but because—well, how would he feel if another man had been comforting his wife, listening to his wife, becoming his wife's best friend?

Yes, he owed Darek an apology for that.

"Maybe Darek doesn't hate you. Maybe he's caught too—an apology, an admittance of sorrow, might allow him to forgive."

"Darek isn't going to forgive me. Ever. Even if I ask."

Joe was quiet as they turned along the south side of the lake. The caravan behind them bumped along, lights scraping the forest.

"He might surprise you," Joe said finally. "I spent ten years of my life hating my father for walking out on my family, for abandoning me, for abandoning Gabe. I hated him and believed I had a right to. The problem was, I was hanging on so hard to that belief that I nearly missed everything God had for me. I nearly left Deep Haven for good, without Mona, without Gabe—nearly missed having the life I have now. Because I clung to the worthless idol of my right to be angry. You're doing the same thing—clinging to your innocence."

They pulled into Jensen's gated neighborhood, and he rolled down his window to key in the code.

"My given name, by the way, is Jonah."

"I know. I've read your books." The gate opened.

"I've always been struck by the words Jonah prays in the belly of the whale, as he's slowly being digested. 'Those who cling to worthless idols turn away from God's love for them.' I was clinging to the idol of my self-righteousness. But my very anger convicted me, just as my father's abandonment did him. I had to forgive—and ask for his forgiveness—to finally find what I was looking for."

"Which was?"

"My life here."

Jensen pulled into the driveway. Sat for a long moment, looking in the mirror at the lights from the other vehicles arriving behind him.

He wanted a life here. With Claire. With these people.

Even if he didn't get clemency—and he knew that was a long shot. So long, in fact, that he'd practically dismissed it. But maybe, if Claire would stick with him through his prison stint, he could return here, to her. Figure out how to build a new life, not as a lawyer, but as a free man. He was pretty handy; maybe he could hang out his carpenter's shingle.

Joe was right. Holding on to his anger, his innocence, had kept him from embracing what he had, right here. Claire. A life. Maybe even a future. Maybe it was time to let go and trust God for what He had, come what may.

If Gibs was right, that started with repentance. But Jensen had no idea how to go about saying he was sorry. Or even where to start.

He got out and opened the garage door. "C'mon, everyone. My home is yours."

The moon overhead felt like an eye, watching him, too bright as Darek scraped out the forest near the north end of Evergreen Resort. Sometimes watery with the fog of smoke, other times bright, the eye was an X-ray, lighting him up—bones and tissue and heart. Examining. Judging.

Accusing.

And the clank of the dozer walking down the forest couldn't douse his father's words, lodged there in his head.

Don't let this consume you, Darek.

How his father could read his mind, Darek didn't know, but as he stood there in the middle of his quiet house, seeing Tiger's unmade bed, his nest of stuffed animals, the rush of fury had nearly done just that.

Consumed him.

It wasn't just the fury, but the cold grip of panic, the hole in his chest that could turn him inside out.

What if he lost Tiger?

He'd been standing there, trying to sort out the terrible noise in his head, when his father walked in quietly.

"I know you're angry, and you have a right to be. But you have a choice. You can keep burning, keep letting this smolder inside, or you can forgive."

Forgive.

"This isn't about forgiveness," Darek said. "This is about betrayal."

He'd gone straight for his closet then, found his goggles and old hard hat, tied a bandanna around his face. In fact, he'd nearly put on his entire old uniform—gloves, the Nomex shirt, a pair of sturdy hiking boots. Then he'd headed out to the property line and climbed aboard the dozer, letting the noise shut out Tiger's cries.

Evergreen Resort was all he had left.

And working to save it would keep him from climbing into his Jeep, driving to Nan's, and stealing his son back.

Stealing. Yeah, that's what they'd call it, despite the fact CPS had done exactly that.

He tightened his grip on the controls, his bones loose from the rumble of the dozer. Dirt and grime layered his skin; sweat trickled down his back. The headlights cut through the shaggy overhang of forest across the fire road. He estimated maybe another half mile he needed to cut, hours and hours of work. Deeper into the back of the property, the tangle of forest slowed his progress, and he'd taken more time to cut a wider swath, digging down to the mineral soil, the unburnable dirt that might hold back the line of fire.

Let Deep Haven burn. He'd protect the resort with everything he had in him.

Darek pushed over a tall blue spruce, watching it wave its arms as it fell. He crushed it onto the forest floor, backed up, went after a beautiful birch.

You don't belong here.

He let those words fuel him.

He'd save his property, get Tiger back, and never, never bring another woman into his life. Their lives.

Darek uprooted a stand of saplings, spindly little poplar offshoots, digging deep and turning over the ground beneath them, exposing their roots, then burying them under the debris of the land.

Oh, he'd been a fool to trust her. Ivy turned out to be just as manipulative as Felicity. And a betrayer, like Jensen.

Jensen. His father brought him up too as he'd stood at the door, watching Darek assemble his gear.

"You've been letting anger consume you since the day Felicity died. You stopped going to church, walked away from God, and you've let it burn away the foundation of who you are, the man you could be."

That hurt, but Darek had ignored him, grabbing a container of water.

His father didn't move from his place in the doorway, blocking Darek's exit. "God says that whoever hates his brother is in the darkness and walks in the darkness. He does not know where he is going because the darkness has blinded him. Don't let your unforgiveness keep you in the darkness, Son. Let God help you forgive. It's the only way you're going to get through this. In fact, forgiveness is not optional."

Darek had rounded on him then. "Are you kidding me? Forgive Jensen? If it wasn't for him, Tiger would be safe at home with his mother. And let's not even talk about Ivy."

"Have you ever stopped to think that, despite the accident, God healed? Even used it for good?"

He hadn't answered, just pushed past his father.

Good? Hardly.

Darek didn't let his father's words take root until he climbed into the darkness of the cab, turned on the dozer, and muscled it through the woods.

If Felicity were still alive, he wouldn't have his son—he knew that. Because at the end, his marriage was headed toward divorce, fast. And the moment he untangled himself from Felicity, he would have hit the road without so much as a backward glance.

No, Felicity's death could never be good, but it had woken Darek up to his son. To what he could lose—what he'd lost.

He blinked back the burn in his eyes.

What he'd lost. His father was back in his head then, following him just as he had earlier when he stepped off the deck. "You think you're the only one to lose a son? The only one who has ever had to forgive someone for killing someone he loves?"

Darek had glanced back at him, frowned.

"Has it occurred to you that God did exactly that for you? You, Darek, were His enemy. Your sin killed His Son. And yet He reached out to forgive you, if you wanted it. Even though you didn't know how to ask. Even when you didn't *want* to ask."

Yeah, but that was different. Darek wasn't God.

He'd told his father that too.

"You don't have to be. Forgiveness starts with you on your knees, taking a good look inside. I know it's hard. You're afraid of what you'll find. But God isn't going to stay away from you, Darek, when you need Him. And I promise, Jesus can help you do the impossible."

His parents' faith always started with "on your knees." Well, they didn't know what it felt like to have everything ripped from them. They didn't know what it felt like to have someone you loved betray—

No. He didn't love Ivy. He couldn't love Ivy, not so soon. . . .

And yet he didn't know how else to describe it, the feeling of wholeness, of . . . well, maybe he might call it love, but . . .

Whatever he felt, it told him the truth. He'd never loved Felicity.

Darek pushed a bundle of debris into the forest, that reality burrowing deep.

Yes, if he were honest with himself, he'd only given in to her because . . .

Because Jensen was with her.

Because Darek wanted to win.

Darek closed his eyes, breathing in hard. Regardless of how Felicity felt, he'd betrayed Jensen. And then he betrayed Felicity by sleeping with her, using her. And then marrying her, knowing he had no intention of truly meaning his *I do*.

He let the dozer idle there, shaking, rumbling, the truth touching his bones.

He'd been blaming Jensen because it felt easier than looking at himself. Seeing his own sins.

Oh, Felicity. For a moment, he let her walk into his mind. Saw her smile at him. The times when she'd sat behind him, massaging his tired shoulders, or called his cell phone just to hear his voice. The times she'd put Tiger on the line, prompting a *da-da* from his tiny son.

Felicity, waiting for him to come home that first year, decorating their tiny cabin, nearly setting the place on fire cooking his favorite meal.

Yeah, he should have loved her. Maybe if he hadn't been so angry . . . angry not only at Felicity but at himself. He'd betrayed himself, the man he'd wanted to be.

His conversation with his mother the night Tiger fell from the bunk nearly a month ago rushed back at him.

Is there forgiveness for someone who kills another man's wife?

I hope so, for your sake.

Maybe she had been talking not only about Jensen but about Darek as well.

Unforgiveness had destroyed his life—or at least his marriage. Unforgiveness had worn a hole of anger nearly clear through him.

Maybe he was a little like the peat fires, his life turning to ash under the surface.

In fact, forgiveness is not optional. His father's words clung to him like a burr. But maybe it wasn't. Not if he wanted to heal. Not if he wanted to learn how to live—really live—again.

Not optional.

Not optional for Felicity. For Jensen.

For himself.

He stared out into the night, the eerie glow of fire against the darkness, setting the sky aflame.

For Ivy.

Please, Darek. . . . Trust me. Ivy's voice. Small. Pleading.

If he were honest with himself, maybe he'd have done the same thing in Nan's shoes. In Ivy's. Taken a closer look to make sure Tiger was safe.

He didn't know what had happened, but maybe . . . maybe he should at least stop to listen. To hear the truth.

Yes, if he hoped to start again, let God seed something new in his life, he'd have to let Him turn over the burning soil, lay Darek bare.

Confess. Repent.

"I'm sorry." It felt weak, even untrue, so he shut off the motor. Let the dozer die. Listened to the wind through the mesh of the cab.

"I'm sorry." He stared up at the eye, dusty against the night. "I . . . I'm so sorry. I . . . Oh, God, I blew it. I really . . ." He closed his eyes. It still felt so . . . trite.

On your knees.

He heard his father again, and for some crazy reason, it seemed right.

So he climbed off the dozer. Walked around to the front, where the moonlight glinted off the scoop. And there, in a puddle of reflected light, he knelt.

The earth was soft beneath his knees, the smell of it raw and honest. He pressed his hands into it, bowed his head. "I'm sorry. I'm so sorry."

And suddenly the heat, always simmering so deep inside that

he'd barely noticed it anymore, rushed out of him, pouring out in the wake of his words. It shook him with its power, the freshness that swept in behind it, like a dousing of more than water. Of life, maybe. He made a sound like a whimper. Like a child, afraid.

Or maybe relieved.

Yes, oh yes. Relieved.

He lifted his gaze, found the eye. "I never mean to hurt Felicity, Lord. But she was right. I was selfish—am selfish. I've hated Jensen, and I . . . I hated Felicity. Or at least I didn't love her as I should have. I didn't cherish her. . . . I betrayed her, Lord."

He sat back on the earth, tugged the handkerchief from his face. Drew off his goggles. The smoke bit his eyes, making them water. "Please forgive me," he whispered.

The wind shifted in the trees. He drew his hand through the dirt, picked it up, let it fall through his fingers. "I want to be a better man, Lord. I want to forgive. Please, show me how."

Show me how.

Darek wasn't sure how long he sat there, just listening to the wind gathering in the trees, trying to hear something—anything.

He laid a hand against his chest. The hole, the dark raging inside—it had vanished. Instead, there was just a scar of some old ache. An imprint of sorrow. But for the first time, it seemed, he could think. He saw Felicity holding Tiger on the sofa. Saw Jensen standing beside him at his wedding. Saw Claire smiling at him from beside Felicity, her gaze landing on Jensen.

Yes, maybe those two were meant to be together.

And he saw Ivy. Sweet Ivy. Holding Tiger on her lap. Rescuing Darek from himself at the art show and standing up for him in front of Kyle.

Ivy, holding on to him, molding herself to him. Belonging to him.

She hadn't turned on him. That thought took root.

Whatever happened, she'd been trying to protect him.

Trust Me.

He heard the words, but they weren't Ivy's.

The smoke had scoured the eye from above, but it was still there. Even if he couldn't see it. It would always be there. Even if he lost Tiger, the resort . . . Ivy.

The thought of her swept in and filled the raw, still-healing places. Warm. Perfect.

Thank You. Thank You for Evergreen. For my family. My son. My faith . . .

Thank You for Ivy.

Tomorrow he'd find her. Listen to her. Tomorrow they'd figure out how to get Tiger back. And then, maybe . . . maybe he'd figure out how to tell Ivy that he loved her.

Yes, loved.

Darek smiled at that, something goofy he was glad no one could see. He got up and was circling back around the dozer when he saw a light jag across the road, quick, as if someone was running.

"Hello?"

"Darek!"

"Over here!"

Casper came into view. "You got a call from Jed. He says the wind's turned. The fire is headed away from Junco Creek."

"That's good, right?"

"Dude—it's headed right for Evergreen Lake, and it's coming fast."

CHAPTER 16

YOU WANT TO LOOSEN the roots, not break them.

Perhaps it was her grandmother's scent in the afghan or the leather softness of the recliner, the embedded history in the paneled walls of the cabin or the taste of her past—stories and laughter and the sense of home—that dredged up the memory. But Claire settled right into the dream, almost feeling the touch of black soil between her fingers, her grandmother beside her, handing her impatiens to repot.

They stood at a picnic table around the back of the house, the lake bright and inviting as it lapped the shore, round planters filled with potting soil ready for the flowers her grandmother had purchased from the nursery in town.

"They're all nice and snug in their baby planters, so we have to replant them without shocking them." Grandma ran her fingers into the roots, lightly loosening them. Then, with her other hand, she held open the hole she'd created in the soil and gently set the flowers in.

Beside her, Claire did the same, digging her fingers into the roots, scraping them loose, then settling the spray of buds into the planter. She worked the soil around in it.

"Not too tight, but enough to make it feel snug. You want the roots to spread out into the new soil, take hold." Her grandmother rested her hands over Claire's, her touch strong, exactly the right pressure.

"Now we water." She handed Claire the watering can and Claire sprinkled the pots.

"Oh, more than that, honey. They need a good, long drink. They're thirsty after their trip from the nursery. A good gardener always keeps her plants well watered."

Thirsty indeed. Claire didn't know when she'd transitioned from the dream to reality, but she lay there in the darkness, the wan fingers of moonlight pressing in through the cabin curtains, across the tweed, plaid-patterned sofa, then across the floor to the recliner. Her grandmother's voice faded with the dream.

Claire sat up and realized she'd fallen asleep in the recliner. In high school, how many times had she come home to see her grandfather asleep here, her grandmother on the sofa, knitting, waiting up for her?

She'd been thirsty after moving to Deep Haven from Bosnia. Thirsty for friends. Thirsty for safety. Thirsty to know that she could heal—that she *would* heal.

Claire got up, went to the bathroom. Her face felt sticky, puffy. She hadn't remembered crying herself to sleep, but maybe. She didn't have to turn on the light to know the layout of the room, the picture of her parents on the counter, the embroidered wall hanging of the John 15 verse—*"Yes, I am the vine; you are the branches. Those who remain in me, and I in them, will produce much fruit. For apart from me you can do nothing."*

She washed her hands, then made her way to her bedroom. Even once she moved into town after graduation, she'd spent many nights here, relishing her grandmother's cooking, then nursing her in the days before she passed.

Claire lay on her quilt, the anger from the evening before now a distant echo inside. The spray of the lilac towering outside her window traced a shadow on the ceiling. The smell of smoke saturated the air—a faraway campfire, maybe.

She could almost hear Felicity's laughter as she tucked in beside Claire on the double bed, whispering what-ifs about Darek. Felicity had loved the eldest Christiansen boy for so long, sometimes Claire wondered if Felicity became her friend just so she could get closer to him. But in those early days, Claire didn't ask questions.

And then Jensen showed up in her life.

She could still see him, standing on her dock in his cutoffs, his shirt flapping in the wind, grinning at her.

How many times after Darek left and Felicity fell asleep by the campfire did Claire and Jensen wind down the night hours talking, their hands propping them up as they stared at the stars?

She'd loved Jensen since that first summer, maybe.

You do that. . . . Coax things back to life.

No, Jensen had coaxed her back to life. Jensen and her grandparents and even Felicity and Darek.

In fact, *God* had coaxed her back to life. With this place. With this life.

Maybe God *was* kind. Because in the aftermath of her devastation,

He'd wrapped her in this safe place. With these safe people. And for ten years, she'd remained. Healed. Grown stronger.

Her words to Angie Michaels filtered back to her.

I'm not hurting them. I'm pruning them so they'll grow better.

Maybe God had used these years to prune her, to heal her so she could bear fruit. She wasn't a disappointment or a failure. She simply needed time to bloom.

She remembered what she'd told Jensen: *I would love to open a nursery in town, maybe do private landscaping.* Maybe Jensen hadn't betrayed her. What if he'd helped set her free?

It didn't mean that she could trust him, but perhaps she didn't have to hate him. Three years of hating Jensen had eaten her alive.

She just had to let him go.

Because she was staying in Deep Haven. And maybe selling the house was for the best. She'd needed this place, but God had healed her. Strengthened her. And now He was giving her the chance to create something new—she could open her own nursery with the money her grandfather gave her. Turn the gardens of Deep Haven lush and beautiful.

Quietly coax things back to life.

Remain in Me and produce much fruit.

That command didn't say *leave.* It said *stay.* And if God wasn't sending her anywhere, then she didn't have to go, right?

Claire rolled over, pulling the quilt over her. Maybe first she'd stay *here* a little longer, scouring up the courage to tell her parents.

"There's only one answer, Darek."

His father stood over the kitchen table, looking at the map

Casper had rolled out, tracing the line of fire as relayed to Casper by Jed, still at the fire camp. He pointed to a pasture west of the Gibson place. "There's a natural fire break here, but if the fire runs west of Evergreen Lake, what's to keep it from turning south?" He looked at Darek, raised an eyebrow. "There's no other choice."

"Dad, if I don't finish cutting this line around our property—"

"And let's say you do. Then what? By the time you start working on the other line, the fire might be too large. You won't be able to set a back burn in time. The fire will overrun the line and not stop until it hits Lake Superior. You need to start now and cut in to Thompson Lake. Then you and all the fire crews can concentrate on burning everything north, starving the fire before it gets to Deep Haven."

"And Evergreen Resort?"

His mother stood in her bathrobe, her arms folded over her chest, her mouth a tight line.

His dad glanced at her, back to Darek. "We trust the Lord for His protection. I've heard you mention at least once that the best thing for Evergreen Resort would be to set a torch to the old cabins and rebuild."

"I wasn't serious, Dad."

"We might not have a choice. But the truth is, we can't hold on to something so hard that it destroys everything else we love. Like our town. We have to trust the Lord to save us, Son, even if it means that He has to burn away the old."

Darek stepped away from the table. He was probably littering dirt along his mother's wooden floor. He stared out at the lake, the dawn spreading across it like flames. "Okay. I'm going to head over to the pasture behind Gibs's place, start cutting in a line." He turned. "Casper, you get on the horn to Jed, tell him to send a crew down to the line. We'll need to set a back burn as soon as I have the fire line built."

He waited for some smart remark like "Roger that, Captain," but Casper only nodded.

"Mom, you pack up and get out of here. I don't know how fast this fire is coming, but you and Gracie and Amelia need to leave."

"I'm not leaving without your father," Ingrid said.

"Casper and I are going to wet down the house, Ingrid. And I don't want you anywhere near danger."

"Thank God Tiger isn't here," Ingrid said. She glanced at Darek. "I'm sorry, Son, but I'm just glad he's safe."

He hadn't exactly seen it like that, but maybe right now he could be thankful his son, so prone to getting underfoot, lost, or hurt, was safely asleep at his grandmother's house.

Small glimpses of grace, perhaps. But after that moment in the dirt, when the burn inside him had finally, truly died, Darek intended to hold on to glimpses of grace.

"I'm taking this walkie," Darek said. "Keep me posted. Stay safe."

He took off down the road, back to the dozer left by the fire road where the property line crossed the Gibson place. He'd take the dozer down the road, then cut in behind the Gibsons' and start by laying a line across the pasture. Then he'd tackle the forest.

He could use some help. Like someone with a chain saw. Someone who knew how to work with him. Someone who had fire training.

Someone like Jensen.

He climbed aboard the dozer, fired it up.

He'd nearly killed his best friend that summer when Jensen abandoned Darek in Montana. Not abandoned, but . . . Yeah, abandoned. Just like Jensen had abandoned Darek when he moved to Minneapolis—even if he hadn't had a choice.

Jensen had missed all those moments Darek shared with others. Like days upon days of backbreaking, honest work, hiking into the mountains to mop up a fire, watching it burn itself out, embers glowing in the darkness. He'd missed seeing the aurora borealis while sleeping under the stars in Washington State, swimming in a glacial lake in Montana.

Jensen's friendship felt closer than his brothers', and yet . . .

Yes, Darek missed him. Maybe if he hadn't been so angry about Jensen leaving—so selfish—he wouldn't have so easily wooed Felicity into his arms. Wouldn't have taken silent pleasure in winning her heart away from Jensen.

He owed Jensen an apology. But they were so far beyond that now, he hadn't a clue how to fix it.

Dawn turned the field to shadow and fire, and as he came into it, the smoke cleared long enough for him to see the low red ball on the horizon, spilling out to melt away the darkness.

He lowered the scoop and began to plow the earth, furrowing it down to bare soil.

Please, let this be enough to push back the fire.

The truth would set her free to love.

Ingrid's words fueled Ivy as she stood on Nan's doorstep, balancing two coffees, breathing out the last of her sanity.

Talk about a breach of ethics.

But Ivy had been up all night, pacing through her decision, and she couldn't live with herself if she didn't try.

God's not impartial. . . . God operates almost entirely on emotion—love.

It had taken her a trip down to the beach, where the waves combed the shore under the moonlight, to scroll through her life and discover that, yes, God might have shown up a little. Like rescuing her from her mother. And giving her a warm bed, even if not a family. Putting Daniel in her life to believe in her, and then . . . and then Darek. Tiger. Ingrid and the entire Christiansen family.

Maybe it was time to give Him a chance.

She'd let that truth sink into her heart, let herself believe.

God had loved her enough to give her a family, and she wasn't going to lose them if she could help it.

So she'd written the best brief of her life to DJ, outlining her actions and, most importantly, her eyewitness perspective on the events in Tiger's life that accounted for his injuries. She'd explained Darek's actions without prejudice, added in her firsthand experience with Nan, and finally summed up her opinion.

Yes, her opinion. But that, too, was what the law was about. A judge was supposed to be impartial, but a lawyer was supposed to be on the side of truth.

She had forgotten that, a little. An admission she put into her resignation letter. Because she couldn't be a prosecutor and a defender. And she was about to leap so far over the line of ethics that it wouldn't matter anyway.

But ethics and truth had parted ways somewhere in the night. And she had to live in truth. Had to live in love.

She'd left the letter attached to the brief with a note to DJ saying that he could accept if he wanted to. Or not.

She was hoping for *not*. But until she knew his decision, she was free to stand at Nan's front door and plead Darek's case.

So she knocked.

Please, God . . . She'd begun the conversation last night at the lake and continued it now. *Please, God, let this go well. Please be on my side.*

The door shuddered.

No, be on Tiger's side.

Yes, that felt right.

The door opened and Nan appeared, looking down at her, frowning.

"Hi, Nan. I was hoping we could have a conversation." Ivy held up a coffee.

Nan stared at it.

"Please? I think—"

"If you're here to defend Darek, I'm not interested."

Ho-kay. She kept her smile, the litigator's face that refused to be rattled. "Actually I wanted to tell you a story."

Finally . . . "Fine." Nan looked behind her, then stepped out onto the porch, accepting the coffee cup. "But Tiger's going to wake up any minute."

"I know. And I don't want him to be afraid or disoriented either. Believe me, I know what that feels like." She blew out a breath. "See, I lived in fourteen different foster homes from the time I was nine years old. I remember every single morning I woke up in a new house—the fear, the strangeness. The hope that this family might want me. Might think I was worth keeping. That this might be the last time I woke up in a new, strange home."

"Tiger isn't in a strange home."

"I know. And I'm thankful for that because as a child, there is nothing worse than having the hover of social services in your life.

I never knew if one day I'd come home and discover them waiting for me. Or coming into school. Or meeting me off the bus."

"If we had custody of Tiger—"

"Seriously, Nan. Have you seen Darek with Tiger? Because you can bet he will never leave this alone. You might somehow get legal custody of Tiger, but I can guarantee that Darek will be in his life. He adores his son. He lives for his son. And I'm so sorry that I can't be impartial, but the truth is, maybe I'm here to help you understand exactly what you do to Tiger every time you fight with Darek or file a complaint or yank him out of his father's home."

"Darek doesn't deserve Tiger."

"Tiger is his son, and he doesn't deserve to have his son taken from him. Just like you didn't deserve to have your daughter taken from you."

Nan drew in a quick breath. "She never would have been on that road if Darek hadn't fought with her."

"He knows that, Nan. Believe me, he knows that. But that still doesn't make it his fault. It was just a horrible, terrible accident."

Nan tightened her lips.

"Here's the truth," Ivy said. "If you keep going with this, you're going to shatter Tiger's fragile foundation. You're going to start a fight between you and Darek and the Christiansens, and the only casualty will be Tiger. Is that what Felicity would want?"

Nan closed her eyes, said nothing.

Ivy softened her tone. "But that's not what I came to say." She slid down onto one of Nan's patio chairs. Set her cup of coffee on the table. "In one of the many homes I lived in there was another foster child about my age. Difference was, she had parents—two of them. They were both fighting over her, and her father had abducted her, taken her across state lines. The mother went a little crazy and attacked him, landing herself in a psychiatric hospital. So when they finally found Corrie, they put her in a home to sort it all out. I'll never forget that night—she was in the twin bed opposite me, weeping. I was so jealous of her—angry that she had two parents who both wanted her—and I wasn't very nice. I might have told her to shut up. But she just kept crying, so finally I asked her what was wrong. She told me that her father hadn't really wanted her, but he couldn't bear her mother getting her."

Nan had turned away from her and was staring at the lake, only her tight profile visible for Ivy to read.

"I know you love Tiger, Nan. Of course you do. But do you want to raise Tiger, or do you just not want Darek to have him? Do you want to punish Darek or bless Tiger?"

"I think you should leave."

Ivy sighed. This hadn't gone at all how she'd hoped. Unless . . . "I love him too, Nan."

Nan looked over her shoulder. "Darek?"

"And Tiger. I see a wounded boy who needs a mom—"

"He had a mom."

"Yes, he did. But he doesn't anymore." She expected the flinch across Nan's face but braced herself for it. "And you can't be it. You're the grandma, and that is a wonderful thing. But it will never be a mom. Please, let Tiger have a family."

"You?"

"Maybe. Or someone else someday. Let Darek start over. Let him be the husband he should have been to Felicity."

Nan sighed.

The day was still a tin-like gray, smoke thick in the air, nothing of the sunrise rescuing the shadows.

"He didn't love her like he should have," Nan said quietly. "She adored him."

Ivy nodded.

"I'm just so angry all the time. It's like a vise around my chest. It keeps me from thinking straight. I need to blame someone. Anyone." She met Ivy's eyes. "I want to blame Darek."

"But the more you blame, the more your anger burns, the more it keeps you from seeing the blessings you still have. You have to stop blaming and forgive. Forgive Darek and Felicity and Jensen." She took a breath. "Forgive me."

Forgive me. She let the words hang there.

Nan frowned at her. "Why?"

Ivy swallowed. "Because I'm the one who arranged the plea agreement for Jensen."

"I don't understand," Nan said, sinking into the opposite chair.

"It's a long story, but I was the one who recommended Jensen be given the community service hours in exchange for a guilty plea."

Nan just stared at her.

"You should know that while I feel great sadness for your loss, Jensen might have been exonerated if he went to trial. I'm not sure he was really guilty of negligence."

Nan looked away. "Me either."

"What?"

"I knew Jensen—of course, we all did. He was a great kid, straight A's, a good athlete. I felt terrible for him when his parents split. I actually wanted Felicity to marry him . . . but . . . she loved Darek, and, well, she would do anything to get him. Including get pregnant." She reached up, wiped her cheek. "I was so angry with her for her behavior, but she was so . . . so happy to marry Darek. And then Tiger came along and I thought everything would be fine . . ." She ran her thumb along the lid of her coffee cup. "I probably should give Darek a little more credit for all he's been through."

"Darek made his choices. But he's trying, Nan. Really, if you could see him with Tiger, you'd know that the child is . . . active. And Darek is doing all he can to help his son grow up safe and healthy."

Nan nodded. "Last night Tiger climbed on the table and leaped onto George's back as he came in the door."

Ivy chuckled.

Nan took a sip of her coffee. Cradled it in her hands. Overhead, the smoke had shifted some, just a hint of rose gold in the sky. "Okay. I'll call Diane at a more decent hour and talk to her."

Okay? Ivy hadn't realized she'd been holding her breath. "Thank you, Nan. I promise everything will be just fine."

Funny how suddenly that line felt true.

Nan nodded. "He's lucky to have you."

"Tiger?"

"Darek."

Ivy shook her head. "Well, he's pretty angry at me right now. I'm not sure—"

"Are you the assistant county attorney or not?" Nan smiled, something kind in her eyes. "For cryin' in the sink, go win your case."

When he woke up, Jensen smelled bacon, and from the kitchen he could hear the sounds of pots banging. It suggested the sense of family—or at least guests in his home.

He'd fallen asleep on the sofa, dressed in a pair of loose but clean jeans and a gray T-shirt. His mouth tasted of last night's pizza as he rose and headed for the bathroom. He brushed his teeth, washed his face, and tried to look presentable, unable to remember the last time he had guests. It had been so long that he'd forgotten, really, what it felt like to have people connected to his life.

Ruby, the Garden house manager, was in the kitchen, an apron tied around her waist, flipping pancakes. "Hello, young man. I hope I didn't wake you."

He poured himself a cup of coffee, shaking his head. "I'm usually up early."

"Grab yourself some pancakes because when the residents wake up, there'll be nothing left."

He helped himself to a plateful, poured on syrup, and took it out to the deck to eat. In the early morning, the smoke lay heavy over the lake and the air smelled charred. In the distance, he thought he could see the peaks of flames, but it might only be the sunlight fighting through the fog.

He finished his coffee, trying to make out Gibs's house.

Claire hadn't been at Pierre's Pizza last night when he'd made his run into town to pick up mattresses from the thrift store and the pizzas Joe ordered. He'd hoped to see her pretty face working the counter or in the kitchen. But apparently she'd gotten off earlier that afternoon.

He wanted to see her. Tell her that he couldn't stop thinking about her, that he wanted to figure out a way to stay, and if she'd wait for him to finish his jail time, he'd be back. They could build a life here.

He brought his plate inside and put it in the dishwasher. "I'm headed to town. Do you need anything?"

"You're so sweet, Jensen. No thank you," Ruby said.

He couldn't remember the last time someone called him sweet.

In town, he stopped by the donut place first, then knocked on Claire's door. It might be too early, but after five days, it seemed terribly overdue.

No answer. So he knocked again. Tried the door handle. It opened. "Claire?" He didn't want to frighten her, so he made some noise. "Are you here?"

He walked through her apartment, found her room empty, her bed made.

Maybe she was at the care center.

He headed there next. Left a donut for the nurse at the front desk, then tiptoed up to Gibs's room.

Gibs lay in his bed, the television on, watching a morning news show. "Jensen!"

Jensen walked in and handed him a skizzle.

"And here I thought I was going to be all skin and bones in this place. You going to keep this up when I move into the senior center?"

"What are you talking about, old man? You're moving home. Claire's got it all fixed up." He went to the window, opened the blinds. Even here in Deep Haven, the light seemed wan, blocked by the smoke to the north.

"Didn't Claire tell you? I've decided to accept your offer to buy the place."

Jensen froze. "What?"

"I told you last week. The answer is yes. I'll move into the senior center, and Claire can have enough money to go to college—"

"She doesn't want to go to college!" Jensen's voice emerged harsher than he intended. He took a breath. Schooled his tone. "Mr. Gibson, Claire is perfectly happy staying here in Deep Haven."

"Says who?"

The question came from a man who could only be Richard Gibson—a younger version of Gibs, with darker hair, less paunch, more fight in his eyes. Richard Gibson. Jensen had been absent, fighting fires with Darek, the last time Claire's parents had visited, but he remembered her father from photos.

Wanda Gibson followed her husband in, holding a quilted casserole carrier.

Jensen found his words. "Uh, says Claire. She doesn't want to move. She likes it here—"

"Have we met?" This from Wanda, who put down the carrier and extended her hand.

"Jensen Atwood. I live next door to Gibs." Okay, that sounded lame. But *I'm your daughter's boyfriend* wasn't right either. "Claire and I are friends." Yes. Better.

"Jensen, I am sure you mean well, but Claire has been stuck here for too many years already. She needs to move on with her life. Go to college, find a career."

"Get married?"

"Yes, of course. Start a family. Figure out where her place of service for the Lord is."

"What if it is here, in Deep Haven?"

Richard laughed.

Jensen didn't. "If you ask your daughter, she would say that she wants to stay. But more than that, Claire belongs here. She . . . she takes care of the rose garden—"

"I am sure they can find another gardener."

"And she plays in a band—"

"The Blue Monkeys. We know." Wanda looked at her husband, gave him a tight smile.

"And she—"

"Works at Pierre's Pizza. We're her *parents*. We know all about what Claire has been doing. And we know what is best for her."

Jensen couldn't help the flood of words, the rush of anger, despite his efforts to tamp it into civility. "With all due respect, no, you don't. If you knew what was best for her, you would have come home ten years ago when she needed to be safe. When she needed to leave Bosnia. You wouldn't have sent her here alone—"

"She had her grandparents—"

"She needed you."

"Listen here—"

"No, *you* listen. Claire is amazing. She's beautiful and kind and everyone here loves her. She does more than make pizza. She reads to the kids at the Footstep of Heaven bookstore, and she volunteers to serve meals at the senior center once a month, knows all the residents' names. And she goes up to Gibs's house every single day to make sure he hasn't burned his dinner."

Richard Gibson glanced at his father.

"She has spent the past week renovating the house so he can move home—"

"No one asked her to do that."

"No one has asked her *anything*. That's the problem. You just assumed, and because she so desperately wants to impress you, because she doesn't want to be a disappointment, she doesn't argue. But she does not want to leave Deep Haven."

Richard blew out a breath. "How long have you been in love with my daughter, Jensen?"

The question pushed him back, sucked out his wind just a little. *I'm not . . . But . . . well . . .*

Yes. He was in love with Claire. Had been for years, probably since that night on the beach when she'd told him her story. When he'd wanted to be as brave as she'd been.

"A while," he said quietly.

"You think she wants to stay here with you?" Richard said.

Jensen tightened his lips. Then nodded. "I hope so."

"Son, I hate to tell you this," Wanda said, "but if I remember correctly, she mentioned you when she left here yesterday."

She did?

"She said something along the lines of 'I can't believe Jensen did this. I never should have trusted him.'"

He opened his mouth. Closed it. Looked at Gibs.

The old man gave him a sad nod. "She's pretty angry. But she'll come around—"

"I'm not buying your land, Gibs. I told you that once, and here's something you should know about me: I don't lie."

Jensen walked out of the room, tossing the bag with the remaining donut in the trash can as he left. He'd lost his appetite anyway, with Claire's words churning in his stomach. *I never should have trusted him.*

Jensen broke into a jog as he headed toward his truck. If he hadn't already searched her apartment, he would have gone back, but instead he drove to the rose garden, then the cemetery. No lime-green Yaris, no red bike.

She wouldn't have gone to Gibs's place, would she? He hadn't seen a light on, not last night, not this morning. Still, he headed back up the hill.

He couldn't bear to let her reactions sluice into his head, to think about how angry—how betrayed—she would've felt at hearing her grandfather's news. *I'm selling the place to Jensen.*

No wonder she didn't believe she could trust him.

I'm sorry, Claire. The thought came so easily, so perfectly. *I'm sorry.* Not the kind of sorrow that admitted guilt, but the kind that admitted pain.

I'm so sorry.

Easy enough words, and they should have been spoken to Darek, to the town of Deep Haven. *I'm so sorry for the pain I caused.*

He keyed in his number at the gate and parked behind the Garden van. Hitting the garage opener, Jensen headed to the four-wheeler and hopped on, glad he always left the keys in the ignition. He zoomed out of the garage intending to check on the sprinkler system.

The sound of a motor, something big and rumbling in the air, turned him toward Gibs's place.

The path was bumpy, just like when he'd taken it the night Gibs fell. He ducked under tree limbs, over ruts, vowing to clear it better. Because he hoped to be making plenty of trips next door when he and Claire ironed this out.

Oh, God, please let us iron this out.

Jensen came out into a clearing west of the house and nearly skidded the four-wheeler as he careened into a bulldozed swath of earth. He stopped, sat with the machine idling, tracing the path all the way to—

Darek sat on his dozer, clearing a path into the forest, on the fire road to Thompson Lake. A tree cracked, fell hard, and he ground it up, pushing a debris pile into the forest.

Jensen debated, then turned the four-wheeler toward Darek.

He pulled up just as Darek backed out of the forest. When he waved his arms, Darek cut the motor, took out his earplugs. His face was nearly blackened with dirt, his eyes red. He tugged the handkerchief from over his nose.

"Wow, am I glad to see you," Darek said over the puttering sigh of the dozer.

Jensen stared at him. "What?"

"We gotta clear a fire line and set a back burn or we won't be able to stop this fire."

Jensen looked at the dozer, at Darek, who was looking back at him as if they'd had a conversation yesterday, something akin to *Hey, wanna go fishing after dinner?*

And then Darek offered a smile.

The effect of it pulled the breath from Jensen, knocked him over inside. He swallowed, scrambling for his emotional footing. Then he managed to nod. "What do you need?"

"Saws. Shovels. People." He paused, looked toward the horizon. Even from here, Jensen could make out the flames. Darek turned back to him. "I need you, Jens. Get me some manpower and then come out here and help me kill this fire."

"You got it," Jensen said.

CHAPTER 17

Ivy HADN'T REALIZED how much larger, how much closer the
fire had grown until she topped the hill above town. From Deep
Haven, the flames seemed little more than a glow on the distant
horizon. However, now only a few miles from Evergreen Lake, she
could make out raging tongues that torched trees like the flames
of some mythical dragon scorching the land. The entire sky had
turned orange for as far as she could see, and smoke billowed out
and pitched the heavens with ash. Occasional plumes of fire suggested the blaze might only be gaining speed.

Ivy felt her pulse in her throat as she pushed the gas toward
Evergreen Resort. Certainly Darek and his family knew that they
might be in danger?

Maybe the specter of the fire would temper her early morning appearance and catch Darek off guard. He'd let her explain, hear her out. Realize that in the face of no good choice, she'd done the best thing she could for him.

Okay, for herself, too. Until last night, she'd wanted to save her job *and* her future with Darek.

Now—well, she turned onto their road, not caring if she had a job to go back to.

She pulled in fast and nearly ran over Ingrid, carrying a laundry basket full of photo albums to the open rear hatch of her Caravan.

Ivy got out, rushed over. "What's going on?"

Looking a decade older than yesterday, Ingrid set down the basket and crushed Ivy to her chest. "I'm so glad to see you." She held on a little longer and then let her go. "We have to evacuate."

Amelia came out carrying a suitcase. She'd clearly been crying, her face streaked, and looked like she'd only just rolled out of bed, wearing sweatpants and a T-shirt, her hair messy. She glanced at Ivy with a frown as she threw her bag in the back.

"Hi, Amelia. I . . . I came to apologize for what happened—"

"Ivy!" Grace ran toward them, rolling her bag, and threw her arm around Ivy's neck. "What are you doing here?" She let go and added her bag in the back end.

"I came to talk to Darek. But—can I help?"

"We have more pictures in boxes in the family room," Ingrid said. "And a few more suitcases."

Ivy headed to the house. She spied John coming around the side, dragging a long hose. Casper was setting up sprinkler heads, pounding them in with a rubber mallet.

"They're going to set up a water perimeter, see if that will help," Grace said.

Amelia stormed past her.

"Ignore her," Grace said. "I think she's more angry at herself for calling 911 than at you."

"Calling 911 was the right thing to do," Ivy said as she followed Grace in. Four large boxes held the family photos, pilfered from the walls. She grabbed a box.

"Can you imagine if Tiger were here right now?" Grace said over her shoulder on the way back outside. "I have to wonder at how God works things out." She shoved the box into the Caravan.

Ivy added hers. "I hadn't thought of that."

Grace smiled. "See? It's all a matter of perspective."

Someday Ivy hoped to be like Grace. Seeing life through God's eyes. "I hope Darek agrees with you."

"He's not here. He's over at Gibs's place trying to cut in a fire line."

They headed back to the house, standing aside for Ingrid, who was toting a box of books.

"Why? Some little strip of dirt isn't going to stop that fire."

Grace handed her a stack of homemade quilts sitting on the granite countertop. "He'll cut a boundary line in the dirt and then set the area behind it on fire so that it burns up all the fuel. That way, when the main blaze hits the parched area, it has nothing to consume and it starves."

"But isn't that dangerous? What if the fire turns on him, jumps over the boundary line?" She pushed the quilts in on top of the boxes in the car.

"That's what the hotshots do—they dig and dig, then burn and stop any little fire from crossing the line. It's called a back burn."

Or craziness. "They could get killed."

Grace gave her a grim nod. "Darek knows what he's doing. And he's worked with the volunteer fire department, so they know too. But yeah, we need to pray for them."

She loved how Grace's go-to was prayer. Ivy would have to start thinking that way too.

"I think that's about it," Ingrid said. She stood in the middle of her family room, the walls bare, looking out to the lake. It glimmered bronze. She shook her head. "Please, God, save our home."

Grace put a hand on her mother's shoulder.

Water hit the sliding-glass doors as John and Casper began spraying the house.

"Amelia—c'mon!"

"Mom! I'm not done packing!" Amelia's voice came from upstairs, nearly frantic.

"I'll get her," Grace said.

Ingrid walked to the bathroom, opened the door, and hooked Butterscotch by the collar. "Sorry, honey, but I couldn't have you running away."

Ivy walked to the sliding doors, peering out toward Jensen's place. He'd have a breathtaking view of the fire, safe on the other side of the lake.

"Ivy, are you coming?"

She nodded, followed the three women outside. "Did anyone get things from Darek's house?"

Amelia looked at Grace. "No."

"Believe me, Tiger's going to need a few things. I know how it feels to have nothing. I'll be right behind you."

Ivy took off down the path toward Darek's A-frame cabin, sweat dribbling down her face. Through the trees, she could make out a distant orange glow.

Flinging open the door, she ran inside to Tiger's room. Looked around. Saw a stuffed tiger, worn and wadded next to his pillow. She grabbed that and a picture of Felicity by his bedside and ran back out.

A glint of color to her left, from the cabin on the shore, caught her eye.

Claire's Yaris?

Ivy glanced down the trail. Ingrid's van had already pulled out.

Someone had to warn Claire. She ran down to the shoreline and spotted a trail. "Claire!"

But no one emerged from the house. She looked back but couldn't see John or Casper. Behind her, the entire forest seemed to glow.

Shoot. Ivy took off along the trail, around the end of the lake toward the cabin.

"Claire!"

She heard her name as if through a fog, something sweaty and dark, and she tore through layers of sleep to open her eyes.

Claire blinked against the brightness inside her room. The ceiling fan whirred—she didn't remember turning that on, but it lifted the tiny hairs on her arms and cooled the sweat on her brow.

She couldn't remember the last time she slept so well, so hard. So at peace.

"Claire!"

The frantic voice seemed familiar but she couldn't place it. "In here," she mumbled.

She got up, pushed aside the quilt, and nearly screamed when Ivy appeared at her bedroom door, sweating, breathing hard.

"What are you doing here?"

"Claire, the fire—everyone is evacuating."

Huh?

Ivy grabbed her by the wrist. "We gotta go."

"No—what are you talking about?" Claire yanked her arm away. "Why are you here?"

"I was at Darek's place and I saw your car. The Christiansens have packed up and are leaving. The fire is coming toward the lake."

"You're overreacting—"

"Am I?" Ivy strode to the back door, the one facing the lake. "Tell me I'm overreacting." She opened the door.

When Claire shuffled to the entrance, her breath faded from her chest. To the north, the entire horizon seemed lit by a blaze, with spikes and waves of flames crowning trees, spires reaching for the sky.

"We gotta go. Now."

"Let me get my things."

"There's no time!"

"There *is* time!" She picked up her grandmother's afghan, swiped a picture of the couple off the end table. "I have books and photo albums—"

"You have to leave them behind, Claire. You have to let them go."

"No. They're my life—"

"No, they're not. It's all just stuff. You're a big girl—I promise; you can live without it."

Live without it. Yes, she could.

Claire grabbed her keys as Ivy took hold of her hand and dragged her through the house, toward the front door.

Smoke layered the air, so thick that Claire bent over, coughing. Her eyes stung, but she felt her way to the car, opened the door.

Ivy swung into the passenger seat. "Drive!"

Claire nodded and turned the engine over. The fire reflected in her rearview mirror as she backed up and pulled onto the road.

The woods to her right had turned to flame, the trees furred with fire, the ground a hot glow. Thankfully, the road looked clear—

She heard the crack just as Ivy grabbed her arm. From the forest, a giant, flaming white pine toppled across the road, its bushy arms blazing, the crown of the tree exploding. Ivy screamed and Claire braked before they plowed into the inferno.

Flames skittered around her car, igniting the woods on the lakeside.

"Back up! Back to the house!"

Ivy seemed to have no problem ordering her around, but Claire wasn't arguing. She put the car in reverse, then whipped around and gunned the Yaris forward, through the war zone. Flames loomed up and around them, grabbing at the car. The clearing smoked over.

"I think we're trapped!"

"Just keep driving!"

Claire broke free of the forest, a ball of hades behind her.

Ivy had her hands braced on the roof. "Is there any other way out of here?"

"There's a trail up by the pasture to Pine Acres—"

"Let's go."

She floored it up the dirt trail toward the pasture, the air now swirling with embers.

And that's when she saw it—a plume of fire over the pasture, growing, a mushroom cloud of flame.

"The pasture's on fire!" Claire said. "We're trapped!"

She sent the car into reverse again, turned around on two wheels, back into the forest.

Another tree fell, this one cutting off their access to the house.

Claire tasted the old panic, rising up, choking off her breathing, her thoughts. She couldn't move.

Except, no. She wasn't staying put. Not this time. "We have to get out!" she yelled. "C'mon!"

But Ivy wasn't moving. She shook her head, her eyes wide, suddenly frozen. It was only then that Claire noticed her clutching a tiny, worn stuffed tiger.

"C'mon, Ivy. You can do this." She grabbed Ivy's hand. "We have to go—now."

"Sheesh, Jens, did you call the entire county?"

Darek held a shovel, wore a five-gallon jug of water on his back, stomping out creepers that threatened to jump the fire line and ignite the grasses of the pasture.

Beside him, Jensen had changed into fire-retardant clothing, a pair of sturdy boots, a red helmet, and goggles, a bandanna pulled up over his nose. He was choking off a handful of sparks, his spade grinding them into the dirt. "I called Marnie in dispatch, and yes, she called the county EMS. You said help, right?"

"It's a regular convention out here." Three local fire departments had shown up, as well as the Jude County Hotshots, who'd arrived shortly after Jensen hauled off in his four-wheeler. They'd taken the road to Evergreen just ahead of the blaze and tried to reinforce the road between Gibs's place and the pasture.

Hopefully any fire would stop before it destroyed the Gibson homestead.

Darek didn't even want to think about the cabins at Evergreen Resort.

Jensen had also returned with three more dozers, compliments of local septic and landscaping contractors. They'd unloaded the machines and tripled their efforts, crawling all the way to Thompson Lake as if they were out for a stroll.

Teams along the line lit the back blaze with their drip torches, chewing up the fuel for the conflagration headed their way.

Now the fire plumed in front of them, burning away at the lush forest, cinders falling like ticker tape from the sky. Air tankers dropped orange slurry, hoping to slow the fire as it advanced. They just had to keep their blaze from rushing back across the swath of dirt until it met the main front of the fire head-on.

While the dozers cut line, Jensen had taken his sprinkler system and rerouted part of it from Pine Acres, dragging hose through the woods until it reached the pasture. He had water shooting full out into the pasture, wetting it down, the pump back at Pine Acres dredging water from the lake.

Overhead, the sky had turned black, ash dripping like snow.

Jensen caught another hot spot, stamping on it. Down the line, Darek saw a crew of Jed's team sawing down a tree burning midway to the top.

"Dare, look out!"

A snag, one of the dangers of deadfall—dead trees still standing—had lit on fire and now came toppling from the heavens over the fire line, into the green.

Jensen grabbed his arm, yanked him away as the oak crashed, sparks flying. One of the hotshots turned his hose on it while another attacked it with the saw.

"Thanks," Darek said.

He saw Jensen smile even through the bandanna.

Yeah, this felt good to him, too.

"We should head over to Gibs's place, see if we can't get the hoses out, wet the roof down."

Jensen nodded.

They started off in a jog down the road.

The fire had plumed as they fought the winds. Darek saw it torching trees near the lake and picked up speed. "Uh-oh, it looks like it jumped the line—"

They rounded the edge of the pasture and cut into the forest toward the homestead. He could feel the heat, see embers swirling in the supercharged air. Ahead of him, in the middle of the road, a car burned, flames licking out of the windows, the acrid odor of burning plastic saturating the air.

"We gotta get back to the line—it's too late to save Gibs's house!"

Jensen didn't stop.

Darek reached out to grab his arm but Jensen broke away, turned on him. "That's Claire's car!"

Claire.

Jensen whirled back around, then cut off the road through the forest toward Gibs's place, still ahead of the fire. Darek followed him, his boots running over smoldering pine needles ready to ignite. Smoke choked his vision, his lungs.

Jensen wasn't slowing, instead hitting away branches with his shovel, shouting Claire's name.

They emerged at the front of the house. The fire had already ringed the edge of the yard, spitting hot spots into the grass, edging toward the house. They rounded the far end of the house, into the backyard, and found the fire there, too, rushing out like a wave toward the beach.

"Claire!"

"Over here!"

Darek turned. Froze.

No.

Ivy stood with Claire in the doorway of the house, at the apex of a ramp, clutching what looked like Tiger's stuffed animal.

Jensen ran to the ramp. "C'mon!" He held out his hand and Claire took it. But Ivy stayed glued in the house, shaking her head.

Darek ran up the ramp. "Ivy, we gotta run!"

She just stared at him, her eyes wide, breathing hard.

"Ivy!"

"No. I can't—"

"Ivy. I'm right here. I'm *right here*. You're going to be just fine. Take my hand."

Around them, more trees torched, another crashing across the yard, spitting embers.

"No—" She clutched the tiger, shaking.

"Please, Ivy. Trust me."

She looked at his hand, back to him, her green eyes locked on his. Then she reached out her hand.

He got a good grip on her. "Stay with me and don't stop running." Then he pulled out the hose attached to his water backpack. They ran down the ramp, following Jensen, who had the same idea, dousing a path to the lake.

Around them, sparks lit the ground like a minefield. The flames reflected in the lake, dropping cinders onto the water's surface.

Another log fell, this time hissing at their feet, and Darek doused it, steam rising in protest. He leaped the log and Ivy followed him, their feet hitting the sand.

Jensen was already in the water, pushing Claire out past the shore. Darek had once taken shelter in a lake during a firestorm that had sucked the oxygen right out of the air and seared the lungs of those above the surface.

"Run for the water!" he said and pushed Ivy ahead, veering toward the canoe on shore. He grabbed the end, started to drag it.

And then Jensen was right there on the other end. He lifted it and chased Darek down to the water, dropping the canoe in. Water seeped into his pants, cool against his hot skin as he splashed deeper.

"Turn it over!" Darek said, but Jensen already had his hands on the gunwale, the keel, still reading his mind. Together they flipped the canoe and dragged it out into the water. The girls were bobbing away from shore, treading water.

Darek held his end up over his head. "C'mere, Ivy. Get under it!" His backpack of water began to float and he shucked it off as she swam to him. He caught her to himself, pulled her shaking body against him. She still held the now-soggy tiger. "Let it go, Ivy, and hold on to me."

She obeyed. He pulled the canoe down over them, seeing Jensen do the same. Claire had ahold of the stern thwart, managing for herself as the murky shadows trapped them inside.

Outside their aluminum covering, the forest fire howled, raging itself to a frenzy.

Jensen was kicking them farther out into the lake. Probably to keep away from any trees landing on them, crushing them in the water.

Smart.

Darek hung on to the bow thwart with both hands, the lake bottom disappearing beneath his feet. Ivy was small against him, trembling, and as they drifted farther from shore, all he could think was to press his lips against her forehead, any remaining anger, the touch of her betrayal, gone. "What are you doing here?" he whispered in the darkness.

"I . . . I came to say I'm sorry," she said softly, her mouth against his throat. "I came to tell you that I talked to Nan, and I convinced her that Tiger needed to be with you."

She did? He couldn't see her, but he longed to search her eyes. "When did you do this?"

"This morning. After I resigned."

"You *resigned*?"

"Yes. I don't know what else to do. I love it here—I really do. And a big part of me wants to stay, but I care too much, Darek. About this town and about you. And I will always run into these sticky, horrible situations as assistant county attorney."

But that's not what hit him, not what tightened his chest. "Are you leaving?" He didn't wait for an answer, just let the words emerge as they should—desperate and raw. "Don't leave, Ivy. Please. I . . . I'm in love with you. I want to be with you."

She stilled and it was probably better that he'd said it in the darkness, but oh, how he wanted to see her eyes. See if she could forgive him, too. "I'm so sorry for what I said. You do belong here. With Tiger. And . . . and with me, if you'll have me. I know I really blew it, but I promise to be more patient, to listen and forgive and to make things right—"

She kissed him. Watery and trembling, her arm went around his neck and her lips found his. Kissing him like, yes, she'd forgiven him.

Yes, she belonged here, with him.

Darek wrapped his arm around her waist, leaning into her touch. Tasting the lake on her lips, her wet hair clinging to his face. *Ivy.*

"What are you two doing over there?"

"Shh, Claire. Leave my best friend alone."

Best friend. Jensen relished the words just a moment before he leaned close to Claire, finding her ear, whispering in the darkness. "I love you too, you know. I've always loved you, Claire, even when I was stupid."

"Stupid?"

"When I was chasing Felicity. I knew she loved Darek, and I was a jerk. Especially since the best day of my life was the day I met you."

Jensen had just about died seeing her Yaris in flames, had another heart attack at the sight of her trapped in the house. But it would finish him off if he had to wait one more day to tell her the truth. "I know your grandfather told you that I offered to buy the land—and it's true; I did. But you have to know that I also rescinded the offer. I am not taking your land—"

"It's not my land," Claire said. She'd turned in the water, and he felt her soft breath on his face. "And if my grandfather wants to sell it, then it's his choice. God has other plans for me."

He did? Oh, he didn't want to be a fool, but . . . "Please tell me those plans include me."

Please.

"Do you want them to?"

He had his hands on the stern seat, holding the canoe steady in the water. Now she wove her arm up, around his shoulder, hanging on.

"Yes," he said. "Very much. I don't know what's going to happen. I'll probably have to do some time. But if you wait for me, I . . . well, I'll follow you, Claire. Here or anywhere. If you let me, I'll be right here, beside you. Cheering you on."

She hooked her other arm around him, pulled herself to his chest. "Or maybe I'll cheer *you* on."

Then she leaned up and kissed him. Softly but taking him by surprise. His sweet, timid, saintly Claire, pulling herself tight against him, making him realize that indeed, so many years ago, he'd chased the wrong girl.

"I love you too, Jens." She whispered it in his ear, then pressed her lips to his neck.

Oh. My. He wanted to put his arms around her, but the canoe just might topple over. All the same, he could see her face in his memory as he leaned forward, kissing her pretty little nose, those beautiful eyes that saw him and loved him anyway.

Despite his mistakes. His sins. Not because he earned it, but because she'd chosen to.

Yeah, maybe Gibs was onto something with all his preaching.

Around them, cinders fell on the water, sizzling. He was treading water, the bottom of the canoe hot, the air under it steamy. They kicked out farther from shore—he didn't know how far, but enough that the water grew colder. Outside, the fury seemed to die, just a little.

"I have to see," Darek finally said from the other end of the canoe.

"Are you sure?" Jensen said.

"What?" Claire whispered.

"He wants to see if Evergreen Resort is still standing."

She said nothing, just laid her head against his chest.

"Ready, Dare?"

"Yeah." But his voice was tight.

Jensen pushed the canoe up, over his head. It fell with a splash, upright.

He hung on to the gunwale then because his strength left him.

The fire had decimated the Gibson place, the home charred timber and ash, still burning in places, the fireplace the lone survivor. Even the dock had burned—was still burning, the old wood dropping into the water with a sigh.

Oh, Claire. He tightened his arm around her. "I'm so sorry."

"We're alive. That's what matters," she whispered.

In fact the fire had run all the way along the shore and then—

Stopped. At the corner of his property where he'd spent hours extending the sprinkler system into the pasture, the fire was dying, defeated by the plumes of spray protecting Pine Acres.

Beyond the shore, more charred forest gave way to the wet green pasture, where now he could make out yellow-shirted firefighters still mopping up the blaze.

He turned and followed the destruction along the shoreline, north.

Evergreen Resort had burned, the cabins along the lake still in flame, the stately evergreens that named the resort toppled into the water. Darek's A-frame home, the one he'd built for Felicity, was an inferno now falling in on itself, only a skeleton remaining.

Jensen held on to Claire as he turned, tracing his gaze along the destroyed cabins to—

The lodge had survived. Jensen just stared at it, and even Claire had a hand over her mouth. The hoses still rained lake water over it, the sprays plumes of rainbow in the sky, but the lodge house stood, glistening in the morning light.

Beyond the mostly unscarred dock, in the water, Casper and John bobbed, holding on to the diving platform.

Jensen glanced at Darek.

He had his hand cupped over his face, his shoulders shaking. Jensen looked back at the property, saw Darek's house crumble inward, embers like water splashing into the air.

He swam over to Darek. "I'm sorry, Dare. I'm so, so sorry."

And then, with the words, something broke free. Perhaps it was the trauma, the emotion of the fire. Or maybe the sense of starting over, a baptism of sorts in the water. But he, too, felt his eyes filling. "I'm so sorry. For everything. I'm so sorry about Felicity and . . . my anger. I was angry at you. I blamed you for Felicity's death—I know that sounds crazy, but I did. And . . . Dare, I . . . If I could take her place . . . I'm just so sorry, man. Please—"

"Shut up, Jensen." Darek looked up at him. "Just shut up."

He frowned, not sure—

"You're not the only one who screwed up here." Darek's voice thickened. "I forgive you already, okay?"

Umm. Okay. Jensen nodded. "Me too."

Then Darek made a face, something that said, *Shoot, man, we're not crying, are we?* and Jensen laughed.

Jensen found Claire swimming up to him. She looked back at shore. "Sorry about your house, Dare."

"Aw, I don't care about the house—look at the lodge. It made it!"

Look at the lodge.

So they did. Shiny and bright, decades of history miraculously untouched by the flames.

Yeah, look at the lodge.

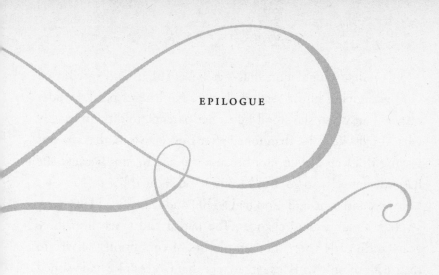

"I'm not ready, Claire. I'm not—"

"Shh." Claire stepped up to Jensen, adjusting his tie, smoothing his lapels. "It's going to be fine. Everything is going to work out."

He grabbed her wrists. "No, I'm not afraid. I'm ready to do the time. I'm just . . . I don't want to be away from you. Not right now."

She rose on her tiptoes to kiss him on the lips, and Jensen just wanted to wrap his arms around her and hold her there. Sink into her embrace and tell himself that he could do this. Leave her here to start a new business, a new life, while he took the prison van down to Stillwater to serve his time. Four years—his mandatory suspended sentence for vehicular homicide—as a result of violating his probation.

He closed his eyes, rested his forehead against hers. *Please, God, help me do this. Give me faith.*

Claire had taught him that—to believe that God cared, that God was giving him a second chance. He'd never been prouder of her than when she stood up to her parents, told them exactly what it felt like to be abandoned after Bosnia. More, that she was staying in Deep Haven, not because she had to, not because she had nowhere else to go, but because God wanted her to.

Apparently she and God had a talk, and it involved Jensen.

Talk about second chances. Too bad it had taken him three years and nearly three thousand hours of community service to realize it was only with his repentance that God's grace had washed his slate clean.

But before man, well, the law was the law.

Jensen took a breath, blew it out.

Claire caught his face in her hands and met his eyes, pouring into him everything he ever needed. "Trust me. Everything is going to be fine."

Yeah. He nodded, although when the bailiff brought him in, settled him alone at the defendant's table, he started to doubt. But this had been his choice—no lawyer, and . . . he had to learn to live with his choices.

He'd said that much to his father when the old man called, offering money for defense.

Jensen still rolled that conversation around his head. *I love you, Son, and I'm rooting for you.*

Huh. Maybe his father had been hit hard on the head. But Jensen took it in.

Behind him, he heard movement, but he didn't turn, not wanting to see Claire, wishing he had talked her out of attending.

He saw Mitch sitting on the prosecution side and tried not to feel betrayed.

Then Ivy came in. He'd known that as assistant county attorney, she'd be forced to bring his probation violation to a hearing. But he expected a smile or something as she walked over to the prosecutor's table. DJ Teague came in behind her. Jensen tried not to be rattled that he'd decided to attend.

Apparently they'd brought the big guns for this hardened criminal.

The bailiff announced the judge—Magnusson—and Jensen rose as she entered. She seemed a stern woman, her blonde hair fluffed back, a pair of reading glasses dangling around her neck.

Yeah, he was going to jail—do not pass Go.

Jensen stared at his hands as the bailiff read the case file number, the charges against him, the reason for the hearing.

"Mr. Atwood, I see here that you are defending yourself. Why is that?"

He looked up. "Your Honor, I knew the terms of my probation, and I violated them. I have nothing to defend."

He knew that, behind him, Claire was cringing, having fought for the past two weeks to get him counsel. But he was tired of trying to wrangle the law and wage a defense.

He'd killed a woman. A friend. His buddy's wife. There was no defense for that, despite the fact that he'd never meant for it to happen.

And innocent or not, he couldn't take one more day of living in this town pretending he hadn't hurt people, pretending that he didn't have some culpability. Going to jail might be a thousand times easier.

Except, of course, for Claire.

"Very well, Mr. Atwood. Prosecution, bring your case."

He heard a chair slide back. "Your Honor, before we get started, I'd like to address the court, if I may."

Jensen looked at Ivy. She stared straight ahead, at the judge.

"Go ahead, Miss Madison."

Ivy stepped up to the podium. "As a clerk in my final year of law school, I worked for Atwood and Associates. I was given a file and asked to find a way to help the defendant in the case escape the mandatory vehicular homicide sentence. See, his father was my boss, and he loved his son, but he wasn't representing the case. So he asked me to help."

Her hands curled around the sides of the podium. "I didn't know Jensen Atwood at all. He was just a case to me, but I was an eager young law student and I wanted to please my boss. So I studied the case and discovered that much of it was circumstantial. The prosecution couldn't prove that Jensen had been negligent, although with his cell phone open in the vehicle, it was certainly suspect. The cell phone usage law, by the way, hadn't held up a single successful conviction in the state of Minnesota at the time. I reviewed the facts, and in my opinion, the state did not have a substantial case. However, knowing the venue where the court case would be tried—here in Deep Haven—and knowing the outcome in the event of a guilty verdict, I proposed a rather unorthodox plea. Jensen would plead guilty, and I submitted a substantial memorandum proposing setting aside the sentencing guidelines and instead offering probation that included three thousand hours of community service."

Jensen couldn't breathe. She'd crafted his plea agreement?

"In a twist of fate, today I find myself wanting to defend Jensen's innocence. But as the court knows, I can't because he's already pleaded guilty and been sentenced for his crime. So I'm recusing myself as prosecutor and joining his defense to plead for clemency."

Then Ivy closed her file. The court fell silent until the judge finally said, "Mr. Atwood?"

He nodded dumbly.

Ivy walked over and sat down beside Jensen. She didn't look at him, just touched his hand. Squeezed.

His heartbeat thundered in his ears. He had no words. Except . . . he leaned over. "Thank you, Ivy."

For believing in him, for giving him a life here, even if he had blown it.

Judge Magnusson finally nodded at DJ. "We'll hear the prosecution's complaint."

DJ stood and outlined the probation violation, his voice tight, ending with "And pursuant to his suspended sentence, the state of Minnesota asks that Jensen Atwood serve out his full sentence at a correctional facility of the court's choosing." DJ took a breath as he closed the file. "Although, granted, he is only twelve hours short on his community service."

Twelve.

Even with the hours he'd earned at the Garden—thanks to Joe Michaels, who'd submitted the appropriate paperwork to Mitch. And Mitch's generosity in allowing him double time for hazardous duty. And the extra hours he managed to put in since then. Twelve hours short.

But twelve hours short was still . . . short.

"Thank you, Mr. Teague. Defense?"

Ivy rose. "I would like to submit a request for clemency to the court, Your Honor. I know this is a bit unorthodox, but in this case, I believe it may be relevant."

The bailiff took the clemency petition.

How Jensen wanted to turn, to thank Claire for the hours

she'd spent writing it, keeping him from balling the entire thing in a wad and throwing it against the wall. But now, it felt like too little, too late.

"Is that all, Miss Madison?"

"Absolutely not, Your Honor. If it please the court, I have character witnesses who will testify to the points laid out in the petition."

"Character witnesses?" the judge asked.

That's what Jensen wanted to say. He looked up at Ivy. But she didn't spare him a glance.

"Indeed, Your Honor. I have a list here of everyone who has agreed to testify." She opened her file folder again.

"How many are there, Miss Madison?"

Ivy paused, glanced at Jensen, then looked behind her. "Well, see for yourself."

Jensen frowned. Turned.

And then he was a child, his mouth gaping open. The courtroom was filled to overflowing, people standing in the back, against the wall. He saw Kyle Hueston and Emma Nelson, Claire's bandmates. Sharron and Noelle, who'd worked with him at the thrift store. Annalise Decker, from the animal shelter, and her husband, Nathan, the real estate agent he sometimes cleaned for. They grinned at him. Beside them were Lucy and Seb Brewster, the mayor, and Caleb Knight, whom he mowed the school football field for every summer. He saw Joe Michaels, of course, and Marnie Blouder from the sheriff's office waved to him. Pastor Dan stood in the back, his hand on his wife's shoulder, wearing a pastorly, affirming grin. Phyllis McCann from parks and rec held up a cup of coffee and winked, and in the front row sat Donna Winters with his favorite Meals On Wheels blue hairs, who'd turned out to give him a thumbs-up. Ruby and the folks from the Garden took up an entire row. Gabe Michaels waved. Beside him sat Grace Christiansen, beaming. And Ingrid, who looked like she might cry.

Yeah, him too.

He felt Ivy's hand on his shoulder. "Who wants to go first?" she asked the crowd.

Every hand shot into the air.

Jensen tightened his jaw, knowing he was way too close to weeping.

And then Darek came forward. He had slicked up, wearing— no, a suit? He held Tiger's hand and now handed him to Nan Holloway, who sat in the front row. Tousled his son's hair.

Tiger waved. "Hi, Ivy!"

A chuckle murmured through the courtroom.

Then Darek turned and faced the judge. "Your Honor, I'd like to be the first witness on behalf of the defense, if I may."

"I hope I didn't embarrass you too much," Ivy said as she closed her apartment door behind her.

Darek had to choose between finding words and simply drinking her in. Her beautiful green eyes, the red hair now falling over her burnt-orange shirt. When he was quiet, she looked up at him with a frown.

"You're not angry, are you?"

Angry? He could hardly breathe with the joy in his chest. He managed to shake his head. "No, Ivy, I'm not angry." He cupped her face, lifted it for a kiss. Just one because if he got going, then . . . well, he knew it was too early to ask her to marry him, but . . . soon.

Very soon.

But not tonight. Tonight was a different kind of night, for someone else. He slipped his hand into hers. "I am glad you told me before you announced it to all of Deep Haven, however."

He would never forget the moment when she'd revealed her part in Jensen's sentencing. The way she sat a little away from him, her hands tucked between her knees as they watched Tiger swing on the community playground. How she hadn't looked at him once, until the end. Then her eyes said it all.

And what was he going to do? "Of course I forgive you," he'd said. "There is nothing to forgive, really. You saw the truth, tried to find justice for us all in a case where there was no justice. How could there be? You did a good thing, even though it was hard on all of us."

He'd folded her into his arms then, and it seemed like he felt the last of something she'd been holding on to slip away. She sank into him, and he didn't know how he'd ever let go.

He didn't plan to.

The air was thick with the scent of rain, the streets and air still soggy from yesterday's drenching.

Jensen had arranged for their family and others who'd lost their homes to rent from the vacation home owners of Pine Acres. Darek had a feeling that Jensen might be footing the bill on a number of the properties. Meanwhile, Darek's family was meeting with the insurance agent and planning to use the extra cash to acquire Gibs's property.

Darek hadn't expected that phone call from Claire's parents, offering his family the land. Nor did he expect, when he asked Claire about it, for her to willingly agree.

"I don't need it anymore," she'd said, and he guessed the way Jensen wrapped his arm around her had something to do with that.

If they were wise, and the family helped with the rebuild, they could afford the land. Someday Evergreen Lodge Outfitter and Cabin Rentals might be more than any of them had ever dreamed. But that's the way God worked, apparently.

He held Ivy's hand as he walked her down the stairs, out to the driveway.

She stopped, glanced at him. "You brought your motorcycle?"

"Just until Casper goes back to college. His Key West pirate adventure fell through, and with Mom and Dad trying to figure out how to rebuild, he's sticking around until the end of the summer. I thought maybe you'd like a ride."

"I'd love a ride," she said and he climbed aboard, helping her on as she swung her leg over. Then, like he hoped, she leaned in, wrapped her arms around his waist, and held on.

Keep holding on.

He backed the bike out of the driveway, but instead of heading toward town, he drove to the cemetery. "I have to stop here for a minute. Do you mind?"

"Of course not. Take your time. I'll be right here, waiting."

He wanted to kiss her, but it didn't seem right, so he parked the bike and left Ivy there.

He'd visited only once, early on with his mother, but he hadn't forgotten where Felicity lay. Someone—probably Claire—had planted a garden, pretty red and purple flowers over her grave.

He palmed the top of the smooth, cool surface of the stone. "Hey, Felicity." He wasn't sure what he wanted to say, but . . . "I'm sorry. I should have loved you better. I should have made it work. And I shouldn't have blamed you for my failures."

He knelt before the gravestone, reading the inscription. *Beloved mother of Theo, daughter, wife.*

Yes. "I will keep your memory alive for him. Remind him of your laughter, teach him to swim and enjoy all the things you loved. I will love him well." His throat tightened. "Thank you for our son. For loving me even though I didn't deserve it."

He crouched there for a moment. Then pressed his hand to his mouth, leaving a kiss on the gravestone. "You are missed."

Ivy sat astride the bike, just as she'd promised, and said nothing as he climbed aboard. She wrapped her arms around him again, however, and they motored down Main Street.

"Where's Tiger?"

"Nan's."

"You're a good man, Darek Christiansen."

He smiled at that. "Trying."

They pulled up to the VFW and he parked the bike. "This is our big hot date?" she asked, wrinkling her nose. But tease played in her eyes.

"Listen. This is the hottest place in town." Indeed, the music already spilled out onto the street, the Blue Monkeys going to town with a Skynyrd song.

"'So don't ask me no questions, and I won't tell you no lies. . . .'"

The crowd was singing along as they walked in. Darek put his hand on Ivy's back, leading her through the room, raising his hand to Jed, who sat at the bar with Pete Holt and a few of the other hotshots. They'd spent the last couple weeks mopping up, making sure no new fires ignited, but the rainfall of the past few days meant they might be leaving soon.

He noticed the new guy, Conner, in the corner, talking with Liza Beaumont. And his dad, sitting at a high top, his chair close to his mom's. She caught Darek's eye as he came in. Her smile filled him with an odd, boyish sense of joy.

Ivy pointed to a chair next to Jensen, and Darek nodded. Jensen stood, grabbing Darek's hand.

Yeah, that had felt good yesterday, standing up in court for his best friend. Forgiving him.

"You ready?" Darek asked.

Ivy glanced at them with a frown.

Jensen nodded.

As they sat, he noticed a dog lying at Jensen's feet. "They let you bring a dog in here?"

"This is Rusty!" Jensen said over the last bars of the song. "He's my moral support."

"And what am I?"

He grinned. "You know what you are."

The song ended with whistles and cheering. And then Emma stepped back and Claire took the mic. She was looking pretty tonight in a simple white-and-blue floral dress, a pair of leggings, and red Converse high-tops. Her dark hair flowed in waves around her face. She looked out into the audience, her gaze landing on Jensen.

"I have a treat for you tonight, folks. You might not know it, but we have another musician in the audience."

Jensen's smile faded.

"If you live near Evergreen Lake, sometimes you can hear the tunes of a lonely harmonica drifting over the water. Those would be the magic melodies of our very own Jensen Atwood! Jens, get up here and join me onstage."

Jensen glanced at Darek, something of panic on his face. "Did you know about this?"

Darek reached into his pocket, pulled out a harmonica.

"I'll get you."

"I dare you," he said.

Jensen swiped the harmonica and took the stage amid the rousing cheer of the crowd.

Ivy slipped her hand into Darek's and squeezed.

"What are we singing, darlin'?" Jensen said to Claire.

"How about 'Ring of Fire'?"

He smiled. "Right." Then he leaned close to the mic and began to blow out the bars. He got the band going, then belted out the song, his voice the tenor Darek remembered.

The crowd sang along, and Darek grinned at Ivy as she clapped, met his eyes.

"'The taste of love is sweet when hearts like ours meet. . . .'"

Ivy suddenly leaned over and kissed him on the cheek.

"What was that for?"

"For being the right bachelor to take a chance on."

"Ha. Right. I don't think you've gotten your money's worth yet."

"Not quite yet," she said but winked.

Claire sang the next verse, laughing, and Jensen finished it, his eyes in hers.

The crowd went wild. Onstage, Claire went into Jensen's arms.

"They're so cute," Ivy said.

Darek leaned over to pet Jensen's dog. "Oh, it's going to get better."

Indeed. Jensen put Claire down and took the mic from the stand. Then he took her hand and knelt in front of her.

Yes, much, much better.

"I can't believe it, but I'm actually a little chilly." Ivy sat straddling Darek's motorcycle, her back against him as they parked on the

Pincushion overlook above Deep Haven. A breeze had gathered in the woods surrounding the parking lot and now rushed over the edge, toward the inky lake below.

"I can solve that."

Ivy snuggled back into Darek's chest and he wrapped his arms around her. He smelled of the outdoors, the wind in his hair, the slightest sense of the hard work he'd done today cleaning the property. They probably had a year or more of work before they could rebuild and reopen. But Darek seemed to be leaning into it, already trying to talk his parents into the improvements that would bring new life to Evergreen Resort.

He seemed a new man since the fire. Instead of letting it knock him over, it energized him. Turned him into a man his parents could count on to rebuild their legacy.

He pressed his lips against her neck, and she shivered, although not from the chill.

"Didn't you tell me you used to bring girls up here during high school to neck?"

"Nope," he said. "Only you. You're the only one, baby."

She gave him a playful swat. "Darek. I can find out the truth, you know. I am a lawyer—I know how to get information out of people."

"Okay, okay, fine. I did bring a few girls here. But it was always about the view. Really. I promise."

She laughed and tucked herself into the curve of his embrace. The view was beautiful, the way the town sparkled under the night sky. A thousand brilliant lights glittering against the velvet darkness. She could point out where the courthouse stood and her little rental behind the Footstep of Heaven Bookstore and of course the lighthouse at the point where he'd first kissed her. Where he'd first made her believe that she could belong here. That this might truly become . . . home.

"Your mom said the funniest thing to me tonight. She said, 'Welcome home.'"

Darek lifted his head. "Huh. She said that to me, too."

"But you've lived here all your life. It's hardly a 'welcome home' for you."

"Maybe, but it sort of feels that way right now. Like I've been gone for a long time, on a trip I didn't know how to find my way back from. Until now. Until you came into my life, Ivy. Maybe you brought me home."

She curled her hands around his arms. "Or maybe God brought us both home."

"You believe that?"

"I'm starting to. I want to."

"Yeah," he said. "So do I."

He rested his cheek against her head, silently watching the view with her. A ship moved across the water, lights floating in the darkness. The rich scent of evergreen and pine fragranced the air as he said, "I love you, Ivy Madison. Welcome home."

AN EXCITING PREVIEW OF SUSAN MAY WARREN'S NEXT BOOK, *WALK ON BY*

CHAPTER I

EDEN CHRISTIANSEN'S CAREER, her love life—even her car battery, for that matter—were frozen stiffer than the late-January cold snap freezing the city of Minneapolis.

The blue-mercury windchill blew through the frosted, thin-paned windows of Stub and Herbs, a restaurant located a couple blocks from the offices of her old haunt, the *Minnesota Daily* newspaper.

Back then, Eden would wander over here for a burger after a week of reporting and find her cohorts gathered around a fresh issue of the paper, newsprint on their fingers, arguing over the editorials and who had landed the stories above the fold.

Back then, it was only a matter of time before she earned

herself a real byline. Maybe in the *St. Paul Pioneer Press*. Or the big fish—the *Minneapolis Star Tribune*.

Back then, her career was hot. Her future was hot.

Maybe, back then, even she was hot.

Now, she looked like she lived on the northern slope of Alaska, dressed in a green down parka, a black woolen cap, and a pair of sensible black UGGs like she might be ready for dogsledding through the streets of Minneapolis.

No wonder her date's attention fell upon the gaggle of under-dressed college coeds who pushed in through the frosted doors, young and hopeful, messenger bags over their shoulders as they thumbed the screens of their iPhones.

"I really like the bleu cheese burger," Eden said, perusing the menu, hoping that the cold snap might be fogging her brain. But who was she kidding? This wasn't even a real date. She could see right through mortician Russell Hayes and his out-of-the-clear-blue offer to take her to dinner. Until last week, Russell had spoken to her as if she were his personal secretary rather than the obits clerk.

Then the NHL lockout ended. After three months of waiting for the owners and players to reach an agreement and end the deep freeze on the hockey season, fans had games to watch, and the Xcel Energy Center was filling seats faster than hot cocoa sales in a blizzard.

And just like that, Russell had sent her an e-mail.

Just because he hadn't mentioned the Minnesota Wild hockey team didn't mean it wasn't imprinted between his eyes. How obvi-ous was it that she, single sister of Wild star Owen Christiansen, suddenly had a little warmth headed her way from the man whom she'd talked to three times a week for the past four years?

Russell wasn't exactly hard on the eyes, either. Funeral directors should be short, squirrelly men, with comb-overs and bad polyester suits. But Russell didn't fit that description. He wore a pedestrian red sweater but filled it out well, and with his brown eyes and short, curly blond hair, he could almost be an L.L. Bean model. He wasn't a big man, but he had wide shoulders, and he'd held the car door open for her and crooked his elbow to help her across the icy parking lot.

Yes, tonight he looked like a man who actually meant his words: "I know we haven't really gotten to know each other over the past four years, but would you like to have dinner?"

But she wasn't a fool. They'd shared a sum total of four sentences since sitting down, and now—

"Last week's snowstorm really kept us busy," Russell said over the top of his own menu.

Really? They were going to talk shop? Which meant . . . tragedy, death, and obit notices for the paper.

Fine. She'd play along. At least it would take her mind off the trouble Owen might be finding tonight.

Oh, she'd promised herself she wouldn't think about Owen.

"My parents said that it would be a banner year for them, if they were finished rebuilding their resort."

Russell closed the menu, and his gaze caught on a couple college jocks who sauntered in and took seats on the black leather stools at the bar. One wore a U of MN sweatshirt. Hockey players. Eden could tell by the long hair dusting their collars, the hint of beard, the swagger. Minnesota grew hockey players like pine trees—big, strong, and everywhere.

Russell turned his attention back to her. "Rebuilding?"

"Evergreen Resort burned last summer during the wildfires."

"I'm so sorry."

"It's okay. My brother Darek is heading up the rebuild. It's going to be spectacular—a sauna, a playground, Wi-Fi, and brand-new cabins—all state-of-the-art."

"Sounds spectacular indeed." He leaned back in the chair. "I didn't know you were from northern Minnesota."

He said it as if he meant it. As if he hadn't scanned the player pages online and picked out every tidbit of information about Owen. She cupped her coffee mug, warming her hands. "I went to the University of Minnesota, and I live here, but I go home as often as I can."

Which, for the last four years, hadn't been often, with Owen's junior hockey schedule and then last year's debut on the Wild.

The door opened and another coed came in, bringing the chill with her. Eden glanced at her and then to Russell, expecting his gaze to be on the brunette.

Nope. He was looking at her. "I've been wanting to ask you out since that first day you answered the phone at the obits desk."

He had?

"I'm sorry it's taken so long." He smiled. He had nice teeth, a warm smile. So he wasn't a big guy—she liked guys who seemed approachable. Human.

Maybe he wasn't here trying to score tickets. She shrugged her parka off her shoulders.

"When Charlotte mentioned she had hired an obits clerk, I guess I thought it would be some temp girl—"

"Reporter."

Oh, why had she corrected him? She wanted to snatch it back. He was right. She *wasn't* a reporter. In truth, Eden was more a classified-sales representative than a reporter. So much for her four years of education at the University of Minnesota School of Journalism.

"Of course. Reporter." He looked uncomfortable now, shifting in his chair. His gaze drifted to the television over the bar. The news had moved on to the sports report. No hockey game tonight, or she would have had to turn him down.

"I wrote a couple rough drafts for the remembrance section last year, while Charlotte was in Hawaii. But she has had an iron fist on that section. I haven't a hope of doing any serious writing."

He frowned. "Really?"

"Of the three interns who passed through obits in the past four years, all of them got jobs in editorial. One with sports, one in entertainment features, and one on the police beat."

"Ouch."

"Yeah. I'm tired of getting passed over."

No, *passed over* didn't quite cut it. Crushed. Mowed down. Flattened. Winged. Clipped. Bodychecked.

Maybe she had a little hockey in her, too.

In her pocket, Eden's phone vibrated. She fished it out in time to see Owen's number move to missed calls. She noted two previous ones and frowned.

"Everything okay?"

She nodded but put the phone on the table. "Owen's at a big birthday bash for the Wild's captain tonight. A sort of fan event. I was just . . ."

Worried.

She smiled and bit back her word. "I was just hoping he has a great time."

"I heard about that party. Private tickets for box-seat holders?"

"How did you know?"

He nodded toward the news. "They just reported on it."

Right. So maybe Russell wasn't a crazed fan. She had her radar set way too high. But just in case . . . "I have tickets. Do you want to go?"

He stared at her for a second; then a half smile hitched up his face. "No . . ."

She didn't mean to let out an audible sigh, but there it was, and along with it died more of her suspicions that he might be just like every other man she'd dated in the past year.

Being Owen's sister had ignited her dating life. She could wear a bag over her face, shuffle around in burlap, and she'd have a lineup of dates. But a real relationship, with a man who might like her? Listen to her? Care about her—and not hockey? Right.

But maybe Russell was different.

"Unless you do," he finished.

She forced a smile. Shook her head.

"You know, maybe you should try to get a job as a sports reporter. With your connections, you could get exclusives with the Wild."

Was he serious? "Yeah, like I'm going to walk into the locker room after the game, maybe interview the players as they peel off their gear? No thanks."

A frown touched his eyes.

"Sorry." Maybe it wasn't all Owen's fault she couldn't get beyond date number one. She simply walked into every relationship with her dukes up. No wonder she spent most nights alone with a good book.

Her phone vibrated again. She glanced at it, then at Russell.

"Take it," he said.

She heard music, yelling in the background. "Hello?"

Nothing. She held the phone up to her ear. "Owen?"

More music, and this time a crash, something like glass splintering, on the other end. Voices, loud and boisterous.

Maybe even angry.

"Owen!" she said, a little too loudly. A couple players at the bar turned, and she ducked her head, pressed a finger to her ear. The noise on the other end of the phone was muffled and it sounded like the phone hit something, and she figured it out.

Owen had probably put the phone in his back pocket and was accidentally dialing her.

Had been all night.

Which meant that no, he didn't need her.

And that yes, he did. Because by the sound of it, Owen was up to trouble. Following right in Jace Jacobsen's bad-boy footsteps.

She pressed End. Took a breath.

"What's the matter?"

Eden shook her head but stared at the phone. Stupid kid. If her parents only knew how many times she'd fished him out of bars and pried him away from rink bunnies this past year. It seemed that Owen's fame had rushed straight to his naive, small-town head. She hardly knew him anymore.

"Can I drive you somewhere?" Russell had leaned forward, his brown eyes full of concern.

She took a breath. "Would you mind driving me to Sammy's Bar and Grill in St. Paul?"

He glanced at the television again, then at Eden. "The Wild party?"

In more ways than one. "Please?"

"Sure." He reached for his coat.

She led the way out to the parking lot, the windchill not

touching the anger heating her cheeks. Owen was going to land in the papers, and then her parents would realize that not only had she failed in her career, but even the job of watching over her brother was too big for her.

Russell opened the door for her, and she climbed into his Nissan Pathfinder, hitting the seat heater button as he started the car. "Thank you."

"It's no problem."

"It's that stupid Jace Jacobsen," Eden said, staring out the window. "He's a bad influence on Owen. Almost since Owen could lace up his skates, he's wanted to be like J-Hammer."

"The guy is a beast on the ice," Russell said, turning onto the highway. "And he didn't get his reputation for nothing. Last season, he had sixty-six penalty minutes. But he also scored three game-winning goals and had forty-two total points."

She glanced at him. Wow. Seriously? "Are you a Wild fan?"

"I live in Minnesota," Russell said. "I also root for the Vikings, the Timberwolves, the Gophers, the Bulldogs, and the Twins."

"Right. Of course." She blew out a breath. "I'm probably overreacting about Owen."

"J-Hammer's rep isn't just on the ice, and we all know it."

They cut off the highway, toward downtown St. Paul, and Russell drove like he knew the way. Sammy's was a sports bar just down the street from the Xcel Energy Center, where the Wild played. Russell parked, and Eden spotted Owen's Charger in the lot across the street. She kept a spare key on her ring for nights like this.

"Thanks, Russell," she said as she climbed out.

"Do you need any help?" he asked, and she tried to test him

for sincerity. Not that he didn't want to help her, but maybe . . .
Oh, see, she read into everything.

He was a nice guy. And she'd blown this entire date. "I'll be
fine. I'm just going to get him and drive him home. We'll be fine."

Russell didn't protest, only nodded. "Sorry about this."

"You're sorry? I'm the one who is sorry. I'll make it up to you.
Maybe get us a couple tickets to a game."

He shook his head. "No need. But I will call you again, if that's
okay."

There it was. Proof that she was the author of her own demise.
She swallowed, regret like a boulder in her throat. "Yes, please."

The cold swirled around her legs and up the back of her jacket
as she stood there letting a perfectly good date drive away. What
was her problem that she had to rush to Owen's aid—especially
since she was probably the last person he'd want to see?

It didn't matter. Someone had to watch out for him. Eden
turned up her collar and marched across the street.

The sweaty heat and raucous noise of the bar flooded over
her, and the smell of cigarette smoke, too much cologne, whiskey,
beer, and chaos tightened her stomach. Bodies pushed against each
other, and she heard the chanting even as she stood at the entrance
and looked over the crowd.

"Fight! Fight!"

Perfect. She plowed through the onlookers, ignoring the pro-
tests, dreading what she heard—the familiar sounds of men hitting each other, laughing, huffing as they tumbled onto the floor.

She reached the edge of the brawl, and there he was. Owen,
power forward for the Wild, a button ripped off his shirt, his long
hair over his face, his nose bleeding, writhing as defenseman Zach
Stoner caught him in a headlock.

"Let him up!" she yelled and ran toward Stoner.

People laughed, and Owen's eyes landed on her, growing wide.

"Stoner!" She grabbed the man's hair. "I said let him up!"

Stoner let go and Owen sputtered as he rolled away, found his feet. "Eden, what the—?"

"Stop right there. You pocket-called me four times. And then I heard the fighting. What was I supposed to think?"

The crowd had dissipated, probably embarrassed for him, and in that moment, Eden was too. Just a little. But more angry because she smelled his breath, saw the red in his eyes. She stepped close to Owen, still only a smidgen taller than her off his blades, and cut her voice low enough that he could still hear her. "You might want to remember you're not old enough to drink."

He glared at her.

She didn't flinch. "Get your coat. You're going home."

"We're just having fun. It's J-Hammer's birthday—"

"Someone has to protect your hockey career, even if you won't."

He ground his jaw, his lips an angry line, and she gave him her just-try-it face.

Owen scooped up his leather jacket from where it hung on a chair and stormed out through the crowd.

Eden was just turning to follow him when she saw the hulking form of Jace "J-Hammer" Jacobsen sitting at the bar. The man of honor seemed like he'd stayed above the fray tonight—at least so far. He wore black dress pants and a gray silk shirt rolled up over his strong forearms. Up close, she could admit that—for others— he might have the ability to take a girl's breath away. His dark-chocolate hair fell in sculpted waves behind his ears and he sported a close-clipped full beard. His dress shirt only accentuated that he maintained the build of a linebacker, all cut muscle and brawn, but she knew he had the finesse of a skater, smooth and liquid on blades. And his eyes, blue as ice—yes, they could look right through a gal. Leave a scorching trail behind.

But she was immune. Because she wasn't a rink bunny, wasn't a crazed fan. Wasn't dazzled by the star power of one of hockey's top enforcers. She was family, thank you, here for one reason only.

Owen.

Yes, Eden was made of ice, and J-Hammer hadn't a prayer of thawing her resolve.

"This is all your fault, Jace Jacobsen. If Owen loses his contract, it's on you."

"Hey—!"

She didn't stick around to listen to his lame excuses. He was the team captain. Who else was supposed to watch Owen's back when she couldn't?

Eden stormed out, back into the frigid January air.

A NOTE FROM THE AUTHOR

WE LIVE IN A BLAME WORLD. For some reason, over the past two or three generations, we've turned into a society that points fingers, that seeks out someone to accuse. We've all heard of the crazy accusations—hot coffee spilled on a lap at McDonald's causes a lawsuit; people trespass onto property and the owner is sued for a slippery sidewalk. We blame creditors for extending us too much credit—as if it is their fault we overspend. And what about the big events, the ones that truly cut into our lives? School shootings. Gas explosions. Car accidents. The truth is, the chaos of the world is frightening, and when something terrible happens—accidents, mistakes, even tragedy—it simply feels better to blame rather than forgive. Forgiving takes a part of us that feels too overwhelming. It might require us to look at ourselves and see if we have a part in the story. One might even suggest that some sins aren't forgivable. It's too much to ask. More, in a society that rushes to blame, we destroy any hope of sorrow—there simply isn't room for it when we're too busy defending ourselves from blame.

We're quickly spiraling into a society without mercy. Without grace. Without forgiveness.

A few years ago, we had a tragedy occur in our town not unlike the events of this story. Different players, different situations, but I used this concept to explore what happens when grief and anger take over and ignite an ember of hatred inside. We lose perspective. We lose our hold on grace.

Hatred turns into a peat fire in our hearts, burning away at our insides. The only hope to snuff it out is forgiveness. Grace. A hard look at ourselves to see if we are measuring others by the measure by which we want to be judged. Or are we measuring them by the pain they caused?

I am thankful that God doesn't measure us by the pain we caused Him. Still cause Him. I am thankful that His measure is Jesus. His measure is grace.

I am excited about this series! I've longed to write a story about a northern Minnesota family and their adult children. We're in this season of life—parenting our adult children. As a parent, you nurture your children, then guide them, then walk beside them . . . and finally stand back as they walk into life. And then you really start praying! These books are about those years . . . watching, hoping, praying your adult children into a legacy of faith. Thank you for taking this first step on the journey with the Christiansen family. I hope you will continue with me as we "come home to the Christiansens."

In His grace,
Susan May Warren

ABOUT THE AUTHOR

SUSAN MAY WARREN is the bestselling, RITA Award–winning author of more than forty novels and novellas whose compelling plots and unforgettable characters have won acclaim with readers and reviewers alike. She served with her husband and four children as a missionary in Russia for eight years before she and her family returned home to the States. She now writes full-time as her husband runs a lodge on Lake Superior in northern Minnesota, where many of her books are set. She and her family enjoy hiking, canoeing, and being involved in their local church.

Susan holds a BA in mass communications from the University of Minnesota. Several of her critically acclaimed novels have been ECPA and CBA bestsellers, were chosen as Top Picks by *Romantic Times*, and have won the RWA's Inspirational Reader's Choice contest and the American Christian Fiction Writers Book of the Year award. Five of her books have been Christy Award finalists. In addition to her writing, Susan loves to teach and speak at women's events about God's amazing grace in our lives.

For exciting updates on her new releases, previous books, and more, visit her website at www.susanmaywarren.com.

DISCUSSION QUESTIONS

1. *Take a Chance on Me* opens with a letter Ingrid writes to her oldest son, Darek, expressing her concerns and prayers for him. Do you think Ingrid should have given Darek the letter—or that she should at some point in the future? Why or why not? How do you work through your prayers or worries, whether for others or for yourself?

2. In her letter, Ingrid tells Darek, "You never seemed to question the beliefs your father and I taught you. Perhaps that is what unsettled me the most, because without questioning, I wondered how there could be true understanding." Do you agree that beliefs need to be tested, questioned, to be fully understood? How do you see each of the main characters—Darek, Ivy, Jensen, and Claire—questioning their beliefs over the course of the story? What are the results?

3. As "the most ineligible eligible bachelor in town," Darek frequently wishes he could start over without the baggage of his past. What circumstances keep him from moving

on? Have you ever wished for a new start? Darek sees a relationship with Ivy, a woman unburdened by his history, as the key to his second chance. What would a second chance look like in your own life? A new job, a move to a new place, a new relationship?

4. After growing up in the foster care system, Ivy is used to being on her own; she's determined to stay impartial in her work and cautious in her relationships. But at the same time, she longs to belong somewhere, to be part of a family. How do these conflicting desires play out in her actions?

5. Jensen sees himself as a pariah in Deep Haven, unforgiven for his role in Felicity's death. How does his perspective change by the story's end? Have you ever had to reconsider a long-held belief about yourself?

6. Darek and Jensen were best friends from childhood, but even before their friendship broke apart, they competed for hometown glory and for Felicity's affection. Similarly Claire is devastated by Felicity's death but still resents the attention her friend always got from Jensen. Is there anyone in your own life with whom you've had a complicated friendship—one tainted by jealousy or rivalry? How did you handle that dynamic?

7. After Felicity's death, Darek gave up his dream of firefighting to work at Evergreen Resort. Years later, he's determined to help the family business survive but still angry over the way his life has turned out, sticking him in a role he never wanted. How do Darek's feelings for the resort change over the course of the story? Have you ever felt burdened by a family legacy? How do you feel about it now?

8. Claire watches as two of her friends get engaged, happy for them while at the same time feeling pain over the inertia of her own life. Why do you think Claire feels so stuck? Have you ever felt as though life was moving forward without you? What did you do about it?

9. As a single father to Tiger, Darek feels he's doing his best to raise his son on his own. But in others' eyes—particularly Nan Holloway's—Darek appears to be negligent or incapable of parenting well. Whose point of view did you agree with? What do you think Darek was doing right as a parent? In what areas did he seem to need help?

10. Felicity Holloway Christiansen is a central figure in this story, one whose life and death have far-reaching impact, yet we know her only through the memories and descriptions of other characters. What was your impression of Felicity, and how did it change throughout the story?

11. Claire believes she's a disappointment to her parents and to God, and she still wrestles with the attack she suffered in Bosnia. Looking at the pain of her past and the uncertainty of her future, she doubts that God really is kind. What changes her mind? In what circumstances have you doubted God's kindness? Did your perspective change over time?

12. Claire's grandfather, Gibs, provides a voice of wisdom and challenge for Jensen—Jensen even learns that Gibs spoke up on his behalf after the accident. Why does he initially fight against Gibs's counsel? How does it ultimately change him? Who in your own life has provided wisdom when you needed it—whether or not you wanted to hear it at the time?

13. After their daughter was attacked, Claire's parents allowed her to move to Deep Haven while they continued their work in Bosnia. But Jensen believes they should have moved home to care for Claire. Do you agree? Have you ever faced tension between obligations to family and friends and the calling you feel God has placed on your life? What did you do?

14. Ivy finds herself in an impossible situation—forced to either sign the petition removing Tiger from Darek's custody or risk having the little boy put into foster care. What would you have done if faced with the same choice?

15. Jensen maintains his innocence in Felicity's death, even when he's challenged to ask for forgiveness. And at the same time, Darek refuses to offer Jensen forgiveness when he hasn't asked for it. Do you agree that Jensen needed to apologize to Darek? To Deep Haven? Should Darek have forgiven him regardless? Can you think of a time when you've been in either man's shoes—either reluctant to ask for forgiveness or forced to forgive someone who seems unrepentant?

16. When Angelica Michaels expresses concern that Claire is hurting the flowers in her garden, Claire explains how pruning the flowers allows them to grow. How does that conversation change Claire's perspective on her own life? Looking back, are there any difficult circumstances in your past that you now see as pruning, shaping you into who you were meant to be? How does this concept affect your outlook on difficult circumstances you're currently facing?

17. Ivy believes that emotions get her into trouble, get in the way of rational decisions, but Ingrid tells her that "God is a God of emotion. And it's good." Which do you tend to trust more— your mind or your heart? Why?

18. As the fire approaches, the Christiansens decide to risk their property for the chance at saving Deep Haven. Did you agree with this decision? Do you think their faith in God for the outcome was rewarded?

More great fiction from

SUSAN MAY WARREN

THE PJ SUGAR SERIES

PJ Sugar came home looking for a fresh start. What she
found was a new career as a private investigator.

THE NOBLE LEGACY SERIES

After their father dies, three siblings reunite on the family ranch to try
to preserve the Noble legacy. If only family secrets—and unsuspected
enemies—didn't threaten to destroy everything they've worked
so hard to build.